Lovestruck in London

RACHEL SCHURIG

Copyright 2013 Rachel Schurig
All rights reserved.

No part of this book may be reproduced, or stored in a retrieval system, or transmitted in any form or by any means, electronic, mechanical, photocopying, recording, or otherwise, without express written permission of the author.

This is a work of fiction. Names, characters, places, and incidents are either the product of the author's imagination or used fictitiously. Any similarity to real persons, living or dead, is coincidental and not intended by the author.

ISBN-13:978-1490488066
ISBN-10:1490488065

For Kristin,
in honor of many years of friendship,
most of which were spent mooning over British movie
stars.

ACKNOWLEDGMENTS

Thanks, as ever, to my wonderful parents, siblings, family, and friends for all of your help and encouragement. A special thank you to my parents, for watching Lucy so I could gallivant around England and write this book!

Thank you to my editor, Shelley Holloway, for all your help, support, and advice.
www.hollowayhouse.me

Book cover design by Scarlett Rugers Design 2013
www.scarlettrugers.com

Like Lizzie, I have always been fascinated by London and the UK. When I went to visit to research this book, I fell even more in love with the beautiful country and lovely people. I apologize for any unintentional errors relating to places or language. I'll be back as soon as I can—please save me a mint Aero!

CHAPTER ONE

For as long as I could remember, I've wanted to live in London.

I'm not exactly sure what the draw was, specifically. I had always felt drawn to the city, to England in general. One of my older sisters, Laura, used to tease me mercilessly for watching *Coronation Street*, a British soap opera carried on a nearby Canadian station that I could pick up on the TV after school when I adjusted the antenna just right. "It's not even a decent soap, Lizzie," Laura would argue, wrestling with me for the remote so she could switch over to *General Hospital*. "I can't understand half the things they say with that accent."

I *loved* the accent. It was so romantic and refined. Nothing like the harsh bellows and sudden outbursts of Spanish from my brothers and sisters. I had been thrilled when Laura joined the school dance team, which practiced after school. For the first time in my life, I had the house to myself, if only for a brief hour. In a family of six children, solitude was practically unheard of, and that hour was priceless, allowing me a daily dose of the melodrama of my favorite British soap.

But my love for all things British had begun long before I discovered *Coronation Street*. My preoccupation probably had something to do with my taste in literature; nearly all of my favorite authors were British. From Jane Austen to Helen Fielding to J.K. Rowling, I spent an inordinate amount of time living vicariously in the cities and countryside of Great Britain. For a self-described bibliophile like myself, the literature connection was a strong one.

And now, at the age of twenty-three, my dream of living in London was about to come true.

"I can't believe we're actually going," I said, bouncing in my seat a little. "Finally!" My friend Callie didn't bother looking up from her magazine; I had been saying pretty much the same thing ever since we had arrived at the airport.

"Mmmhmm," Callie murmured, idly flicking the page.

I sighed. I knew Callie was excited as well, though she might not be quite so effusive as I would like. But I simply couldn't contain my excitement. Callie and I had both been accepted into a graduate program at Kingsbury University's London Campus. We would be spending the next nine months studying literature and poetry, respectively. I had heard of the program right after starting my student teaching internship the previous fall and was immediately intrigued. Nine months in my dream city? Nine months of studying the subject I loved, before settling down into a teaching career I was feeling less and less excited about? I had jumped at the chance and convinced my classmate Callie to go for it as well. And now, after imagining it for so long, I could hardly believe it was real.

Feeling too keyed up to sit still any longer, I grabbed my purse. "I'm gonna walk around a little," I told Callie. "Watch my stuff?"

Callie finally looked up from her magazine. "Will you get me a water?"

"Sure."

She smiled her thanks. "Don't be long," she said, looking down at her watch. "You don't want to miss the flight."

Fat chance, I thought as I walked in the direction of the airport shops. I wouldn't miss this flight for the world.

The airport in Detroit was much bigger and more crowded than I had remembered. The last time I had flown from Detroit Metro—the last and only time I'd been on a plane, period—had been a good fifteen years ago, when my entire family flew down to Orlando for a Disneyworld vacation. I smiled, thinking of how stressed out my father had been shepherding his six kids through the airport. It hadn't been the calmest start to a vacation, all of the kids seeming to have some kind of meltdown at some point before wheels-down in Florida. My oldest sister Maria, sixteen at the time, had been angry she had to leave her boyfriend behind, at Spring Break no less, for such a baby vacation. My brother Carlos, fourteen, thought it was hilarious to tease and torment Laura, who was completely terrified of flying and kept breaking down into noisy tears, probably secretly enjoying the drama and attention for all it was worth. And the twins, Matias and Samuel, had been, well, the twins. Rambunctious and loud, chasing each other through the lines of passengers, and generally driving my parents crazy. It was a wonder that I had even been born; the twins would have retired most parents.

A display of books caught my attention, and I changed course to head into the small book and magazine shop. I made it a habit never to pass up a display of books. I had plenty to read for the flight, probably too much, in fact (did anyone really need four books for a ten-hour flight?), but you never knew when you might find your next can't-put-it-down read.

A shrill ring came from my purse, startling me. It took a moment for my brain to kick in and realize it was my new cellphone, the ringtone unfamiliar. I'd needed something I could use in the UK and had thus retired my trusty old flip phone for an upgrade only the day before.

"Hello?" I said, finally figuring out how to answer the touch screen.

"Mom is crying. I hope you're happy."

I rolled my eyes. "She is not."

"Okay, she's not," Sam admitted. "But she is sniffing a lot. And Dad's been out in the garage ever since they got home from dropping you off."

I felt a pang. To say that my parents hadn't been thrilled about my study-abroad choice was an understatement. People in our family just did *not* move away from home, even for nine months. It was unheard of.

"What are you doing over there, anyhow?" I asked, trying to get my mind off the idea of my parents being sad or worried.

"It's Sunday," my brother said, as if that should be self-explanatory.

"So you're there for the food," I said, smiling. "I shouldn't be surprised."

"Hey, if she's gonna make Sunday dinner every week, the least I can do is come over and eat it."

I'm going to miss him, I realized suddenly, my heart constricting slightly. Out of all of my siblings, it was Samuel, the younger of the twins and three years my senior, that I felt closest to now that were all grown. Unlike the others, he didn't tease me for wanting to spend all of my time with my nose in a book. He was overprotective, just like all the rest, but he also encouraged me to do the things that made me happy.

"What's she making?"

"The usual. Enchiladas, rice, veggies. She got those corn tortillas you like, the ones from the bakery downriver."

I groaned. If I missed anything while I was gone, it would be the delicious authentic cooking I could get right in my very own kitchen.

"Are you the only one mooching off her cooking tonight?" I teased, trying not to dwell on my sudden rush of sadness.

"What do you think? Everyone is coming tonight. They have to be here to complain about your ridiculous, money-wasting decision, don't they? How else will they lament the fact that you're throwing away a perfectly good teaching certificate to gallivant with foreigners—"

"I'll be the foreigner in this situation."

"Yeah, well, that's not the point, is it? The point is you have an opportunity to get a nice, stable, union job with good benefits. And instead you choose to go overseas to read books all day. Major scandal, little sis. I heard a rumor our tias will even be here. All the cousins."

I heard Sam laugh on the other end of the phone and smiled in spite of his words. Of course my family, including my aunts and cousins, would be together tonight to discuss my leaving. They were always in each other's business, everyone had an opinion. It drove me crazy.

"I was starting to get a little homesick there, Sammy," I said. "Thanks for snapping me back to reality."

"Don't be too hard on them," he said, serious now. "They all just care about you."

"They're all just nosey," I corrected.

"Seriously, Lizzie. They all want what's best for you."

"I know," I said softly. "But their ideas of what's best are sometimes different from mine."

Samuel was quiet on the other end of the phone for a moment. "Hey," he finally said, his voice lighter. "Don't sweat it, right? Why do you care if they'll be gossiping? Won't you be well on your way across the ocean by dinner time?"

"Not really. We have a layover in New York first."

Sam snorted. "New York City? That's as good as being half a world away from this place."

I laughed.

"I'll let you go," Sam said. "Just wanted to wish you luck."

"Thanks, Sammy."

"You call Mom when you get there tomorrow, okay?" His voice was suddenly gruff, and I felt a lump in my throat.

"It will still be night in Detroit," I said. "There's a five-hour difference."

"Then call when you know she'll be up. Don't forget, Lizzie."

"I won't." I paused. "Love you, big brother."

"Love you, too," he said. "Be safe, okay? You don't take any crap from those limey boys."

"Got it…Bye, Sammy."

"Bye."

I hung up, pushing my phone back down in my purse, determined not to cry. My family had been giving me so much crap about leaving that I hadn't really had an emotional goodbye with any of them. Now the thought of nine months without them seemed endless. What if I was making a mistake? I'd never been away from my siblings before. I'd gone to a local college, living at home while I took my classes, and my brothers and sisters had all lived within ten minutes of the house, along with numerous cousins and aunts and uncles. They were a constant presence in my life, a loud, overwhelming, overbearing presence, but one I had never been without.

They'll be there when you get back, I reminded myself. *Your family will always be there. This is the only time in your life you'll be able to do something like this.*

It was true. It was only a matter of time before I was back home for good, settling into that teaching career my family had so encouraged, probably getting a house within walking distance of my folks. Just like my sisters before me.

Just like that, the fear vanished, replaced by an almost panicked urge to get on the plane, to put as many miles between Detroit and me as was humanly possible. I pulled out two waters from a cooler and made my way to the counter to pay. As I waited in line, I glanced at a clock on the wall. We should start boarding the flight to New York in about twenty minutes. Not long at all now. The flight to New York was short, our layover shorter, and then it'd be on to London.

Almost there, I told myself, smiling at the clerk as he rang me up. *You're almost there.* I glanced at the clock again as I took back the waters, quickly calculating in my head. *Less than half a day.* In ten hours, I would be touching down at London Heathrow, my UK adventure beginning at last.

***

"I should have known this would happen," I grumbled eighteen hours later as Callie and I finally stepped off the plane. Bedraggled and exhausted, we stumbled along, blindly following our fellow passengers down to customs. "Everything was way too perfect, there was no way it could continue."

Callie yawned loudly. "I'm so tired I can't feel my eyelids." She turned to me. "Are my eyes even open right now, or am I hallucinating?"

"They're open," I said. "But just barely." Someone jostled us from behind, and I reached out for Callie's arm. "Come on, let's get a move on. The sooner we get out of the airport, the sooner we can go to sleep."

Callie blinked out at the waning early evening sun shining through the glass windows of the terminal. "God, what time is it? This is so disorienting."

I looked at my watch, but found I couldn't remember how many hours to add in order to get local time. I would have to figure that out. But for now, I just wanted my luggage. "Come on," I said again, pulling Callie along in my wake.

Our flight from Detroit had been inexplicably delayed, causing us to miss our connecting flight from JFK. Callie had gotten on the phone with her father, some bigwig in the insurance industry who apparently spent half his life on an airplane. He managed to pull some strings, getting us on a flight to Boston. From Boston we could connect to London. All told, the delays and missed flights had added an extra eight hours to our trip. I had never been so tired in all my life, not even the time I stayed up for forty-eight straight hours to finish a term paper for a dreaded political science class.

But our luck finally seemed to turn now that we had arrived. We got through customs easily, managed to find our luggage, and even got our tickets for the train into town without having to ask anyone. I was relieved—the airport was a mass of people rushing about, much bigger than any of the terminals I had visited over the last twenty-four hours. I felt irrationally afraid of having to stop and ask for help. Surely these sophisticated Londoners would know just by looking at me that I was a clueless American from a small town.

Once we had lugged all of our bags onto the train, we collapsed into our seats in relief. Callie closed her eyes immediately, laying her head on my shoulder. "Wake me up when we get there."

As the train slowly began its ascent from the bowels of the airport, I found my energy reviving. I was looking at the British countryside! Well, not quite—it was more like the outskirts of a British city. In fact, it didn't look all that much different from home. But still! I was nearly in London!

Home felt very far away now, but I found that I wasn't scared anymore. Sure, I had never had cause to take a train or subway in my life, but I'd managed to figure out how to get on the Heathrow Express just fine, hadn't I? While Callie snored softly beside me, I pulled out my already worn guidebook and reviewed the information I had previously committed to memory

Heathrow Express to Paddington Station. Get Oyster cards at the underground and take the Circle line to King's Cross. From there, switch lines to Angel station and take a taxi to Fulton Street. The thought of so many steps, particularly on little sleep, and carrying luggage, made me nervous, but I tried to push the thoughts down. I could do this. I knew I could.

Trying to keep my stress at bay, I turned again to the window. As the buildings grew closer and closer together, my excitement grew. *This is going to be amazing,* I told myself. *Everything you want it to be.*

I had very high hopes for my time in London. I didn't just want an experience—I wanted *the* experience. The perfect, life-changing opportunity I had always dreamed of. In a city so far from home, where no one knew me, I would finally be able to leave my old image behind. In London, no one would know that I was a nerdy bookworm who spent more time in the library than out with friends. No one would know that I was the baby sister of five loud, bossy siblings. That an exciting night in my family's life consisted of all the cousins coming over to eat my mom and tia's cooking in the backyard. No one would know that I'd only traveled outside of my state once, that I'd never been abroad. No one would know that I had so few boyfriends I could count them on one hand—with several fingers left over. In London, I could reinvent myself, find some excitement for once in my life. Work on the novel I had always dreamed of writing. Have fun. Maybe even fall in love.

I smiled to myself as the train began to slow. *It could happen,* I thought. *Anything could happen.*

CHAPTER TWO

"This is boring," Callie whispered. "I am officially bored."

Much as I hated to admit it, I agreed with her. We'd been in London for three days now, and so far, it wasn't much different than my time at Wayne State University back in Detroit.

Since our arrival at the college, we'd had to sit through endless orientation sessions covering topics ranging from our future classes to life and safety in London. We hadn't even had the chance to get into our apartment yet, all of the study-abroad participants being required to sleep in University accommodations during orientation. So, after being in London for three days, I had yet to see any of it besides our room and the few blocks between lecture halls. I could barely even remember the ride in from Heathrow, as jet lagged and exhausted as I had been.

"Just another hour," I whispered back. "Then we'll be free."

A group of the girls from our hall were going to a pub that night for dinner. I was trying to be cool about it, but inside I was thrilled. Going to a pub sounded so quintessentially British. Plus it was a relief just knowing that

I wouldn't be sitting in the residence hall with Callie, both of us passing out as soon as we finished eating, our bodies not yet adjusted to the time change. The girls who had asked us were exactly the kind of girls I had always secretly admired—the girls whose hair always somehow managed to stay styled and sleek, who always had dates, who could sit comfortably with a group of friends in a bar, gossiping and having fun. I had never been one of those girls.

I tried to turn my attention back to the professor in front of the room. At least eighty years old, he was blessed with an abundance of white hair on both his head and face. He seemed to be wheezing a bit, every word coming out in a raspy whistle. I struggled to concentrate, but the prof couldn't possibly make his subject sound more boring if he tried. He was rambling on about the various tracks we could sign up for. Normally I would be into it, I loved planning my schedule. One of my favorite fall-time activities was pouring over the course catalogs, researching my professors, and generally spending hours finalizing just the right schedule. Callie always told me I was missing the point of college as she herself signed up for whatever classes applied to her degree requirements and allowed her to sleep in until at least eleven.

True to form, I knew exactly what I wanted my course focus to be in the program, and had pre-selected all the classes I was hoping to take. I prayed my choices wouldn't be as boring as the old man was making them sound.

"Okay," a clear, female voice called out. With a start, I realized that the man had finished speaking and our coordinator, Valerie, had taken his place at the dais. "That's all we have for today," Valerie said. "I encourage you to take a good look at the course catalog tonight as we'll want your final decisions tomorrow. I'll be available in my office all morning for those who have questions about any of the tracks."

Next to me, I could feel Callie sit up straight, her attention suddenly renewed. I could practically hear her mentally urging the coordinator to let us out early. Valerie started to explain the registration procedure, information we all had in our course catalog. "Come on, come on," Callie whispered.

"So if there're no more questions, you can all be excused to enjoy what's left of this lovely fall day."

Callie let out a loud sigh of relief as the students began gathering up their things. "I thought she was never going to say it," she muttered, swinging her book bag up onto her shoulder. "I swear, I thought we were going to be stuck in here forever."

"Have I ever told you that you're a bit dramatic, Cal?"

My friend snorted and we made our way down the row and out into the corridor beyond the lecture hall. "I figure one of us should be," she said. "When I started hanging out with you, I thought I'd finally found the Latina bombshell to round out my social circle. And instead, I got quiet-as-a-church-mouse Lizzie."

"I'm so glad to hear I've dispelled your stereotypes about Latina women," I said, my voice dry. "But I am sorry to have been such a disappointment to you all these years."

Callie slung an arm over my shoulder as we stepped out into the weak sunlight outside the lecture hall. "You know I'm only kidding," she said. "I love you dearly and would have failed all my classes had I not picked the seat next to yours in that first English class." Callie looked up at the sun and sighed. "Did she call this a lovely fall day? It's about forty degrees out here and cloudy."

"You're in England," I reminded her, pulling my jean jacket a little closer around my shoulders. I didn't tell Callie, but secretly I loved it. Weather like this made me want to curl up inside with a good book. *Not tonight*, I reminded myself. *Tonight you'll join the world of people who actually go out.*

"Callie!" A voice called from behind us. We turned to see a classmate, Meredith Hall, waving at us from down the sidewalk.

"Pub night's off," she said, catching up to us. "Johanna and Tonya are panicking about their class schedule. Apparently they haven't looked at the catalog once. Plus there's that novel we were supposed to read for Patterson's seminar in the morning. None of us has even touched it."

I groaned. I, of course, had finished the novel the day after it was assigned. "Really?"

"Lizzie's feeling a little claustrophobic in the dorms," Callie explained.

"Me, too," Meredith nodded, flipping her blonde hair behind her shoulder. I was momentarily distracted. I could spend my life's savings at the best salon in London and I'd never get my hair that sleek or shiny. "But I've heard Patterson is really tough," Meredith was saying, "and he has final say over his class list. If we start off on his shit list, I bet he won't let us in."

I couldn't help but scowl. Here I was, ready to not put my entire focus on schoolwork for once, and the cool girls I had always admired had suddenly been struck with a sense of academic responsibility.

"What about Friday night?" Meredith asked. "We'll be finished with orientation and everyone should be settled by then. Besides, we won't have to get up early the next day, so we'll have plenty of time to party."

I felt a flicker of excitement that was quickly dashed. "We have theater tickets," Callie said, excitement clear in her voice.

"We *do*?"

Callie nodded, smiling. "I booked them months ago."

I gaped at her. Had I entered into some kind of bizarre universe? *I* wanted to go to a bar and Callie, of all people, was declining in order to go to the *theater*?

"You haven't heard what show we're seeing yet," Callie said, obviously dying to be asked.

"What show are we seeing?"

"*Ships Sail.*" Callie said the title as if she expected me to burst into cheers. Instead, I stared at my friend blankly.

"Oh, come on," Callie said, disappointed. "You know, *Ships Sail*. The new play starring none other than…" she paused for effect. "Jackson Coles!"

Meredith gasped. "Oh my God, you lucky bitch!"

"Wait a second," I said, staring hard at Callie. "Jackson Coles, the werewolf guy?"

Callie rolled her eyes. "Only you, Lizzie, would describe the hottest, biggest name in Hollywood as 'the werewolf guy'."

"But that's who you mean, right? That guy in the *Darkness* movies?"

"Of course that's who I mean." Callie was clearly getting annoyed that I was not more thrilled at the prospect of seeing a major Hollywood star live on stage. "Lizzie, how do you not know about this play? It's been all over the news lately." I raised an eyebrow. "Fine, all over the celebrity news."

"Big difference," I muttered.

"Yeah, Lizzie, she has a point," Meredith said, her eyes wide. "This is a really big deal." She leaned in a little closer and lowered her voice. "This is the play that he goes full frontal, isn't it?"

I groaned, finally realizing that I had, in fact, heard about the play. Personally, I had never quite seen the appeal of Jackson Coles, though I had to admit I was in the tiny minority of girls my age who felt that way. Jackson Coles was *the* big thing, the hottest movie star of the year, and the year before that, come to think of it. He had broken onto the scene in a likely way; the star of a massively popular franchise of paranormal romance films geared toward teens, though, by all accounts, pretty darn popular with women of all ages. And Jackson Coles, with his golden hair, icy blue eyes, and killer British accent, was a huge part of that appeal. My cousin Sofie had dragged me to the theater to see the first movie, *Darkness Rise*, and that was more than enough to tell me that the *Darkness* franchise was not my cup of tea. Movies full of vampires, werewolves, and sorcerers were just not my thing, not even if the werewolf in question looked like Jackson Coles. The franchise had started when Jackson was only sixteen, and now, five films later, showed no signs of slowing down. Jackson had further endeared himself to the female population by his current turn in the West End production of *Ships Sail*, a horribly overwrought script (in my opinion at least) that had the one saving grace of requiring its lead to strip down to the buff. Thus the reason, I was sure, that Callie had purchased tickets months ago in anticipation of our arrival in London.

"I don't believe it," Meredith was saying dreamily. "You're going to get to see Jackson Coles. Right up close and personal. *All* of him."

"I know!" Callie squealed. "I'm so excited, I can't even tell you!"

After the girls fawned over Jackson for a few more minutes, Meredith left us to head back to her dorm. Callie and I started off down the sidewalk toward our own room.

"I have to say, Lizzie, I thought you'd be a tad more excited about this. You love theater. And they were really hard tickets to get, you know?"

"I'm sorry, Cal. I just don't really get the hype about Coles. Isn't he just another pretty boy?"

Callie looked scandalized. "He obviously takes his work seriously. I hardly think he'd do a boring old play if he wasn't a serious actor."

Not wanting to hurt my friend's feelings, I made an effort not to laugh.

"You're bummed about missing pub night, aren't you?"

"Yeah," I said. "I was really looking forward to going out with a group. I never do stuff like that."

"You're with a group all the time," Callie argued. "I've seen that family of yours."

"It's not the same, Cal. I always just have one or two girlfriends, you know? It would be nice to have a bigger social circle."

"You will," my friend assured me. "We have nine months, Lizzie. And look at how many nice people we've already met."

"True," I agreed. I usually had a very hard time relating to the girls in my classes. They seemed to speak a language I didn't understand, one peppered with celebrity gossip and fashion chatter. It wasn't that I didn't have an interest in clothes; I just never understood how someone could think of that many things to say about a handbag. I had been hoping that the girls here, the ones who obviously cared enough about their studies to go through with an expensive and accelerated graduate course, would be enough like me that I'd feel comfortable around them.

"Come on," Callie said, putting her arm around my shoulder once more. "It's not that bad. We get to move into the apartment tomorrow, right? That will be fun."

Through my disappointment, I felt a rush of excitement. Moving into the apartment was the thing I was most looking forward to, the thing that would make me feel like I was a real Londoner, and not just a visitor. I couldn't wait to find our local newsagent, to find the closest Tesco for groceries, the nearest pub to pop into on our way home.

"You're right," I said, smiling at my friend. "Tomorrow is definitely something to look forward to."

***

"We cannot live here."

I felt my stomach sink. "It's not that bad."

Callie spun to face me, a wild look on her face. "Are you kidding me? Not that bad? Lizzie, no. No, no, no. There is no way we're living here!"

"But...it's all arranged! Our stuff will be delivered by this afternoon, and we signed a lease. What are we supposed to do?"

Callie was breathing hard, staring around at the tiny room. The garden view, two bedroom that had been advertised was, in fact, much more like a basement-level studio with a couple of shoulder-height, rickety partitions to divide the space. Though we had been assured it was fully furnished, all I could see by way of furniture was a cheap folding table in the kitchen area and a couple of glorified cots in what were, presumably, the "bedrooms." Even with the scarce furniture taking up so little space, I couldn't see how we could possibly fit all of our things here. Even worse, a dank, sulfur smell seemed to permeate the air, and the relatively few surfaces in the flat were filthy.

"I'm not doing it," Callie said decisively. "I'm not staying here."

"But...but we signed." I was feeling panicky now. Money was not nearly the issue for Callie that it was for me. What would I do if we were on the hook for the rent? What better could we find for my scholarship and student loan-funded, paltry budget?

"It's false advertisement," Callie said, crossing her arms. "They can't show us fake pictures of an apartment and expect us to take it." Seeing the worry on my face, Callie took my arm and led me to the door. "We are done with this horror of an apartment, Lizzie. Just forget we ever assaulted our senses with it. I'll call my father. He'll take care of getting us out of the lease."

"That's all fine and good, but where the heck are we gonna live?"

"We'll go apartment hunting," Callie said dismissively, leading me to the hallway and shutting the door firmly behind us. "It will be fun!"

I stared at her in disbelief. Fun? We knew nothing about London real estate. How on earth were we supposed to find something? Especially with our budget. But Callie was already pulling out her phone and dialing. "Dad?" she said a moment later as she pulled open the front door and stepped out onto the sidewalk. "Dad, you will not *believe* this..."

I followed her outside, feeling numb. I sank down on the porch steps, watching as Callie walked a few feet away. Though she was out of earshot, by her facial expression and excessive hand gestures, I could tell my friend was really selling the issue to her dad.

I looked down the admittedly grungy street and sighed. I'd had such high hopes for this apartment. Callie and I had both agreed that we weren't going to have the authentic London experience if we were living in a dorm miles away from everything. The residential office at the school had given us a list of nearby flats that were within our budget, and I had spent an afternoon emailing back and forth with estate agents, pouring over pictures and maps, until I finally settled on this one. And look at where all that work had gotten me.

"Okay," Callie said, slipping her phone back in her purse. "My dad's on it."

"What's he going to do?"

"He's having his secretary call an estate agent, someone he trusts, and he'll send us a list of acceptable flats within the hour."

I felt a growing dismay. "Cal, you know my budget is not very big—"

Callie waved me off. "He knows our budget. He'll negotiate with the agents. It will be fine."

I had a sinking feeling Mr. Owen was planning on subsidizing the difference in price of a decent place. Before

I could voice this concern, Callie was pulling me up from the stoop.

"Cheer up, Lizzie. You worry too much. Everything is going to be peachy, promise."

"Cal—"

"No arguing. Come on, let's go get some lunch while we wait."

***

An hour and a half later, we were climbing the stairs from the Underground at Marylebone station, blinking in the sudden sunlight. After several days of riding on the tube, I still wasn't used to it. I found it disorienting to hurdle through the damp dark so far below. Coming back to the surface was a shock to the system every time. Most days, I kind of enjoyed the feeling of being so off-kilter; it was a reminder to me that I was trying something new, that I was outside of my comfort zone, just like I'd wanted to be. But after the earlier apartment fiasco, and the distinct lack of fun I'd had since my arrival, I wasn't feeling so keen on new experiences. For the first time, I was starting to wonder if maybe I should have stayed home after all. London was not what I had expected it to be.

"Okay, the first place shouldn't be far. Connie said she picked it because of how close it was to the tube…" Callie peered at the map, not noticing that she was blocking the path of several harried people trying to make their way off the tube. I gently took her shoulder and moved her out of the way, wishing I could have a small amount of my friend's confidence. Since we'd been in London, I had been terrified of bothering anyone or getting in the way. Cal, while sometimes annoyingly oblivious, obviously didn't put as much energy into worrying about what people thought.

"Okay, I think if we head this way…" Callie led the way down the busy street, turning off on a side road, and then another before stopping in front of a gorgeous, red brick mansion. "Callie…" I said, a warning note in my voice.

"Oh, don't be such a worry wart. Let's just check it out."

We rang the bell and were buzzed up, meeting a professionally dressed woman outside the apartment door. The mansion appeared to be divided into several apartments, I guessed at least four. The woman introduced herself as the building manager and let us in. My first impression was light. Sunlight poured in from the front windows, brightening the modern decor. Everything in the apartment was clean and minimal, decorated in creams and whites—pale wood floors, white furniture, ivory walls.

"Oooh, it's pretty," Callie cooed.

"Oooh, it's expensive," I shot back. But Callie was already off, exploring the space. "These are proper bedrooms," she called to me from the hallway off the living room. Sighing, I followed her. The rooms were small, but adequate, plenty of room for a bed, desk, and dresser. We even each had a window.

"Small closets," Callie murmured to herself, before testing the mattress on the bed. "Not bad."

"Callie—"

"Let's see the kitchen."

Resigned, I followed her to the kitchen. It, too, was on the small side, but completely adequate, with stainless steel appliances and marble counters. "I love it," Callie declared.

"How much?" I asked, facing my friend across the counter.

"My dad said it was in the budget." Callie shrugged.

"Cal, we're in Marylebone right now. Do you know how ritzy this neighborhood is? There is no way this is in our budget."

"I'm sure it's fine—" Callie began, but I turned to the property manager.

"Do you have a fact sheet on this place that we can take with us?"

Reluctantly, the manager pulled a sheet from her handbag and handed it to me. I took one look at the price and burst out laughing. "Yeah, that's what I thought."

"Lizzie, it's really not a big deal—"

"It was nice meeting you," I told the agent, grabbing Cal's arm to pull her toward the door. "Thanks for your time."

Downstairs, Callie pulled her arm free. "I *liked* that place, Lizzie!"

"It was a thousand pounds over our budget!" I cried. "A thousand pounds, Cal. That's almost two thousand dollars! Two thousand dollars extra a month!"

Callie pouted, but didn't respond. "Let me guess," I went on. "Your dad was just going to pay the difference?"

"What's the big deal?" Callie shot back. "He has the money. Why does it matter?"

"I'm not mooching off your father," I said. "We talked about this when we first agreed to live together."

"You'd be contributing! You would pay what you can, and he'd handle the rest."

"No," I said firmly. "Absolutely not."

Callie sighed. "Fine. But it's going to limit our options."

"Then it's going to limit our options," I said. "I'm not taking money from your dad. Let me see the links for the rest of the apartments."

Reluctantly, Callie handed over her phone. I scrolled through the email, noting that the list didn't include prices but mentally crossing off several places based just on their location and square footage. I might not be an expert in London real estate, but even I knew a spacious two bedroom in Notting Hill, just off the high street, was going to far exceed our budget.

"These don't look too bad," I said, pointing at the list. "Let's start here."

We looked at four more flats before we found one we could even begin to compromise on. Even then, Callie thought it was way too small, I thought it was way too expensive, and both thought it was too far from transportation.

"It's clean though," I murmured, running my hand across an empty bookshelf. "The bathroom was practically gleaming."

"It's a fourth-floor walk-up," Callie muttered.

"Think of how toned our quads will be."

"There's not room in that second bedroom for a desk."

"Then I'll work at the kitchen table," I said.

Callie turned to me. "Do you really like it, Lizzie?"

I shrugged. "Not particularly. It will be a bitch getting to class every day. And the rent still seems high for the location. But it would *work*. It's the first place we've seen that would actually work."

Callie sighed. "I don't want to settle. Could we at least look at the rest of the flats?"

I glanced back at the list on the phone. Of the flats I hadn't dismissed out of hand, only two remained. "May as well check out these two, at least," I agreed.

The first was a no-go from the start, as it was another basement location without windows. "I cannot live somewhere without light," Callie said firmly. "I'd rather go back to the residence hall."

Though the price was the lowest we had seen, I agreed with her. "One more chance," I said. "Let's cross our fingers."

I fell in love with the last flat at first sight. It was situated over an Italian restaurant in Kentish Town, not too far from our Islington campus, fairly near a tube stop, and even closer to a bus stop. The restaurant was already gearing up for the dinner hour, and I was immediately charmed with the atmosphere. It felt homey and comfortable, conversation and laughter ringing out between the patrons and staff. It almost felt like home.

The hostess directed us to a short, older woman who introduced herself as Mrs. Idoni. After explaining that we were there to see the flat, she showed us up the stairs. "It will smell like garlic *all* the time," Callie whispered in my ear as we climbed.

"Sounds yummy," I whispered back.

The flat was nearly spacious, compared to many of the other options. An open plan living area included a couch and armchair, dining table, and kitchenette. The wood floors appeared to be original to the building, and a large window with a built-in bench seat overlooked the street below. I was grinning before we even made it to the bedrooms.

"Perfect," I whispered, standing in the doorway to the second room. It overlooked the back street, the view slightly shabbier, but branches from a large maple tree blocked most of it anyhow. An old iron bed was pushed against the wall, a rickety desk under the window. It was smaller than the first bedroom, but cozy, comfortable, and romantic somehow. I knew it was meant for me.

"I see that look on your face," Callie said. "You're already mentally unpacking, aren't you?"

"I like it, Cal," I said, turning to my friend, my face alight. "I can see us here. There's plenty of room, there's actually some character. And we can jump right on the bus a few blocks down. Plus we're really close to Camden, which is supposed to have lots of shopping and nightlife. What do you think?"

Callie was watching me closely. Finally, she sighed. "It does have the biggest living area," she said. "And the bedroom closet is better than the place in Wandsworth. Plus it's a lot closer to school."

I felt excitement rise up in my chest. The street outside had looked bustling, and a warm buzz could be heard from the restaurant downstairs. This was what I had imagined when I pictured living in London—excitement, movement, a buzz of noise.

"How loud does the restaurant get at night?" Callie asked Mrs. Idoni.

"A little loud," the woman said, her accent an interesting mix of Italian with a slight British overtone. "We close at eleven on weeknights, midnight weekends."

I figured the noise and the admittedly present smell of garlic were responsible for the low price. But what was the point of living somewhere with no character? I glanced at the fact sheet Mrs. Idoni had given us and took a deep breath. "I think it's priced high," I said, hoping the woman wouldn't catch the nerves in my voice.

"I get husband," she said, turning to go downstairs.

"What do you think?" I asked Callie. "Should we go for it?"

"It's the best we've seen," Callie said. "Besides that gorgeous place in Marylebone. Are you sure you don't want to go back there? Just see it one more time?"

"Sorry, Cal. Not happening."

Callie sighed. "Fine then. I think we should take this place."

"I'm going to try to bring him down a little," I said, trying not to let my excitement carry me away. "It's still out of our budget."

Mr. Idoni appeared a moment later, a skinny, bald man with a bushy salt and pepper mustache who towered over me. I gulped and tried to give him my most winning smile. "We really like the flat, but it's priced a little high for us."

"It's a fair price," he said, rubbing his chin. "You students?"

I nodded. "We just got to town this week. Look, if you can come down two hundred pounds, we can sign for nine months instead of six. You'll have reliable tenants, and you won't have to worry about renting it again for at least nine months."

He watched me carefully for a moment. "I come down one fifty. No more. You sign for nine months."

I considered. That would put us about one fifty over our budget. Split by two people, it wasn't too bad, considering. "Okay," I said, holding out my hand. "You have a deal."

Mr. Idoni shook my hand, finally gracing me with a smile. "You are a good negotiator. I like that."

"My dad taught me well," I said, smiling back. "When can we move in?"

Mr. Idoni agreed that we could have key to the apartment the next day. Resigned to spending one more night in the resident hall, we headed back to campus, Callie calling her father once more to tell him the news and arrange to have our things delivered to the new flat. We decided to take the underground from Camden Town so we could check out the neighborhood. As we walked to the tube station, I felt better than I had all week. Camden buzzed around us, the Thursday nightlife already picking up. The weather had remained mild all day, with a hint of summer still in the air. We had a flat in a great location, and we'd be moved in by tomorrow. And, best of all, I'd taken control and made it happen.

CHAPTER THREE

"I can't believe you're making me sit through this," I muttered as we made our way down the crowded aisle.

"And I can't believe you don't want to see this!" Callie shot back. "Lizzie, we are talking about a major movie star here. How many people can say they've seen *the* Jackson Coles up close and personal like this? Besides—oof," Callie muttered, having tripped over someone's bag. "Sorry, can I just get by?" We continued our struggle down the aisle and plopped unceremoniously into our seats. "Besides," she said, slipping off her coat. "I thought you were totally into theater and art and all that crap."

I made a face at her. "I am into *all that crap*, I just thought that since it was our first night in our new flat in London, we might want to be, you know, out in London."

"Is this not London?" Callie asked. "Last I checked, we were smack dab in the middle of the West End."

I didn't respond as I struggled out of my coat. The seats were incredibly close together. I felt claustrophobic already. I imagined London out there, just gearing up for the Friday night crowds. I could picture the energy, the pulse of the city, and felt a pang. After all of my daydreaming that my time in London would be a fresh start for me, my opportunity to experience more of life than the library, here I was, spending my first Friday night in town doing something totally old-school-Lizzie—seeing a play. So much for my exciting new life.

"I know that we're in London," I said. "I just thought we would want to do something a little more exciting than go see some old play. Do you even know what this is about?"

Callie stared at me blankly. "What part of Jackson Coles naked are you not understanding here, Lizzie?"

I snorted.

"Look," Callie said, finally seeming to catch on to the crux of my disapproval of the evening. "I promise tomorrow night we'll go out somewhere more exciting, okay? We'll find some hot restaurant, and some hotter club to hit afterward, okay?"

I felt a familiar rush of nerves at the image Callie painted—though I was desperate to change my ways, the idea of clubbing still made me feel slightly nauseated. *All the more reason to get out there and do it*, I thought. *Get over your shyness once and for all. And in what better place than London, where no one knows you and no one has any idea of how big of a dork you really are.*

The lights started to dim, and Callie immediately sat up straighter in her seat, eager, I was sure, to see all of what Jackson had to offer. I couldn't help but smirk at her as I settled back into my own seat. As I did so, my arm brushed the man sitting next to me. I looked over at him in the dimming light to see that he was watching me, a smile just evident on his face. "Sorry," I whispered, bringing my arm back to my side of the armrest—no easy feat in such close quarters.

"No problem," he whispered back in a British accent. There was something familiar about his face, but I couldn't place it, and then the lights went off completely, and we were plunged into darkness. I turned my attention back to the stage just as the curtain went up.

I hadn't expected much from the play, but even I hadn't imagined just how bad it would be. Jackson wasn't much of an actor, and he seemed to think that being in a serious play meant he had to grimace at all times and deliver his lines in the most affected, melodramatic voice I had ever heard. It might not have been so bad had the production not taken itself so seriously. As it was, the entire thing just screamed pretension. By the time Jackson dropped his pants in the last scene of the first act, I was having a hard time not giggling at the ridiculousness of it all. "Shut up," Callie hissed, hitting me with her elbow. I slapped a hand over my mouth, sure that I was about to start snorting. I heard a rustle from the seat next to me and turned my head slightly to see that the man there was watching me again, a big smile on his face. He, too, seemed close to laughter, and that set me off all over again. He shook his head at me, and I turned away quickly, knowing I'd lose it if he laughed. Luckily the curtain was already falling on Jackson, standing proud on stage, even his nakedness unable to dispel the painfully serious look on his face. As the audience broke into applause, I was finally able to laugh.

"Holy crap," I said to Callie. "That was absolutely ridiculous." The woman in front of me turned to glare at me, and I lowered my voice. "Callie, you can't actually think that was good."

"Who cares?" Callie asked, grinning. "He's gorgeous. Oh my God, I can't believe I just saw Jackson Coles naked."

I shook my head in amazement. "But the play is so bad," I persisted. "By the time he got naked, it just seemed completely silly."

"Again I ask, who cares?" Callie shook her head. "I'm gonna go get a drink. Wanna come?" I shook my head, not eager to fight my way through the throngs of people streaming up the aisle toward the lobby.

"Alright, I'll be back," Callie said, standing. "You know, Lizzie, you might like it more if you let yourself get into it. I think you're focusing on the wrong things."

"Well, I would rather not focus on some stranger's package right in front of my face," I muttered to myself as Callie squeezed down the aisle. I heard laughter from next to me and turned my head, having completely forgotten about the guy sitting there. As I took in the sight of his face under the full lights I gasped, realizing immediately who was sitting next to me, listening to me bash Jackson Coles.

Thomas Harper, Jackson's co-star in the *Darkness* films, grinned at me, and I was sure I was going to faint.

Shit, I thought helplessly.

"Are you enjoying the show?" Thomas asked. I felt a blush flood my cheeks and Thomas's grin grew. "I couldn't help but notice you had a case of the giggles there."

"I'm so sorry," I whispered, feeling completely ridiculous. "I had no idea that you were…who you…I didn't realize, I'm sorry."

"It's okay," he said, waving a hand dismissively.

"No it's not," I said, mortified. "You know him. I shouldn't have—"

"Lizzie, can I tell you a secret?" he asked, leaning toward me. I started. How did he know my name?

"I completely agree with you. I think it's the stupidest play I've ever seen in my life. Your giggling was well-founded."

I could only stare at him. I had no idea if he was kidding or not.

"How do you know my name?" I whispered.

Thomas shrugged. "I heard you and your friend talking. I wasn't trying to eavesdrop," he said quickly. "It was just hard not to overhear, what with these seats being so bloody close together."

"Right?" I asked, forgetting my embarrassment for a moment. "I've never felt this cramped up in my life. It's worse than an airplane."

Thomas laughed. "You're completely right. I'm Thomas, by the way." He held out his hand to shake mine, and I hoped he couldn't tell how damp my palms were. "So, Lizzie, what would you rather be doing tonight? Did you say it was your first night in London?"

"Our first weekend," I corrected. "We've been here since Monday, but we had orientation and meetings and all of that." I realized I was rambling and ordered myself to stop talking. Thomas didn't seem phased. Instead he leaned closer.

"Orientation? What kind of orientation?"

"I'm studying here," I said. "At Kingsbury University."

"Wow, that's a great school," Thomas said, flashing me another grin. I was momentarily distracted. He was really quite handsome, not as flashy as Jackson Coles, but much more my type. Thomas had dark brown, wavy hair, which he kept neat, as opposed to Jackson's mess of golden hair, styled to within an inch of its life to look perfectly tousled. Thomas's features were handsome in more of an understated, classic way. His eyes were a bright green, and I was finding it difficult not to stare at them. With a flash of panic, I realized that he was talking. I had completely been zoned out, staring at his face. I struggled to catch the thread of what he was saying, praying I hadn't been too obvious.

"...says that the professors are pretty tough, but you get your money's worth," he was saying. "He managed to scrape pretty good grades. Of course my mother is convinced he's the smartest student to ever grace their halls." He winked at me and I fought down my panic. Who was he talking about? His brother, maybe? I smiled, hoping he didn't catch on to my cluelessness. "So what are you studying there?"

"Literature," I said, relieved he had moved on.

"Ah, then you'll be able to tell me if my brother was right about the professors—his course was in literature as well."

It *was* his brother then. I smiled for real now. "I'll be sure to let you know," I said, shocked to hear a flirting tone in my own voice. I didn't think I had ever flirted with a boy in my life, though I had watched Callie plenty of times. Apparently I hadn't failed miserably, because Thomas's grin grew wider. "I'm going to hold you to that, Lizzie," he said, his voice deep and soft. It sent shivers down my arms.

Callie chose that inopportune moment to return. "God," she said, plopping into her seat. "It's a mad house out there. The line for the bar was a mile long."

I looked at Thomas, not knowing if I should introduce them. He smiled at me and pulled out his phone. "I need to make a call," he murmured, standing.

"So you'll be happy about this," Callie was saying, completely oblivious to the man at my side. "I got a text while I was in line. Apparently Meredith and all of them are hitting a club on this side of town after they eat. I bet we could totally make it. So you'll get your exciting London night after all."

"Great," I said, barely hearing her. I felt completely gob smacked. I wasn't sure what'd had the biggest effect on me—the shock of realizing who Thomas was and what he had overheard me say, or the few moments of conversation we had shared. I did know one thing though; in real life, Thomas Harper was the most attractive man I had ever seen.

"We aren't really dressed for clubbing," Callie murmured, looking down at her jeans. "I guess if I shove my cardigan in my bag, I can make due with the tank top I have on underneath." She looked over at me. "You're another story, but there's not a lot we can do about it now."

I had dressed to go to the theater in a pink and brown flowered, gauzy shirt dress over leggings and brown, ankle-high boots. With my jean jacket and a pink scarf, I had thought I looked pretty cute. Seeing my face, Callie backtracked. "I mean, you look fine, of course, just not really clubby."

Still too overwhelmed by my Thomas Harper encounter, I didn't even allow myself to worry that I was so woefully unprepared for my first clubbing experience. I wondered if I should tell Callie what had happened, but knew my friend would absolutely freak out. I doubted Thomas wanted every girl in the theater under the age of thirty alerted to his presence. Trying not to be obvious, I craned my neck down the aisle, looking for him. Was he coming back for the second act? Had he been mobbed by girls in the lobby?

The lights started to go down, and I felt an odd sense of disappointment. Just before the theater was plunged entirely into darkness, Thomas reclaimed his seat, leaning over to me.

"Almost missed the start. What a disaster that would have been."

I snorted just before the curtain came up, earning myself another elbow from Callie.

Feeling brave in the dark theater, I leaned closer to Thomas. "You're going to get me into trouble," I whispered. "My friend really, really like Jackson Coles."

"Is it his phenomenal acting skills or his well-renowned humility and self-effacing attitude?"

I had to slap a hand over my mouth again to keep from laughing again. "Sorry," Thomas whispered. "I'll be good now, promise."

Thomas managed to stay quiet for nearly five minutes before leaning over to whisper something else in my ear, this time about the pedantic vocabulary of the script. During those minutes, I frantically struggled to remember everything I could about the man beside me, cursing myself for not following the celebrity gossip like Callie. Though I had to admit, Thomas wasn't the kind of guy who found himself in the gossip section all that often. In fact, if Callie hadn't forced me to watch the most recent *Darkness* movie that very afternoon, in preparation for seeing Jackson tonight, I might not have even realized who Thomas was.

To the best of my knowledge, Thomas Harper had a supporting role in each of the *Darkness* movies. Was he a rival to Jackson's character, or a friend? I couldn't remember. As far as I knew, he hadn't starred in any other movies, and a lack of celebrity dating seemed to leave him out of much of the Hollywood gossip. Did he have a girlfriend now? I couldn't remember seeing anything about him in the week of living with Callie in the dorm and being forced to watch entertainment news shows before bed every night.

The second half was far more enjoyable to me than the first half had been. How could it not be, when I had Thomas so often whispering in my ear, making fun of the seriousness of the actors and the ridiculousness of the script? Even the thrill of brushing my arm against his on several occasions would have been enough to improve the play, let alone the feel of his breath on my neck when he would lean in to whisper to me. By the time the curtain came down, I was a trembling mess of tension and excitement.

"Wow, guys," Thomas said, glancing around as the audience rose to its collective feet in applause. "I mean really, wow."

I laughed, glad to not have to worry about being loud now. "They are, apparently, really impressed."

"I suppose we should stand, too. Heaven knows I don't want him looking out here and seeing me on my arse. It will be all over the press that I'm a jealous wanker by morning."

I stood with him, clapping along with the rest as the cast took extended bows.

"I have to thank you, Lizzie," Thomas said, leaning toward me again. "I was afraid that was going to be a terrible evening. You made it bearable."

My stomach started flipping uncontrollably, like I was on a roller coaster. "I could say the same for you," I said. "The second half was somehow much better than the first."

He grinned at me, sending my stomach into overdrive again. "Do you have plans after this?"

"I don't know," I whispered, surprised. "Callie said something about going out…"

"I could meet you somewhere," he said, talking fast now. The lights were starting to come up around us. "Would that be cool with you?"

"Yeah," I said, without thinking. "That would be great."

"Here," he handed me his cell phone. "Put your number in."

I did as he asked, trying to keep him from seeing how much my fingers were trembling. "I'll be a few minutes," he said. "I have to go backstage and pay my respects. But I'll text you when I'm out? Find out where you are?"

"Sure," I breathed, completely overwhelmed by the situation, by the nearness of him and the feeling in my fingers when they had brushed his when he took back the phone.

"I should go," he said, looking around. The audience was gathering their things, the house lights on now. "I'll text you." He brushed my shoulder, fleetingly, meeting my eyes once, before he was gone, gracefully weaving his way through the crowd to a door near the stage.

I let out the breath I was holding in a rush of air. Had any of that really happened?

"Lizzie? Are you listening to me? Who were you talking to? You look all pale."

I turned back to my friend. "I do? Sorry. Must be more tired than I thought."

Callie looked concerned. "Do you want to skip the club? We could always call it a night, go out tomorrow instead."

"No!" I practically shouted, causing Callie to raise her eyebrows. "I mean, no, I'm fine. I want to go."

"Well, Meredith sent me the address." Callie started to force her way down the still-crowded aisle. "It doesn't look far. We could probably walk, save our money for cab fare home."

"Sounds good," I said, distracted. I wondered how I could get Callie onto the topic of Thomas Harper. I was desperate to know more about him. As it turned out, it wasn't so hard. As we made our way through the lobby and out onto Shaftesbury Avenue, crowded with theater goers, Callie seemed unwilling to talk about anything besides the *Darkness* series.

"I still can't believe we were able to see Jackson in such an important role," she gushed, slipping her arm through mine so we didn't get separated in the crowd. "I mean, just this afternoon we were watching him on screen in our flat. And tonight we saw him in person!"

"It's pretty cool," I said, looking for my angle. "So, how many *Darkness* movies are there now? I'm so out of the loop."

"Five," Callie said promptly. "But the sixth comes out next year. It's supposed to be the best one yet! And just think, we'll be over here when it happens. Oooh, maybe we could go to Leicester Square for the premiere!"

"That would be cool. Um, so what about the other cast members? Who, uh, who else do you like?"

If I sounded as awkward as I felt, Callie didn't notice. Or maybe she was just too excited to be talking about her favorite movies to care. "Well, there's Lola Fischer, of course. The female lead. She's a huge deal, you know, she was even dating Jackson last year. Major scandal, he was supposed to be with some British soap star. And Killian Cooper, he's a pretty big star. He's the bad guy, remember? A vampire, Jackson's major rival. Supposedly in werewolf mythology, the only being that can kill a werewolf is a vampire, so the two of them are always fighting for power—"

Eager to keep Callie from getting too far into werewolf mythology, I interrupted her. "What about, um, Thomas Harper? He's in those movies, right?"

"Oh yeah. He's really good. Cute, too, but he's got nothing on Jackson. He spends half his time doing indie movies no one's ever heard of, so he's not as famous as the others. I heard a rumor his part gets a lot bigger in this next movie though. We're supposed to find out what kind of powers he has, because it's never been really clear. At first, they made it seem like he was just a sidekick for Jackson's character, but they're setting it up for him to be a bigger deal. I wouldn't mind, I've always liked him."

"I don't think I've ever seen anything about him in any of the magazines," I pushed. "Does he have a famous girlfriend?" I was sure I sounded ridiculously obvious, but Callie just scrunched up her face.

"You know, I don't think I've ever heard him linked to anyone. Which is totally weird. Maybe he's gay."

My stomach sank. It would be just my luck for the first cute guy I'd ever flirted with to turn out to be gay. And a nice punch to my confidence, if I couldn't even tell the difference between actual flirting and a guy just being nice. Callie was still going on about *Darkness*, now explaining in intricate detail the relationships between the main characters. I tuned her out, replaying my interactions with Thomas at the theater.

"Oh, here we are," Callie said, stopping suddenly in the middle of the pavement, causing several people behind us to have to veer around us, muttering about tourists. Callie grabbed my hand and pulled me up to the bouncer. A small line snaked out from the door, but he took one look at Callie, who was smiling and, I noticed, had already removed her sweater, and let the two of us through.

"How do you always do that?"

"I have the best luck with bouncers," Callie said, as if getting past a line at the club was the easiest thing in the world. "You just have to remember that they want pretty girls in here. It's good for business. So you smile and you show them how confident you are and you have no problem."

"Yeah, I'm sure I'd have no problem at all," I said drily. Callie was scanning the room for our classmates, and I took the opportunity to check out our surroundings. I'd been to a few bars over the years, mostly with Callie or Sofia, my favorite cousin, but I'd never really been in an actual nightclub. I was surprised by how dark it was; I had been expecting bright, colored lights everywhere, but only saw them on the dance floor. The area around the dance floor was occupied mostly with overstuffed, hot-pink furniture. Between the pounding music and the crush of bodies, many of which seemed to have on very little clothing, I was overwhelmed in minutes.

"There they are," Callie said at last, pointing to a booth toward the back. We made our way to our friends, Callie getting hit on by no fewer than three guys on the way. Meredith, Tonya, and a few other girls I knew by face alone welcomed us, scooting over so we could squeeze into the booth. Sitting on the edge, my butt practically off the cushion, I couldn't say I was exactly comfortable, but I tried to keep a smile on my face. I was out clubbing with my new friends. Wasn't this what I had been waiting for?

I managed to hold out for a full minute before I pulled my phone from my purse. No text yet. I wondered how long it would be for Thomas to get out of the theater. There was probably a huge line of well wishers and groupies waiting for their chance to talk to Jackson.

I turned to the girls, trying to follow the conversation, but it was hard to hear from the end of the booth, and even harder to hear over the music. I could really use a drink to help calm my nerves, but I had yet to see a waitress in our section of the club. Suddenly the music changed and all the girls squealed. "I love this song!" Callie shouted, pushing me out of the booth, so she could get up. Before I realized what was happening, most of the girls had gotten up, and Callie was pulling me toward the dance floor.

"Callie—" I started to argue, but my friend wouldn't hear it.

"You're a great dancer, Lizzie. No fear, okay?"

I allowed myself to be pulled onto the floor, though I was unable to obey Callie's command of no fear. I was very scared. Dancing was a huge part of my culture at home. Most family parties ended up with a makeshift dance floor, and we had more family parties than anyone I knew. I was more than proficient at salsa and merengue. But that music was very different from this club stuff, and I hadn't danced in front of strangers probably ever in my whole life.

"Just loosen up," Callie shouted in my ear. "It's dark in here, no one is watching. Just have fun!"

That was one of the nicest things about Callie—no matter how different we were, she would never tease me, or judge me for being afraid of something new. Determined to trust that my friend had my best interests at heart, I tried to fall into the beat of the music, realizing after a minute or two that it really wasn't all that different.

Two songs passed before I felt the buzz of my phone in my jean jacket pocket, where I had slipped it for safekeeping on the dance floor. I pulled out the phone, nearly dropping it in excitement when I realized I had a text from an unknown number.

Hey, Lizzie, this is Thomas. Still up for that drink?

I wanted to squeal the way the girls had when their song came on. Instead, I satisfied myself texting him back the name and address of the club.

Be there in five.

I looked over at Callie, now dancing enthusiastically to something by Katy Perry. Somehow, I wasn't ready for my friend to know about Thomas yet. I was freaking out enough by the fact that he was famous, without bringing a screaming fan girl into the equation.

"Cal," I shouted into her ear. "I'm gonna go get a drink. Want something?"

"Vodka and cranberry," she shouted back. I gave her a thumbs up and headed off the dance floor, pulling out my phone on the way and sending a quick text back to Thomas. *I'm at the bar.*

I leaned against one of the bar stools, my nerves growing by the moment. Thomas was actually coming. He hadn't blown me off or changed his mind. I could hardly believe it. The bartender finally noticed me, and I ordered Callie's drink and a gin and tonic for myself, knowing my nervous stomach couldn't handle anything sickly sweet. As the bartender handed my change back, I felt a hand on my shoulder and nearly dropped the coins.

"Hi," Thomas said, smiling down at me. "Sorry I scared you."

"It's okay," I squeaked, knowing my face had gone red again. It drove me crazy how quick I was to blush.

He leaned down closer to my face. "It's loud in here."

"I know," I shouted back. "A little too loud for me."

"There's a section back there that should be a bit better," he said, pointing to a roped off area. "If my buddy is working, we can go back."

"Let me go take this to Callie," I said, holding up the pink drink.

Thomas nodded. "I'll meet you over there."

Careful with the two drinks, I made my way to the dance floor, wondering if there was any way to disappear behind the roped off section without arousing suspicion. I handed Callie's drink off to her and leaned in to shout. "I met a guy!"

Callie couldn't have looked more shocked if I had told her I was going to do a strip tease on the bar. "You did?"

I nodded. "At the bar," I lied. "I'm gonna go talk to him."

Callie still looked gob smacked. "Want me to come with you?"

"No, I'm fine."

"I don't know, Lizzie. This is a new town. And you don't exactly have a lot of experience with guys. What if something happens? Your brothers would murder me."

"I have my phone," I reminded her. "And we're not going to leave the club. I'm a grown-up, Mother, it will be fine."

Callie laughed, having called me Mother in similar situations a number of times. "Okay. But you text me if you need me, okay? Or come get me. I'll be here or at the booth."

I nodded and gave a little wave, trying not to be irritated with my friend for being so shocked. *You'd have been overprotective, too,* I reminded myself. *This* is *a strange city.*

I met Thomas at the velvet rope where he introduced me to a staff member named Bill. "Bill and I go way back," he shouted in my ear as we shook hands. "He used to tend bar in my local."

Bill unhooked the rope and stepped aside so Thomas could lead me up a short flight of stairs. I found myself in a small loft area overlooking the dance floor. We could still hear the music, but velvet drapes around our booth muffled the sound quite a bit.

"That's better," Thomas said, settling into the booth. "I can at least hear you now."

"Do you come here a lot?" I asked, amazed that this section of the club existed without anyone below knowing it.

Thomas shook his head. "To be honest, this isn't really my scene. I'm much more of a pub guy when I want a drink."

I grinned, glad to hear it for some reason. Maybe Thomas wasn't too glamorous for me after all. "What about you?" he asked. "Pub or club?"

"Uh," I felt suddenly uncomfortable. "Pub, I guess. But I don't really do much of either."

"A university student who doesn't go to the pub? I'm shocked."

I shrugged. "I should warn you right now, I'm kind of a goody-two-shoes."

"Me, too!" Thomas cried, looking thrilled. He leaned into me and spoke in mock confidential tones. "Would it shock you to know that I spent last New Year's Eve in my flat studying lines for a film I was about to start shooting?"

I laughed. "I spent last New Year's Eve at a party at my uncle's house, so I'm not one to judge."

"One time my brother convinced me to steal a Coke from the newsagent down the road," Thomas countered. "He said he would tell all my friends I was a baby if I didn't. So I did."

"You returned the Coke an hour later, didn't you?"

"Twenty minutes," he said, grinning. "And I cried."

I laughed, wondering why I had felt nervous about talking with him. He was wonderful.

"Tell me about school," he said. "Why London?"

"I've *always* wanted to come to London," I said.

"Are you enjoying it so far?"

"We haven't seen much of the city. We were stuck in orientation sessions the first few days, and were suffering crazy jet lag at night. Then we had this whole apartment fiasco. It hasn't been quite what I expected." I paused, not wanting to admit the underlying disappointment I had been feeling about my London adventure so far. "Anyhow. This is our first night really off campus."

"So you've been here all week and you haven't seen the city yet? We'll have to fix that." The implication in his words made my heart thud in my chest. I couldn't seem to wipe the smile from my face.

"I think the big draw for me was the literary history here," I went on, trying to control the giddiness that threatened to overwhelm me. "My favorite authors are British; I couldn't think of anywhere else I would want to study literature."

"Funny, my favorite authors are mostly American," he said, taking a sip of his beer. "Patterson, King, Grisham." He gave me a rueful grin. "Not exactly high-minded literature."

"There's nothing wrong with genre fiction," I said firmly. "Take it from an English major; people who only read the classics are usually boring and uptight."

"Cheers." Thomas rapped his bottle lightly against my glass. "Did you study literature at your university in the States as well?"

I nodded. "My BA is in English. I also have a teaching certificate."

"A teacher, eh? My mother was a teacher."

"So are my sisters," I said, feeling depressed suddenly. "But I have a ways to go. This program is nine months long."

"Nine months is a long time to be away from home. Where is home, by the way?"

"Detroit, Michigan. You know, where they make the cars. Motown, Kid Rock."

"I've seen *Eight Mile*, you know. I'm quite familiar with Detroit."

I laughed. "Well, I don't actually live in the city. The suburbs. Sterling Heights, to be exact. Much more *Pleasantville* than *Eight Mile*."

"Thank you for putting things in movie language for me," he said, winking. "Taking pity on the brainless actor is kind."

"You started it!" I cried, smacking his hand as he laughed. "So where are you from?"

"I grew up in Surrey, but the family's all up in Edinburgh now."

"Oooh," I sighed. "I can't wait to get up there."

"It's a beautiful city," he said. "They moved right when I started working in London, so I never lived there full time, but it's really nice to be able to visit them now."

We chatted for a while about family. I learned that Thomas is a middle child, his older brother is married and living outside Edinburgh, and his younger sister still lives at home. He seemed fascinated by the idea of my five siblings, and wanted to know all about my family, cousins and aunts and uncles included.

"My grandparents on both sides immigrated from Mexico," I explained. "My mom's mom moved back there after her husband died, and my dad's parents are both gone. But we have a huge family all nearby, more than a dozen cousins, and I don't even know how many second and third cousins. It gets pretty crazy when we're all in the same place, which happens all the time. We have more family dinners and parties than anyone you'll ever meet."

"Wow," he said. "I only have three cousins all together."

I laughed. "Then your house is probably much more peaceful than mine at Christmas."

"I think it would be nice to have a bigger family," he said. "You must have had lots of built-in playmates when you were little."

"I did," I agreed. "My best friend is actually my cousin Sofia." I felt a pang. It had only been a week but I missed Sofie like mad.

"It's pretty brave of you, coming all this way on your own, for such an extended stay." I looked up and saw that he was watching me closely, something about his expression making me think he could tell what I was feeling. Slightly embarrassed, I reached for my drink.

"I don't know about brave," I said, after I'd drained the rest of it. "But my family sure wasn't thrilled about it."

"They thought it was too far?"

"They thought I should be putting my hard-earned education to work getting a real job, not spending more loan money on something frivolous."

"Higher education is frivolous?"

"It is to them." I reached for my drink again, my hand coming up short when I realized it was empty. Talking about my parents' expectations always stressed me out.

Thomas noticed and gestured for a waitress. "Another gin and tonic and another Heineken, please."

"Thanks," I said, grateful.

"You're welcome. We can change the subject if you want."

"No, it's okay. I just have some guilt issues when it comes to my career," I laughed lightly, hoping I didn't sound too melodramatic, but Thomas only said, "I can relate."

"My parents are big on stability. They saw their parents struggle so much when they came to America. My dad worked a bunch of terrible jobs before he got hired at Ford. For him, a job with a good union, good benefits, that's like the holy grail."

"Your brothers and sisters agree?"

"Oh God, yes," I laughed. "Two brothers are at Ford with him, another is an electrician, and both the girls are teachers."

"So you followed in their footsteps?"

I was saved answering by the waitress's return with our drinks, and it was a good thing, too. I had been about to admit that the thought of teaching had lately filled me with a panic I couldn't explain. I hadn't admitted that to anyone, not even Sofie or Callie. What was it about Thomas that made me feel so chatty?

"What about you?" I asked, eager to stop thinking about my career prospects. "What did your folks think about acting?"

"They're supportive, now. It was a different story at first. They sent all three of us to really good schools, education was really important to them. I think they had visions of all three of us becoming barristers, like my dad."

"What does your brother do now?"

"He's a barrister." Thomas laughed. "He's the good son. But my sister is making noise about wanting to give acting a shot. They'll really kill me then." He winked at me, making my tummy flip all over again. I found that I was staring at his eyes while he talked. They were the most expressive eyes I had ever seen, flashing and twinkling, their green depths seeming to darken depending on his tone. *If I spent enough time with him I could read his mood in his eyes*, I thought. *Without him saying a word.*

"You said they weren't thrilled with the acting at first. Weren't you really young when *Darkness* came out?"

"I went to an open call when I was seventeen," he said. "I actually auditioned for Cooper." When I looked blank, he laughed. "Jackson's part. I take it you aren't a fan?"

I blushed to the roots of my hair. "Um…"

He laughed again and patted my hand, the contact sending a rush of shivers down my arm. "Don't worry about it. It's actually pretty refreshing. Anyway, I went to the audition kind of on a lark. I really liked drama in school, and kept telling my parents I wanted to study it at university. I figured if I could manage a callback in a major show, they might take me seriously. I was blown away when I was cast."

"And they let you do it. That's pretty cool."

"At that point, they couldn't have stopped me," he laughed. "I had visions of Hollywood superstardom in my eyes. I was impossible for months."

Just then, my phone beeped. I groaned as I looked down at it. "The girls are leaving."

Thomas sat up straighter. "I could take you home," he said. Was I imagining the eagerness in his voice?

"Thank you, but I should go with Callie. The other girls don't live on our side of town, and we're too new here for me to be leaving her on her own."

"You sound like a nice friend," he smiled at me, and I noticed, for the first time, that he had dimples. Or maybe they only appeared when he smiled a certain way. I had already mentally catalogued at least four different smiles to obsess over when I was alone.

He stood with me to walk me down the stairs. As soon as we were out of our protective alcove, the club noise hit me all over again. I had to lean up to yell right in his ear for him to hear me, brushing my arm across his as I went. I wasn't complaining. "Look, I'd introduce you but I'm afraid Callie will go all fan girl on you. Are you up for that tonight?"

"Hmm, can I take a rain check on the fan-girling?"

I laughed. "Sure."

As I scanned the room for Callie, Thomas took my hand. I looked up at him, surprised, as a rush of warmth shot through my fingers. "I'd like to see you again," he said, leaning down so I could hear him. "Would that be okay with you?"

I couldn't speak. Being so close to his face, his hand holding mine so firmly, I was overwhelmed with the desire to reach up and kiss him. I'd barely have to stretch at all. Instead, I nodded wordlessly, earning another grin from Thomas.

Five distinct smiles, I thought to myself. *I wonder what they all represent.*

"Tomorrow?"

I nodded again, pretty sure that *my* grin had turned downright goofy looking.

Thomas squeezed my hand before releasing it. "Text me when you get home then, we can set a time and you can give me your address."

"Sounds like a plan."

He nodded across the room. "I think I see your friend. Talk to you soon?"

Before I could respond, he was brushing his lips lightly across my forehead, squeezing my hand one last time, and turning away. I stood gaping after him, still feeling his lips on my forehead.

"There you are!" I turned to see Callie weaving across the room toward me. "Who was the cutie?"

"Just the boy I met," I said, unable to wipe the grin off my face.

"Oooh," Callie sing-songed, sounding distinctly tipsy. "You like him, I can tell."

"Yup. I do." Callie clapped her hands, stumbling slightly, and I reached out to put an arm around her shoulder. "Come on, drunky. Let's get you home."

We only had to wait a few minutes for a cab, much to my relief. Callie was drunker than I thought, and I was far too keyed up to worry about keeping my friend upright and steady. In the safety of the cab, I could let Callie slump into the door, giving me the chance to pull out my phone. First, I changed the unknown number to Thomas's name, feeling a little thrill as I did so. I had a cute boy in my contact list! Then I sent him a quick text, thanking him for the drink and giving him my address. Within seconds I had a new text in my inbox.

I thought we could make a whole day out of it. Start with breakfast. Is ten too early?

I beamed to myself in the darkness. I wouldn't have refused if he said he wanted to meet at six a.m.

Ten is great, I wrote back. *Can't wait.*

CHAPTER FOUR

I woke up the next morning well before the alarm went off. I'd had trouble falling asleep the night before—I was just too keyed up. My evening with Thomas had filled me with a buzz of energy I couldn't have dispelled if I wanted to. And knowing that I was going to spend the entire day with him…I was practically bouncing off the walls as I gathered my shower things and headed down to the bathroom.

Twenty minutes later, my excitement had turned to panic.

"Callie," I whispered loudly from the doorway to my roommate's bedroom. "Callie, wake up."

She snorted loudly in her sleep, threw an arm over her head, and rolled over to face the wall. Throwing good manners to the wind, I walked to her bed, bent over her sleeping form, and shouted, "Callie, wake up!"

She sat up, gasping and looking around the room in a panic. "Who's there? What's going on?

"Callie, I need your help."

She turned, hand on her heaving chest, to see me standing beside the bed and narrowed her eyes. "What the hell, Lizzie?" She flopped back against her pillows. "You scared me to death."

"Sorry," I said, reaching for her arm again. "I owe you big time. But I really, really need your help."

"With what?" she glanced at her alarm clock. "Jesus, Lizzie, it's not even nine a.m. It's *Saturday*."

"I have a date." I gave her arm another tug. "And I have absolutely no idea what I'm doing."

"Wait, what? You have a date? With who?"

"Remember the guy I was talking to last night? In the club?"

Suddenly her face cleared. "Wait a second. The club. That all seems so hazy. I totally forgot you hooked up with a guy!"

I rolled my eyes. "I did not hook up with him. I talked to him and had a few drinks."

Callie pulled herself out of bed and hugged me. "You picked up your first guy in a bar. I'm so proud of you."

"You're ridiculous," I said, laughing. "It's not that big of a deal."

"Yeah, right," she said, pulling back to peer at my face. "You're totally into him. I can tell. So you talked to him that whole time? Good for you. God, I drank a lot." She pulled her robe on. "Was he nice? Cute?"

"He was amazing," I said, figuring there was no point in hiding how much I liked to him. Cal would see right through it. "And he's taking me out again today."

Callie squealed and started jumping up and down, holding my hands.

"You have a date? Seriously? That is so awesome! I'm so happy for you! And we just got here too, look at you—"

"Cal, focus!" I shouted. "I'm desperate here!"

"What's the matter?" she asked, stopping her bouncing at once.

"I don't know what I'm doing," I repeated. "I never go on dates, and I don't know what to wear or how to do my hair. I'm no good at this stuff, Callie! I'm a mess!"

"Okay, okay, just calm down," she soothed, wrapping an arm around my shoulders. "Let me just get some coffee first, and then we'll figure it out, okay?"

She led me to the kitchenette, depositing me into a chair at the tiny dining table before setting to work on the coffee maker.

"First thing's first," she said, glancing back over her shoulder. "Where's he taking you?"

"I don't really know. He just said he wanted to spend the day with me."

Callie stopped what she was doing and turned to face me. "That's *adorable*!"

"Yeah, well it will be less adorable if I show up looking like the lame dork we both know me to be."

"You're not a dork, Lizzie," Callie said firmly, turning back to the coffee maker. "And he apparently liked you just fine last night, or he wouldn't be asking you out again."

"Yeah, well, it was pretty dark in that club."

Finished with the coffee, Callie poured us each a mug and joined me at the table. "Okay," she said, taking a sip. "What time is he getting here?"

"He said he'd pick me up at ten." I cast a worried glance at the clock over the microwave. "Which means I only have an hour to figure out how to look half way decent."

"You're worrying too much," she said firmly. "This is going to be fine." She peered into my face for a minute. "You really like him, don't you? What happened last night?"

"He took me to the…uh, VIP section of the club," I said, feeling my stomach flip at the memory. "It was…it was great. We talked so easily, you know? And he's really sweet."

Callie beamed at me. "This is awesome, Lizzie. It's so good to see you excited about a guy. And the VIP section, eh? Sounds like a keeper."

I played with my coffee mug for a minute, wondering if I should just come clean with Callie. My friend would be furious if she knew that I was going out with one of the actors from her favorite film franchise and hadn't told her. I took a deep breath.

"Cal, there's something I didn't tell you yet."

"Oh, Lizzie, you made out with him, didn't you? Girl, what have I told you? Never make out with boys in clubs. It's *so* tacky."

"I did not make out with him." I said firmly. "I just...I actually met him at the theater. He was sitting next to me, and we got to talking. He came to the club to meet me."

"Wow," my friend said. "So he *really* likes you then. Or he's a stalker." She raised her eyebrow. "Should we be concerned?"

"No," I scoffed. "Of course not. But, Cal...okay, so the reason he was at the play is because he knows one of the actors."

Callie went very still. "Which one of the actors?" she asked, her voice controlled. I glanced across the table and allowed myself one small grin.

"Jackson Coles."

Callie was silent for a good twenty seconds. "You're going out with someone who knows Jackson Coles?" she finally managed, her voice squeaky.

I nodded. "That's, uh, that's not all. He doesn't just *know* Jackson Coles. He works with him."

Callie reached across the table and grabbed my arm in a death grip. "Elizabeth Medina, you tell me who you're seeing right this second."

"Thomas Harper."

The kitchen was so quiet I could hear the drip of the leaky faucet. Then Callie let out an ear splitting shriek. "Holy shit!" she cried.

"Callie, shh, you're going to wake up the neighbors!"

"You're going on a date with a movie star, Lizzie! A frickin' movie star!"

"He is not a movie star," I said, then stopped myself. For all intents and purposes, Thomas *was*. It was just hard to think of him that way after spending even five minutes with him. He was just a boy—a really cute, really nice, really comfortable, really gorgeous boy.

"He is, too. He's in one of the biggest movie franchises in history. Oh my God. Oh my God."

"Callie, get it together. You are doing nothing to help my nerves."

"No wonder you were so eager to go off and talk to a boy you met at the bar. I mean, I never thought you had it in you. I was sure you'd be back on the dance floor in minutes. But, seriously, if it was Gideon from *Darkness*, of course you wanted to talk to him."

"It had nothing to do with that," I said firmly, ignoring Callie's insinuation that I was a baby about men. "I talked to him in the theater before I even knew who he was. Besides, you know I never even liked those movies."

"Well, don't tell him that." Callie raised her eyebrows. I flushed, remembering that I had pretty much already let that slip to Thomas in the club. How stupid could someone be?

He still asked you out, I reminded myself. *Even though you pretty much insulted his work, he asked you out.*

"Maybe that's why he likes me," I murmured, more to myself than to Callie. "Maybe he likes that I don't fall all over him for the movie thing."

"Could be," Callie said thoughtfully. "Or maybe he's just happy to get some attention. It probably gets lame being overshadowed by Jackson Coles all the time."

I made a face, amazed than anyone would prefer Jackson over Thomas. Then I realized we had yet to address my problem. I stood. "This is all very interesting. But you said you would help me. It's getting late."

"Fine," Callie said, picking up her mug as we stood. "Let's pick an outfit first."

***

Half an hour later, I was ready. Callie waited with me at the window seat, both of us staring out at the street below for a sign of Thomas. "Is he driving, do you think?" Callie asked for the fifth time. "I bet he drives. I bet he has a gorgeous, flashy sports car. Lizzie, *please* let me go down and meet him."

"No," I said, also for the fifth time. No way was I subjecting Thomas to Callie freaking out on him. And she would, too. There was just no way she could keep her shit together when it came to an honest to goodness celebrity, let alone one who had worked in such close proximity to Jackson Coles.

"Are you sure you don't want to change your shoes?" Callie asked, looking down at my ballet flats. "Those heels I showed you look so good with skinny jeans."

For all my panic earlier, in the end, I had pretty much picked out my own outfit. Callie had encouraged me to borrow a short pink skirt and pair it with her highest heels. I had put my foot down, deciding I was already way too nervous to pull off heels, which were hard for me in the best of circumstances. I had settled on skinny-leg dark jeans, a yellow long-sleeved tee, and pink ballet flats. I had agreed to borrow Callie's turquoise blazer though, which was much more stylish than any of my own jackets. Paired with the same pink scarf from the night before and a pair of silver hoops, I thought I looked cute enough. More importantly, I was comfortable and felt like myself. I had a feeling Thomas would see right through me if I showed up looking like I'd stepped out of a fashion magazine.

"These shoes are better for me," I said. "Thanks, though."

"And your hair," Callie said wistfully. "I'm still not sure. Should we have gone ahead and straightened it?"

I had the exact same hair as my mother and my sisters—long, dark, and curly. Unlike my sisters, who managed to coax their curls into luxurious waves, I had never managed better than frizzy corkscrews. "If we straighten my hair, it will end up frizzy if there is even a touch of humidity. And this being London, that's not like, unheard of."

When I had suggested my normal braid, Callie was so horrified I thought she might cry. In the end, I agreed to let my friend complete some kind of complicated, loose French braid that hung softly over one shoulder. It felt soft and pretty, and I had to admit, I liked the look.

"Well, what about lipstick? I mean, that lip gloss is nice and all, but this is *Thomas Harper* we're talking about." Callie had started to say Thomas Harper with the same reverence she usually reserved for talking about Jackson Coles. Yet another reason I wouldn't be inviting her downstairs.

I was saved having to have the lipstick argument yet again by the arrival of a nondescript, green car on the curb below. "He's here!" Callie squealed as we watched Thomas step out of the car and onto the sidewalk. In a more subdued voice, she said, "That's his car?"

I could care less about his car. Just the sight of the top of his head had sent my heart galloping in my chest. I took a deep breath and turned to Callie. "Do I look okay?"

"You look great," my friend said, wide-eyed. She looked almost as nervous as I felt. "I can't believe this is real."

I felt a flash of panic. Thomas had seemed like such a normal, nice guy last night. But what if Callie was right? What if he did act like some big movie star? What if I wasn't what he was expecting? What if he was disappointed with me? Sensing my panic, Callie suddenly reached out and grabbed my hands. "You'll be fine," she said firmly. "You'll be *better* than fine. You just be yourself. He's lucky to get to spend a day with you, Lizzie. I mean that."

Touched, I hugged my friend quickly before grabbing my purse. "I'll text you, okay?"

"You better!" Callie called after me as I headed through the front door.

Thomas was waiting for me outside the restaurant, just as we had arranged. He looked ridiculously handsome to me, dressed in dark jeans and a green crew-neck sweater that brought out the brightness of his eyes. "Hi," I said, feeling suddenly breathless.

"Hey." He smiled at the sight of me. Did I catch his eyes flick down over my outfit. "You look great."

"Thanks."

Thomas led me to the car and opened the passenger door for me. I knew Callie would still be watching from the window, and allowed myself a small grin. The door-opening would score big points with my friend, I knew.

"So, what did you have in mind today?" Thomas asked, turning his attention to his side mirror and peering out at the approaching traffic.

"Um..." I said, my nervousness returning. *What did I have in mind?* I thought. Besides wanting to kiss him, which I don't think would go over all that well, my mind was a complete blank.

But Thomas was continuing. "If you don't have any objections, I was thinking I could take you on a little tour of the city."

"Yeah?"

"Yeah," he turned back to give me one more devastating smile before finding a gap in the traffic and pulling out. "It's completely unacceptable to me that you're not having any fun here yet. We need to correct that immediately."

I smiled, relaxing back into my seat. "I've had fun," I said. "It's just not...quite what I thought it would be."

"What did you think it would be?"

I was quiet for a moment, considering that. How dumb would it be to tell him that I had expected it to be life changing? Thomas looked over at me, obviously waiting.

"Epic," I finally whispered. "I was expecting it to be epic."

A grin broke out over his face, making the breath catch in my throat.

"We can do epic."

***

"Okay, no judging," Thomas said, setting the parking break. "I'm fully aware that this place doesn't actually look all that epic, but I promise you won't be disappointed."

I looked up at the unimposing facade of the brick building in front of us. "We do have diners back in Michigan, you know."

Thomas laughed and reached for the handle of his door. "Just trust me."

I pushed my own door open and joined him on the sidewalk in front of the restaurant. Through the front window, I could see the Saturday morning diners clustered around tables and the counter. It looked crowded.

"I hope you're hungry," Thomas said, smiling down at me. "No epic London day should ever be attempted without a full English breakfast in your stomach."

I was surprised to realize that I was in fact hungry—starving was more like it. I hadn't managed more than a piece of toast this morning, so intense were my nerves. Now that I'd had time to get used to being in Thomas's presence, I realized those nerves had completely gone, replaced entirely by hunger pangs.

Thomas led me into the restaurant, calling out a hello to a passing waitress. "You got a seat for me, Maggie?"

"Try the back corner," she called over her shoulder as she hurried off with a coffee pot in her hand.

"You're on a first-name basis with the staff here?" I asked, raising an eyebrow at him. Thomas nodded as he took my elbow, leading me through the crowd.

"I come in a lot. I told you, best breakfast in London."

I decided to take his word for it. To my eyes, the place looked completely unremarkable, no different really from any of the generic diners I frequented at home. The somewhat rickety table was covered in a frayed red tablecloth, a pair of plastic-coated menus stuck between a cheap plastic vase of flowers and a ceramic bowl holding sugar packets.

"No need for that," Thomas said when I reached for the menu. "I promise I'm not one of those guys who makes a practice of ordering for his date, but since the goal here is to show you the best breakfast in London, I hope you'll trust me."

I was so thrown by his casual use of the word date that I wouldn't have been able to argue if I wanted to. A moment later, the same waitress appeared, looking harried.

"All right, Thom?" she said, leaning her hip against our table.

"Great, thanks," he said. "This is my friend, Lizzie. Lizzie, this is my Maggie, without whom I would starve and die from caffeine deprivation."

I felt a strange flash of jealousy at his familiar tone. *Seriously, Lizzie?* I thought. *You're gonna be that girl?* Besides the utter absurdity of being jealous over a guy I'd known for less than twenty-four hours, Maggie appeared old enough to be his mother. She wore her long red hair in a braid through which quite a bit of white was showing, and there were copious laugh lines around her mouth and eyes.

Maggie rolled her eyes at Thomas, but held out her hand for me to shake. "Nice to meet you."

"Nice to meet you, too," I said. Maggie held my gaze, a small smile playing at her lips. I got the impression the older woman was evaluating me for some reason. "Thomas has been raving about the food."

"Well, he certainly eats here enough to know something about it, I guess."

"I'm telling you," Thomas said, leaning back in his chair, completely at ease. "Best breakfast in London. And clearly I'm not alone in my opinion." He looked around the room. "Business looks like it's booming."

Maggie sighed. "My new girl called in ill this morning. Says it's something she ate, but I'd bet the whole shop it was something she drank, if you know what I mean. I've been run off my feet all morning."

Thomas patted her hand. "We'll make it easy on you, then. Two fulls and a pot of Earl Grey."

Maggie scribbled something on her pad before looking up at us. "I'd stay and chat, but like I said..."

Thomas waved his hands. "Get back to work, lazy bones."

Maggie slapped his shoulder as she headed off to put in our order.

"Don't let her grumpiness fool you," Thomas said. "She's actually really nice."

I smiled in response, watching as he took a sip from his water glass. I found it unbelievably strange to see Thomas in this environment, so comfortable. I'd watched him on a giant screen in a movie theater, for God's sake, and now here I was, watching him tease a waitress in a dingy little diner. It was just too bizarre.

"What?" Thomas asked, and I realized I'd been staring.

"Sorry," I said, shaking my head. "I just keep thinking how weird this is, hanging out with a movie star."

A loud laugh erupted from behind me, and I spun in my chair to see Maggie returning with a pot of tea. "A movie star? Him? You must be joking."

I flushed, feeling embarrassed. I knew it was totally uncool to give any impression of being star struck. But Thomas was laughing.

"Thanks a lot, Maggie." He winked at me across the table. "We can't let the pretty girl think I'm a star, just for the morning? You really have to mess up my game like that?"

"Sorry," she said, plopping the teapot down on the table. "It just sounds too ridiculous. Little Thomas Harper, a star." The sounds of her laughter lingered as she headed to the next table.

Thomas shook his head. "She's got a point, you know. I'm hardly a movie star."

"You're in one of the most successful franchises of the decade!" I argued, already forgetting my internal instructions about not sounding star struck.

"Being in a movie is different from being a movie star, believe me. I'll bet you that Maggie is the only person in this place who even knows my name."

"I knew your name."

"Yes," Thomas said, his voice suddenly more serious. His eyes met mine across the table, and he held my gaze. "Yes you did."

I squirmed slightly, feeling something in his expression, some kind of intensity I wasn't used to. But then Thomas was smiling, looking like his normal, easy-going self again. "Don't forget, I've spent a great deal of time in the company of Jackson Coles. I am fully aware of what it takes to be a movie star."

I was impressed, and slightly surprised, to find not a trace of jealousy or bitterness in his voice.

"You don't sound like it made the most positive of impressions on you," I said.

Thomas shrugged. "I've never really been too interested in that, to be honest. I'm not gonna lie, the money would be nice," he winked at me and I felt my stomach flutter. There was something about the way he teased, the way he always seemed to be slightly amused by the world around him, that I found incredibly appealing. Thomas continued. "I didn't get into this business for the fame part, you know? It was always about the acting for me."

"You love it," I guessed.

"You have no idea." The seemingly ever-present half smile had disappeared from Thomas's face, replaced by the same look of intensity that had so affected me a moment earlier. "Acting is the most fun I've ever had. It challenges me like nothing else in my life, but when I get it right, the thrill is indescribable. I can't ever seem to get enough."

"Wow," I said, my voice soft. Somehow I hadn't expected that kind of passion from him. It gave me a sad little ache in my chest; had I ever felt that way about anything? Ever in my life? I didn't think so. Maybe my writing, but that was just a hobby. It wasn't like I could share that with anyone.

"What about you?" Thomas asked, as if reading my thoughts. "Do you enjoy your work? Studying literature?"

"I love studying literature," I said. "But I'd hardly call it work." I couldn't help the sigh that escaped. "Work is what will come next."

"What do you mean?"

"Once I'm done with my program here," I clarified. "I'll be going back home to teach."

"I think you mentioned that last night," Thomas said, nodding. "A teacher. Now there's a noble profession."

I did my best not to snort. There was no point in dragging all my baggage into our perfectly nice Saturday breakfast. Instead I twisted the paper from my straw around my fingers, not meeting his eyes.

"I don't know about that, but it is what I'm qualified for, so it's what I'll be doing."

The ache in my chest intensified, mutating slightly until it felt more akin to panic. I was getting used to this feeling; it seemed to appear every time the subject of my future teaching career came up. I looked up and noticed Thomas was watching me, a shrewd look on his face.

"Is teaching what you want to do? I recall a lot of talk last night about what your parents wanted you to do, but not a whole lot about what you wanted to do."

I had a sudden urge to tell him about my doubts, but was saved from embarrassing myself by the arrival of our food. "Here you go," Maggie said, sliding two plates off her forearm neatly onto the table. "Two full English breakfasts and a pot of Earl Grey."

"Looks great, Maggs, thanks," Thomas said, smiling up at her.

I was looking down at my plate. It didn't look too different from the breakfasts I found in diners at home, except for the puddle of beans, mushrooms, and a fried tomato. And there was something strange next to my eggs.

"Blood pudding," Maggie said, grinning. "It's better than it sounds," she called over her shoulder as she walked back to the kitchen.

I looked up at Thomas, feeling faintly ill. "Blood pudding? Does it actually have, you know, blood in it?"

"Yes," he said, looking slightly sheepish. "But I promise it's really good. Just try not to think about it, yeah?"

"I don't know." I poked the purplish mass with my fork, uncertain.

"Look, if you don't like it, you don't have to eat it," Thomas said, nudging my hand. "But you gotta at least try it."

At the feel of his hand against mine, I looked up and met his gaze. I thought of all the things in my life I had refused to try, all the things that seemed too scary or weird or out of sync with my family. And then I thought of how I wanted this trip to be the start of something new, the start of someone new. I smiled at him and took a bite.

In the end, I didn't care for it much, and Thomas plucked it from my plate to finish it himself, allowing me to concentrate on my bacon, eggs, and sausage.

But I was very, very glad I'd given it a chance.

CHAPTER FIVE

"This is amazing," I said. "Seriously, I don't think I've ever seen this many people in one place in my life."

"It gets pretty crowded," Thomas agreed, taking my elbow to guide me past the group of tourists that had stopped in the middle of our path to take pictures.

"Is it always like this?"

"Saturdays are the worst," he assured me. "Or the best, depending on how you look at it. That's when the antique stalls are open. But there's always some kind of crowd in Portobello Road. It will be worse this afternoon, actually. We got here early."

As we made our way down the street market, I had a hard time keeping my jaw closed. No matter what Thomas said, I couldn't imagine the crowd ever getting larger than this.

We wandered from stall to stall, checking out the plethora of goods. In addition to the antiques, there were stalls upon stalls of vendors selling clothing, produce, street food, jewelry, books… all of it stretching on and on as far as I could see, no end in sight.

"This is amazing," I said again. A bookstand caught my eye, and I looked at Thomas hopefully. "Do you mind?"

"Not at all."

I could have spent the entire day just pouring over the books. Leather-bound ancient volumes, early editions, long out-of-print favorites. It was like a dream come true. I had to struggle not to spend half my rent money on a leather-bound, perfectly preserved copy of *Pride and Prejudice* from the early twentieth century. When Thomas swooped in to buy it for me, I recoiled. "No," I said firmly. "I mean, thank you, my gosh, what an offer. But no, please. I couldn't take it."

"I'd like to buy it for you," he said, searching my face. "It would mean a lot to me."

"It's too much," I insisted. I smiled at the stall owner. "Thank you." I grabbed Thomas by the elbow and dragged him away. "You can buy me a crepe instead. Those smell amazing."

We stood in line at the crepe stand, watching the cook spread batter paper thin onto hot round griddles. It smelled heavenly, and I cursed the long line in front of us. Breakfast seemed a long time ago.

"You a Jane Austen fan?" Thomas asked, his voice a bit too casual.

"Yes, I am," I said, turning to him. "But don't you dare even think about going back to buy that book."

He held up his hands. "I wouldn't! I'm just curious. Your entire face came alive when you saw it."

I felt a little embarrassed. "It's my favorite book. It always has been. My mom read it to me when I was little—it was her favorite, too. I'm named after Lizzie Bennet."

"Ah, I was wondering if you were a Liz or an official Lizzie."

"Lizzie. Which is a pretty big deal, cause I'm the only one of my siblings who wasn't given a family name." I ticked the names off on my fingers. "Maria, Carlos, Laura,

Matias, Samuel. All good, Hispanic names, all family names. There are like, six Marias in our family. Lots of Sofias, too. My mom is Sofia, and my favorite cousin is named after her. So is my niece. They're all connected. I'm the only one who's different." Saying it like that made me feel sad, somehow, though I had always been so proud of my literary name.

"So your love of books was assured from birth." Thomas reached over and took my hand. I wondered when the heat-shooting effect of skin-to-skin contact would wear off.

"My mom always said she had a feeling I'd love books as much as she does. She used to read to me when she was pregnant." I did not mention the fact that my mother had only just learned to read English before I was born. As an undocumented immigrant's daughter, Sofia Flores had been in and out of school her entire childhood as the family moved from place to place, finally dropping out entirely to help her mother clean houses at the age of thirteen. It wasn't until her own children were in school that she decided to learn to read in the language they would be using in school. She practiced right along with Laura and Carlos when they brought their schoolwork home. By the time she was pregnant with me, she had fallen in love with the language. *Pride and Prejudice* was the first novel she had ever finished.

Thomas squeezed my hand. "You okay? You went away there for a second."

"Yup," I said. His eyes searched my face, kind and curious, and I knew, in that moment, that I would tell him that story one day. Knew I could trust him with all of my stories.

"Next!"

Thomas pulled me up to the front of the line, and we made our choices, me going for the cinnamon and sugar while Thomas picked the Nutella and berries. Walking down the road in the bright sunshine, Thomas eating with his left hand so he didn't have to let go of my hand, I decided it was the best thing I had ever tasted.

***

Half an hour later, Thomas was maneuvering his car through the busy traffic of Westminster. I found I was having trouble keeping my eyes off of his profile; with the sun shining and the sky blue behind him, his hair rustled by the breeze from the open window, he was beyond attractive. The fact that his face diverted so much of my attention away from the sights of central London around me was testament to that.

"Having fun?" he asked, turning his head slightly to look at me. I blushed, wondering if he could tell I'd been staring.

"I'm having a great time," I said, hoping he could tell from my tone how much I meant that.

"But not epic yet." It wasn't a question.

"I don't know," I said, considering. "I think it's been pretty epic so far."

"Pretty epic isn't epic," he scolded. "Don't worry. We'll get there."

Thomas made a turn, and suddenly I could see a flash of water in the distance. "Is that the river?" I asked, feeling excitement coarse through me.

"It is indeed," he said. "And our next stop."

Thomas turned again, following winding streets. We seemed to be getting farther from our destination; I was sure the river was quite far behind us now.

"Here we are," Thomas said, pulling over suddenly and deftly parking in a spot not much bigger than the car. He turned to me and grinned. "We're lucky. I have a friend who lives and works in Westminster, and he lets me use his spot when he's out of town."

"These are private spots?" I asked, noticing the bumper-to-bumper cars lined up on the streets.

"Yeah." Thomas unbuckled his seat belt. "Parking is a premium down here. I usually don't bother. The Tube is much faster."

As I climbed out of the car, I couldn't help smiling to myself. I'd been so worried Thomas would be different from me, a glamorous movie star out of my league. Instead I found he traveled London by Tube, just like me.

"Do you have everything?" he asked, as he donned a blue baseball cap. "I figure we won't need the car much from here out."

I patted my purse. "Yup."

Thomas took my hand again, thrilling me, again, and started off down the street. "I'm glad you wore good walking shoes. I was scared you would show up in heels or something and we'd have to take the car everywhere. Parking in London is a nightmare."

"I'm not much of a heels girl," I said. "I usually fall in heels, actually."

Thomas led me down a few blocks. It was a beautiful neighborhood, the white stone buildings old and imposing. "Where are we, exactly?"

"Westminster," he explained. "We actually parked pretty close to Buckingham Palace. Lots of these buildings are related to the government. I should probably know what they are, but...." He trailed off, winking down at me. After a moment, he went on. "In just a minute, when we pass this building, we should be able to see...yup, there."

I stopped short. We had come around a bend and now, fully visible, Westminster Abbey stretched up in front of us, Big Ben towering beyond, the London Eye just barely visible in the distance. "Wow," I whispered. "I've wanted to see this my whole life."

"It's not bad, right?"

"It's really, really cool." I felt breathless with excitement. *This* was how I pictured London—ancient buildings full of history, beautiful architecture, the bustle of locals and tourists around me. I felt, just then, a world away from home. We crossed the street and walked around the Abbey, joining the crowds of tourists swarming the lawn outside the north entrance.

I pulled out my camera, snapping madly. "Here," Thomas said, holding out his hand. He took the camera from me and directed me in front of the Abbey. "Smile!"

A passing tourist paused at his side. "Would you like me to get you both?" the man asked, his accent American.

"That would be great," Thomas said, handing over the camera and jogging the short distance to my side. He draped an arm around me, his hand resting gently on my arm. I was sure I could feel tingles from the contact all the way to my toes. "Smile," called the man. *What an unnecessary direction*, I thought, suppressing the urge to burst out laughing. Standing there outside Westminster with the sun shining down and Thomas's arm around me, I was pretty sure I'd never be able to stop smiling.

"Cheers," Thomas said, retrieving the camera. "We appreciate it."

"Is it a good one?" I asked, as Thomas gazed down at the display. I peeked around his shoulder, seeing the two of us smiling up at me. *We look good together*, I thought, and a thrill ran through me. *We look like a couple.*

"You'll have to print me a copy," Thomas said. "Okay, now to business. Did you want to tour the Abbey, or just walk down to the embankment?"

"I want to go inside," I said automatically.

"Inside it is then."

Thomas insisted on purchasing our tickets, though I did my best to convince him to let me contribute. In my head, I was adding up his costs from the day; breakfast, street food at the market, now tickets. It made me feel anxious.

"Let me get mine."

Thomas was having none of it. "You're my guest today," he said firmly.

Once we'd passed through the doors, I had to blink to adjust my eyes. It was much darker inside. It was also quiet, in that vast echoey way of sacred places. It made me think of mass at home, sitting with my family in our usual pew, waiting for the service to start. It made me want to whisper. Then I looked up at the towering arches of the ceiling and thoughts of home slipped my mind entirely.

"Wow," I said, my voice soft. "This is...wow."

"Come on," Thomas said, taking my hand. "It's even better when you're properly inside."

We strolled through the abbey hand-in-hand, examining the nave, the choir, even the coronation throne. "I wish I could take a picture of this," I said, gazing at the wooden chair on which countless royals had been crowned.

"Because of the history?" Thomas asked, releasing my hand so I could lean in closer to the chair.

"No," I said, flashing him a grin over my shoulder. "Because someday I'll get to see hottie William sitting on this thing, getting *his* crown."

Thomas laughed. "He might not be so hot by then."

We headed down the nave, and Thomas pointed out the various tombs and graves of famous Britons we passed. "There are people here?" I asked, looking down at the floor. "Like, buried under our feet?"

Thomas nodded. "Some of the richer guys are in crypts in the walls. But there're loads of famous people in here. Queen Elizabeth, Bloody Mary, Isaac Newton, Darwin—"

"Darwin is here? *Charles* Darwin?"

"He is." Thomas looked down at the map he had grabbed at the door. "This way." He led me down the nave, studying the floor, until we found a plain white marble floor stone. "Here he is," Thomas said, pointing down. "Darwin."

"That's incredible," I said, shaking my head. "That they would put a scientist here, with all the royalty."

"If you like that, wait till you see the poets. This will be right up your alley."

In a corner of the Abbey, we came to a grouping of plaques on the floor. "What is this?" I asked.

"Look at the names."

My eyes scanned the graves. "W.H. Auden…Charles Dickens…Kipling…Tennyson…"

I turned to Thomas. "They're buried here, too? All of these writers?"

He nodded. "And there are memorials for other great writers and poets that are buried elsewhere. There's Shakespeare, the Bronte sisters…"

To my horror, I felt tears come to my eyes.

Thomas noticed immediately. "What's wrong?"

I shook my head, trying to smile. "It's stupid," I said, wiping my eyes.

"Tell me."

"I just think it's so beautiful," I said, gesturing around. "The way they honor science and literature and poetry and religion all at the same time. So many people think those things threaten each other, that they can't exist together."

"Those people are wrong," Thomas said, his voice soft.

I looked up and saw that his eyes were trained on my face, his expression serious. I smiled, though the tears were back. "They're wrong," I agreed.

Thomas took my hand. This time, he didn't let go.

***

After the Abbey, we walked down to the embankment, and I got my first look at the River Thames. "What do you think?"

I was quiet for a minute. "It's, uh, browner than I thought it would be."

Thomas threw his head back and laughed. "It's very muddy."

"It's nice," I backtracked, feeling embarrassed. "Just, you know, brown."

We strolled along the embankment, still hand in hand, and I told Thomas about the river in Detroit. "It forms the border between the US and Canada," I said. "There's this island park, Belle Isle, that we always go to in the summer. One of my uncles has a boat, and we all go out together with a picnic to eat on the island."

"You're going to be homesick," Thomas said, watching my face.

"Yeah, probably. I miss it already. It's weird, you know, how you can't wait to get away from something your whole life, and then end up missing it."

"Why did you want to get away from home? You said you are close with your family, right?"

I was quiet for a moment, wondering how to explain. "I love my family," I finally said, my voice soft. "But I've always felt…trapped, I guess." Thomas waited for me to go on. "Oh, I don't know if that's the right word." I shook my head. "Stifled, maybe? Confined? Like everything was already decided for me."

"What was decided for you?"

"Like, my school. There was never really any discussion about where I would go. My parents just assumed I'd be at the local college, just like my sisters. The day I suggested I might go away to school, that I wanted to live on campus…" I remembered how my mother had actually cried at that announcement, how she'd had to excuse herself from the dinner table. And my sisters and Carlos had yelled and Matias had sneered until finally I backed down. "You would have thought I was telling them I was disowning them," I said, shaking my head again.

"You told me last night that you had some guilt issues about your career. Let me guess, there was never really any discussion about that either?"

I was momentarily stunned that he'd remembered my comment from the night before. It filled me with a comforting warmth, taking the sting out of the topic of conversation.

"Yeah," I admitted. "My parents have been talking about me being a teacher for as long as I can remember. Stability, benefits, protection. That's about all that matters in their eyes."

Thomas stopped walking, oblivious to the people around us. "What matters to you, though, Lizzie? If they had asked, what would you have told them?"

I looked down, embarrassed, but Thomas placed a hand under my chin, gently directing my gaze at him. "Go on, you can tell me."

"I've always wanted to be a writer," I said, feeling myself blush. I'd only ever admitted that to Sofie. "Besides my family, books are the thing I love most."

Thomas's face lit up. "What do you like to write? Can I read your stuff?"

I laughed, pulling on his hand so he would start walking again. The other pedestrians were starting to grumble about us blocking the sidewalk. "I doubt you want to read my stuff."

"Why would you say that?" Thomas asked, running a few steps to catch up with me. "I'd love to read what you've written. What is it? Poetry? Literature?"

"Nothing so high-minded," I said, trying to avoid his gaze. I was totally wishing I had kept my mouth shut now.

"Okay...mystery? Thriller? Romance?"

"I write love stories," I said, averting my face. I was completely blushing now. He was going to think I was so stupid.

"That's awesome," he said, and I was surprised to hear the sincerity in his voice. I chanced a glance at his face and saw that he was smiling—in a nice, non-mocking sort of way.

"You think so?" I asked.

"Of course," Thomas said. "Why wouldn't I?"

"It seems like most guys are pretty critical of romance." I thought of the number of times my brothers had mocked me for my dog-eared collection of drugstore paperbacks.

"All the best stories are love stories," Thomas said, placing a hand on my back to gently guide me away from the embankment. We crossed the road and headed off along a tree-lined street, leaving the river behind us. "Really," Thomas went on. "Try to think of one classic film or book that doesn't have an element of romance. Even action flicks have a love story sub-plot."

"I guess that's true," I said, trying to think of an example that didn't support his theory.

"Love stories are like, the common thread," Thomas continued. "The thing everyone wants in their own life. What do we connect with more than a great love story?"

I was grinning now. "I completely agree."

Thomas smiled back. "Everyone is looking for a good love story. If you can write that, if you can connect with people over something so elemental, I think you're really doing something."

He literally couldn't be more perfect if he tried, I thought. Maybe it was the look in his eyes or the way he was so unquestioningly supportive. Or maybe it was simply all the talk of love. Regardless, Thomas was still smiling at me, and I was overcome, once again, with the desire to rise up on my tiptoes and kiss him.

"Come on," he said, tugging my hand a little and dispelling the mood. "We're almost to Leicester Square. There's a great gelato place up here. Then I'm taking you to the best bookstore in town."

I allowed myself to be hurried along, thankful I hadn't done anything stupid. *How awful would that have been?* I asked myself. *To have kissed him when all he's got on his mind is gelato.*

***

Several hours later, I was completely exhausted. We had wandered through Leicester Square, Thomas pointing out where the *Darkness* premieres had been held as we ate gelato outside a café. He had then taken me to Foyles, a sprawling bookstore that I would have been content to stay in for the rest of the day. Thomas eventually had to drag me away, promising I could come back just as soon as I wanted. Then we headed to Trafalgar Square, pausing with the other tourists to sit at the base of Nelson's Column and take pictures of each other.

After we had made our way up Regent Street, pausing to window-shop as we went, we took a few minutes to do the tourist thing again in Piccadilly Circus. Night was beginning to fall, and I felt slightly revived by the excitement of the neon signs and bustle of crowds heading out for dinner. Finally, Thomas turned to me. "You tired yet?"

"Exhausted," I admitted, laughing. I felt like we had walked through the entire city. I was completely overwhelmed by the knowledge that there was so much more of London out there. I'd barely scratched the surface.

"Let's catch a bus," he said. "We need to head back toward the embankment, and I'm not sure my feet can handle it. He pointed the way down the street to a bus stop, and we rambled over in that direction. As we neared the shelter, my attention was caught by a poster in the glass window.

"Hey, that's you!"

Thomas turned, confused, and looked in the direction I was pointing. When he saw the *Darkness* poster on the side of the bus stop, he snorted. "Just barely."

"Come on, I can totally see your face."

"Yeah, behind Jackson, Lola, Killian, and a bunch of other people. It's no big deal, Lizzie."

"Isn't it weird though? To just be walking down the street and see yourself on a bus stop?"

Thomas shrugged. "I don't really think about it. I mean, yeah, the first time it happened, it was weird. But now I just try not to let it bother me."

"I have to say, I'm kind of surprised."

"About what?"

"Well, we've been together all day, out and about in London. I would have thought that someone would recognize you. I would have thought you'd have fan girls following you around, demanding autographs. Or paparazzi taking your picture. *Darkness* is such a huge franchise."

Thomas laughed. "Fan girls have never paid any attention to me. I guess my face just isn't that memorable." He winked at me, making my heart flutter. "The only time someone asks me for an autograph is at a premiere." He touched the brim of his cap. "Hats work wonders. Sunglasses, too, if it's closer to a release and there's more buzz. Well, not for someone like Jackson, but for me it's probably more than enough."

Not for the first time, I marveled that anyone would possibly think that Jackson was in any way more appealing than Thomas. My train of thought was interrupted by the arrival of our bus, a bright red double-decker. "Wanna ride on the top?" Thomas asked, his eyes sparkling.

"Do you even need to ask?"

I didn't even try to hide my delight at hurtling through the London streets on the top level of the bus. We crossed the Thames at Westminster Bridge, another thrill. I felt Thomas's eyes on me more than once, but I couldn't manage to wipe the huge smile off my face. I was confident he wouldn't judge me for it.

"The next one is us," Thomas said, standing and taking my hand to pull me from my seat. I wasn't entirely sure I'd be able to walk down the aisle, let alone the stairs, while the bus was still moving, but I followed him anyway. I managed to get off the bus in one piece and followed Thomas down to the South Bank. Ahead of me, the London Eye towered over the skyline.

"Oooh," I said, a suspicion hitting me. "Is that where we're going?"

Thomas nodded. "Best views in town."

We joined the line at the London Eye. Thomas had pre-purchased our tickets but I decided, for once, not to press it. The city was lighting up around us, and I couldn't wait to see what it looked like from one hundred and thirty meters in the air, though I tried not to think too much about how high that really was.

When we reached the front of the line, we were directed to a glass pod. I was surprised by the size. It was larger than my living room at home and could have easily fit twenty people, though only four others joined us. The pods hadn't seemed nearly so large from the ground.

Thomas led me over to the glass wall as the pod began to move. "It's slower than I thought," I said, placing my hands on the railing. So far, all I could see was the darkness of the river—we were pretty much still at ground level.

"It takes a half hour to go all the way around," Thomas explained. "We won't be to the very top for a while yet."

Once we started to pick up some elevation, I found it more and more difficult to talk. The city looked amazing stretched out around us, the lights of the buildings and cars blazing in the darkness. In addition to my amazement at the beauty of the view, I was also feeling more than slightly nauseated. I hadn't told Thomas how afraid of heights I was.

"You doing okay?"

"Yeah," I said, looking up at him. I saw that his eyes were focused on my hands on the railing. "Why do you ask?"

"You've got quite the grip on the railing there. Your knuckles are turning white."

"I may have a slight fear of heights," I mumbled, looking down.

"Why didn't you tell me?" he asked. He abandoned his spot next to the window and stood behind me, his arms wrapping around me to reach for the railing. Suddenly trapped in the cage of his body and arms, my breath left me in a rush. My back was pressed against his chest, his arms strong and secure around me. It was a strange feeling; I felt both more secure than before while simultaneously feeling that I was on the precipice of some great fall. Instead of causing more fear, I felt exhilarated, almost as if I wanted to jump, *wanted* to fall.

"I would have planned something different," he said, his mouth close to my ear. Tingles immediately burst out along the skin of my neck. He was so close, I could feel his breath, warm and steady.

"I wanted to see the view," I whispered back, my voice unsteady.

"I like that about you," he said. Was I just imagining it, or was his voice equally shaky? "Even when you're scared you do things anyhow. You don't let anything stop you from an experience you want."

"Do I?" I asked. I had never thought of myself as being a brave person; was that how Thomas saw me?

"Sure," he said, and his arms tightened slightly around me. "Standing up to your family about coming here, leaving everything behind for nearly a year. Going hundreds of feet up in the air just to see a good view even though you're scared of heights."

Agreeing to meet you at the bar, I thought to myself.

We were coming up to the top of the arc now, London lit up below us. The view was breathtaking—or was that just the feel of Thomas's arms wrapped so securely around me?

"Beautiful," I whispered.

"*You're* beautiful," he whispered back, his mouth brushing up against her ear. "And brave. You…you captivate me, Lizzie."

For the first time in my life, I *felt* brave. I felt strong. And I felt beautiful. So I turned away from the view before me, turned toward Thomas, and did the thing I'd been wanting to do all day. I kissed him.

And as far as I was concerned, it was pretty damn epic.

CHAPTER SIX

"You're mooning," Callie said, looking at me over her coffee cup.

"I am not mooning." I insisted, but she only snickered in return.

"Okay. That goofy smile on your face has nothing to do with Thomas. Sure."

I giggled—I couldn't help it—and Callie's face lit up. "Oh my God. You have it so bad. Was that a giggle? You never giggle."

"Maybe it was a chuckle," I said, winking at her.

"I know a giggle when I hear one," she said. "So are you gonna spill, or not? You promised if I got out of bed you'd give me details."

Callie had been in bed when I came home the night before. Understandable, since it was nearing two a.m. by the time I finally finished kissing Thomas goodbye at the door. At the thought of those kisses, the smile broke on my face again and Callie snorted.

"Okay, for real. Deets."

I picked up my teacup and leaned back in my chair. Callie and I had found this restaurant the day we moved our stuff in. It was located on a quiet little street in Camden Town. They served hot coffee and tea and a variety of sandwiches and were open for breakfast. I had a feeling we'd be spending quite a bit of time here on weekends.

"Okay," I said, wondering where to start. "So pretty much he's amazing and perfect and I had the best day of my life."

"Wow." Callie's eyes were big over her mug. "What'd you guys do?"

"He took me all around the city," I said. "We did a bunch of the tourist stuff, but he also took me to special places he liked." I thought about our dinner in a tiny little pub in Bethnal Green. It had been Thomas's local when he was still living in the East End and the bartenders there knew him by name. We had sat there for hours after our dinner of shepherd's pie, drinking dark beer, kissing across the table, and talking about everything and nothing.

"You're doing it again," Callie said, a warning note in her voice. "Mooning."

I laughed. "Okay, I'll start from the beginning." I told her all about our day, about the things we had seen and how Thomas had been so easy to talk to. When I got to the part about the London Eye, I felt a blush form across my cheeks.

"I knew it," Callie said, pointing at me. "You kissed, didn't you?"

I buried my face in my hands, laughing. I was fully aware that I was not acting like myself, but I couldn't have cared less. "We kissed a lot," I corrected.

Suddenly Callie was giggling, too, reaching across the table to grab my hand as we both laughed. It was silly and girly and unlike me, but way more fun than I thought it would be. I suddenly understood, at least a little, why girls acted like this together.

"Was he a good kisser?" she asked, still grinning. "I bet he was, wasn't he?"

"He is an amazing kisser," I said, resting my chin in my hands. I thought about stealing kisses across the table in the pub, about kissing in the car when he dropped me off, about how he had then walked me to the door where we kissed some more. I was pretty sure I had been kissed by Thomas more often than I'd ever been kissed in my life—total.

"Who's an amazing kisser?"

We looked up to see Meredith standing at our table, Tonya beside her.

"Hey, guys!" Callie cried, ignoring the sharp kick I lodged at her shin under the table. I hoped she got my meaning; I did not want Meredith and Tonya knowing who I had been kissing last night. "What are you doing on this side of town?"

"We were shopping in the Camden market," Meredith said, grabbing an empty chair and pulling it up to the table. Tonya followed suit. "We wanted to stop somewhere for coffee, and we saw you two through the window."

"That's a nice coincidence," Callie said.

"So," Meredith said, turning to me. "Who's this amazing kisser?"

"A guy I met," I said, feeling shy. "His name is Thomas, we went out last night."

Callie must have sensed my desire to keep Thomas's identity a secret because she didn't elaborate.

"Oh, is this the guy you snuck off with in the club?" Tonya asked. She was giving me a strange look; half impressed and half disbelieving. I nodded.

"He's really cute," Callie said. "I saw him yesterday when he picked her up."

"Wow." Meredith smiled. Was I imagining it, or did she sound kind of condescending. "Good for you, Lizzie." Nope, definitely not imagining it.

"Thanks," I said, feeling awkward.

Callie asked Meredith and Tonya what they had gotten up to the night before, and I soon lost interest in the conversation. From what I could make out, the girls had gone out to a club and spent most of the night taking careful notes of the way British girls dressed to go out. I couldn't imagine putting so much effort into caring what strangers were doing, but they seemed happy enough as they made fun of the total skanks and complete losers they had run across.

I had been zoning out with my tea for a good ten minutes when my phone beeped in my purse. With a thrill of excitement, I pulled it out, smiling when I saw Thomas's name on the screen.

"I know that look," Tonya said, rolling her eyes. "You're one of those girls who goes head over heels for the first guy she meets, aren't you?"

"No," I said, stung. "But Thomas is pretty special."

"There are lot of pretty special guys in London," Meredith said, that same condescending tone in her voice. "Take it from me, you don't want to get tied down already. We just got here! Live a little."

Behind her, Callie stuck out her tongue, and I smiled, grateful. "I'm gonna take this," I said, standing.

"What'd I tell you?" Tonya said as I walked away. "She's totally gone. After one date!"

I ignored her and accepted the call. "Hello?"

"Hey," Thomas said, his voice deep and sexy, that slightly amused note present. It was enough to make me shiver, just that one word.

"How are you?" I asked, stepping outside. I leaned against the brick side of the restaurant, holding the phone closer, as if in doing so I could get closer to him.

"Would you think I was a total prat if I told you I missed you?"

My stomach did its familiar flipping routine. "I miss you, too," I said.

"Ah, but you didn't answer my question," Thomas said, laughing softly. "Prat or not?"

"Not," I said. "Definitely not."

"What are you doing?"

"Finishing up breakfast with Callie," I said. "We ran into a few girls from school, they're talking about going shopping."

"Right," he said, sounding slightly disappointed. "You probably want to go with them."

"Actually," I said, peeking through the window. The girls were all laughing, talking. I knew Callie wouldn't mind if I bailed. "I'm not really in a shopping mood."

"Is that so?" Thomas asked, his voice a notch lower. "Would you perhaps rather hang out with me?"

"How soon can you be here?" I asked, feeling breathless.

"I'm already in the car," he admitted, laughing. "I was going to play it cool and tell you I was heading out from brunch, but the truth is I was hoping I'd be seeing you."

I gave him the address of the restaurant and went back inside, grinning like a fool.

"I take it you aren't coming shopping?" Callie asked, raising an eyebrow at me.

I shook my head and she laughed, shaking her head. "You have it bad, Lizzie."

"Did you have a boyfriend back at home?" Meredith asked. Though her expression was pleasant enough, something about her tone continued to make me bristle.

"Not recently," I told her.

"Lizzie's always been way too busy with school for boys," Callie said, and I immediately wished she hadn't. I knew that she didn't mean anything by it, in fact, there was clear fondness evident in her voice. But I could already tell Meredith and Tonya wouldn't see it as quite the compliment.

"Well, that explains it," Meredith said. "No wonder you're so eager to hook up over here."

"I'm not hooking up," I said, my face hot. "I met a nice boy, and we've had fun together."

"You're pretty, you know," Tonya said, looking at me closely. "If we changed up your clothes a little and did something with your hair…have you ever considered relaxer for those curls?"

"I'm not looking for a makeover." I was having trouble keeping an edge out of my voice. Meredith and Tonya were looking at me the same way girls always had; I was nothing more than the mousey book nerd. Clearly I was in dire need of their help if I wanted to impress the guys.

"Yeah, but now would be the perfect time to reinvent your look!" she persisted. "No one here knows you, you could be a brand new person! Mer, wouldn't she look amazing with like, really sleek, full curls? With your coloring you could totally go exotic."

"Leave her alone, Tonya," Meredith said. She winked at me, and I felt an urge to slap her. "Lizzie obviously does just fine all on her own."

Her words were benign, maybe even kind, but all I could hear was condescension. My temper rose another notch, and a million snappy retorts came to my mind. Before I could decide on one, a shadow fell over the table and I looked up.

"All right, Lizzie?" Thomas asked, smiling down at me.

I allowed myself one quick glance over at Tonya and Meredith, just long enough to be convinced that they definitely recognized him. Both of their mouths had dropped open, their eyes wide. I hadn't wanted to deal with the inevitable questions and attention that would come from their knowing about him, but in that moment, I was suddenly really glad that he had decided to come in instead of waiting for me in the car.

"Girls, this is Thomas," I said, struggling to keep from laughing at their expressions. "Thomas this is my roommate Callie and our classmates, Tonya and Meredith."

"Hello, ladies." His eyes flickered to each of them in their turn before returning to me.

Callie grinned up at him. "Hey, Thomas," she said. "I've heard so much about you."

"All good, I hope," he said, his eyes never leaving mine.

"I guess you'll never know," I said, winking. Meredith and Tonya still had yet to close their mouths.

"What are you two up to today?" Callie asked.

"I was thinking we could head over to Hyde Park," he said, raising his eyebrows at me for my approval. "I figure if the weather is cooperating, we may as well enjoy it."

"Sounds good," I said, grabbing my purse and standing. "God knows it will be cold soon enough."

"It was nice to meet you," Thomas said, resting a hand on my back as he nodded down at the girls. "I hope you have a nice time shopping."

"Bye," Callie called out cheerfully as we turned to go. At the last moment, Meredith seemed to snap out of it. "Uh, bye," she called, her voice over-eager in my ears. "So nice to meet you!"

I stifled a laugh as Thomas led me outside, his hand never moving from the small of my back.

"What's up?" he asked as we stepped into the sunlight. "You're looking a bit mischievous."

"Those girls aren't really my favorite people," I told him. "Not Callie, of course, but the other two. They were being slightly, uh,—"

"Bitchy?" he asked. I laughed.

"Just a little. It was kind of worth it to see their faces when you came in, though."

"I take it they recognized me."

I nodded. "And I have a feeling they're the type of people for whom that kind of thing would really matter."

"Well, next time I see them, I'll casually mention Jackson, really rub it in."

I liked the idea of him planning to see my classmates again.

"So I figured we could walk around the park a bit and maybe stretch out somewhere to read or chill. I have a blanket in the boot." At my blank stare he pointed at the trunk. "The boot," he repeated.

"If you say so," I said, shaking my head. He opened my door for me, and I climbed into the car. "So, reading in the park. Sound good?"

"Sounds perfect." I felt a little rush of happiness as he closed my door and circled around to his side. Last night, I had mentioned in passing that my favorite thing to do on a nice day was to sit outside and read. The fact that he had remembered, and wanted to indulge me, made the goofy smile pretty much permanent.

"Did you need to stop back at your flat for a book?" he asked, sliding into his seat and looking across at me.

I shook my head, feeling slightly embarrassed. "I have one in my purse."

He raised his eyebrows. "Really?"

"Yeah, I pretty much always carry a book."

"Even out to breakfast with your flat mate?"

"You never know," I said defensively.

"True," he said, smiling.

"A girl's got to have a book," I muttered to myself, hearing him laugh as he started the car.

Hyde Park was gorgeous in the fall with its large expanses of lawn, walking trails, towering trees, and stretches of flowers. Thomas and I wandered around for a while, holding hands. He told me about a gallery event he'd be going to the following weekend. "My mate Charlie is a photographer," he said. "He's really good. It's his first big show."

"Wow," I said. "That's awesome. Where is it?"

"The Utopia Gallery, over in Chelsea. Chelsea is really high-end so hopefully there will be plenty of posh folks over there to buy his pieces."

I laughed. "I hope so, too."

He looked at me out of the corner of his eye. "Would you, er, maybe want to come with me? If you're not busy."

"That sounds great," I said, eager to see him again and more pleased than I liked to admit that he was willing to plan something a full week out.

"My friends will like that," he said, smiling at me. "I don't usually bring many girls around. How does this look?" he gestured to the ground next to a large Oak tree. I nodded and he spread out the blanket, a well-worn quilt. I wondered where he had gotten it, whether it meant something to him or not.

We settled onto the blanket, and I pulled my copy of *Jane Eyre* from my purse. "Why don't you bring girls around much?"

He shrugged. "I don't really date much in general," he said. He seemed a little sheepish. "It's kind of hard to meet people. And a lot of girls start to act strange around me when they find out what I do for a living."

I wondered, not for the first time, if part of the reason he liked spending time with me was because I wasn't much of a fan of the *Darkness* series.

"Tell me about your friends," I said, feeling a rush of attraction for him when his face lit up. There was something nice about a guy who clearly loved his friends.

"There's Charlie, like I said. He's the photographer. We met when I first moved down here, we were actually flat mates. And through him, I met the rest of the group. Sarra is his sister and Mark is her boyfriend. They both work in the City. And then there's Meghan and Carter, Sarra's friends. The four of them went to university together."

"You see them a lot?"

He nodded. "They pretty much became my family in London. They took me in when I was lonely and sad."

"It's hard to picture you sad," I mused. "You're seriously one of the happiest people I've ever met."

He shrugged again. "I generally am. I like my life." He looked over at me. "But I guess I am still a little lonely."

I took his hand, feeling brave. "Then I'm glad I can keep you company."

We smiled at each other for a moment, his gaze sending shivers up and down my arms. "So," I finally said, when I was sure I was about to be overcome with the desire to reach out and kiss him madly, right there in the middle of the park. "How'd you meet Charlie?"

"I had just moved down to London," he explained. "The first *Darkness* film had just gone into post-production. At the time, we had no idea it was going to be such a hit, and just another obscure actor, I couldn't book another job to save my life." He stretched out on the blanket and propped himself up on his elbows, getting comfortable. I was momentarily distracted by the lazy lankiness of his limbs. He had pushed the sleeves of his sweater up, and I could clearly see his forearm muscles flex as he settled onto his elbows. I had a thing about guys with strong forearms, and I had to force myself to redirect my attention to his face.

"So I was depressed and running around auditioning all the time, and about to completely run out of money when I got to talking to a bloke in the pub. He was a starving artist as well, his parents had completely cut off supporting him because he dropped out of school." Thomas laughed lightly. "We commiserated over a pint about the impending doom of having to go to university. We were totally hammered by the time we realized we could save a bunch of cash by becoming flat mates." He gave me a quick grin. "I'd like to claim our ignorance was the result of our youth, but by all accounts, we haven't improved much since then."

I laughed. "How long did you live together?"

"Four years. *Darkness* took off a year after I moved into his flat, and suddenly it wasn't so hard to book jobs, but I was happy where I was. I promised Charlie I would never tell a soul when he got teary the day I moved into my own place."

I swatted his arm. "You're mean. He sounds like a good friend."

"The best," Thomas agreed, catching my hand in his and holding it there. "He can be a little flighty—he never did lose that artist vibe. But I'm thrilled his career is finally taking off."

We sat in the park for a good two hours, reading and chatting. Every time I looked up from my book, I would find Thomas's eyes on me. He would grin, unabashed, and continue watching me after I returned my attention to my book.

"What?" I finally asked, reaching a hand up to my face. "Do I have something in my teeth or something?"

He shook his head. "You just look really happy when you're reading. I like to watch you."

Late in the afternoon, it started to get chilly. "Fall's in the air," Thomas said, taking my hands and rubbing them between his own. "You want to head out?"

"Sure," I said, reluctantly. I had my first day of classes in the morning, and I had plenty of work to catch up on, but I didn't particularly want to say goodbye to him just yet.

When we got to the car, I could tell that he wasn't quite eager to say goodbye either. "You hungry?" he asked. "My stomach is growling like crazy. What would you say to getting some take-out and heading back to my place? We could watch some telly or a movie."

"I wish I could," I said, feeling disappointed. "But I have school work to do back at the flat."

"Ah, big first day tomorrow, huh?"

I nodded, feeling a jolt of nerves. I hadn't thought much about school all weekend, but now my anxiety was coming back full force. It was important to me that I do well, to show my parents that I hadn't wasted my time over here. That getting my masters in literature was a worthwhile thing. That pressure, combined with not knowing many people in my classes, was a sure-fire trigger for my anxiety.

"I'll drive you back," Thomas said.

A new emotion joined the anxiety—disappointment. I'd had such a nice, easy time with Thomas in the park, but I was nowhere near ready for our day to be over. "Well," I said, knowing I was only pushing back the inevitable, "maybe I'd have time for a quick meal first. I mean, a girl's gotta eat, right?"

"Sounds totally logical to me," he agreed seriously as he started the car. "So, where to?"

"There's an Italian place under our flat," I suggested, trying to dispel the immediate thought that maybe I could invite him up after.

"I love Italian," he said, pulling out into traffic. As we headed out across London, I did my best to ignore the little voice in the back of my mind warning that I was getting in too deep, way too fast. *It's just dinner*, I told myself. *No big deal.*

But as Thomas reached across the gearshift to take my hand and the now familiar tingles erupted over my skin, I knew that I was lying to myself. It may be too soon, and it may be too fast, but there was no ignoring it: I was falling for him.

CHAPTER SEVEN

"Alright, missy," Callie said, plopping her tray down next to mine and collapsing into her seat. Callie did everything this way—from talking about cute boys to choosing a seat in the cafeteria, the girl was dramatic. "I want details and I want them now. And you owe me, too, because I barely saw you this weekend."

I winced. "Sorry." I'd been so wrapped up in my Thomas-induced happy bubble that I hadn't thought much about ditching my best friend our first full weekend in a new city.

"It's okay," she said, taking the plastic lid off her container of salad. She ripped a dressing packet open with her teeth and doused the lettuce with fat-free ranch. "You know I would have done the exact same thing in your situation."

I managed not to snort at that, but just barely. I couldn't count the number of times Callie had ditched me over the years because she just had to go on a date with some total hottie. But I appreciated her not giving me a hard time about seeing Thomas so much over the weekend.

"We had a great weekend," I told her as she stabbed a bunch of lettuce with her fork. "What exactly do you want to know?"

"The last we discussed this, you were telling me what an amazing kisser he was," she said, raising her eyebrows. "So what kind of kissing are we talking, here?"

"Um...nice kissing?" I wasn't sure what she was getting at.

Callie threw a napkin at me. "Lizzie, come on! I want the deets here! Was it on the mouth kissing? Hickey-induced necking? Did you French?"

"Oh *gross*." I threw the napkin right back at her. "Did you seriously just ask me if we Frenched? What are we, thirteen?"

"Lizzie, I've like, never heard you talk about kissing a guy before. I just want to know how major it was!"

"It was pretty major," I said, trying not to feel embarrassed. She was right, I had never really done the post-mortem make-out breakdown before. It was hard to, when you were as kissing inexperienced as me. "But nothing more than kissing."

"Okay, that's a start," she said. "Were you in public during said kissing?"

"Some of it," I said.

Her eyebrows shot up. "So some of this kissing occurred in private, huh? That's promising!"

I laughed at her. "You're ridiculous. We kissed in his car on Saturday night and in the flat yesterday when he walked me up after dinner."

"He was in the flat yesterday?" she cried. "Where the hell was I?"

"You weren't home yet. He dropped me off after dinner, and I invited him in for a bit." I blushed, thinking about kissing Thomas in the doorway...and then again on the couch.

"And you just went in your room and studied after that?" she asked, her expression thunderous. "I cannot believe you didn't come out when I got home to tell me all about it."

"Sorry, sister," I said, taking the top off my bottled water and taking a swig. "I had a ton of work to get done for today."

"Yeah, 'cause you were out getting frisky while some of us studied all day Saturday."

"Uh huh. I'm so sure you studied all day Saturday."

"Well...I guess it wasn't all day." She flashed me a grin. "But I did spend a few hours working at Starbucks. You would not believe the hot barista that served me. I think he was Scottish. Or maybe Irish? I can never tell accents."

"Hi, girls!" I looked up and tamped down a groan. Meredith was standing at our table, giving us—or rather, me—her most friendly smile. "Can I join you?"

"Of course," I said, moving my tray out of the way to make room for her. Like Callie, she too had opted for a salad for lunch. Unlike Callie, she had skipped the giant brownie. I felt a little trickle of guilt as I looked down at my turkey sandwich and fruit cup. Girls like Meredith probably would faint at the mere idea of eating carbs. Reminding myself how ridiculous that was, I made a mental promise to myself to stop worrying about what a girl I didn't even particularly like thought of me.

"How was your day yesterday?" I asked Meredith. "Did you buy anything nice?"

"Just these jeans," she said, pointing down at perfectly fitting slim-cut denim. She beamed at me. "But enough boring shopping talk. Tell me about Thomas."

I groaned on the inside. I had known this was coming. My one moment of glee at showing her up with Thomas yesterday now hardly seemed worth the gossip and inquisition that I was sure would follow.

"I met him at the play Callie and I saw on Friday," I said, and she nodded.

"Callie told me. But how on earth did you get him to ask you out?"

"Wow, Mer," Callie said, her voice dry. "You sure know how to make a girl feel good."

Meredith slapped a hand over her mouth. "Oh no, I so didn't mean it like that, Lizzie. I promise! Of course you could get any guy you wanted!"

"Thanks," I said, meeting Callie's eyes across the table. She shook her head slightly, and I felt better—at least I wasn't the only one who thought Meredith was kind of a brat.

"I just meant, you know, he never dates anyone. Like anyone. So it seems so crazy that he just randomly starting talking to you. In a theater, no less!"

"How do you know he never dates?" I asked. Her comment did seem to jive with what Thomas had told me, but how did Meredith know that?

"I did some research last night," she said, smiling smugly. "I mean, I knew who he was, of course, as soon as I saw him. But then I got to talking with Tonya, and I realized that I didn't really know that much about him, you know? Which is totally weird for someone cast in all five of the *Darkness* movies. He really flies under the radar, doesn't he?"

I tried not to think too much about the mention of her talking about Thomas with Tonya. I made a mental note to ask Callie if they had been talking about us during the shopping trip, before deciding I didn't really want to know.

"Thomas is pretty private," I told Meredith. "He doesn't really like all the fame stuff."

She raised a perfectly sculpted eyebrow at me, clearly not buying it. "Of course," she said. "That's really cool." She took a sip of her water before continuing. "But I did manage to find some stuff about him. Apparently he's into all these artsy roles when he isn't shooting *Darkness*, and he hasn't had a girlfriend in more than a year."

"I don't really know, Meredith," I said, unwilling to give her any of the information that she was clearly after. "We've only had a few dates. I'm hardly an expert."

"Hey, Lizzie," Callie said suddenly. "Didn't you need to talk to Fenton before his class starts?"

I looked at her blankly for a moment, wondering what on earth I would have to say to our twentieth century poetry professor before we'd even had our first class. A quick stomp on my foot under the table brought me to my senses—she was giving me a way out.

"Oh yeah," I said quickly, hoping Meredith hadn't noticed the pause. "I do. Did you want to come with?"

"Sure," she said, wrapping her unfinished brownie in a napkin and slipping it in her purse. "We'll see you later, Meredith."

"Okay, girls," she trilled, waving at us. "Lizzie, by the way, I totally love that sweater on you!" I looked down at my faded blue cardigan. It was old and comfortable, not exactly raggedy, but certainly not up to Meredith's fashion threshold.

"Uh, thanks," I said, bemused. "See you."

After we'd made our way out of the cafeteria, Callie let out her breath with a huff. "That girl is shameless. I should have warned you. From the way she and Tonya were talking yesterday, I got the feeling they were looking for ways to get in good with Thomas."

"I'm not surprised," I said. "Though I admit to feeling a small amount of satisfaction when he showed up yesterday and wiped the condescending smile off her face, I would have much preferred for them to have not met."

"We'll just have to do our best to avoid her from now on."

I looked at her in surprise. "I thought you liked those girls."

Callie shrugged. "It was fun hanging out with everyone on Friday, but Tonya and Meredith are totally shallow. I can do without that drama."

I felt a momentary flash of guilt for being surprised Callie would notice that. It wasn't that my friend was shallow, but I did seem to have the habit of assuming all girls who looked like Callie and Meredith were somewhat the same. Callie might spend a ridiculous amount of time styling her hair every day, and she might enjoy clothes and celebrity gossip as much as any teenage girl, but the similarities with Meredith ended there.

By the time Callie and I got off the tube in Kentish Town that afternoon, my head was spinning. They had led us into a false sense of security during orientation, we knew that now. Our professors were not messing around. I had so much homework to do, I had no real idea how I would finish it in one night. The full enormity of our decision to finish our masters in three terms had finally hit us full on, and we were both feeling distinctly screwed.

We hunkered down in the living room with our books and laptops, stopping only when we were too hungry to carry on. "We should have stopped at the shop on our way back from campus," I told Callie, staring at the meager offerings in our fridge. Studying always made me hungry, and I knew the cheese and whole grain bread were not going to cut it.

"Screw this," Callie said, grabbing her purse off the counter. "We live upstairs from a restaurant, for God's sake." She walked to the door. "I'll be back with something edible."

"Here," I said, reaching for my purse. "Let me give you some cash."

She waved me away. "Pay me when I get back. Who knows, maybe I can get a deal." She batted her eyelashes at me and flipped her blonde hair over her shoulder. "I think Mr. Idoni likes me."

She came back ten minutes later with a pizza box. "So much for the discount," she muttered. "He asked me if I had something in my eye. Said I looked crazy blinking so much."

I laughed. "Sorry, babe," I told her. "I guess your charms don't work on everyone."

"You should see it down there," she said, sighing as she set the pizza box on the kitchen table. "The restaurant is totally full and the sidewalks are packed with people. Everyone's soaking up the last of the sunshine. And we're stuck up here."

I peeked out the window and saw that she was right. The street down below was bustling, immediately making me wish I was out there amongst the throngs of people.

We sat at the window seat, eating our pizza straight from the box. "We could always take a little break," Callie said, after she'd polished off her third slice. I thought I detected a pleading note in her voice. "I mean, maybe it would actually be good for our work if we got outside for a little while before we tackle the rest. Get out spirits revitalized."

"Oh, what the hell," I said, turning to grin at her. My friend's mouth dropped open in surprise.

"Seriously? You want to put off studying?"

I shrugged. "It's going to get cold soon enough, and we'll be wishing for a day like this. Besides," I pointed at the stack of books on the kitchen table. "There's no way in hell I'm going to be able to finish all that tonight regardless."

She beamed at me. "Wow, Lizzie, what's come over you? First you're picking up movie stars in clubs, now you're actually agreeing to put off your schoolwork. I hardly know you."

I ignored her comment and went to get my sweater. "Just get your purse before I change my mind."

After pulling on my sweater—and discreetly checking my phone for any missed messages from Thomas—I met Callie at the door. She slung an arm over my shoulder.

"Come on, London Lizzie."

"London Lizzie?"

"I've decided your new personality needs a new nickname."

I laughed and pushed her arm off. "Hey, don't be mad," she said. "I'm a big fan of London Lizzie."

As we headed out into the dying sunshine, leaving our schoolwork behind, I had to admit that she had a point. In some ways, I felt like a new Lizzie. And I was a pretty big fan of her myself.

CHAPTER EIGHT

I saw Thomas twice over the next week. On Tuesday night, he took me out to a Mexican restaurant called Cocina for dinner. We ate empanadas and drank salty margaritas while Thomas asked for my commentary on the authenticity of every item we ate. I proclaimed it passable, and Thomas said he would add it to his list of good restaurants on the South Bank.

Callie and I had both had Thursday morning free, a rare stroke of scheduling luck. Since we could have a later night, I asked Thomas if he wanted to join us both for dinner on Wednesday. Now that I was used to the whole actor thing, I was eager for them to get to know each other. But Thomas had to decline, due to a long-standing trivia night with his friends at a local pub. We made plans to have a late lunch the next day, and I tried not to feel too disappointed. It was ridiculous that I could miss him after just one night. Plus we were talking on the phone at least once a day, and texting on top of that. If Callie or Sofie had told me they were communicating that often with a guy they just met, I would have been worried about them.

Callie cheered me up by stopping at a video store on her way home and coming away with the entire *Darkness* series on DVD. We got pizza from Mr. Idoni (who, oddly, seemed more inclined to give me a discount than he did Callie) and holed up all night watching the films. I certainly enjoyed them more now that I knew Thomas, though I still found plenty of opportunities to roll my eyes. Why did girls my age find vampires and werewolves sexy? I was quite sure that it wasn't just my personal bias that convinced me that Thomas was the best actor of them all. As the series progressed, I became more engrossed in the story. Callie pointed out this was probably related to the fact that Thomas's role, Gideon, got progressively bigger with each film. I went to bed that night and dreamt of being saved from a werewolf attack by Thomas.

On Thursday afternoon, Thomas picked me up from campus and took me to lunch. I had just finished my first Regency British Lit class, by far my favorite time period, and I was way over excited. Thomas listened patiently as I gushed about the syllabus and reading list and extolled the virtues of Professor Kimberly Houghton, whom I had fallen totally in love with after her first impassioned lecture on feminism in Jane Austen novels. Most people would have quailed under the ferocity of my enthusiasm, but Thomas seemed genuinely interested, even asking me questions about my favorite authors of the period.

When he dropped me off at campus, we finalized our plans for the following evening. Thomas thought the rest of his friends would probably arrive at the gallery around eight thirty, so he said he'd pick me up at home around eight. "We'll probably get dinner after," he said. "But if my friends get to be too much, you just tell me and we'll go out on our own."

"Should we have a code word?" I teased. "I can hardly tell you they're on my nerves right in front of them."

"Smart, Medina," he said, tapping the side of his nose. "How 'bout you tell me I'm hunky, and I'll know you want to bail."

"Hunky?"

"Yeah, isn't that something Americans say?"

I laughed and kissed him. "I'll see you tomorrow."

He picked me up at eight on the dot. This time I asked him to come up. Callie was planning to go out with the hot Starbucks barista that evening, and I thought it would be nice for the three of us to have a glass of wine before we all headed out. I was pleased to see Callie and Thomas hit it off right away. She did a great job of hiding her star-struckedness, and after a few moments of polite chatter, she was her normal bold, confident self, teasing us both and insisting we stay for a second glass of wine.

We left my flat later than planned, but Thomas didn't seem bothered by it. I was getting used to how even keeled he was, and found it strangely appealing, if just for the novelty of it. Back home, my family was typically late for everything, as there were so many of us, but there was always an undercurrent of stress and anger as we rushed to get out of the house. Thomas, on the other hand, just let it go, turned the radio on in the car, and softly hummed along to the Rolling Stones as he made his way through London traffic.

The nearer we got to Kensington, the more nervous I got. As eager as I'd been for Thomas to meet Callie, I was terrified of meeting his friends. He obviously thought very highly of them; their names peppered his conversation and featured prominently in most of the stories he'd told me about his life. What if they didn't like me?

"You ready?"

I turned to see Thomas was watching my face closely in the darkness of the car. I hadn't realized he had even parked.

"Sure," I said, trying to smile.

"You're nervous," he guessed and I nodded. "Don't be nervous. They'll love you."

"What if they think I'm some dumb American?"

He laughed. "They are so not like that. Come on, buck up. It will be fine. You'll love Charlie's stuff."

"Okay," I said, taking a deep breath. "I'm ready."

The gallery was packed by the time we made our way inside. Thomas whistled softly. "Well done, Charlie," he muttered, looking around at the crowd. He glanced at me and smiled. "I just got nervous for him. He must be freaking out right now."

"Let's go find him," I said, taking his hand, completely touched by his reaction for his friend.

We found Charlie surrounded by a group of people. He caught sight of Thomas over their heads and his face lit up. He held up a hand to wave and Thomas gave him a thumbs up. I saw Charlie's eyes flick over to my face before he redirected his attention to the woman talking to him.

"There you are," said a cross sounding voice. Thomas and I turned to see a short, frizzy-haired brunette approaching us. "You're late."

She stood on her tiptoes and kissed Thomas's cheek before turning to me. "Hello, Lizzie. Thomas told me all about you."

"Lizzie, this is Sarra," Thomas said.

"Hi, Sarra." I felt shy. "You must be so proud of your brother."

"He's done well, hasn't he," she said, looking around. "Granted, he's still a whiney little slob, but at least he's not totally hopeless."

Thomas laughed. "You'll get used to her," he told me, pushing her shoulder good-naturedly. "Sarra has no idea the meaning of the phrase good first impression."

"Oh, hush," she said. "You'll make her scared of me."

I smiled, feeling instead immediately at ease. There was something appealing and comfortable about Sarra's easy, brash demeanor. I had the feeling that what you saw was what you got.

"Where's Mark?" Thomas asked.

"Everyone is over here, oohing and ahhing over the pieces." She led us across the room, stopping to snatch up a champagne glass from a passing waiter. Thomas took two and handed one off to me. I was grateful; maybe it would be easier to face all of his friends with a little champagne in me.

"Oy, everyone," Sarra announced to the small group viewing a black and white photo of an empty field. "Tommy is here, and he's brought a girl with him."

"Ignore her," Thomas instructed again as his friends turned to face us.

"Hello, Lizzie," a tall, thin blonde said, reaching out immediately to grasp my empty hand. "We're so happy to meet you. Thomas has told us all about you."

I felt a warm blush rush to my face, but forced myself to smile back. "You must be Meghan."

She beamed at me. "I am. And this is Carter." She released my hands and gestured to the man next to her.

"All right, Lizzie?" he asked, in what was fast becoming my favorite Brit greeting. I nodded at him, smiling.

"Nice to meet you."

"This is my boyfriend, Mark," Sarra said, poking the man beside her. He was short, like Sarra, and slightly round. He was wearing a truly ugly plaid wool sweater and had a scruffy beard. He smiled brightly at me, his eyes twinkling behind round glasses. He and Sarra couldn't look any more different from Carter and Meghan, who appeared to be the epitome of good looks and sophistication.

"Hiya, Lizzie," Mark said, shaking my hand. "Sarra hasn't shut up about meeting you for days."

Everyone laughed, and Thomas rested his arm lightly over my shoulders. I thought I saw Sarra and Meghan share a little smile behind Mark's head, but I couldn't be sure.

"We were just looking at Charlie's pieces," Meghan said, pointing at the photo.

"They're great," Thomas said, taking a step forward to peer at the black and white shot.

"Tommy is the only one of us who knows anything about this crap," Mark said.

"Well, I saw enough of it when I was living with him," Thomas said. "He had every square inch of that flat covered in his prints."

"I think they're nice," Meghan said, squinting at one. "I would put this up on my wall."

"You can't afford it." We all turned to face the newcomer, and I immediately recognized Charlie himself.

"How's it going, mate?" Mark asked, clapping him on the shoulder. "You making a killing?"

"I'll be able to pay my rent this month," Charlie said, laughing. "So, this is the famous Lizzie, eh?"

I looked up at Thomas. "All right, what did you tell them about me?"

Everyone laughed. "Sorry, Lizzie," Meghan said. "We're just very excited about the fact that Tommy is finally dating."

"You all are really helping me to impress her," Thomas said, his voice dry. "Thanks for that."

I found his hand behind my back and squeezed it.

"Sorry, mate," Charlie said. "We just like to see you getting out there."

"You make it sound like I'm a disaster with girls," Thomas said. "It's really hurting my rep here." His friends laughed again.

"You have nothing to worry about," I told him, no longer feeling shy. Thomas's group was clearly friendly, kind, and crazy loyal to each other. I already liked them.

"Let me talk you through some of the pieces," Charlie said eagerly, pushing his thick plastic-rimmed glasses up on his nose. "I was really going for a minimalist feel here. This here, with the emptiness of the field juxtaposed with the buildings, I think it really represents the inherent loneliness of urban life in the twenty-first century."

I saw Sarra roll her eyes behind his back, and the others nodded, clearly zoning out already, but I was happy to see Thomas taking a real interest, asking his friend questions about the composition and his lighting choices.

Before we had managed to look at more than a dozen photos, Charlie was pulled away again to talk to some important-looking guests. Before he left, Thomas clapped him on the shoulder and looked him straight in the eye. "Well done, man. This is really something to be proud of."

Charlie beamed at him before allowing himself to be pulled away.

I felt a rush of affection for Thomas and, on a whim, leaned up to kiss him.

"What was that for?" he asked, smiling down at me.

"You're a good friend," I told him. "I like you."

"I like you, too," he said, kissing me again.

"Seriously, you guys are so cute!" Meghan was standing next to us, her hands clasped in front of her.

"Dear Lord," Thomas muttered. "If I'd known they were going to be like this, I wouldn't have brought you."

"It's okay," I told him. "Can't you tell how crazy they are about you? They just want you to be happy."

"You make me happy," he said, his voice low, sending my heart rate galloping away.

We milled around the room with Thomas's friends, drinking champagne and people-watching. Meghan and Sarra stayed close to my side, asking me questions about my life in America and my program at the University.

"Give her a break," Thomas finally said, his voice stern. "She doesn't need the third degree."

"We're interested!" Sarra cried, pushing on his arm.

"It's okay," I assured Thomas, but he wrapped an arm around my waist and pulled me away. "Come on," he said. "Let's take a little break from the inquisition."

With Thomas's arm around my waist, we left the gallery and strolled down the street. It was chillier than it had been since I'd arrived in London, and I wished I would have worn a better coat over my Callie-approved little black dress.

"I like them," I told him. "They're really nice."

"They can be a little nosey," he said.

"They care about you. Anyone can see that."

"The, uh, last girl I dated turned out to be kind of a disaster," he said, looking down at me. He was clearly uncomfortable with the topic, and I pushed down the jealousy that had sparked at the mere mention of another girl.

"What happened?" I asked.

He sighed. "I brought her to a party with the cast. She, uh, made a pass at Jackson. Right in front of me."

My mouth dropped open. "Bitch!"

He gave me a brief smile before grimacing again. "Yeah, well, I thought she actually liked me. It kind of messed me up for a while. I didn't date for…well, until this week, I guess."

"I'm sorry that happened to you," I said. "You deserve so much better."

"It's no big deal," he said, his usual smile replacing the grimace. "I got over it. Just taught me to be more careful, that's all."

We were both quiet for a moment. "She was crazy," I finally muttered. I snorted a little, disapproving. "Jackson Coles. Honestly."

"I wouldn't call it crazy," he said, a slight edge to his voice. "Most girls would pick Jackson."

"No way," I said firmly. "No girl in her right mind would pick Jackson. Not over you."

"Wow," Thomas said, his voice clearly amused.

"What?"

"You really like me, huh?"

He laughed and I pushed him. "You suck."

"No way," he said, wrapping his arms around me and pulling me to him. "You can't fool me now. I'm onto you."

As he brought me close to his body, I stopped pushing and let myself melt into him. "I guess you're okay."

"That's good enough for me," he said, his lips finding mine. "But I still think you really like me."

***

After Charlie's show, the seven of us ended up in a nearby restaurant. "This place is way too posh," Sarra muttered as the hostess showed us to our table. She pushed her frizzy hair out of her face and looked around. "I mean, look at these chairs. Who do they think they're kidding?"

"I think it's nice," Charlie said, shrugging out of his leather jacket. "And it's my special night, so you'll just have to deal with it."

"Your special night?" Sarra asked, incredulous. "What are you, seven years old?"

"I think it's nice, too," Meghan said, patting Charlie's arm. "Let's just sit down, okay?"

Thomas pulled my chair out for me—Sarra did have a point, the velvet-upholstered behemoth was a bit much—and I sat down between him and Charlie.

"They make a great martini," Charlie told me gleefully. "Almost all gin."

I laughed. "Can't go wrong there." A waiter arrived to bring us menus, and we placed our drink orders. I followed Charlie's lead and ordered a dirty martini, though I'd never tried one before. Back at home, I was usually a fruity cocktail kind of girl. When my drink arrived, I was pleased to find it was good—a little different, but good. Charlie hadn't been lying about the gin.

"I'm starving," Mark muttered, rubbing his stomach. "Why am I not seeing any real food on this menu?"

"It's all real food," Meghan said. "Just because they don't have burgers and chips doesn't mean it's not real food."

"So, Lizzie," Charlie said, leaning toward me. "Thomas tells me you're a literature major. What books are you studying this term?"

Charlie and I fell into an easy conversation about books; I was pleased to find he was nearly as much of a bibliophile as I am, though his tastes focused more on fantasy and darker works. We only stopped talking when the waiter appeared, and we both realized we hadn't made our choices yet. After a hurried look over the menu, I ordered a pasta dish that looked interesting.

After the waiter took our order, I stood. "I'm going to use the restroom."

"Restroom," Sarra said, shaking her head. "What a stupid name for the loo."

"Sarra!" Meghan admonished. "You'll make Lizzie feel bad."

"Why? Did she come up with the word?" Sarra countered.

"We'll come with you," Meghan said, shooting Sarra a dirty look.

"I never understood that," Sarra said as the three of us made our way to the restroom. "Why do girls always have to go to the loo together?"

"Oh Jesus, don't start on that again," Meghan said, then muttered to me, "Every time I say I'll join her, she goes off on this kick. It's so annoying." She opened the door and looked at Sarra. "If you didn't want to come, you should have said so."

"Oh yeah, like I want to sit at the table with all those blokes. You know what they're like when they're together. I can do without the endless recapping of the weekend's football matches, thank you." She glanced at me. "That's, uh, soccer."

"I know what football is," I said, laughing. "My family watches plenty of South American football matches on TV."

After we'd visited the stalls, Sarra and Meghan joined me at the sink. "So, Lizzie," Meghan said, rubbing soap into her hands, "Thomas says things are going well for the two of you."

I blushed. "Well, it's only been a week," I pointed out.

"You wouldn't have guessed from the way he's been talking," Sarra muttered, earning herself an elbow jab to the ribs from Meghan.

"He's been, uh, talking about me?" I asked, feeling my heart rate start to increase.

"Oh God, yeah," Sarra went on, oblivious to Meghan's death stares in the mirror. "Sunday brunch, all we heard about was your date on Saturday. When we saw him Wednesday night at trivia, it was even worse. And I must have gotten at least four texts from him about this evening, warning me to be nice and not make you feel uncomfortable."

"Texts which you clearly took to heart," Meghan said drily. "Way to embarrass her."

My heart now seemed to be attempting to gallop straight out of my chest. It made me feel both elated and strangely terrified to know that I wasn't the only one doing the head-over-heels bit. As happy as I was to get this outside confirmation that Thomas really liked me, it also made me feel a sense of pressure I hadn't experienced before.

Meghan was watching me closely. "Sorry about Sarra," she said. "If you're like, not on the same page, don't freak out."

I realized that she was worried they were scaring me off, and I tried to smile at her in the mirror. "Well, like I said, it's only been a week, but I think he's pretty great."

"He is," Meghan agreed. "We love him like a brother."

Sarra nodded. "So we want to make sure you're nice to him," she said cheerfully.

"Sarra!" Meghan admonished as my cheeks darkened further. "You're scaring her!"

"I'm just saying," Sarra said, leaning into the mirror to brush a hint of lipstick off her teeth. "If we would have been proactive about that Franny witch, he wouldn't have gotten his heart broken so badly."

"She broke his heart?" I asked, feeling a sinking in my stomach. I hated the idea of him caring about someone else so much that she could hurt him like that. What was wrong with me? First Maggie the waitress and now his ex. Who would have known Thomas could bring out such jealousy issues in me?

"He was pretty upset about it," Meghan said, still watching my face in the mirror. "It hurt his feelings, you know. To think that she was just using him to get to Jackson Coles."

"I would never do something like that," I said, meeting her eyes. "I really like Thomas. And I could care less about Jackson Coles."

"Yeah, he told us how you guys met," Sarra said, her eyes sparkling. "Well done, you. That guy is such a tosser."

Meghan snorted. "Yeah, well, Thomas is still friends with him. So if you're going to be with Thomas, you'll probably end up meeting him. And a lot of other big-wig celebrity types, too." She was still watching me closely, as if trying to gauge my reaction.

I shuddered slightly. "That scares me, a little," I admitted. "It's so not my scene."

I felt a little clench of fear in my stomach. Was I really going to have to rub elbows with people like Jackson? I would so totally embarrass myself—and probably Thomas, too— in a situation like that.

"It's not Thomas's either," Sarra said. "He only goes to the industry stuff when he has to."

"Well," I said, trying to banish the scary thoughts. "Maybe he'll get tired of me before I have to worry about any of that." I tried to laugh, to show them the thought of Thomas tiring of me didn't cause me to feel like I might throw up, but they weren't fooled.

"Don't count on it," Meghan said. "Sarra wasn't joking. He's crazy about you."

"But…it's only been a week," I repeated, stammering in my embarrassment.

She shrugged. "I've never seen him like this."

Sarra stopped messing with her frizzy hair to meet my gaze. "Me either."

"Wow," I whispered.

"So," Sarra went on, smiling though her voice was even and firm, "I hope you keep that in mind. 'Cause we really don't want to see him get hurt."

I followed them out of the restroom, feeling numb. Thomas really liked me, so much so that his best friends thought they should warn me against hurting him. So much that I, apparently, had to start worrying about meeting his work colleagues, who just so happened to be movie stars. I felt faint.

"Hey," Thomas said, catching my hand as I sat down. "You okay? You're looking a little pale."

"I'm fine," I said, trying to smile. He watched me for a minute before turning to Sarra and Meghan, glaring at them. They both met his gaze, unabashed, and Thomas turned back to me, leaning close to my ear.

"I don't know what they told you," he said, "but you shouldn't listen to them. They think they're my big sisters or something."

"It's fine," I assured him. "They didn't say anything."

"They didn't threaten you?" he asked, obviously not believing me.

"Well…I wouldn't call it a threat. They may have warned me—"

He made a scathing noise in the back of his throat and started to pull away, to yell at his friends, no doubt. I pulled on his hand, keeping his head near mine. "We're fine, Thomas," I assured him. "Don't worry about it."

He looked into my eyes for a long moment before finally smiling. "Okay."

Feeling better than I had since I first went into the restroom, I leaned forward and kissed him lightly.

As he pulled away to say something to Charlie, I caught Meghan's eye across the table. She was watching us, an inscrutable expression on her face. After a moment, she smiled at me, and I somehow knew I had her in my corner.

CHAPTER NINE

After we'd been seeing each other for three weeks, Thomas offered to cook me dinner in his flat. I jumped at the chance; I'd been dying to see the place. Usually we spent time at my flat, or went out. When I mentioned to Callie that I thought it was kind of odd, she pointed out that he was probably just trying to make me feel comfortable by keeping our dates to places that were on my turf or neutral. "Inviting a girl to your flat *means* something," she told me wisely. "He probably hasn't wanted to make you feel pressured."

"Awesome," I said, my fingers slipping over the strands of hair I was trying to braid. I would have to start over. I pulled the braid out and concentrated. "I wasn't feeling any pressure at all until I talked to you."

"Sorry, sister," she said, perching on my bed. "I'm just telling you the facts."

She probably had a point. Thomas had been nothing but respectful to me, not pressuring me in any way. It made sense that he hadn't invited me over to a place where he would naturally have the upper hand, comfort-wise. But now he *had* invited me over. Was he looking at tonight as the night to take things to the next level? Oh God, what if he thought we were going to sleep together? The very thought filled me with a mixture of panic and eagerness. I messed up my braid again.

"Let me do that," Callie said, coming to stand behind me. "Relax. You don't have to do anything you don't want to do. Thomas isn't that kind of guy."

"I know," I said, trying to even out my breathing. "I just...I don't *know* what I want to do."

"Then you should tell him that," she said. "'Cause if you have any doubts, that means it's not time, not yet. You should tell him you're not experienced in that kind of stuff. If he's not willing to wait for you to figure it out, he's so not worth your V-card."

"Please," I muttered. "Can we please not use that term? You know I hate it."

"What should I call it then, Lizzie?" she asked, a truly wicked smile coming over her face. "Your virtue? That's what they'd say in those romance novels you love. Or your innocence? Your flower?"

"Ew!" I cried, trying to slap her hands as she howled with laughter.

"Seriously, though," she said, swatting my hands away. "You shouldn't do anything you don't feel totally comfortable with."

"I know." I looked down at my fingers and fiddled with my bracelet. It wasn't like I was opposed to pre-marital sex, though that kind of thing was drilled into my head at church and home since I was old enough to know what it meant. I just hadn't dated anyone that I would remotely considering doing that with. But Thomas...Thomas wasn't like anyone else I'd ever met.

"Regardless what you decide, you *should* tell him that you haven't had sex. It's not something to be embarrassed about."

"Can we stop with the after-school special now?" I asked. "It's starting to gross me out."

"Fine," she said, finishing the braid and stepping back to admire her handiwork. "I just want to make sure you're comfortable with whatever happens."

"I'll let you know if I need to have a heart-to-heart," I said, scrunching up my nose at her in the mirror. She slapped my shoulder.

"So, what are you doing tonight?" I asked as we headed into the living room. "Another date with the sexy barista?"

"I wish. I have to get that paper for Patterson done. I'm so far behind."

I felt a slight pang. My paper wasn't finished either. Between the time I was spending with Thomas and the time I was spending working on my novel, my course work was definitely suffering. And I wasn't even a full month into the program yet. *I'll do it Sunday*, I promised myself. I had already agreed to have dinner with Thomas the following night as well—he'd gotten reservations at some super swanky West End restaurant, and I didn't want to tell him to cancel them just so I could stay home and study. *Sunday*, I told myself again. No excuses.

"Your cab is here," Callie called from the front window. "Wait, what did Thomas say it was called? A small cab?"

"Mini-cab," I corrected, grabbing my purse.

"We've been here a month, and I still don't understand half the things they say," she muttered. I laughed.

"It's just to differentiate between the cheap services and the black cabs. The official taxis need all kinds of tests and registrations and stuff. A mini-cab is cheaper."

"Whatever." She settled onto the couch with her laptop, and I felt another pang of guilt that I wasn't working on my paper. *Sunday*, I repeated to myself.

"Have a good night," she called.

"You, too. Good luck on the paper."

The ride to Thomas's flat in Bayswater took about twenty minutes. He had told me that he lived within walking distance to Hyde Park, and I kept an eye out for it while the cab driver weaved in and out of traffic, occasionally shouting things in an unfamiliar language at pedestrians and bikers. We finally turned onto Bayswater Road, and the park came into view, stretched out to my left as far as I could see. "Wow," I murmured, still not used to the pockets of natural beauty scattered around this teeming, massive city.

We turned off Bayswater Road and the cabbie made several turns in quick succession. I was having trouble keeping my bearings and was sure I would have a hard time finding my way back out to the tube stop if I ever needed to take public transport.

"Here you are," the driver said, stopping abruptly. I peered up at a white stone building that seemed to stretch, without break, down the whole block. Belatedly, I realized that I was actually looking at nearly identical, attached apartments. The porch of Thomas's building had a bright blue flowerpot beside the door, making it easy to distinguish it from its neighbors.

I stood on Thomas's front step and let my eyes scan across the names on the buzzer until I found his. I hit the button and waited.

"Lizzie?" his voice came from the speaker, scratchy and distorted.

I held the button down. "Hi, I'm here."

"I'll come down."

I shook my head slightly, smiling to myself. Of course he would come down to personally fetch me. A moment later, the heavy wood front door swung open, revealing Thomas standing in the foyer, a broad welcoming smile on his face. He was barefoot, dressed in faded blue jeans and a green T-shirt, his hair mussed. He had a kitchen towel slung over his shoulder, and I detected a hint of flour on his cheek as he bent forward to kiss me hello. My throat immediately went dry at the sight of him. Why was he so sexy when he was all casual and messy like this? I placed my hand on his cheek, feeling the stumble below my fingers, and kissed him back.

"Come on up," he said, after we'd pulled apart. He held the door wide for me to squeeze through. "Dinner's on the hob."

"Hob?" I asked, following him up a set of creaky wooden stairs. I tried hard not to stare at his butt, which looked ridiculously good in those faded jeans.

"A stove to you," he said over his shoulder. "We really need to work on your British vocabulary."

"I learn something new everyday."

He stopped in front of a white door on the first landing. "Here we are," he said, looking slightly nervous. He pushed the door open for me and waited while I entered the flat first.

I was standing in a cozy living room. Thomas had filled his space with bookshelves, comfortable seating, large potted plants, and lots of squishy pillows. There was a fireplace against the far wall, and I could already imagine snuggling up with him in front of the flames. Several black and white photographs of various London landmarks covered the walls. I suspected Charlie's handiwork.

I realized Thomas was watching me expectantly. I again had the feeling he seemed nervous. "What do you think?"

"It's fantastic," I told him, watching as his face cleared immediately.

"Yeah?"

"Of course." It occurred to me that maybe he had been nervous waiting for my reaction. I reached out for his hands. "I really love it, Thomas. It feels warm and comfortable—like you."

"I'm glad." He pulled my hands gently until I was standing directly in front of him, the tips of our toes touching. "I want you to feel comfortable here."

I took a deep breath, feeling that familiar flip of my tummy. "I'm always comfortable with you," I said, my voice soft.

"Good—oh bollocks!"

I laughed as he suddenly released me and ran for the kitchen. "You better not burn my dinner!" I called after him.

I followed him into a large, modern kitchen and watched as he pulled a frying pan from the gas burner. "That was a close one." He grabbed a spatula and flipped something breaded and delicious-smelling in the pan. "I think I saved it."

I perched onto one of the bar stools and inhaled deeply. "That smells good. What is it?"

He set the pan on a hot pad and raised an eyebrow at me, his eyes sparkling in a way that made me feel tingly all the way down to my toes. "I don't know if I should divulge that information to someone being so cheeky. Didn't you just order me not to burn your dinner?"

I stuck out my tongue at him and he laughed. "What are you, five?"

He looked so cute, standing there in his kitchen, barefoot, a counter full of cooking things behind him, smirking at me. Without thinking, I slipped from the stool and wrapped my arms around his neck, pulling his face down to mine and kissing him eagerly.

"What was that for?" he asked, grinning at me. There was something in his expression that I liked, a surprised sort of happiness. As if he couldn't believe his good luck. Amazing to think that I could cause that kind of reaction.

"I just like you."

"Hmm, I should cook for you more often." I released him and walked to the counter. "Can I help with any of this?"

"Nope." He nudged me out of the way with his hip. "I'm just about done."

"Let me at least set the table."

"Already done. You could grab that wine and go pour, if you're so set on making yourself useful."

I grabbed the bottle of red from the counter and walked out to the dining area. Night had set in since I'd arrived, and I was struck by the view from the picture windows. I poured the wine into each of our glasses then stood by the window, looking down at the streetlights illuminating the concrete below, until I felt him come up behind me. His hands slipped around my waist. "Ready to eat?"

I leaned back against his chest, wishing I could just stand there in his arms instead. "Sure," I said. "Though you still haven't told me what we're eating."

He released me and, ever the gentleman, pulled my chair out for me. "I made eggplant. It's a new recipe, hopefully it will be good."

"Wow." I slid into my chair. "I had no idea you were so into cooking."

"I enjoy it," he said, taking his own seat. "I like trying new stuff."

He started dishing food onto each of our plates and my mouth actually watered. "That's nice. We tend to eat mostly the same stuff at my house."

"What stuff?"

"Well, my dad pretty much won't eat it unless it's Mexican," I said, rolling my eyes. "Or Tex-Mex, at the least. Though he does make an exception for burgers." I met his eyes. "Real sophisticated."

"My dad subsists almost entirely on roast and potatoes," Thomas countered, his voice dry. "I feel your pain."

The food was delicious. Though I had never had much interest in cooking before, I found myself surprisingly interested in Thomas's descriptions of how he had prepared things and where he shopped for his ingredients. He was so cute when he got animated about the things he cared about; clearly cooking was one of those things. It was very comfortable, sitting there with him, eating yummy food and chatting while looking out those huge windows at the garden below. I had told Thomas I loved his home and I meant it—I could easily envision many more nights like this. It actually gave me a moment of disquiet, realizing how readily I felt at home here.

"I'm stuffed," I said, once we had finished eating. I leaned back in my chair and rubbed my stomach, glad I had worn a flowy dress. I had never been the type of girl to pretend I didn't have an appetite, and I had eagerly accepted seconds when he offered. "That was really good. Thank you."

"You're welcome." He leaned over the table to kiss me softly. I knew that I probably had garlic breath, but he wasn't complaining so I decided not to worry about it.

"Let's do the washing up," he said, pulling back so he could stand up. He wiggled his eyebrows at me. "Come on, Miss. Time to earn your keep."

I laughed and helped him gather the dishes, taking the stacks into the kitchen where I loaded the dishwasher as he put away the leftovers. When we were finished, he held up the half-empty bottle of wine. "Another glass?"

"Sure."

With our glasses refilled, we made our way back to the living room. Thomas pulled me down next to him on the couch and I snuggled against his chest. "This is great," he murmured, kissing the top of my head. "Would you think I was a total wanker if I told you that having you here in my house is the best I've felt all week."

I brought my knees up into my chest so I could snuggle in further. "Nope. It's the best I've felt, too."

I could feel his chest move with his slight laughter. "Glad to see we're on the same page."

We sat in comfortable silence for a moment. "This is good wine," I finally said, taking a sip.

"I like it," he agreed, looking down at his glass. "This is a malbec. I've been reading up on wine pairings, it's kind of interesting. I used to think that kind of stuff was bollocks, but I'm starting to think that maybe they have a point."

My stomach dropped a little as I wondered how much the bottle had cost. Once again, I had allowed Thomas to handle everything. Most every time we had gone out, he had insisted on paying my share, usually taking care of the bill before I could even object.

"Dinner's on me tomorrow," I burst out. "No arguments this time."

He pulled away a little so he could look down on my face. "How did we go from wine pairings to that?"

I felt my cheeks heat a little. I probably sounded crazy. "I was just thinking about how much you probably spent on this bottle of wine. And that got me thinking of all the meals you've bought me over the last few weeks. I think it's more than my turn."

He shook his head. "There's no competition, Lizzie. It's not something to like, keep score over."

"I'm not keeping score," I said, feeling stupider by the minute. "But I'm also not comfortable with you always paying for me. So just let me get the next one, okay?"

It was his turn to look uncomfortable. "How 'bout you get the one after next, yeah?"

He was hiding something, I could tell. "Why? We're supposed to be having dinner tomorrow, right? Why can't I pay for it?"

"Well, I already made reservations…"

"So?"

He looked very uncomfortable now. "The place I booked is…not really budget friendly."

I felt a rush of embarrassment, though I wasn't sure why. I was a college student. I wasn't working. Of course he didn't expect me to have money for some swank place—and he was right; I didn't. But I'd already made such a big deal of paying for the next meal. What could I say now? I would sound even sillier if I demanded we go somewhere else.

"Oh," I said, my voice small.

"Lizzie, come on." He turned on the couch so he was facing me. "Don't feel awkward about it, okay? It's not a big deal."

"It's a big deal to me."

He sighed. "Look, I know a guy who works there, okay? He's a sous chef and it's his first job in a real gourmet place. I've been telling him I'd come check it out. That's all this is."

"Okay." I would sound very childish if I argued with that. But I still didn't like the idea of him buying me another dinner, especially one that was clearly going to be expensive.

"You'll get the next one, okay? I promise. No arguments from me."

I knew he was trying to make me feel better, but I somehow felt worse. Not knowing how to explain that to him, I set my wine glass down and settled back into the couch, determined to pretend like this whole awkward conversation had never happened.

Thomas wasn't quite so willing.

"I'm getting the feeling that money is kind of a sensitive issue. Should we talk about that?"

"What's there to say?" I asked, my face flooding with color now. "I'm a poor college kid."

"Which is what anyone would expect," he said. "Not many people have much money when they're in university. So why are you so touchy about it?"

When I didn't respond, he sighed. "Lizzie, we should be able to talk about stuff, you know? This is going to come up again. This is at least the sixth time you've acted uncomfortable about me paying for something."

"It's more than just being broke because of college," I mumbled. "Money has always been...well, it's always something I'm aware of."

He was quiet, waiting for me to continue. *Oh, what the hell*, I thought to myself. He was right, the money thing would come up again. I may as well tell him why it bothered me so much.

"My parents both grew up poor. Like, really poor." I looked up at him, feeling defensive, ready to jump at any judgment in his eyes. But he was merely watching me, the same familiar expression on his face that he always wore when he listened to me talk. "My mom was born in the States, but her parents were undocumented, so they could never settle in one place. She was in and out of school..." I thought about her telling me how much education mattered, how I should never take it for granted. "Anyhow." I cleared my throat, trying not to get emotional about any of it. "My dad was born in Mexico and came to the States with his family when he was ten. They were poor, too, but they could stay in one place because they had papers. They settled in Detroit, in Mexicantown. That's where he met my mom."

"Were they young when they got married?"

"Twenty." I smiled, unable to imagine having been married at that age. "Anyhow, when my dad got the job at Ford, it was such a huge deal for them. They were able to move out to the suburbs, buy a house. It was stability."

"That's why it's so important for them that you get a good job," he surmised.

"Yup. They're almost fanatical about making sure their kids are middle class."

"There's nothing wrong with that." He was watching me carefully. "With them wanting the best for you guys."

"No, there's not. And they took great care of us. We always had more than they did when they were growing up. A comfortable house, food, clothes. They paid for us to go to college. They worked really hard, you know, and we had a nice life."

"You're proud of them."

I nodded. "I am. But other people…"

"What?"

"People gave us a hard time, at school. There are some people…well, I guess certain people have ideas about Mexicans…about immigrants." I felt uncomfortable, squeamish even. I had never talked about this with anyone outside of the family, not even Callie. "We got teased a lot. Called names. They said things about our parents, about illegals mooching off the taxpayers. That people like my dad were stealing jobs."

"That's bullshit," Thomas said, his voice low. "You didn't listen to that crap, did you?"

I shook my head. "I know who my father is. I know how hard he worked for us and what he deserved. But it's hard to get away from those stereotypes, you know? Every time there was an immigration debate in our country, it would start up all over again." I was quiet for a moment, thinking of the way my dad's face would close up when those stories would be on the news. "It was ridiculous, really. Because if my parents taught us anything, it was to be reliant on ourselves, to work hard so we could be independent."

"You don't like to be beholden to anyone," Thomas said, his voice quiet. I nodded. "I get that."

I looked up at him. "Do you?"

"Sure. And I think it speaks highly of your character."

I smiled at him, feeling shy, but didn't tell him how much I liked the sound of respect in his voice.

"Look," Thomas said, running a hand through his hair. "For years now, I've watched guys like Jackson splash their money around as if it made them more worthy. I'm not like that, Lizzie. I hope you know that." I tried to assure him, but he held his hand up to finish. "I'm not going to lie and tell you that money is a huge issue for me. I'm not rich or anything, but the *Darkness* franchise means I can be comfortable. If I offer to pay for you, it's just because my dad raised us that way, you know? That you pay for a girl when you ask her out. And I'm the one doing all the asking…"

I laughed. "So I should be the one asking more, is what you're saying?"

He gave me a quick grin before his face got serious again. "I just don't want you to think that I'm trying to show off, or be flashy, or anything like that. I promise you, Lizzie, I am so not that guy."

He looked so worried, so concerned with how I thought about him. I couldn't help but slide closer to him on the couch and take his hand. "I know that, Thomas. I know what kind of guy you are."

"You do?" He turned his head to look at me, bringing his face within an inch of mine. He was looking at me so intently, his eyes boring into mine, as if he had a lot resting on my answer. I nodded and moved in closer. "Of course I do."

I wanted to tell him how grateful I was that he listened to me, that he didn't judge me or make me feel stupid. And I wanted to tell him how I never once felt like he was showing off or splashing his money around, how he was so much better than that. How I knew what a good guy he was. But before I could tell him any of that, he was closing the distance between our mouths and kissing me.

I released a happy little sigh and decided I would show him instead. I brought my hands to his face and kissed him right back.

CHAPTER TEN

Thomas hadn't been joking when he said the restaurant he had booked wasn't budget friendly. I had never seen prices like that on a menu, not anywhere.

"Jesus," he muttered, looking at the menu. "Dom told me his new job was posh, but he didn't say it was out of control."

I laughed at the look on his face. He had surely been to numerous swanky places over the course of his recent career success. It was cute that he wasn't jaded by it.

"And is it just me," he went on, "or does none of this stuff sound like real food?"

"You sound like Mark now," I pointed out. "Are you going to start complaining that the decor is too poncey as well?"

He laughed. "Those two are something else, aren't they?"

"They are," I agreed, thinking about my meeting with Mark and Sarra. "It seems kind of strange that they would be friends with Meghan and Carter."

"Sarra and Meghan were roommates at university," he explained, taking a sip of his ice water. "Meg might come across as sophisticated, but she's no snob. Her parents were really into appearances and were always pushing her to hang out with a certain 'class'." He made quote marks as he said the word, and rolled his eyes. "She hated being told what to do. I think meeting Sarra was the perfect situation for her."

"You couldn't accuse Sarra of caring about appearances."

Thomas laughed. "You said it." Without warning, his face seemed to cloud over, the laughter slipping away as quickly as it had come. "Crap," he muttered.

"What? What's the matter?"

He was looking over my shoulder. Before I could turn to see what had grabbed his attention, he was leaning toward me. "Look, a bunch of people from the movie just came in. I'm going to need to say hi to them, and they'll probably invite us to sit with them."

"Oh," I said, my stomach dropping. This is what had him so visibly bothered? Was he worried about me meeting them? Did he think I would embarrass him, or something? *Don't be stupid*, I told myself firmly. *This is Thomas.*

"I'm really sorry," he said, meeting my eyes. "I wanted to enjoy this night with just you. And some of those guys…well, they can kind of be jerks. Stuck up." He smiled ruefully at me. "Nothing like you."

I felt a warm rush of affection for him. *See?* I told myself. *Stupid to think the worst.*

"Don't worry about it," I assured him. "Really, I don't mind. I've known some snobs in my day. I can hold my own, you know."

He gave me a quick grin before someone on the other side of the room called out his name. "Hey, Harper!" Thomas looked up, his face the picture of surprise, and I stifled a giggle. Without looking at me, he winked minutely, making me want to laugh harder. But then his friends were upon us and I looked up, my breath catching in my throat. Standing at our table were Jackson Coles, Lola Fischer, Killian Cooper, and a few people I didn't recognize, but who, by the looks of them, were fabulously rich and good looking, if not famous.

"Hey, guys. I didn't know you'd be here tonight. This is my girlfriend, Lizzie. Lizzie, these are some of my coworkers." At the word girlfriend, every head snapped in my direction. *Don't blush*, I ordered. Under the table, I felt Thomas's fingertips brush across my knee. The contact calmed me enough that I could smile up at the group.

"Hello," I said, glad to hear that my voice was even.

"Hey," Jackson said, his voice a lazy drawl. He reached out for my hand, surprising me by leaning forward and kissing it. "It's really great to meet you." He looked directly in my eyes as he spoke, his face mere inches from mine. It was a ridiculous performance, especially with Thomas sitting feet away. Was this supposed to be attractive to me? Did girls actually fall for this? Under the table, Thomas stepped on my toes. Sure I was about to laugh, I merely nodded in return. Jackson released my hand and stood tall. "You guys should totally join us, yeah? We were just about to sit down."

Thomas met my eyes across the table. "What do you think, Lizzie?"

I appreciated him deferring to me, particularly in front of his friends. He must know how nervous I was; demonstrating to me that I was in control of our situation made me feel better immediately. "Sure, that's nice of you to offer."

Thomas gestured to the waiter, explaining the situation as the group moved over to a table in the corner. I couldn't help notice that every eye in the room followed them. Even in a place like this, a place dripping with wealth and reputation, Jackson Coles and his group were the most noteworthy people in the room.

Thomas pulled out my chair for me and rested a hand at my back as we made our way to Jackson's table. He leaned in close to my ear. "You sure you're okay?"

"I'm fine," I replied, smiling at him. He kissed me softly on the lips before we completed our trek. As we joined the group at the table, I couldn't help but notice Lola Fischer's eyes were glued to my face.

After requesting a bottle of Cristal for the table from the waiter, Jackson turned his attention to Thomas. "So, Harper, is this why you've been so MIA lately?" Jackson was slouched back in his seat, taking up half the table, the picture of lazy confidence. Thomas scooted his chair marginally closer to mine and rested his hand on my knee under the table.

"As opposed to what?" Lola asked. I was surprised at the throatiness of her voice. In the films, her voice was sweeter, girlish and high-pitched. "Like he's usually some party animal."

"Fair point," Jackson said, grinning. "But it's nice to see you've been keeping busy."

Something about his tone made me blush, and I tilted my head down so he wouldn't see. I had a feeling he'd be happy to know he'd embarrassed me. He seemed the type.

"I keep busy with lots of things," Thomas said, his voice even. "I've been working a lot since we wrapped."

"Ah, yes. The hardest working man in the industry," Jackson said. "How's the work going, mate?"

The two men fell into conversation about their respective work. I was surprised to hear that Jackson seemed genuinely interested in what Thomas had been up to. Maybe he did take the whole acting thing seriously after all. Across the table, though Lola and Killian were deep in conversation, I couldn't help but notice the actress's eyes continuously flicking in my direction. I tried to ignore it.

"So, where'd the two of you meet?" Lola asked suddenly, leaning across the table so that I got an eyeful of her ample cleavage.

"You'll enjoy this, Jax," Thomas said, and I could hear the smirk in his voice. "We actually met at your show."

I kicked him under the table, but he showed no sign of reaction. I was going to kill him. Now I'd have to talk to Jackson about that stupid play, and Thomas knew how much I hated it.

"Really?" Jackson said, his face lighting up. "How about that. I take it you were in the audience?"

"Yes," I said, trying to ignore Thomas as he turned to face me, laughter evident in his eyes. "A friend purchased tickets months ago. It was actually the first night out we had in London, so it was very memorable. It was wonderful," I added. It wasn't totally a lie. I had met Thomas there, and that had been pretty wonderful.

"Great, great," Jackson said, nodding seriously. "So glad you enjoyed it. And glad it brought the two of you together. Who knows, Tommy," he continued, but his gaze remained on me. "If things work out, you'll have me to thank."

"Oh, for sure." I wondered if I was the only one at the table that could hear the amusement in his voice.

The waiter returned with the Cristal. "Are you ready to order?" he asked.

"Oh shite," Lola said, looking down at the menu. "I haven't even thought about it. Is anything here suitable for the Gershin Diet?"

Jackson made a scathing noise in the back of his throat. "Christ, Lola, what the hell is that? Just order a salad like you always do."

"The Gershin Diet is *the* big thing," she scoffed. "You just wait, you'll be hearing all about it soon." Her eyes flicked to me. "It makes such a difference when you can't drop those last ten pounds."

Her implication was obvious, but Thomas leaned in close to me and said, in a voice just loud enough for Lola to hear, "Don't even think about it. You're perfect the way you are." I grinned at him, feeling warmth spread through me. In fact, I felt confident enough to order the steak I had been eyeing, getting me an approving pat on the thigh from Thomas, who ordered the same.

"So, Leslie, is it?" Lola asked once the waiter had gone, her voice dripping with saccharine sweetness. "You're from the States then?"

I nodded. "It's Lizzie. And yes, I'm from Detroit."

"Mmm. And what brings you to London then?"

Did this chick end every sentence with the word *then*? "I'm here for school. I'm doing a graduate course in literature at Kingsbury."

"Ah, she's a brainy girl," Killian said, his first words to me. They did not sound complimentary.

"I don't know about that," I said, determined to stay pleasant. "But I do enjoy books."

"How long are you here?" Jackson asked. I was starting to feel slightly on the spot, with all of the very famous eyes on me.

"Nine months," I said. "I love it so far. It's already going too fast." Thomas squeezed my knee under the table.

"And what do you miss most about, um, *Detroit*." Lola said the city's name like it was a dirty word, and I was suddenly visited with the urge to kick her under the table.

"Culturally or personally?" I asked, my voice taking on some of the fake saccharine that had characterized Lola's so far.

The actress smirked at me. "Culturally? We are talking about the States here, right? Would we really say they have much culture to offer?"

"Lola," Thomas said, a warning note in his voice.

"Oh, I'm just joking," Lola said, perhaps sensing she had gone too far. "One thing you'll learn about we Brits, Liz, is that we take the piss out of everything."

"Mmm," I said.

"Now that Lola's done being so rude," Jackson said, "what *do* you miss about home? Personally *and* culturally."

"I miss the *Daily Show*," I said, trying to calm myself without taking obvious deep breaths. "It's the best political satire, very funny, very clever. And my family, of course."

"Are you very close with your family?" Jackson asked, leaning slightly toward me.

I nodded. "I am. I have five siblings, and we see each other all the time."

"Wow." It was strange, being the focus of Jackson Coles's attention. He was watching me rather intently, his eyes trained on mine. Suddenly, I could understand why people found him so captivating. Just in the few moments since I'd met him, I could tell he had a way of making someone feel like she was the most important person in the room. It was natural charisma like I hadn't experienced before. Behind him, I saw Lola narrow her eyes slightly. "You should really cherish that, Lizzie," Jackson said, his voice soft. "There's nothing more important than family."

I nodded, trying not to focus on how trite he sounded. Charismatic or not, he didn't strike me as the most genuine person in the world. It felt like a performance to me, the Jackson Coles show. I could see how girls got swept up in it, but I found it lacking. I felt Thomas's fingers brush my leg again and I smiled. The difference in the men was palpable.

"So, Thomas," Lola said, her voice louder than the setting warranted. "Why weren't you at Dizzy's party last week? You missed the most wild time." She leaned across the table toward him, twirling a lock of red hair on her finger. I had the distinct impression of someone trying hard to redirect the focus of the table. I had a feeling Lola wasn't happy unless she was the focus, regardless of the setting.

"I had plans," Thomas said. "Besides, the last time I went to one of Dizzy's parties, I was bored out of mind."

Lola laughed. "You would say that." She gave me a little knowing smirk. "Thomas is far too good for us all, you know. Our shenanigans are beneath him."

"Don't be silly, Lola," Thomas said, a hint of irritation evident in his voice. "You know I love nothing better than watching a bunch of spoiled rich kids get hammered."

Lola only laughed. "Naughty boy." She turned to me. "See what I mean?"

Thomas must have caught a whiff of the same predatory tone in Lola's voice, because he wrapped an arm casually around my shoulders. "Lizzie is well acquainted with my stodgy old-man ways, aren't you darling?"

I met his eyes and smiled. Thomas may have been doing a bit of acting himself, but I knew it was for my benefit and I was grateful. "Indeed I am."

"I need the loo," Lola said, standing suddenly. "Come with me, Lizzie?"

I shot Thomas a questioning look before standing to join her. "Sure." I was sure she had some kind of agenda. Were we going to be buddies now? Or was I about to get the Lola version of Sarra and Meghan's bathroom warning?

In the bathroom, Lola made a beeline straight to a stall. "Christ, I have to pee," she muttered. "I drank far too many martinis for so early in the night."

"Were you at a bar before this?" I asked as I entered my own stall. I was determined to be pleasant, no matter her agenda.

"No, dear," she said, her voice dripping condescension. "In the limo. Jackson always makes sure his transportation is well stocked."

Glad she couldn't see me in the stall, I indulged myself in a massive eye roll. "That sounds nice."

I heard her toilet flush. "It is one of the perks."

A moment later, I joined her at the sink to wash my hands. "Speaking of perks," she said in a tone just a shade too casual, "will you be joining Thomas at the Hot Under Thirty party next month?"

"Um, we hadn't discussed it."

She made a little clucking noise and shot me a pitying glance. "I suppose it is a bit early for him to be expecting you to put up with such a ridiculous production. Lots of girls think a celebrity event like that is all glamour, but it can be such a pain. Dieting, finding the right dress, having your picture taken. All the gossip and pressure."

"Mmm," I said noncommittally. Was this her angle then? Was she trying to scare me off?

"Of course he'll have asked you to Holman's Christmas party." When I didn't respond, she continued. "Mark Holman? The executive producer of *Darkness*? He throws a huge party in Cannes every Christmas, has the entire cast down to his villa for a weekend in early December."

"That sounds nice."

"Lizzie, you would not believe it." Her tone was indulgent. "It is *the* event of the entire winter. It's not just the *Darkness* cast, there are more celebrities than you could even imagine. It's like a who's who of London *and* Hollywood." She gave a twinkly little laugh that made me want to smack her. "You absolutely must insist that he bring you."

"Christmas is quite a ways off," I said, determined to keep my tone detached. I wasn't sure if she was trying to scare me off or if she was simply bragging; regardless, something about this girl had my guard up.

"Oh, poor you," she cooed, pulling a lipstick out of her purse. "I'm sure Thomas will still be interested in you. But you're smart not to get too attached." She gave me a knowing look in the mirror. "These showbiz boys can be so fickle."

Heat was rising to my face now, but I was determined not to let her see that she was getting to me. "True. But then, so can we college girls. Who knows what will happen between now and Christmas?"

She gave me a look in the mirror that indicated she wasn't buying it. "Well, it's wise of you to keep your options open. Personally, I never could see how anyone put up with those of us in the industry. The pressure of it is can be absolutely ridiculous. Not to mention the schedule."

Her words set off a little alarm. "I haven't felt much pressure from Thomas," I began, but she cut me off.

"Oh no, dear, I didn't mean from Thomas. I meant from the fans. And the press. Blimey, they can be an absolute terror."

"Why would I need to worry about fans and the press?"

She gave me a pitying look. "Sweetie, you just have no idea what you're in for, do you?"

"Thomas said he doesn't get much press attention," I said uncertainly, remembering the jolt I'd gotten from seeing his face on the *Darkness* poster.

"Well, right now he might not," she said, leaning up against the marble counter so she could face me directly. "Because we're between releases. It lets some of the cast fly a bit below the radar." She smiled smugly as if to indicate there was nothing that could make *her* fly under the radar. "But you just wait until the New Year when we start gearing up for the next film. He'll be gone all the time, you know, promoting. There are loads of responsibilities when you have a movie coming out. And, of course, you already know about the increase in his role's importance this time around. I have a feeling things are about to get very big for our bloke out there."

I was so disturbed by the picture she painted that I didn't even bother to get annoyed at her use of "our" in describing my date. "He didn't say much about his part in the next film," I muttered. "Is it really that much bigger?"

She nodded, her eyes gleaming in a way that felt unpleasant to me. "It is. I have a hunch this could really be his breakout. But that's fun for you, right? To be dating a movie star, all your girlfriends will be so jealous." She gave that same tinkling laugh. "That is, if the two of you manage to find the time to date, what with his schedule."

The worry must have been evident on my face because she suddenly reached out and patted my shoulder. "Oh, don't fret, dear. He seems to really like you. I'm sure he won't let you slip away so easily." The almost gleeful expression on her face couldn't quite be masked by her words, but my head was spinning too much to care.

"We should head back," she said, turning back to the mirror to give her red hair a final shake. She sighed. "I'm really not sure about this red. Fredrico tells me it looks divine, but I think it's a bit dark for my coloring."

Too preoccupied to ask, or care, who Fredrico was, I mutely followed her from the bathroom and back out to the table. My stomach felt like it had settled somewhere down by my knees. Objectively, I knew Lola was just trying to get to me, to put me back in my place. She probably hated the idea of a poor American nobody playing in her sandbox. But none of that changed the impact of her words.

Were things really about to drastically change for Thomas? The thought of press coverage made me shudder. I had no desire to be in any kind of spotlight. Besides, my time in London was limited. Was there a point in getting more seriously involved with a guy who was about to be swept up in a whirlwind of promotion and appearances?

"You okay?" Thomas whispered when I sat next to him. I nodded, feeling numb, and tried to smile. "You look freaked out," he persisted.

"I'm fine," I murmured, not meeting his eyes. I was saved more inquisition by the waiter arriving with our food, but I noticed Thomas's eyes remained stubbornly on my face.

Lola firmly grabbed the reins of conversation at the table, reminding everyone of industry dinner parties they had all attended, and comparing the various fine dining options around the city. She was in her element, the attention of the table (and most of the room at large) directed at her, opining about all things high-end and expensive. I was grateful for her blather; having never dined at any of Marco Pierre White's restaurants, I was saved from having to participate in the conversation, allowing me plenty of time to ponder what Lola had warned me of.

"Are you sure you're okay?" Thomas asked again when the waiter came to clear our plates. "Did something happen?"

"Just tired," I told him, hating myself for the lie. "I should get home. I have that paper to work on tomorrow."

"Okay," he said, clearly unconvinced. "If you're sure everything's okay."

I nodded, but I knew that, too, was a lie. I had a feeling things between us were far from okay.

***

"Where have you been?"

I frowned at the wall of my bedroom and did my best not to sigh into the phone. "Hello, Maria," I said. "It's nice to talk to you, too."

"Don't be cute," my big sister snapped over the phone. "We've been trying to reach you, you know. Mom said you haven't returned any of her calls in more than a week. And Laura tried you this weekend as well. Where have you been?"

"I've been busy," I said. "With school. You know, school? The reason I came over here?"

"You're not too busy to call your family, Elizabeth."

I sighed, feeling guilty. The truth was, school had little to do with my lack of familial communication. Like everything else, Thomas was the thing that was distracting me from calling home. "I'm sorry," I said, knowing she wouldn't drop it until I sounded suitably chastised. "It's hard with the time difference. I always think to call in the morning but it's still late over there. Once I get to class it slips my mind."

"Then you need to plan better," she said firmly. "Mom is very upset."

"I really am sorry, Maria," I said, more sincerely this time. "I promise I'll call her as soon as we get off the phone."

"Okay," she said, sounding mollified. "I just don't want you to forget your responsibilities to your family. You wouldn't have even been in college if it wasn't for Mom and Dad working so hard."

"I know, Maria," I said, starting to get irritated again. What did she want from me?

It was quiet for a moment. It was strange, talking to her after all this time. For most of my life, I hadn't gone an entire day without talking to one of my siblings. And now it had been, what, almost two weeks since I'd talked to any of them?

"So," I said, feeling awkward. "How is everyone at home? How are you?"

"Fine," she said, sighing to indicate that she was actually far from fine. Maria had a bit of a martyr thing going. "Though my kids are driving me insane." She went into a long narrative involving José Junior's behavior issues at school, and how her husband was absolutely no help in disciplining him. "It's just like Carlos when we were little," she said. "The little prince of the family. Dad let him get away with murder, and José seems determined to do the same with JJ."

"Carlos turned out okay in the end," I reminded her. "You know JJ will, too."

She scoffed. "Carlos is twenty-nine with no long-term girlfriend. He spends all of his money on those stupid tech toys. I'm not sure I would call that okay."

Maria had married José at age twenty-three, the summer after she graduated college. Her first child, Sofia, had been born only two years later, José Junior two years after that, and she was eager to be pregnant again. In her mind, no one could be described as "okay" unless they were settled down and working toward a family. She had been particularly incredulous about my decision to spend the year after graduation in a foreign country, on my own.

"Speaking of dating," she said. "What's this Sofie tells us about you having some British boyfriend?"

I groaned silently to myself. I should have known Sofie would be unable to keep gossip that juicy to herself. My inability to find a boyfriend had been a source of family conversation for years.

"It's not a big deal, Maria," I lied. "I just met him. He's very nice and has been showing me around the city. It's nice to know someone who's familiar with everything, you know?"

"Sof said you were smitten," she said, ignoring me. "I hope you're not getting serious with this boy, Lizzie."

I bit back a curse. "Maria, you've been bugging me for years to start dating so I could get ready to settle down," I reminded her. "Now you're going to give me a hard time?"

"I've been bugging you to start dating viable boys," she corrected. "Boys who live here. Boys who are settled and could take care of you."

"I don't need someone to take care of me."

"Don't get all moody with me. You know I mean someone who could take care of your family. Don't you want children?"

"Give me a break," I snapped. "You're as bad as Auntie Sonia. This is the twenty-first century, you know? Women don't need men to take care of them. Besides, I'm twenty-three, for Pete's sake."

"And I was married by that age," she argued. "Mama already had two children when she was twenty-three."

I closed my eyes and concentrated on taking deep, calming breaths. This was not the first time I had received this lecture from a family member, and it certainly wouldn't be the last.

"I just hope you're not spending all your time there with some boy you'll probably never see again when you get home, that's all," she said. Her voice had softened, but I somehow found myself even more upset by these words. "It's hard not to be worried when you stop calling your own parents, and then we hear it's because you have a boyfriend, some stranger none of us have ever met."

"You don't need to worry about Thomas," I said through clenched teeth. "Okay? Can we drop it?"

"What about school?" she plowed on. "Isn't it hard to keep up with your studies when you're spending all your free time with some boy?"

"He's not some boy, Maria, he's—"

"Because you told us the whole reason you were going through with this study abroad thing was to make yourself more marketable to school districts when you came home, you know. You'll hardly do that if you can't keep your grades up."

"Oh my God," I muttered, wanting to strangle her. "I am doing fine in school." I felt a twinge as I said it, knowing the paper I was struggling to finish was not my best work. I really should have spent the last two days working on it, like Callie had done, instead of putting it off until Sunday.

"We worry about you, Lizzie. I just want to make sure you aren't doing anything over there that you'll regret when you get home."

"Thank you for your concern," I said, my voice tight. The thing was, I knew my family wanted what was best for me. I really did. I just wished they would consider what I wanted for once.

Maria was quiet for a moment. I wondered if she could tell that she had stepped over the line this time, that I was actually angry instead of just annoyed. Probably not.

"Oh, did you hear about the drama with the Hernandez girls?" she finally said, and I was relieved. For the rest of the conversation, she could fill me in on family gossip, leaving me free to seethe in my own head. I'd been dealing with my family butting into my life for as long as I could remember. Normally I was able to deal with it; probably because I inevitably ended up going along with whatever advice they were giving. But now, half a world away, the meddling somehow felt more intrusive. Couldn't they see that I was an adult now? I had gone across the freaking ocean. What else could I do to show them that I could make my own decisions?

The worst part, of course, was that Maria had voiced some of the things I had been thinking myself, particularly since my conversation with Lola the previous night. I was letting my grades slip. And I was getting in way too deep with a guy that I wouldn't see again after I left London.

I hung up in the worst mood that I'd been in since arriving overseas. I was worried about Thomas and what I should do, and Callie wasn't even around to talk me down. Having finished her paper the night before, she was now out with some of the girls from our class. I sighed and returned my attention to my laptop, determined to finish the paper before it got much later. As I read over the last paragraph, I felt a knot form in my stomach. My paper was a mess, no two ways about it. I was rushed and it showed.

Maria's words rang clearly in my mind. *Isn't it hard to keep up with your studies when you're spending all your free time with some boy?*

I frowned and ordered myself to suck it up and finish, good or bad.

I hated it when my sister was right.

CHAPTER ELEVEN

"Well, Lola Fischer sounds like a total bitch," Callie said firmly the next day as we enjoyed a coffee break in a small café near campus. "I hope you're not letting yourself get all worked up over this, Lizzie."

I took a sip of my latte, wondering how to put my worries into words. It probably would have been easier had Meredith not joined us at the café. She was so excited about my Saturday dinner with celebrities that she had barely let me expound on the conversation with Lola.

"Lola Fischer," she said, a dreamy look on her face. "And Killian Cooper. Not to even mention *Jackson Coles*. I'm so jealous I could puke. Lizzie, you are so lucky!"

"Lucky?" Callie shot her an incredulous look. "Seriously, Mer, did you not just hear what she said? Lola was horrible to her. Those people totally ruined her dinner with Thomas."

Meredith shrugged. "Lola Fischer could be a bitch to me any time, so long as I got her autograph."

I narrowed my eyes. "She probably would have loved it if I asked for an autograph," I muttered. "Then she could be confident that we were both in our rightful places in the universe."

"Don't let it bother you," Callie urged. "You said that Thomas doesn't seem to like them much. I doubt you'll have to see them all that often."

"That's the thing, though," I said, fiddling with the cardboard heat guard on my cup. "Lola made it sound like they all *will* be together a lot, once the new movie comes out."

"That's not for months," Callie said.

"But they have promotions and appearances. She made it sound like Thomas will be really busy all the time."

Callie shifted uncomfortably. "They do go all out for those movies. When the last one came out, they flew Jackson and Lola to the States, even. They did all the late night shows—"

"And morning shows," Meredith cut in. "And radio interviews. And the entertainment magazines."

"Great," I muttered, ripping the wrapper clear in half. "You're making me feel so much better."

"Sorry," she said, looking abashed. "I don't want to put you off, or anything."

"What do you guys know about this new movie?" I asked. "Lola said Thomas's part is supposed to get bigger."

The girls exchanged a worried look. "I did hear something about that," Callie said, not meeting my eyes.

"What? What did you hear?"

"Oh, Lizzie, weren't you paying attention at all when we watched those movies?" she asked. "It's obvious they're building up to a big reveal about Thomas's character. There were so many hints."

"I heard he finally discovers that he's a werewolf, too," Meredith said, her voice dropping in excitement. "Which is totally going to put a rift between Gideon and Cooper."

"And that's a big deal?" I asked.

"They're setting it up for him to be the main rival to Jackson," Callie said. "At least that's what all the speculation is. It would make his role much bigger."

"Great," I muttered. "He didn't say anything about that."

"That surprises me," Callie said. "Don't you guys talk about his work?"

I nodded. "Well, yeah. But he's much more excited about his new movie. *Hostile*. It comes out in February."

Meredith scrunched up her nose. "Never heard of it. It's probably one of those boring independent films he's always doing." She snorted. "Seriously, Lizzie, if he keeps up that kind of thing, you have nothing to worry about. No one ever became famous by being in a bunch of stupid plays and art house movies no one ever heard of."

Callie shoved her shoulder. "Be nice!"

"I didn't mean it was a bad thing!" Meredith protested. "Isn't Lizzie sitting here getting all upset because she doesn't want to date someone mega-famous? I'm just trying to make her feel better."

"It's fine," I said, when Callie appeared to be ready to argue. "I'm not worried so much about the fame part, though it doesn't really appeal to me. I'm worried about how busy she said they'll be. Is there really a point in getting serious with someone when he's about to be traveling all over the place? I'm not here for that long to begin with."

"Wait a second," Meredith said, holding up her hands. "You said getting serious. Are you guys getting serious? Already?"

I squirmed, wishing again she wasn't here for this conversation. "I don't know," I said. "It feels that way. I mean, I know it's been really fast, but…"

"You like him," Callie said firmly. "You like him a lot. I can tell. And he's crazy about you, Lizzie. There's nothing wrong with admitting that. Sometimes things get serious fast."

I met her eyes. "But shouldn't I be worried then? If I already feel like this after, what? Three weeks? How will I feel in a few months when he takes off to be some big shot movie star?" I sighed deeply. "Maybe I should get out before I get any deeper."

"You're insane, you know that?" Meredith said, shaking her head. "I have never met a person who would look at dating a movie star as a bad thing. You're saying you should dump him before he becomes more rich and famous? Are you hearing yourself?"

I ignored her and focused on Callie. "I don't want to get hurt," I told her. "Doesn't it seem like getting hurt is kind of inevitable if I stick with it?"

"I don't know," she said, clearly struggling. "You guys are so good together, Lizzie. Anyone can see that. But you were never going to be able to stay together long term. Actor or not, we are going home in less than a year."

My stomach dropped at her words. *Doesn't that prove my point?* I asked myself. *If I'm already feeling dread at the thought of leaving him, how much worse will that be in June?*

"Here's an idea," Meredith said. "Why don't you stop worrying about everything and just have fun with him? For as long as it lasts."

Callie stared at her. "You know, she actually has a point."

"You sound so shocked," Meredith said drily.

"We should go," I said, looking at the clock on my phone. "Class starts in twenty."

We headed out of the café and back to campus, Meredith and Callie argued the entire way about Lola Fischer and whether or not it was worth dealing with her bitchiness to be close to such a big celebrity. I let them argue, lost in my own thoughts. I had hoped talking to Callie would help me figure out what I should do next. But now I was more confused than ever.

When class started ten minutes later, thoughts of Thomas were forced from my mind. After collecting our papers, Dr. Patterson passed back our tests from the week before. I had been worried about the test, having not quite finished the required reading. But I was usually good at exams, particularly ones with essay portions, so I had been confident I had managed to scrape a B at least.

I had been wrong.

"I got a D?" I gasped under my breath, staring at the foreign letter on my test.

Callie heard me, and her head snapped over to stare at the grade. She raised her eyes to mine and I could see shock in them. "Holy crap," she muttered. "I've never seen you get less than a B."

"Me either." I stared at the paper, disbelieving. I had never gotten a D, not once in my whole life. I couldn't believe it.

"Don't worry," Callie said, correctly judging that I was about to freak out. "You'll make up for it with the paper. Everyone's allowed a mess-up now and then."

But I wouldn't make up for it with the paper. Patterson clearly was a tough grader, and I knew I hadn't done anywhere near my best on the paper. I had put it off to the last minute and rushed through it. Just like the reading for this exam. All because I wanted to spend time with Thomas.

"Lizzie, relax," Callie said, a worried expression on her face. "It's going to be okay. Breathe."

I closed my eyes, trying not to freak out. My studies had always been important—more than important—to me. I couldn't believe I was messing up this badly so early in the program.

You'll just have to do better, I told myself as Dr. Patterson started his lecture. I opened my notebook to a clean sheet of paper, determined to take perfect notes.

You're here for school, I told myself firmly. *Not for dating. Not for wasting time on your silly novel. God, get a grip, Lizzie Medina.*

As I furiously scribbled down every word Patterson said, I did my best to drown out the memory of Maria's voice, warning me that the time I spent with Thomas could have a negative effect on my schoolwork. There was just no point in worrying about that now, not when I had to pay attention to the lecture.

But no matter how hard I tried, I couldn't manage to get rid of the small knot of fear in my stomach.

***

As I went through the motions of the rest of my day, I tried hard to ignore the growing realization that I had to slow things down with Thomas. I couldn't keep letting my schoolwork suffer. And after everything Lola had said to me, I knew it was only a matter of time before things changed between us. I knew it was smarter to take a step back now, but I didn't want to admit that to myself. The fact was, I was already head over heels with Thomas. The thought of not seeing him as often hurt my stomach. It was far easier to pretend I could ignore it.

But as soon as I got home, something happened that made it impossible to pretend anymore.

Logging into my email, I smiled to see a message from Sofie. I opened it, eager to hear from my cousin.

Girl, you failed to mention that you were now paparazzi fodder, her email began, without so much as a greeting. I frowned. What was she talking about?

The caption doesn't identify you, but I know that Medina hair when I see it. So this is your life now? Dinners with celebrities and photographers clamoring to get a shot of you? You're such a lucky bitch. Love you! P.S. Call your mother. She's worried sick and your sisters keep bugging me to find out if I've heard from you.

My heart beating fast, I clicked on the link under her note. It led to some gossip site and there, on the very front page, was a picture of Thomas and me leaving the restaurant on Saturday night. *Thomas Harper leaves The Wilton with date,* read the caption. Below that picture was another, this one of the rest of the *Darkness* cast leaving twenty minutes after us.

I felt dizzy. I was on the Internet. My picture was right there, for anyone to see. I was grateful that my name wasn't printed, but would that be the case next time? It seemed unlikely that I would be able to avoid having my picture taken so long as I was out in the city with Thomas.

With trembling fingers, I opened a search engine and typed in Thomas's name. Immediately links began filling the screen. There were reviews and articles about his smaller plays and films, as well as a dearth of information linking him to the *Darkness* movies. I clicked on one of those links and found myself on a flashy site called Hearts of Darkness. *The web's number one site for the* Darkness *fanatic at the heart of us all!* screamed the tagline.

For the next half hour, I clicked around the site, feeling sicker by the minute. There were links to interviews, articles, and promotional appearances by each of the cast members—including several of Thomas. As I clicked through the pictures, I saw Thomas at premieres, out around town, and attending parties with the other cast members. There was Thomas, dressed in black, posing next to Jackson. And another with Lola. And another with...holy crap, George Clooney? My head spinning, I clicked on the last photo on the page. My breath left in a little sigh as I took in the picture of Thomas, heartbreakingly handsome in a tux, his arm around a slim blonde girl in a red evening gown. He looked slightly younger in the shot—he also looked very much taken with the woman on his arm. *Thomas Harper with long-term girlfriend Francis Cavanaugh.*

I shut my laptop, feeling slightly dizzy. I wasn't sure I could handle all of this. The celebrities, the parties, the press. This wasn't a world I wanted to visit. It wasn't me. I thought about the picture of Thomas with the woman who was obviously the same Franny that Sarra and Meghan had warned me about. I tried to imagine myself in her place, in an evening gown on Thomas's arm at some glittery party or premiere. I couldn't picture it. I didn't belong somewhere like that, with people like that. I was a plain Jane bookworm from Detroit Michigan, not someone who rubbed elbows with celebrities and wore dresses that cost more than my rent.

It was no use. I would just have to tell Thomas why I was concerned, maybe tell him we should take a step back. He would understand. Maybe I was misreading things, maybe he'd be relieved to take a bit of a break.

When he called that night, I took a deep breath, ready to spill it all, but he didn't give me a chance. "I have to go up to Edinburgh this weekend," he said. "There are some reshoots to do for *Hostile*. I was thinking maybe you would want to come with me."

Wow. I had not been expecting that. "Uh, Thomas, I don't know if that's such a good idea."

"Why?" he asked. "We'll get you your own room, if that's what you're worried about."

"It's not that…it's just…"

"What's up, Lizzie?"

So I told him everything. About the warning his friends had given me, the things Lola had said, and how freaked out I'd been when I'd seen myself on the Internet. "It was weird, Thomas. I saw all these pictures of you, doing all this important stuff. I don't fit in with that, I just don't."

He surprised me by laughing loudly. "Important?" he asked. "Are you kidding me? I can think of nothing less important than putting on fancy clothes and poncing around with a bunch of spoiled, self-centered celebs."

"But—"

"Lizzie, I do that stuff, on occasion, because I'm obligated to. It's the worst part of my job. But I'm very lucky that it doesn't happen all that often. Every few years when one of these movies comes out, there's a big deal made about it. Then it all calms down and goes back to normal."

"Those weren't all *Darkness* events," I argued. "There was stuff in there from your outside work."

"The outside stuff is nothing like the *Darkness* stuff. Honestly, Lizzie. It's smaller crowds, very little attention." He paused for a moment and I could tell he was smiling on the other end of the phone. "The only people who care about the other stuff I do are fellow nerds who like boring old arty stuff. I promise."

I didn't know how to argue with that, but I couldn't get the image of him and Franny at the premiere out of my mind. I shook my head. "I don't know, Thomas. I just don't think I'd fit in with all that. Our lives are very different."

"But that's the whole point," he said. "I want to show you how wrong you are about all of this. You have this idea of my life that is totally inaccurate. I want to show you the truth."

"But—"

"No, just listen. Come to Edinburgh with me. Meet my family. You'll see how boring and normal I really am. If you come up and see where I grew up, meet my family and the drooling old dog, and you still think I'm too glamorous for you, I'll let you go off and leave me without a fight. Promise. I won't bother you again."

I felt trapped by his words. How could I refuse him? Even if I didn't trust him, how could I talk myself out of a full weekend in Edinburgh, with Thomas?

"You know you've always wanted to go to Edinburgh," he said, as if reading my mind. "Go on, Lizzie. Say you'll come."

"Fine," I said, completely out of arguments. "Fine, I'll come. But only as an experiment, okay? I'm not saying this is going to work out."

Thomas laughed softly, the sound warm and intimate against my ear. "But you will, Lizzie. You will."

CHAPTER TWELVE

"I'm so jealous," Callie moaned, watching me zip my little suitcase. She was stretched out on my bed in her bathrobe, nursing a cup of coffee. It was strange to see her up so early, and I knew only the lure of my exciting weekend away could have dragged her from her bed before ten.

"It's not that big of a deal," I assured her. "It's just a weekend."

"A weekend away," she corrected. "In one of the most romantic cities in Great Britain. With a flipping movie star."

I sighed. "It's not like that, Cal. We might not even be together at the end of the weekend."

"You keep saying that," she said, raising an eyebrow at me. "Seriously, Lizzie. If you think you're on the verge of a breakup, why did you agree to go away with him in the first place?"

"So that *he* can see that," I said, sitting on the edge of my bed. "Once he sees how out of place I am, he'll come around and agree that us taking a break is for the best."

Callie smirked. "You keep telling yourself that, babe."

"What's that supposed to mean?"

She sat up straight so she could look me in the eye. "It means, Lizzie, that you're totally crazy about this guy, and you're dying for any chance to be with him."

"That's not...I mean...that's not what this is," I spluttered, my face going red.

She smirked. "Uh huh. Sure. Girls *always* go away with guys to meet their families in order to prove how wrong they are for each other. Yup. Happens all the time."

"Our situation is not exactly typical, Cal."

"Are you kidding me? You think you're the first girl to date a guy with a different background? A different lifestyle? I can name five chick flicks off the top of my head with that exact same conflict."

It was my turn to smirk. "Give me a break." I stood, pulling my bag from the bed and extending the handle so I could pull it along behind me.

"*Pretty Woman*," she called out from my bed. "*Notting Hill*." I turned my back on her and headed down the hall with my bag. "*Love Actually*!"

"That's only three," I shot back over my shoulder. "Besides, are we really taking chick flicks as gospel now?"

"Fine then," she called triumphantly. "How about literature?"

I scowled at the wall as I made my way into the kitchen to wait. I heard Callie jump off the bed and pad down the hall. "*Jane Eyre*," she said from the doorway to the kitchen. "*Little Women*." I glared at her, knowing I had no retort. How many times had I told her we could look to literature as an accurate representation of the human experience? I couldn't exactly take it back now. She grinned, knowing she had me, before laying her trump card on the table. "*Pride and Prejudice*."

"Fine," I said. "I won't argue that in very specific cases, things can work out. But that doesn't mean—"

"Uh, huh." She leaned against the door jam, crossing her arms. "Like I said, you keep telling yourself that."

I was saved from answering by the shrill sound of the buzzer. I felt a swoop of nerves deep in my stomach. Thomas was here.

"Ooh, I wonder if the studio sent some big fancy car." Callie squealed, rushing to the bay window to look out into the street below. Being an independent film, I presumed they didn't have those big budgets for fancy cars, but apparently I was wrong. She squealed again. "Looks like a Jag to me. Very shiny."

I went to the wall and hit the buzzer, hoping it would work. The system had a tendency of malfunctioning at the worst times, like when you were already in your pajamas and waiting for your order of Pad Thai to arrive. The sound of feet on the steps let me know that it worked, this time. Before I could settle my nerves, there was a knock on the door. He was here.

I gave a frightened look to Callie and was rewarded with a thumbs up and a rather smug grin. Taking a deep breath, I turned and opened the door, revealing Thomas in the hallway.

Dressed in baggy faded jeans, a hooded sweatshirt, and a dark pea coat, he looked almost too good to be real. His normally neat hair was windswept and messy, the waves hanging down across his forehead. Best of all, he looked happy to see me. Really, really happy.

"Hi," I said, all of my nerves disappearing. I was sure I was returning his grin, probably looking much more goofy than he did, but I didn't care.

"You ready?" he asked, after a pause. I realized we were staring at each other and could almost feel Callie's silent laughter from behind me.

"Yup," I said, trying to get a hold of myself. I glanced at my bag. "Let me just get—"

Before I could finish the sentence, he had slipped past me to grab the handle of my bag. It was a nice touch, and so totally Thomas it made my chest ache a little. I was having a hard time imagining not being able to see him whenever I wanted.

"Oh, hey, Callie," he said, catching sight of her at the window. "Sorry, I didn't see you over there."

"Hi," she said brightly, giving him a wave. "Lizzie tells me you have some reshoots to do, huh?"

He nodded. "Yeah, only a few scenes, shouldn't be too bad."

"Will there be lots of movie stars there?" she asked, clearly having been dying to ask this question since she first set eyes on him.

"Callie," I said, a warning note in my voice, but Thomas only laughed.

"Maybe a few. Want me to get you some autographs?"

"Would you?" she cried, her face alight.

I rolled my eyes, but Thomas chuckled again. "Sure thing."

"We should go," I said, eager to prevent Cal from embarrassing herself further.

"Have fun!" she called after us as we headed to the front door. "And remember what I said, Lizzie."

I turned back to glare at her, but she grinned in return, winking at me. I pulled the door shut behind me and followed Thomas down the stairs and out to the car the studio had arranged, noting that Callie had been right. It was a Jag. And was, indeed, quite shiny.

***

The flight to Edinburgh was short, not even two hours in the air. "You Europeans are so lucky," I said, staring at the window as the ground dropped, Heathrow sprawling out in all directions below us. "You're so close to everything. If I flew two hours from Detroit, I'd be in, like, Kentucky."

"I wouldn't mind seeing Kentucky," Thomas said. "Isn't that where the chicken comes from?"

I laughed. "It's pretty ubiquitous in the States."

We were comfortably ensconced in first-class seats, which I tried not to let bother me. Thomas had assured me that the studio paid for everything, but I couldn't help feeling funny about the free ride. *It could be worse*, I reminded myself. Callie had been predicting a private plane, something I was pretty sure I wouldn't be able to handle.

A thought occurred to me. "Hey, if I wasn't here, would you be flying British Airways?"

"What do you mean?"

"Callie was sure there'd be a private plane."

He searched my face. "Are you disappointed there isn't?"

"No," I said quickly. "Of course not. I was just wondering if you were like, slumming it for me. So that I wouldn't be freaked out by the glamour of your career."

"I hardly call this slumming it, Lizzie," he said, his eyes twinkling.

I narrowed mine. "You know what I mean."

"Nope, sorry. You lost me."

I knew he was teasing me, and I couldn't keep the corners of my mouth from tilting up slightly. "I'm merely wondering if you forwent the usual comfort of a private flight just for my sake."

He shook his head. "Nope. First of all, this isn't a *Darkness* production, it's a low budget film. And, besides, they reserve the private flight experience for the big guys. Jackson Coles, he'd have a private plane. I have to put up with the horrors of commercial." He winked at me. "I promise this is not an elaborate plan to make you think I'm normal."

I laughed. "If it was, you wouldn't be doing such a great job. Comped first-class flights are hardly normal where I come from."

He shrugged. "It has its charm. But if I were really trying to impress you I'd take you up by train. It's a gorgeous trip, you'd love it."

"I've always wanted to travel by train," I admitted. "It seems so romantic."

"You don't travel by trains in the States?"

I laughed. "Not in Detroit. Everyone drives. I mean, we *have* trains. There's Amtrak service. I know people who take the train to Chicago. But it's not that popular, at least not in the Midwest, or as cheap or convenient. It might be bigger on the east coast, for commuters."

"That's a shame," he said. "I love train travel. When I was first down in London working, right after we finished filming the first *Darkness* and I was desperate for more work, I used to take the train up to my Mum and Dad's all the time. I'd stay until the last possible second, wishing they'd convince me to give it up, and then take the sleeper back down to the city to be back at work Monday morning."

"You wanted them to tell you to give it up?" I asked, surprised.

"Oh God, yes," he laughed. "I hated it. Hated the loneliness, the pressure. Hated the endless auditions and the grotty apartment. Hated working in the restaurant and coming home smelling like bacon grease every night. I missed home so bad, it was like missing a limb."

"Wow." I felt a rush of sympathy for him, wondering if I could ever stand to be on my own like that. At least here I had Callie. I was struck with a sudden ache for my family at home. "You must really be close to your family, huh?"

He looked over at me and smiled, diffusing the mood. "Yeah, but maybe that was overstating a little. A small limb, you know. Like a pinky."

I laughed. I had noticed how he could do that, how he could subtly alter the atmosphere of a situation with a quick smile or wink, even a look in his eyes. He had a knack for making things feel...easy. Smooth. Not in a manufactured or dishonest way, I never had the impression he was trying to mask his true feelings. He just seemed to exude the attitude that it was, generally, better to be good-humored. It was so different from the tempestuous, loud, and brash upbringing in my family's home. It appealed to me in a very vital, undeniable way.

"So," Thomas said, pulling me from my contemplation. "What did you want to see this weekend?"

I felt a rush of excitement as I considered. It had been a dream of mine, for years, to go to Edinburgh. I knew I'd finally get the chance to visit once I moved to London, but the idea that it was actually happening seemed too good to be true. I tried hard not to dwell on how making the trip with Thomas heightened the appeal considerably.

"I want to see everything," I said eagerly. "The Castle, Princes Street Gardens, the Palace of Holyroodhouse." I realized he was grinning at me and tried to rein it in a little. "Sorry, that probably sounds way too touristy for you, huh?"

"Not at all," he said. "I was just thinking how cute you are when you get excited about something."

I blushed. I could see the fondness in his eyes when he looked at me. It was slightly alarming how happy it made me. I had a feeling he was trying hard not to be overly affectionate. He hadn't taken my hand or tried to kiss me once. My disappointment over that fact was also alarming.

"Besides, those places are touristy for a reason—they're awesome."

I grinned, happy that he got it. "We don't exactly have nearly thousand-year-old castles where I come from."

"Let alone ones that are set atop an ancient volcano," he agreed. "You'll love the castle. And the Royal Mile is pretty amazing. Have you heard about the ghost tours?"

I nodded and made a face. "I don't know, they sound kind of intense."

"They can be, but there are some with a more historical bent. It's definitely worth doing. I'll hold your hand if you get too scared, and I promise not to make fun of you."

Trying not to dwell on the idea of holding his hand, I said, "Will you have time for a ghost tour? With you working, I figured I'd be on my own for the sightseeing stuff."

"You might have to do some stuff alone, but the shooting schedule isn't too bad. I should be able to get away quite a bit." He met my eyes and grinned a little. "I'd really like to be with you when you first start exploring, if you don't mind."

"Of course I don't," I said, wishing he would stop looking at me like that. It made it so hard to not reach out and grab his hand—or start kissing his face uncontrollably.

"So today I should have the rest of the morning and lunch to hang out. Then I'll head over to the studio, and you can set off on your own for the afternoon. Then we'll go over to my parents' for dinner, if that sounds okay."

I felt a tremor of fear at the idea of meeting his family. He obviously cared about them very much, and I found that I wanted them to like me for reasons I couldn't quite articulate.

"That sounds perfect," I said, hoping he couldn't detect the nerves in my voice.

"They can't wait to meet you," he said, as if he could read my mind. "I've told them all about you."

"You have?"

"Of course," he said, his voice soft. "They...uh, they've never really heard me talk much about any girls I've seen, so it's a bit of a big deal for them, me bringing someone home."

If he had hoped to make me feel less nervous, he failed miserably. If it was a big deal for them, what was it for me?

I had to turn away from the intensity in his eyes. I busied myself with looking out the window, though thick clouds obstructed my view, as I tried to bring my heart rate down.

Maybe this was a mistake, I told myself. *Why did you agree to come with him? It's far too dangerous. You obviously have no self-control when it comes to this guy.*

Next to me, I heard Thomas pull a book from his backpack, and I relaxed slightly. Reading prevented awkward discussion. I pulled my own paperback from the seat pocket in front of me, eager to get lost in the well-worn, dog-eared pages of *Wuthering Heights*.

I tried valiantly to follow along with Catherine's struggles, but found my brain unwilling to obey. Instead it fixated, for the entirety of the two-hour flight, on the words Thomas had said about introducing me to his family. And the way he had looked at me when he said them.

***

"Is it everything you thought it would be?"

I turned to Thomas, wondering if he could read the amazement on my face. "This is incredible," I said, beaming at him. "It's just how I imagined!"

We were standing on the corner of St. Giles Street and the Royal Mile, staring down the cobblestone street toward the Firth of Forth, a sliver of bright blue off in the distance, just barely visible beyond the spires and storefronts of Old Town.

There was a thrum of excitement in my chest that had not dissipated since the moment our plane had landed. Thomas had led me through the airport, which bustled pleasantly, nothing at all like Heathrow, and out to the taxi queue. He apologized for the lack of a private car on this end, winking at me to show he was joking, and helped me throw my bag into the taxi, teasing me for calling it a trunk rather than the boot, like the locals.

The driver led us directly to our hotel on St. Giles. As we neared the city center, the buildings around us became more and more picturesque, stone and brick replacing concrete and sidings, and the streets became narrower and busier. Suddenly, in the distance, I could see the castle, perched atop the volcano, a grand and imposing sight against the green of the hill.

As our driver crawled up the winding roads further into Old Town, I lost sight of the castle behind the buildings, but I could tell we were close when we finally pulled up in front of the hotel on St. Giles.

"This is perfect," I had told Thomas, staring up at the brick façade. Riots of flowers hung from hanging baskets over the front door, and green ivy clung to the stone below the windows of the rooms above.

"I've stayed here a few times," he said, hoisting both of our bags from the ground. "It's pretty comfortable and you can't beat the location."

My room was perfect. Small and nothing near lavish, but comfortable and stylish. The double bed was made up with a crisp duvet, the furniture looked new and modern, there was a small writing desk in the corner, and the bathroom was fitted out with marble and a rain-style showerhead.

Once we'd stowed our stuff, I grabbed my purse and camera, and we headed out into the city. I was afraid Thomas would get sick of me. I was having a hard time containing my delight at the things we were seeing. Everything was so romantic, so old and charming. I couldn't help imagining the millions of people who had called this place home over the years, who had lived and dreamed here, created memories, struggled and died. It felt magical.

"Ready for the best views in the city?" Thomas asked as we stood in line to buy our tickets to the castle.

"I've been looking forward to this," I said, grinning up at him.

As Thomas had said, the castle was set atop an ancient and long-dormant volcano. It towered over the entire city, providing views that literally took my breath away. "That's Leith down there," Thomas pointed out. "The old royal yacht is docked there, we could go visit it if you want. And there's the Firth of Forth."

"Incredible," I breathed. "It's so beautiful."

"So are you," Thomas said softly. I looked up to see that he was staring down at me. The wind was strong this high up, whipping at our hair and stinging our cheeks. He looked beautiful, windblown and a little messy, his cheeks red and his eyes bright. In that moment, I wanted nothing more than for him to kiss me.

His phone rang, effectively ruining the moment. He sighed and pulled it from his pocket, speaking briskly with an associate producer. From the sound of it, they were confirming the time for the car to arrive to pick him up from the hotel. I took the opportunity to collect myself, turning away from the magical view and busying myself with examining a nearby sign.

"Sorry," Thomas said, joining me.

"It's okay," I said brightly, determined to stay in safer waters until lunch. "Look at this sign, it says that there's a cemetery here for the soldiers' dogs. That's adorable. Let's find it."

We examined every inch of the castle. I repeatedly asked Thomas if I was boring him, but couldn't seem to stop myself from wanting to visit every building, read every marker and sign. The history nerd in me was having a ball.

"We need to leave if we want to get lunch before my call," he finally said, looking down at his watch. "Is that okay?"

"It's fine," I said, regretfully. I would have stayed for several more hours, but I didn't want Thomas to miss lunch before work. We made our way back down the Royal Mile and stopped in at a little pub. "Well, we're in Scotland now," Thomas told me once we had found seats. "So you're going to try Haggis, right?"

"Nope," I said. "Sorry. Don't even think about it."

He laughed. "Oh, come on. You have to at least try it."

"I absolutely do not," I said, shaking my head. "No way."

"That's okay," he said, leaning across the table to whisper. "It's totally as disgusting as you think it would be."

I laughed. "Careful. They'll figure out that you're not really from around here."

"I think the accent was a pretty good giveaway."

We both ordered burgers and fries, which I remembered to call chips when I told the waiter what I wanted. Thomas suggested we try a cider, which was apparently very popular in the UK. "Oooh, this is good," I said after I had tried mine. "Much nicer than beer."

"Can't beat a good cider," he said. "Sometimes it's too sweet, but Magners is a good bet."

While we ate, Thomas told me about the scenes they would be shooting. They were on location outside of the city, and Thomas was glad the weather was cooperating. "Shooting outside, in Scotland especially, can be a real crapshoot. During principal filming, we had to cancel or reschedule I don't even know how many times. It got to be a real mess."

"How long does it take to shoot a scene?" I asked, pouring some more ketchup onto my burger.

"Depends. Today is only a partial scene, just a few lines. Should probably take a couple hours."

"A couple hours? Just for a few lines? Wow."

"A lot of it is getting set up, readjusting cameras for different takes. It can be kind of tedious. Tomorrow will be longer. My call's at seven a.m."

I made a face. "Sorry, that kind of sucks."

"It's okay. For the most part, I love it. So, what do you think you'll do this afternoon?"

"I thought I'd head down to the Palace of Holyroodhouse," I said. "See where the queen stays when she and the family are here."

"They don't stay all that often," he said, stealing one of my fries. "Even though it's the official residence. They have another palace, Balmoral, to use when they're in Scotland."

"Must be a tough life, choosing which of your many palaces to stay in."

After lunch, we walked back to the hotel so Thomas could change and grab some stuff. "You'll be okay?" he asked. "I know it's a different city, but if you don't wander too far from the Royal Mile you shouldn't get lost."

"I'm not worried," I said, patting my purse. "I have my guidebook and a map."

"Okay." He stood there on the pavement outside the hotel, looking awkward for a moment. "Um, have fun, yeah? You can call me if you need anything."

"I'll be fine," I said. "Thanks for a great morning. And good luck with the shoot."

"Thanks." Finally he patted my arm and climbed into the car, waving at me before it pulled out into traffic. I stood, watching him go. That was the second time today I had gotten the feeling that Thomas was stopping himself from kissing me. And it was the second time that I wished he would have.

CHAPTER THIRTEEN

I had a very enjoyable day exploring Edinburgh on my own. After I toured Holyroodhouse, I made my way back up the Mile, browsing in a few shops. Then I headed for the Princes Street Gardens where I wandered through the flowers for a good two hours, enjoying the gorgeous views of the castle above me. I soon found that the only downside to Edinburgh was how hilly it was. Walking toward Holyroodhouse and Princes Street Gardens had been downhill. Getting back to the hotel was another matter entirely. By the time I reached St. Giles Street, I was out of breath and my legs burned.

Since I had at least an hour before I was expecting Thomas, I decided to stop in the little café next to our hotel. It had caught my eye when we first checked in, with its sunny yellow, bright exterior and large picture windows. Inside was equally charming, with creaky hardwood floors, a sloping ceiling, and a set of stairs leading up to a second level of seating. I found an empty, spindly wooden chair in the window, ordered a pot of Earl Grey and a muffin, and pulled out my travel journal, eager to get my recollections of the city down in writing before I forgot anything.

Before I could get started, a couple outside caught my eye. They were a bit older than I, maybe in their late twenties, and were walking arm in arm. He said something to her that made her burst out laughing, throwing her head back and clutching his arm for support. He looked down at her, his expression amused and…something else. Then it hit me. He was in awe of this woman, as if he couldn't believe his good luck in being there with her, in being the one to make her laugh. The love on his face was so plain it made my heart ache.

I turned the page in my journal and started to scribble fiercely. But I wasn't writing about Edinburgh or the sightseeing I had done. Watching the couple, I was struck with the strongest flash of inspiration I'd ever had in my life. Suddenly, I had to write. The compulsion was so intense I couldn't ignore it. So for the next hour, I sat in the café, my tea growing cold as I worked on my novel, my hand growing sore as I filled pages and pages of notebook paper.

"It really kills me, you know," Thomas said, startling me. I jumped in my chair and looked up at him.

"You scared me," I said , laughing as I put a hand to my heart.

"Sorry," he said, pulling a chair out and joining me at the little table. "I said hello, but you were pretty engrossed."

"I had the best idea for my book," I said, not even feeling the sheepishness that usually accompanied any mention of my writing. "I had to get it down."

"That's what I thought," he said, shaking his head. "I said it really kills me."

"What does?"

"Seeing you write like that when you won't let me read your stuff. The look on your face when you're writing…you're so into it. Like you're transported into the story. I want to go there with you."

I smiled at him, feeling shy now. "Maybe someday I'll let you."

"Were you finished?" he asked. "I can call and tell them we'll be late if you want to keep going."

"No, it's fine," I said, closing the notebook and snapping the lid back on my pen. "We should go." I shoved my things into my purse and stood. "How did you know I was here, anyhow?"

He pointed to the glass. "Saw you in the window when the cab dropped me off."

"Oh my gosh," I said, slapping a hand to my forehead. "I didn't even ask you how it went today. Sorry, I get so flakey when I'm writing."

"It's okay," he said, placing a hand at my lower back to steer me around the tables and out to the sidewalk. I shivered at his touch, wishing he would tighten his grip. *Stop it*, I told myself, my inner voice more feeble than firm.

"So, how was it? Everything go okay?"

He sighed. "It was alright, but we're behind already. Pray for good weather tomorrow. It might be a long day."

I made a face. "Sorry."

We entered the hotel and headed up the stairs to our floor. There was an elevator, but the building was old, and required you to walk up and then down two half flights of stairs after getting off on our floor. It was faster and more direct to take the stairs.

"Do you need much time getting ready?" he asked once we had reached my door. He glanced down at his watch.

"No, I'm just gonna change," I said.

"Okay. I'll meet you out here in fifteen?"

I agreed and headed into my room. I wasn't sure what to wear, though Callie had helped me pick a few nicer outfits. I wished she were here. Surely she would have some idea of the protocol involved when going to meet your soon-to-be ex-boyfriend's family in their home for dinner.

In the end, I decided on a navy shirtdress, cinched at the waist with a slim brown leather belt. My hair was windblown from my walking around the city, so I re-braided it. I decided to keep my makeup simple, not wanting his parents to think I was trampy. I added a pair of silver hoops and stared at myself in the mirror. I wondered what they would think of me, then immediately wondered why I cared so much.

You know exactly why, I thought to myself. *You can call this weekend an experiment all you want, but you're crazy about their son and you want them to like you.*

There was a knock on my door, and I realized I had exceeded the fifteen minutes. "Hang on!" I called, rifling through my bag for my brown boots. I pulled them out and opened the door, revealing Thomas in the hall. He, too, had changed for dinner. He looked adorable in baggy khakis, and a white button-down shirt under his green V-neck. I loved when he wore green; it completely brought out the color of his eyes. I realized I was staring at him. "Sorry," I said, stepping back so he could enter. "I just need to put my boots on."

"You look great," he said, swallowing hard in a way that brought color to my cheeks.

"Thanks. You, too."

He sat down at the desk chair, facing me as I pulled my boots on. I noticed that his eyes lingered on my legs, and my blush deepened.

"Ready?" I asked as I straightened, trying to keep my voice light.

"Sure," he said, standing. "There's a cab downstairs."

We were quiet as we headed down the stairs. He seemed preoccupied, and I wondered what he was thinking. His silence did little to ease my nerves. In the cab, he turned to me and smiled.

"How was the rest of your day? Did you go to Holyroodhouse?"

Relieved by the small talk, I told him about my visit to the Palace and the Gardens. "The walk was a killer," I told him. "I didn't realize how steep all those streets were when I was going down them."

He nodded. "I bet I'd get into really good shape if I lived in town."

Before I could stop myself, I snorted.

"What?" he asked, bewildered.

I colored once more. "Well, come on, Thomas. Good shape? You're already in fantastic shape."

His eyes met mine, intense in the dim light of the cab. I was sure he would laugh, make light of it somehow, but he remained silent, staring at me. "Thank you," he finally said, his voice low. It sent a delicious shiver down my spine.

We were quiet for the rest of the trip, the atmosphere in the cab heavy. I was acutely aware of how close Thomas was sitting to me, how I'd be able to brush his knee if I only moved my leg a fraction of an inch. I stared out the window at the darkened streets, unable to get the image of his face at the castle—right before I thought he might kiss me—out of my head. It had now been three days since our lips had touched. Instinctively, I knew he was holding back on purpose. Giving me time to make up my mind and decide where we would go from here.

"We're close now," Thomas said, his voice quiet in the darkness.

We had passed out of the city, the houses here getting farther apart, separated by large yards and, in some cases, fields and clumps of trees.

"When did they move here?" I asked.

"Right after I finished school," he said. "They assumed I'd be going off on my gap year then starting at university, so it was a good time to move without disrupting me too much. Bryony was only just about to start secondary school, so it wasn't much of a disruption for her, either."

"And your brother was at university already?"

"Paul had graduated," he said. "He was already well on his way to becoming a barrister. What a disappointment I turned out to be."

He was laughing, but I frowned. "Don't say that. They must be very proud of you."

"I don't know about that. But they're happy that I'm happy. That's good enough."

Thomas directed the cab driver to a well-lit, rambling stone house far back on a stretch of rolling green grass. "Here we are," he said, looking over at me with a nervous expression.

"You know," I said, smiling at him. "You're not helping my nerves by being nervous yourself."

"You have nothing to be nervous about," he said intently. "They will be crazy about you. Promise."

"Then why are *you* nervous?"

"I'm more worried about what you think." He gave me a small smile, looking strangely sad for a moment. Without thinking, I reached out and squeezed his hand. His eyebrows raised; he looked surprised but pleased. Then the driver was pulling up in the circular drive, and I remembered what we were doing. I dropped his hand and looked up at the house. "Wow," I murmured. "This is pretty great."

The house was made from various shaped, multi-colored stones. Behind the house stood a rocky hill covered in scrubby trees. The proximity of the stone-covered hill gave the impression the house had grown up right out of the ground—it fit its surroundings so perfectly.

"Here goes," Thomas murmured, opening his door. He handed the driver a few bills before leaving me in the cab. Through the windshield, I watched as he came around the front to open my door, reaching out a hand to help steady me as my feet hit the gravel of the drive. "You okay?"

"Yup." I tried to smile up at him but my stomach was doing somersaults.

"Then let's go."

The door swung open before we reached it, and I had the impression of gangly teenage limbs before a young girl flung herself at Thomas.

"Tommy!" she cried, hugging him tight. He laughed and hugged her back. "Save me," she moaned. "They're all doing my head in."

"Stop being so dramatic, Bry," he said, releasing her. "And meet my friend."

"Oooh," she said letting go so she could peer at me. "You're the girl."

"Watch it," Thomas said, tugging gently on her ear. "Haven't you learned any manners at that fancy girls' school of yours?"

She grinned at me and held out a hand. "Bryony Harper," she said. "You must be Elizabeth. Pleased to meet you."

"Better," Thomas said, shaking his head at her, the corners of his lips twitching up like he was trying not to smile.

"Hi, Bryony," I said, shaking her hand. "Nice to meet you as well."

"Come on," she said," dropping my hand and grabbing Thomas's. "You seriously need to get in there. Like, now. I don't know how much more I can take."

Thomas shot me a sardonic look, but allowed himself to be pulled inside. I followed, smiling. I liked Bryony already. She was cute, tall and skinny with a mess of brown waves that reminded me of a messier version of Thomas's. In the darkness, I thought I had caught a glimpse of green eyes. She was clearly crazy about her big brother, which earned her big points in my book.

The entryway of the Harper house was cozy and a bit messy, with several pairs of boots scattered about and a pile of jackets teetering on a wooden bench. "Mum!" Bryony called out. "Dad! The prodigal whatever returns."

"Prodigal son," Thomas said. "And don't be a brat."

A woman in her mid fifties appeared in the hallway. She too had Thomas's trademark brown waves and green eyes. He hadn't gotten his height from her though—she was even shorter than I was, and pleasantly round. "Thomas," she said warmly, wiping her hands on the dishtowel she held before reaching for him. "It's good to see you, dear."

He hugged her back. "Good to see you, too, Mum. Food smells great."

"Thank you, dear." She patted him on the chest and peered around him, eyeing me where I stood in the doorway. "Is this Lizzie?"

"Hello, Mrs. Harper," I said, trying not to fidget. "Thank you so much for inviting me."

"Of course, dear." She lightly smacked her son's arms. "Introduce us properly."

He laughed and turned, holding out his hand so I would join them. "Mum, this is my friend Lizzie Medina. Lizzie, this is my mother."

I noticed he refrained from calling me his girlfriend. It gave me a little pang. I reached out a hand to Mrs. Harper, but she was already pulling me into a hug. "We've heard so much about you," she said, squeezing me tightly. Strangely, I was overcome with the strongest sense of homesickness as I took in the cozy smell of her—mint and some kind of baking. I squeezed her back without thinking, closing my eyes for a moment and feeling a lump in my throat.

She pulled back and looked at me full in the face for a long moment. "I'm glad you're here," she said quietly. "You're probably missing a home-cooked meal, being so far from your family. Poor girl."

I nodded and smiled at her, unsure if I could speak. For some reason I felt more like crying.

"Let's go through," she said, gesturing at the door through which she had come. "Dad and Paul are in the lounge with Mary."

"Mary's the sister-in-law," Thomas told me.

"More like witch-in-law," Bryony muttered, earning herself a smack from Mrs. Harper's dish towel. She didn't look angry though—in fact, she looked like she was trying not to laugh. Much like Bryony, I liked her immediately.

There was a more formal, and clearly empty, sitting room off the hall, but Mrs. Harper turned the opposite way to take us through the kitchen, which smelled incredible. "We're in the lounge tonight, dear," she told me. "Since it's just family. It's much cozier back there."

Cozy was exactly the way I would have described the lounge. A large stone fireplace dominated the back wall, next to which was a set of French doors. The garden was dark, but I could make out a throng of trees and green things. The opposite wall featured a huge flat-screen TV, around which the rest of the family was gathered.

"Oy, you lot," Mrs. Harper called. "We have company!"

"Tommy. Good to see you, mate." A man I could only assume was Paul had risen from a slouchy green corduroy couch to shake hands with Thomas. I did a little double take; they looked almost identical, except for the glimmer of grey I could make out at Paul's temples. He was clearly several years older.

"All right, Paul?" Thomas shook his brother's hand, a smile on his face. "Meet my friend, Lizzie."

Paul turned to me, his eyebrows rising. "So this is the lovely Lizzie then, eh?" He leaned forward to kiss my cheek. "It's great to finally meet you. My brother's been going on about you for weeks now."

I giggled at the look on Thomas's face. "So that whole conversation we had about everyone behaving themselves was for nothing, eh?"

"I don't know what you mean," Paul said, winking at me. "Lizzie, this is my wife, Mary."

Mary was gorgeous, tall, slender, and blonde, and dressed impeccably in cream linen trousers and an oversized grey cashmere sweater. I wasn't quite sure where Bryony got the witch part. She seemed perfectly pleasant to me as she reached out to shake my hand.

Mr. Harper was still sitting in his rocking chair, staring intently at what I was pretty sure was a rugby match on the screen. "Hello, son! Hello, Lizzie," he called over his shoulder. "Be right with you. Important bit here."

Thomas rolled his eyes at me and I grinned.

"Gilbert Harper you get over here this minute and properly greet our guest," Mrs. Harper said. She may have been the shortest person in a room full of exceptionally tall people, but she clearly was the boss. Mr. Harper stood immediately, shooting his wife an abashed expression as he shook hands with his son. "Dad, this is Lizzie," Thomas said. Did I detect a note of pride in his voice? It made my stomach feel funny.

Mr. Harper shook my hand, smiling down at me. His eyes twinkled behind wire-rimmed glasses, and the smile on his face was genuine. "You're very welcome here, Lizzie."

"Thank you. It's so nice of you to invite me."

"Sit, Lizzie, sit," Thomas's mom said, waving me over to the couches.

"Can I help you with anything, Mrs. Harper?"

"Don't be silly, dear, you're our guest. And please call me Anne." She flicked her towel in the direction of her daughter, who was lounging on the arm of a love seat. "You, on the other hand, can join me in the kitchen."

Bryony sighed dramatically before jumping up and following her mother. I headed to a seat near the fire, eager to check out the framed photographs on the mantle.

"Oh God," Thomas said, following me. "I begged her to put those away."

I shot him a grin over my shoulder. "Oh, look at you in your little school uniform," I said, laughing at a shot of a very small Thomas dressed in short pants, jacket, and beanie, scowling up at the camera. "Not very happy in this one, are you?"

I glanced at him to see a nearly identical scowl on his features. "I was livid that I had to go to school. School meant no time for running around outside playing cops and robbers with my mates. And I thought I looked like a complete prat in that uniform."

I laughed. "I think it's cute."

Mrs. Harper had numerous pictures of each of her children. Shots of Thomas and Paul playing soccer, Bryony on horseback, all three kids on Christmas morning. For the first time, I noticed a larger framed photo in a place of prominence over the mantle. "I was there today!"

Mr. Harper must have heard me, because he came up behind us. "Ah, yes. One of my favorite views in Edinburgh."

The photo showed the back walls of a church in ruins, surrounded by trees, an endless hill stretching up in the distance. I had seen the exact same view behind The Palace of Holyroodhouse that very afternoon, and had, in fact, taken a picture from the same precise angle. The ruined seventeenth-century abbey on the Palace grounds had captured my imagination at first sight, and I had used up half my memory card taking pictures there. I was sure my shot wouldn't look anywhere near as gorgeous when I got around to printing it.

"Charlie took that," Mr. Harper said. "You've met Tommy's friend Charlie, haven't you? He's an ace with that camera."

"Wow," I said, staring up at the photograph. "It's really good. How beautiful."

"It was a birthday present for me a few years ago," Mr. Harper said, smiling as he rocked back on his heels. "Knew it was one of my favorite places to go sit and read. He's a good lad, that Charlie."

I smiled at Thomas, who sighed. "My parents always like my friends more than they like me."

"Quite right, too," Mr. Harper said, clapping his son on the back and making me laugh.

At the end of the mantle was a picture of Thomas's parents. She was dressed in a short white dress, he in a brown suit. From the clothes and their hairstyles, I imagined the picture was from the seventies. "Is this your wedding?" I asked.

"Ah, yes," Mr. Harper said. "Look at my Anne. Still as pretty as the day I met her." He winked at me. "We eloped that day. I thought her father was going to kill me when he found out."

"He should have, too," Mrs. Harper said, coming toward us with a plate of hors d'oeuvres. "Stealing his little girl away in the dead of night."

"If I recall, my dear, the whole thing was your idea."

She winked at me. "More than likely. Here, Lizzie, help yourself."

I wasn't sure what the food on the plate was, but I took a napkin and a few items. "Thanks."

"Bryony!" Mrs. Harper called. "Bring those drinks!"

Mr. Harper followed her as she went to serve Paul and Mary. "What am I eating here?" I asked, looking down at my napkin.

"Ah, this is real British home entertaining," he said, laughing. "You've got Angels on Horseback and Scotch Eggs."

I took a bite of the egg, surprised to find that it was pretty good. I leaned in toward the wedding shot again. "Your parents look so happy."

Next to me, he nodded. "They've always been pretty happy."

"You never told me their names." I turned to him. "Gilbert and Anne? Those are the names of one of my favorite literary couples."

He gave a dramatic mock-shudder. "Anne of Green Gables? My mom loves that book. Terrible. She used to read it to us as kids."

"Then you were lucky," I shot back. "It's a wonderful book."

"It's a boring book. Especially when you're a five-year-old boy."

I shook my head in mock-sadness. "I feel sorry for you."

Across the room, I caught Mrs. Harper's eye. She had paused on her way back to the kitchen, and was watching us, a small, knowing smile on her face. For some reason, it made me feel shy, and I quickly turned away.

I found a seat on one of the couches and turned my attention to the rugby game. I had absolutely no idea what was happening on the screen, but I figured it was better than what I had been doing—flirting with Thomas. I hadn't even realized I was doing it until I caught Mrs. Harper looking at us. As soon as I let my guard down with Thomas, it was like I had no control over myself. Out of the corner of my eye, I could see him watching my face.

It was a relief when Mrs. Harper returned to announce dinner ten minutes later.

***

The meal was delicious. Anne had cooked a beef roast, as Thomas predicted she would, with fixings of potatoes, carrots, and onions. Wine flowed freely, even for Bryony, which surprised me until I remembered that the drinking age here was eighteen. I was pretty sure Thomas had mentioned she was only seventeen, but the family was obviously liberal when it came to drinking at home.

Beyond the comforting goodness of the food itself, I was pleasantly surprised by the banter at the table. The family was clearly very fond of each other; they kept up a steady stream of conversation and teasing throughout the meal. It was so different from a meal back home—there was no yelling, no fighting, no curses in Spanish. But somehow it felt familiar, too. As Bryony jumped up to help her mother clear the plates, I realized what it was. They loved each other, just like we did, and were incredibly close—they just had a different way of showing it. We demonstrated all of our emotion through a filter of passion. We were in each other's business, sharing opinions, getting in fights. That's how we showed love. The Harpers clearly had the same feelings for each other, but they were calmer about it. Sarcastic rather than passionate. Clever instead of tempestuous.

After dinner, the family endeavored to teach me bridge. I finally understood why Bryony had complained to Thomas that they were driving her crazy when conversation turned to her exams. Her parents were dead set on her attending the same university that Paul and Mr. Harper had attended. Bryony had other plans.

"I don't understand what the point is in spending all that cash on university when I already know what I want to do," she said firmly. "It's daft, Mum."

"An education is not daft," her mother said, rearranging the cards in her hand. "Look at Lizzie, there. She's going above and beyond, getting a higher degree when she already has her teaching license."

I gave Bryony a sympathetic look. I knew it wasn't my place to get involved, but I felt for her. I'd been in her shoes.

"You don't need a degree to be an actress," Bryony huffed. "Look at Thomas, he didn't go to university."

"Leave me out of it," he said, concentrating on his cards. I frowned at him.

"Thomas most certainly would have gone to university if he hadn't gotten that first part," Gilbert said. "And you will, too. We never said you couldn't study drama. We'd just like you to do it while getting a full education."

"You'll love school, Bry," Paul said. "I did. I bet Thomas regrets not going to university."

"I repeat: leave me out of it," Thomas said.

"But it's a waste of time," Bryony cried, throwing her cards down. "Thomas didn't just happen to get the role in *Darkness*. It wasn't some stroke of luck. He auditioned for it. That's what an actor does. It's what I should be doing after exams. Auditioning and getting experience." She looked at Thomas, her eyes pleading. "*Tell* them."

"What will you do for money?" he asked, finally meeting her eyes. "Do you have any idea how hard it is to support yourself in London?"

"You managed."

"It was terrible." His voice was flat. "At least if you're in university, Mum and Dad can help you with expenses."

"Yeah, until I graduate. Then I'll be in the same position. Looking for work and needing to support myself. Only now it will be four years later."

She looked like she was going to cry. I wondered if she had hoped Thomas would be on her side in this, that he would help her convince her parents. I felt a rush of sympathy for her. I could remember how it had felt to tell my own parents that I wanted to come to London, without the backing of a single one of my siblings.

"You're being overly dramatic," her mother sighed. "We have company."

"Lizzie doesn't care," she scoffed. "Thomas already told me, she went against *her* parents coming here, they wanted her to stay at home." She glared at her brother. "You said it was one of the things you liked best about her, how brave she was. So why don't you feel the same way about me?"

I felt heat come to my face. It was nice Thomas had said that about me, but his sister had a point. He should be helping her.

"Bryony," Mr. Harper said, his voice firm. "It's rude to bring up Lizzie's situation when you don't know anything about it. Besides, you haven't even taken your exams yet. Let's drop this, please."

"Fine," she fumed. "That's just fine. But I'll tell you now, no one can force me to go to school. You all just think about that."

Mary, who had been mostly silent throughout dinner and cards, cleared her throat. "Where did you get that lovely flower arrangement, Anne?" she asked. "You didn't arrange them yourself, did you?"

Conversation shifted to Anne's gardening. Apparently she was somewhat of a gardening aficionado and even had a greenhouse in the back garden. As the four older family members discussed the renovations Anne and Gilbert were planning to make to the yard, I noticed Bryony had sunk into a moody silence. I could understand; she was forced to stay downstairs because they had company, and she had clearly been raised to be polite. But it was plain on her face that all she wanted to do was go upstairs and cry. I had been there myself, many times.

What was harder to understand was the reason that Thomas, too, barely said a word for the rest of the evening.

CHAPTER FOURTEEN

We traveled back to the hotel in silence. It was clear to me that Thomas was upset about something, but he declined my offer to talk about it. I would have been more worried if I wasn't so exhausted. The day of travel and sightseeing had caught up to me, and I was yawning so much it eventually made Thomas laugh.

"I was going to ask if you wanted to get up early with me to have some coffee before I have to go to work," he said as we entered the hotel. "But I think you should sleep in."

"Sorry," I said. "I wish you could sleep in, too."

"What are your plans for tomorrow?"

"I read about something called a literary pub tour. I might check it out. There's also a writers' museum, apparently."

He nodded, smiling at me in a fond sort of way. "Both of those things sound right up your alley."

"When will you be finished?"

"Definitely dinner time." We had reached our rooms now. "Hopefully a bit earlier. I'll call you, yeah?"

"Sounds good." I looked up at him, feeling awkward. "Thanks for taking me to meet your family. I had a really nice time."

His face lit up. "Yeah? They loved you."

"I liked them, too."

"I'm glad." He looked down at me for a moment, his face shifting slightly until he looked almost sad. "I worry that I'm not doing a very good job of convincing you. And we're already almost out of time."

"Thomas," I said, my voice catching, but he just shook his head and leaned in to kiss my cheek.

"Sleep well, Lizzie."

He watched as I opened my door and stepped into my room. Before I let the door close, I looked back at him. He was standing in the same spot, with the same expression on his face, watching me until the door closed between us.

***

I did sleep in the next morning. I decided to start my day in the café next door. I ate waffles and bacon for breakfast and managed to get an entire chapter written before my pot of tea got cold.

I made my way down the high street to The Writers' Museum, eager to spend a few hours in the company of the Scottish greats. After soaking in every piece of information I could find on Robert Burns, Sir Walter Scott, and Robert Louis Stevenson, I spent far too much money in the museum gift shop.

I was disappointed to discover that the literary pub tour was an evening activity, and wondered if I could convince Thomas to go with me that night. With a few hours now open to me, I decided to find Greyfriars Kirk. The cemetery was a little spooky; according to my guidebook it was rumored to be haunted. Wishing Thomas were with me, I wandered around until I found the statue of Greyfriars

Bobby near the other entrance. According to the plaque, the statue honored the loyalty of a nineteenth-century terrier who had guarded his owner's grave for more than a decade. I took some pictures, knowing Callie would love the story. She was very much a dog person and had two terriers at home.

As I left the cemetery my phone rang. "Hey," Thomas said when I answered. "Good news; I'm officially free."

"You are?" I asked, pulling the phone away from my ear to look at the clock. It was only four p.m.

"Yup, and I'm heading back toward the hotel now."

We made plans to meet there in a few minutes, and I set off down the winding stone streets. As soon as I laid eyes on Thomas, I knew he was in a better mood than he'd been in the taxi last night. Maybe he'd just been stressed out about the day's work.

"How was the day?" he asked, as we set off toward the Royal Mile.

"Great." I told him about writing in the morning and visiting the cemetery and museum.

"I can't say I'm too sorry to have missed that," he laughed. "Three hours in a writers' museum?"

I hit his arm. "For your information, it was wonderful."

He laughed. "So what do you want to do tonight?"

I shook my head. "You're the one who's been working all day. What do you want to do?"

"I think we should do a ghost tour," he said. "You really can't come to Edinburgh without learning a little bit about the spooky history."

"Is it going to scare me?" I asked, wary. I had read in my guidebook that some of the tours featured ghost sightings and something terrifying called a "poltergeist experience."

He shook his head. "We'll go to that one I mentioned before that's not so intense. It's creepy, but nothing jumps out at you or makes you scream. It's more historical."

"Okay," I agreed, deciding it would be good for me to be less of a baby. We walked down the high street until we reached the entrance for the Mary King's Close tour. At the ticket booth, we found that the next two tours were sold out. Thomas turned to me. "What do you say we book a later one and go get some dinner while we wait?"

"Sounds good." I had skipped lunch and could definitely eat. Thomas gave me a wicked little grin.

"Good. It will be even scarier when it's dark out."

I made a face at him and he turned back to the ticket counter to confirm our spot. I handed him some money for my ticket and was surprised, but pleased, when he took it.

With nearly two hours to kill, we walked down the Royal Mile until we found a pub that Thomas knew. "This place is good," he said, holding the door open for me.

We found a little wooden table near the back wall. The pub was small and cozy. Even at the early hour, it was nearly filled with talking, laughing groups of people. The walls were littered with pictures of patrons and signs of quotes or short expressions. The one closest to my head read, "Don't be afraid to follow your dreams."

"That's appropriate for you," Thomas said, pointing at the sign.

A waiter appeared, and we both ordered bangers and mash (sausages and mashed potatoes to me) and glasses of cider, which was already becoming my favorite drink.

"Speaking of dreams," I said, once we were alone again. "Why don't you have your sister's back on the acting thing?"

He sighed, running his hands through his hair. "Well, for starters, it was really hard when I was starting out. Our parents won't pay for our living after we're eighteen unless we're in school. It's a hard and fast rule with them."

"I get that," I said. "But surely you understand how she feels. She has a dream for her life and no one is supporting it."

He scowled. "That's not true. They just want her in school. Lots of parents wouldn't be okay with their kid studying drama at university, but they've already said they didn't mind if she did that. I call that pretty supportive."

I met his gaze evenly. "I'm not saying she shouldn't be in school. But she was looking to you for support. All she wants to do is the same thing you did. And all you could do was tell her to leave you out of it."

He sighed again. "I know. I *wasn't* very supportive. It's just...Blimey, Lizzie, my parents were so disappointed when I didn't go to school. If I tell them I think she shouldn't go either..."

"You're scared they'll be disappointed in you all over again."

He nodded.

"Look, I know all about parental disappointment." I made a face at him. "But I also know how she must be feeling. Like she's all on her own and everyone's against her. Couldn't you try to find a way of being supportive without flat out telling her she's right and school's a waste of time?"

He gave me a half smile. "I guess I could try."

Our food arrived and we dug in. For such simple food, I was surprised by how delicious it was, and we both fell into the comfortable silence that indicates good eating. "Tell me about your shoot today," I said after a few moments.

Thomas's face lit up. "It went really well. I'm excited about the film. I think it will be my best work."

"Wow. What's it about?"

He launched into a detailed explanation of *Hostile*, his eyes lit up and shining, his excitement clear. At first glance, the movie appeared to be a basic heist mystery, with Thomas in the role of unsuspecting pawn. But, according to Thomas, the writing and directing took it beyond the ordinary.

"At its core, it's really about the things that drive us and the things that hold us back. I think it speaks to everyone, it's very representative of man at our most basic elements." He caught sight of my smile and shot me a rueful one of his own. "I sound like a pretentious prat, don't I?"

"No," I said, shaking my head. "You definitely don't. I was just thinking how cute you are when you get passionate about something."

The words left my mouth before I could even consider their impact. As he stared back at me, his gaze darkened, and I realized that I didn't care. It was the truth; he was rarely more attractive than when he was talking about his work. His love and passion for it was so clear. I found it inspiring. And he should know that.

"You light up when you talk about work," I said, my voice soft. "I can tell you love it. I can tell it matters to you. I don't know many people that feel that way about what they do for a living." I swallowed, thinking of my dad and brothers, the way they forced themselves through every shift, living for the weekend. "I think it's amazing. I really do."

"Funny," he said, reaching across the table to brush my hand with his fingertips. "That's the same impression I get when I see you writing."

I blushed. "I don't know about that. I love to write, but it's a hobby."

"It doesn't have to be," he argued. "If you really love it, and you're willing to work hard, why couldn't it be more?"

His words filled me with a longing I didn't want to think about, so I laughed it off. "For all you know, I'm terrible."

"Then let me read your work."

I let out a shaky laugh, fully aware that my next words would connect us beyond this weekend, experiment or no. "I will. Soon. I promise."

He leaned back in his chair, pleased. "I can tell you this: after all these years working with creative people, I'm pretty convinced that talent is a very small part of the equation. There's a lot that can be learned, and taught, so long as you have the passion to go for it. I think you have that passion, Lizzie. You shouldn't let it go."

I stared at him. No one had ever talked to me like this before, as if my life was full of possibility. As if dreams could be real if I only reached for them. I blinked back tears and smiled at him, hoping he understood how thankful I was. From the way he returned my gaze, unblinking, I was pretty sure he did.

After we ate, we made our way back up the winding street, stopping in a few stores. It was getting colder now, autumn settling in, so I bought a pair of cashmere gloves. I was tempted to also purchase a cashmere tartan cape, but decided it wasn't wise to spend rent money on something unnecessary, no matter how soft and pretty it was.

We arrived at Mary King's Close just before our tour began. I was feeling apprehensive as I followed the crowd down a winding staircase. Mary King's Close was an ancient street buried far below the current city. It had been closed up and built over centuries ago, only to be excavated in modern times. Thomas was right; the history portion was interesting and the tour was just creepy enough without being full-on scary. The passageways were narrow, dark, and cold. It was amazing to me that we were walking around on real streets, where people had actually lived and worked centuries ago, the whole thing buried below the bustling city above.

"That was great," I told him, as we emerged into the evening darkness an hour later. "I'm glad you suggested it."

"I'm glad you liked it."

"I am a little creeped out though. I don't think I can go to bed quite yet."

"Let's take a walk," he said. "We can go down to New Town, maybe walk in the gardens, get a drink or something."

The streets were quiet, nearly deserted. Thomas told me about the previous summer when he had performed in the

Edinburgh Fringe, a huge theater festival. "It was never this quiet," he said. "It's a crazy atmosphere in August."

"I wish I would have been here for it." I tried not to think about how next August I would be back in Detroit, maybe even getting ready to start in my first classroom. I shivered and Thomas looked at me.

"Are you cold?"

I shook my head. "I'm fine."

We made our way to Princes Street Gardens at the base of the castle. The view was amazing, the castle all lit up against the night sky. "Wow," I whispered, tipping my head back to stare up at the façade. "Gorgeous."

"It's not bad." Thomas's voice was close in the darkness, and I could feel his eyes on me. I had a brief flash of him in the London Eye, the way he had looked at me before we kissed. I closed my eyes.

"Yesterday, you said you weren't doing a good job of convincing me. What did you mean?"

He laughed softly in the darkness, the warm sound bringing goose bumps to my arms. "I could have killed Bryony last night. There I was trying to convince you that I was a normal, very non-celebrity kind of guy. And what did she do? Brought up my acting career. The exact thing I was trying to make you forget."

"I don't want to forget your career," I said, thinking of his face in the pub when he told me about the new movie. "Your career is part of who you are."

"But it's the thing that's making you think we shouldn't be together."

I was quiet, thinking about how unfair to him that sounded. I loved the passion and excitement Thomas showed for acting. Was I then going to hold it against him that he was successful in it?

"I'm scared," I whispered. "That's kind of what it all comes down to. I've never been…in love before. And I fell for you so fast, Thomas. It took my breath away. When I talked to Lola and I saw those pictures…it just seemed so impossible to picture myself there. The way Franny was, all dressed up at some glittery event. I don't belong with the glamour crowd, Thomas."

"Stop," he said, holding up his hands. "First of all, if you ever did come to one of those events with me, you'd be the most gorgeous woman there. No question. If you didn't fit in, it would be because you were better than most of the people there. Kinder. Smarter. Funnier. More caring. You're one of the most interesting people I've ever met, Lizzie. Please don't ever let yourself feel less than someone else just because they have fancy clothes. It's…it's ridiculous. So many of those people are fake, and spoiled, and entitled. And you…you're *you*, Lizzie."

He was looking at me with that same expression from the pub: his face alight, his eyes bright, and the sincerity of every word he said plain on his face. He really believed the things he was saying about me. I shook my head in disbelief.

"I wish I could make you see yourself the way I do." His voice was sad.

"I miss you," I said, wanting nothing more than to reach out for him, to feel the warmth of his arms around me, the softness of his lips on mine. Four days without a kiss was long enough.

"Lizzie," he said, closing his eyes. "I know you're scared. I know it seems like a lot. But we could take it slow. We could take it together. Make sure you have enough time for your studies and Callie. If there's something about my career that bothers you, or scares you, or you're uncomfortable with, we could talk about it. Figure it out together. We wouldn't even have to go to any premieres or movie events. I promise—"

I didn't need to hear anymore. I had stopped caring about all of it, the things that scared me, somewhere around the time that I saw Thomas in my apartment the previous morning. I had come to this country to take chances, to overcome fears, and try something new. If Thomas was with me to help me deal with the fears, well, how could I ask for anything better than that?

"You know," I interrupted, feeling a smile tugging at the corners of my mouth. "I pretty much just told you I loved you. Did you catch that?"

His expression turned immediately to shock. "You did?"

I took a step closer. "Uh huh. I said I'd never been in love before and that I fell fast for you."

His shock was quickly giving away to his familiar teasing smile. "I don't know, Lizzie. It sounds a little vague to me. Maybe you better spell it out for me."

I reached out and grabbed the lapels of his pea coat. "I love you, Thomas Harper. I think I did from that first date. And I'm done being scared."

The grin on his face was so overwhelmingly joyful that it took my breath away. Before I could catch it, he was kissing me, his arms wrapped tight around me, pulling my feet clear off the ground.

"I love *you*, Lizzie." He laughed gently against my mouth. "Actually, I'm a little ticked you got to be the first to say it."

I laughed and kissed him again, realizing how crazy I had been to think I could give this up.

We left the park and caught a cab back to the hotel. I didn't want to let go of him for a second, now that I was decided. I leaned into his chest the entire way back, kissing his knuckles, his palms, the skin below his ear. I was reliving the sensation I'd had up in the London Eye that first date, like I was about to fall and wished I could just jump. I held onto that feeling all the way back to the hotel.

And, because I'd realized I kind of like being the first to take a big step, I walked straight past the door to my room and followed Thomas into his instead.

Wrapping my arms around him and pulling him to the bed was a lot like falling—or, rather, like jumping, since I was the one taking the leap. But I wasn't afraid anymore. Not one bit.

CHAPTER FIFTEEN

As autumn settled over London, I found myself getting into a routine. It was a routine that made me feel deliriously happy, but a routine all the same.

Thomas had started shooting a new film in London. His being busy was good for me, I think. It helped give me a little space when my willpower was faltering. I still wished I could spend every minute with him, but the feeling was less desperate now. Knowing he loved me back did that for me. On a few occasions we ran into Jackson and Lola in restaurants around town. Though I was sure I would never be friends with either of them, I managed to take these encounters in stride.

My schoolwork improved, too. Thomas and I went out less and spent more time in one of our flats so we could both work. We spent long Sunday brunches out with his friends, everyone reading the paper while I scribbled scenes from my novel in a notebook. Thomas went out of his way to include Callie in our plans. She came with us to trivia night at the pub, her knowledge of fashion and pop culture a plus for the team. Before long, I noticed she was flirting with Charlie. When I told Thomas this, he simply rolled his eyes. "Charlie is way too flakey to keep up with someone like Callie," he told me. "He'd forget half their dates, and she'd dump him before the week was out."

As it got colder out, I started feeling slightly melancholy. I confided to Callie one night in mid-November and was surprised when she nodded her agreement.

"It's weird," I said, curled up next to her on the couch. "I'm happier here than I've ever been." I started to count on my fingers. "School is going well. Thomas is fantastic. I love his friends, and we all have fun together. So what's my problem?"

"It's the season," she said, leaning her head back on the couch pillow. "We're getting close to the holidays."

I hadn't really thought of it, but I immediately realized that she was right. "Thanksgiving is next week," I said glumly. "I can't believe I didn't think of it before. I love Thanksgiving. No wonder I'm sad."

"We'll go out to dinner on Thursday," she said, smiling weakly at me. "It won't be the same, but at least we'll be together."

When I told Thomas about our plans, he asked if he and his friends could join us. Callie had no objections, so he told me he would handle making the reservations. "I'll pick somewhere you both like," he assured me.

But when we met at Thomas's flat on Thursday evening, it was soon clear that he hadn't made reservations after all. Instead of buzzing us up, he met us down at the front door so he could walk us to his flat himself.

"You're being kind of weird," I told him, looking over at Callie.

He turned at his door to face us. "Okay, we have a bit of a surprise for you girls."

I looked over at Callie again, wondering if she knew anything about this. She looked as clueless as I felt. "What kind of surprise?"

"Well, we knew you guys were bummed about missing Thanksgiving. And we didn't want you to spend your holiday in some crappy restaurant eating the same kind of stuff you normally do. So we decided that we would throw you a little party."

Thomas flung the door open and the familiar smell of turkey flooded the hallway. Through the open door, I could hear chatter and laughter, the sounds of friends gathered in one place.

"What is this?" Callie asked, a smile breaking out on her face.

"Come on," Thomas said, taking both of our arms and leading us into the room. "I'll show you."

"Lizzie!" Meghan called out once she caught sight of me from the kitchen. "Hi! Hi Callie! Happy Thanksgiving!"

I froze in the living room. Meghan was joined in the kitchen by Carter, who appeared to be wearing a frilly flowered apron over his sweater and slacks while he mashed potatoes, and Charlie, who was stirring something in a metal mixing bowl. Sarra was perched on the counter, not working, with a glass of wine in her hand.

"Hi!" she called out. "We made food!"

"*You* made nothing," Carter said, grabbing the glass from her hand to take a slug of wine. "You've been sitting here bossing us around all day."

"I've been delegating," she said. "It's an important job. Do you think Gordon Ramsey cooks every plate of food himself?"

"I don't believe this," I murmured, feeling like I might cry. "You guys cooked for us?"

"Yeah, come see!" Charlie called, holding up his bowl so I could see what appeared to be very liquidly whipped cream. I turned to Thomas, who smiled at me broadly, before looking back at Callie. She looked every bit as shocked as I was.

We joined the others in the kitchen as Charlie eagerly told us about all the dishes they had made. "The turkey's in the oven, I've been in charge of basting," he said proudly. "And Carter made dressing and some kind of gloppy sweet potato thing. Oh, and Meghan made roasted vegetables and corn pudding."

"I can't believe this," I said, looking around at all of them. "You guys…"

"We wanted you to have a great day," Meghan said, coming over to kiss my cheek. "I know you'll both be missing home, but we wanted you to remember that you're with friends."

To my utter surprise, Callie buried her face in her hands and burst into tears.

"Cal!" Meghan cried. "What's wrong?"

"This is so nice," she sniffled, not looking up. Thomas wrapped an arm around her, smiling at me.

"We love you girls," he said. "Happy Thanksgiving. Now quit your crying and help Meghan set the table."

She gave him a quick one-armed squeeze and wiped her face with her hands. "Sorry," she gulped, her voice shaky. "I just…I wasn't expecting this. I love Thanksgiving."

"We'll have a wonderful time," Meghan assured her. "Come on."

They each gathered up a stack of plates and headed over to the table. I turned to Thomas. "So, what did you make, mister?"

He waggled his eyebrows at me. "My dish is a surprise."

"Is that code for you forgot to make something?"

He gave me a mock-scandalized look. "I'll have you know, I've been slaving away here all day!"

"Hey, Lizzie," Charlie called. "Come help me. Is this supposed to look like this?"

I joined him at the mixing bowl and explained that he needed to use a whisk for whipped cream. "Or a mixer, if Thomas has one."

We found the mixer and finished up the whipped cream, sticking it in the fridge to stay cool until dessert. Mark arrived from work, bearing still-hot rolls from the bakery down the street.

"I think that's everything," Meghan said. "Everyone grab a dish and find your seat."

The table was beautifully set. Meghan had brought her own china, decreeing that Thomas's stuff was too cheap and bachelor-esque. A huge bouquet of orange and red flowers sat in a cut-glass vase. And Charlie had printed out black and white shots he'd taken of the eight of us over the past two months, framed in silver and scattered around the table. There was plenty of wine, the food smelled amazing, and everyone seemed happy and excited. I couldn't have asked for a better Thanksgiving.

"Hang on!" Thomas cried, before I started to fill my plate. "You haven't seen my special dish yet."

Sarra crossed her arms. "He's been talking about this secret dish all day. Meghan made an entire turkey! Have some perspective."

He stuck out his tongue at her as he turned to run back to the kitchen. "Do you know what this is?" I asked Meghan, but she only smiled at me.

He returned a moment later, carrying a covered casserole dish. Grinning at me, he pulled off the lid to reveal a layer of tamales, my very favorite food.

I stared at him. "What...what is this?"

"I may have emailed your cousin," he said. "To ask her what your favorite Thanksgiving food was. She said your family always had tamales, in addition to the traditional stuff. She even sent me your mum's recipe. It might not taste quite as good as hers, but I wanted you to have a taste of home today."

I couldn't believe he had gone to so much trouble. It was my turn to get teary.

"Can you guys be sappy some other time?" Charlie called out. "I'm starving."

"Wait!" Callie said. "We haven't said what we're thankful for yet. It's tradition! Everyone has to go around and say what they're giving thanks for this year."

Charlie grumbled about cruel and unusual punishment, but, under a glare from Callie, he dutifully said he was thankful for how many photos he'd sold lately.

"And I'm thankful for all these new friends," Callie said, smiling around at everyone.

"I'm thankful for my lovely girlfriend, Meghan," Carter said, kissing her cheek.

"Aw, how sweet of you," Meghan said. "I'm thankful for my big promotion and all the cash I'll be making." Everyone laughed as Carter rolled his eyes.

"What about you, Thomas?"

He smiled at me. "I'm thankful for second chances. Lizzie?"

I felt a lump in my throat as I looked back at him. I thought of all the trouble he'd gone through to give me a true Thanksgiving, the trouble they'd all gone to. I looked around the table at my new friends and brushed away a tear.

"I'm very thankful for my London family," I said. "You've made this place like home for me."

"Hear, hear," Mark said, raising his glass. We all clinked our wine glasses together.

"Okay, enough sappiness," Sarra said. "Can we please eat?"

It wasn't quite like the feasts we'd had at home. The sweet potatoes were sticky and the turkey was slightly dry. And, try as he might, Thomas's tamales just weren't the same as my mothers.

But I didn't think I'd ever had a nicer Thanksgiving.

CHAPTER SIXTEEN

As Christmas approached, I had trouble keeping my spirits up. In many ways, I would have rather been right here in London, with Thomas, than anywhere else in the world. But a part of me—an obnoxiously loud part of me that seemed to grow louder every day—wanted nothing more than to be at home with my family for Christmas. Thomas and I spent the first weekend in December up at his parents. I helped Bryony with her Christmas shopping and Thomas and I both joined his mother in baking cookies. I enjoyed getting closer to his family, but it did little to keep me from missing mine.

One Saturday early in December, Thomas and I were curled up in my living room, trying to keep warm under the thick quilt my grandmother had made me years ago. My apartment was perpetually drafty, and the small space heater Callie had bought did little to stop the chill.

"You'd think some of the heat from those brick ovens down there would warm things up," Thomas muttered, readjusting his end of the quilt to cover more of his arms. He was studying the script of his new movie, set to begin filming just outside London in the new year, while I tried to work my way through a boring as all get out critique of *Dante's Inferno*.

"I guess Mr. Idoni keeps it pretty well ventilated," I said, wiggling my toes against his calf. After we had spent most of the morning distracting each other from our work, I had banished Thomas to the other end of the couch.

"Hmph," Thomas muttered. "He just had to follow proper fire safety procedures, didn't he? Fat lot of good that does us."

"It does us plenty of good," I said, kicking him lightly. "Considering how I live up here and all."

"Yeah, yeah," he muttered, grabbing my foot under the blanket. "Now stop kicking, or I start tickling."

I raised my eyebrows at him. Before I could decide if I wanted to take him up on the challenge, my phone rang. I looked at the screen and my face broke into a grin. "It's Sofie!"

"You take it," Thomas said, squeezing my foot. "I'm gonna go downstairs and see if I can talk that miser into comping us a pizza to make up for the cold."

"Good luck with that," I said, making a face at him before accepting the call. "Sof? Hi!"

"Lizzie!" The sound of my cousin's voice, so familiar and far away, sent a sharp pain through my chest. The homesickness I had been feeling grew exponentially. "How are you, chica?"

"I'm good." I struggled to keep my voice even, waving at Thomas as he slipped through the front door. "How are you?"

"Bored as hell," she said, laughing her deep, throaty laugh. "We're all at your house. I've been stuck cooking with all the old ladies all day, and you aren't even here to make it halfway decent."

Another pain. I had forgotten they would all be together today preparing food for Christmas. Christmas was a huge deal in our family, and consisted of several parties and get togethers, both with each other and with our larger church community. The second Saturday in December had long been set aside for the women in the family to get together and make countless tortillas, tamales, and cookie dough to freeze in preparation for the season. Sofia and I had always hated it, complaining bitterly the entire time. So why did I now feel like I'd give anything to be there, sitting with my sisters, cousins, and aunts, rolling out dough, sounds of gossip and laughter filling the kitchen?

"Lizzie? You there?"

"Yeah," I said, swallowing past the lump in my throat. "I'm here. Sorry I'm not around to bitch with. I'm amazed they let you out of the kitchen long enough to call me."

"I escaped to your bedroom," she said. "So, how's it going? How's that boyfriend of yours?"

"He's great," I said, trying to tear my mind from thoughts of home. My mother always made spiced hot chocolate on the cooking day, and by evening they would be adding copious amounts of brandy to it, my old tias getting more and more giggly as the night wore on.

"You okay, chica? You keep fading out on me."

"I miss you," I said, squeezing my eyes shut. I knew I wouldn't be able to hold the tears in for long. "I miss all of you. It's really hitting me that I won't be home for Christmas, and I…I…" I was crying now, my body shaking with sobs. I felt a hand on my shoulder and looked up; Thomas was standing in front of me, a pizza box abandoned on the coffee table, concern etching his face.

"Oh, babe," Sofie was saying on the other end of the phone. "We miss you, too, all of us. But it will be okay. I know it sucks this year, but you'll be home next Christmas, and all of this will be just the same as always. Okay?"

"I know," I gasped, trying to hold the phone and wipe my eyes at the same time. "I'm just being silly." A tissue appeared in my hand, Thomas sliding his arms around me as he joined me on the couch. He pulled me close, and I rested my head against his chest, feeling better already. "I'm sorry."

"Don't be sorry," Sofie said. "Seriously, girl, if I was away from home for that long, I would have broken down months ago. I completely get it. We complain about this bat-shit family all the time, but I know I'd be a mess without them."

"I'm okay," I assured her and Thomas both. "I just need to get my mind off it."

"Are you sure? We could talk about it some more. Maybe it would help."

"Nah," I said. "Probably better to not think about it. Hey, listen. Don't go telling my sisters about this. Or my parents."

"Who do you think I am?" Sofie asked, sounding offended. "We never tell on each other."

I smiled, which somehow made me want to start crying again. "You should get back down there before they hunt you down. Love you."

"Love you, too. Hey, call me any time, okay? I'm always here."

"Thanks. Love you."

I hung up the phone and looked at Thomas, smiling ruefully. "Sorry about that."

"Homesick?"

"Just a little." I gave a rueful laugh.

"Tell me."

I shook my head. "I don't really want to talk about it."

"Lizzie, it's not good to keep this stuff bottled up." He gave me a stern look. "Aren't we supposed to be all open and crap with each other?"

I snorted. "Yes, the first sign of a good relationship is being open 'and crap' with each other."

"Well, yeah." He smiled and kissed the top of my head. "So tell me."

I snuggled into his chest, sighing. "Christmas is my favorite time of year. It's a huge deal in my family. We have all these parties, everyone dropping in at each other's houses. About a week before Christmas, we celebrate Posadas, which is this Mexican tradition."

"Do they do that in Spain? I think I've heard of it."

"Maybe. In Mexico it's this week-long thing, they hold parades in the town and the children go from door to door, playing Mary and Joseph, you know, like they're looking for a place to stay. Our grandparents grew up doing it, but once they came to the States they were on the move so much, it kind of fell out of practice. So now we celebrate it in one night, instead of seven, at this huge party at the church." I smiled, remembering the year Sofia was chosen to be Mary and how she had thrown a temper tantrum that the costume made her look ugly.

"On Christmas Eve, we all go to Mass together, the whole family. They do this candle light service and we sing all the hymns." My voice shook slightly and Thomas's arms tightened around me. "Then we go back to my aunt's house and eat and pass presents and just…just…"

"Spend time together," Thomas said softly, kissing my head again.

I nodded, sniffling. "I've been trying not to think about it, but I miss it. I know it's not a big deal and it will all be the same when I'm home next year but…I cant help it. I miss it."

"Why aren't you going home, then? You have two whole weeks off of school."

"A plane ticket wasn't in the budget," I told him. "My scholarship covered my flight here and back, that's all."

"I'm sorry," he said, pulling me closer. "I can't imagine how hard that is, to be away for so long."

I sniffed, trying to get myself together. "It's okay, really. I shouldn't be complaining so much. It was my choice to come here." I looked up at him and managed a real smile.

"And I'm so glad I did." He kissed me softly and I sighed against his mouth, my emotions at war with each other. I couldn't imagine not being here with him, so why was I so disappointed that I couldn't go home? "Let's eat that pizza," I finally said. "You risked life and limb to get it for us."

I tried to get back to my reading after we ate, but it was hard to concentrate. Thomas kept an arm wrapped firmly around me while he read the script. I knew I was preventing him from making his usual notes, but I couldn't seem to find the strength to pull away.

"Want some hot chocolate?" I asked eventually, needing something to do.

"Oooh, is it your special hot chocolate?" Thomas asked, his eyes gleaming. I had introduced him to my family's spiced drink as soon as it started to get cold out, and he bugged me to make it almost every day he came over.

"Sure," I said, climbing off the couch. "Just 'cause you're so nice."

It had probably been a bit of a mistake to make the hot chocolate, knowing that my family would be drinking the same thing later that night. As soon as I smelled the mix of chocolate and spices, I felt like I was transported directly back to my mother's kitchen. But I put it out of my mind and poured out the sweetened drink into mugs for us both before walking back out into the living room.

"Here ya go," I said, handing him his mug. He had abandoned his script and had opened his tablet. "Whatcha doing?"

"Buying us plane tickets to Detroit," he said, his voice casual.

I nearly dropped the other mug. "What?"

"And it's too late for you to complain because they're non-refundable," he said, tapping something on the screen before setting the tablet on the coffee table.

"Thomas." I stared at him, at a loss for words.

"Listen, Lizzie," he said, pulling on my empty hand until I was sitting next to him again. "I want you to be able to go home for Christmas. It would make me happy if I knew you were with your family. So let me do this for you."

"It's too much," I whispered.

He shook his head. "It's not. Consider it your Christmas present. You're not allowed to return a Christmas present. It's bad manners."

I was crying again. "I can't believe you."

"Come on, love." He took my mug and set it next to the tablet and set his down beside it. Then he wrapped his arms around me. "Just say okay."

"Okay," I whimpered, way too overwhelmed by his act to protest. There was no sense in arguing; I wanted to go home. And the fact that he cared about me enough to offer was so amazingly sweet. How could I tell him no?

"Uh, I bought myself a ticket, too," he said, sounding sheepish. "I probably should have asked you about that part first."

I pulled back to look up at him. "You want to come with me?"

"If it's okay," he said, looking distinctly uncomfortable now. "I kind of just assumed we'd be spending the holiday together. Sorry. Was that...was that okay?"

"Of course it's okay," I cried, throwing my arms around him again. "I'm so happy you're coming with me! Leaving you would have been as bad as missing it!"

His arms tightened around me, and he exhaled a relieved sounding sigh. "I wouldn't want to be without you either. Especially at Christmas."

"This is amazing," I said, my excitement growing. "When did you book it for?"

"The day before Christmas Eve. Your classes are done the Friday before, right?"

"Right," I said, bouncing on the couch a little. I knew I should ask him about the price, offer to pay him back somehow, but I couldn't seem to make myself put a damper on this, not yet.

"Do you think your parents will mind? Shite, I wasn't thinking that I was pretty much inviting myself over."

"Are you kidding?" I asked. "Do you have any idea the number of people who will be at our house celebrating? I've told you how big my family is, not to mention people from church and the neighborhood. One more person is nothing."

"Good," he said, smiling. "It's great to see you this happy."

"Thank you." My voice was low and sincere. "Seriously, Thomas, thank you so much for this."

"You're welcome, love," he said. "You're more than welcome."

***

It was weird to be in Detroit again. Everything looked different to me somehow, though I was sure things like road signs were the same as they'd ever been. Predictably, Thomas had booked us a direct flight, so no layover nightmare this time. And he'd sprung for first class. Of course, he didn't tell me that until we reached the airport, not that there was anything I could have done about it. My irritation about the expense lasted exactly as long as it took me to figure out how to extend my seat into a fully reclining bed.

"Are you kidding me?" I asked him, incredulous. "This is amazing!"

"Right?" He grinned at me. "The few times the studio has flown me to the States, they've sprung for first class. It's pretty awesome."

It was, by far, the most comfortable trip I'd ever experienced. I'd never given much thought to becoming wealthy; my parents had always stressed the importance of being middle class, comfortable, and secure. But it'd be worth it to make good money if only to fly first class internationally.

Thomas and I spent several amusing minutes discussing what kind of profession I could go for that would allow me to make fast money, our ideas becoming more and more ridiculous. Thomas thought I would make a good Ponzi scheme manager. I was partial to trying a life as a drug mule.

Well rested and comfortable, we deplaned at Detroit Metro and made our way to the baggage claim. Before our bags had even arrived, I heard a familiar voice call my name.

"Lizzie!"

I spun around and saw Sofia flying toward me, my brother Samuel behind her. Completely forgetting Thomas or the crowd around me, I flung myself at her, crying and jumping up and down.

"You're home, you're home!" she cried, kissing my cheeks.

"You're both making a scene," a familiar voice said. I opened my eyes and saw Samuel standing next to us, smiling down at me, his hands shoved into his pockets. I released my cousin and threw my arms around my big brother. He squeezed me back, much harder than he ever had before.

"I'm so glad you're home, mi hermana," he whispered in my ear before releasing me.

"Is that the hottie?" Sofia whispered, looking over at Thomas. He was standing a few feet behind us, allowing us a private reunion. I held out my hand to him and he joined us, smiling.

"Thomas, this is my cousin, Sofie, and my brother, Samuel. Guys, this is Thomas."

Thomas shook Samuel's hand before bending to kiss Sofie's cheek. "I've heard so much about both of you."

One look at Sofie's face and I knew she was totally won over. Samuel was a little harder to read, but he smiled at

Thomas and asked if he wanted help getting out bags from the now-moving carousel.

After they'd left, Sofie threw her arm around my shoulders. "Okay, he is totally fine. And that accent! How the hell'd you manage this one?"

"He must be attracted to my charm and smoking good looks," I said, laughing.

Sofie laughed, too. "Does this mean you've finally harnessed the power of your Latina hotness?"

"Sure, Sof."

"Car's this way," Samuel said, lugging my suitcase behind him. Thomas was a few steps back with his own bag, a somewhat bewildered expression on his face.

"Twenty bucks says Sammy threatened him," Sofia whispered, obviously having caught the expression herself.

"Sorry," I muttered, falling back to walk next to my boyfriend. "What'd he say?"

"I'm not quite sure," Thomas said, shaking his head. "Some of it was in Spanish. I think the gist was that I better not hurt you, or I'd find myself short a bollock."

I should not have been surprised. Carlos once saw me kissing Jeremy Higgins behind the bleachers in junior high. He reamed him out so much, Jeremy had run home crying and never talked to me again. Normally, I would have been pissed at my family's interference, but the look on Thomas's face was so funny that I had to laugh. I also knew, out of all my brothers, Samuel had the most interest in my actual happiness. It was hard to get mad at him for being protective.

It was freezing outside, much colder than it had been in London. "Crap," I muttered, pulling my coat tighter. "I forgot what cold really felt like."

"We've had snow all week," Sofie said. "Auntie Sof has been hysterical, thinking flights were going to be cancelled and you wouldn't be home after all."

After Thomas had announced his ticket purchase, I had immediately called home to tell my mom the news. She had screamed and cried and told the rest of the women of the family, so that all I could hear on the other end of the phone was shouting in Spanish. I'd heard from her several times since, calling to confirm flight details and ask questions about the kind of food Thomas would eat. I had not heard from my father.

"How's Dad?" I asked Samuel as he opened the trunk to stow our bags. He raised an eyebrow at me.

"How do you think?"

My stomach dropped a little, but I forced the worry out of my mind. I knew my dad wouldn't be thrilled about me bringing a boyfriend home, let alone a boyfriend that lived on a different continent. *He can just deal with it*, I thought to myself as Thomas and I climbed into the back seat.

As we got under way, Sofie asked us questions about our flight. I declined to mention the first class part. I knew Sof would eat it up, but I wasn't sure how Samuel would take the expense. They in turn told me all the latest gossip from home. My sister Laura was redecorating her living room, and she and her husband, Frank, were apparently arguing over every detail. The aunts were convinced this was all a diversion because they were having trouble getting pregnant.

As Samuel and Sofie argued about the radio station, I turned to Thomas next to me. "How you holding up?" I asked.

"Great," he said, giving me a thumbs up.

Sofie heard us. "You have no idea what you're in for, Thomas. Has Lizzie told you how insane our family is, or was she hoping you wouldn't notice?"

"She may have mentioned that you're a little loud," Thomas said easily.

Sofie and Sam both laughed. "Just a little," she said.

"Don't forget bossy, intrusive, and tempestuous," Sam said.

"We're not that bad," I said. "Would you guys believe that I've actually started to miss the noise?"

"Nope," they said in unison.

As we headed toward Sterling Heights, we fell into comfortable conversation. Sofie and Sam were both very interested in Thomas's job. Sofie, of course, was a huge fan of *Darkness*. Sam was won over when Thomas casually mentioned he'd met Matt Damon at a studio party the previous year. "Don't be shy about using that one on all of my brothers," I whispered to him. "They're all pretty big Jason Borne fans."

As we pulled onto our street, I felt a thrill of excitement mingled with apprehension. Cars lined both sides of the street, and I was sure most of them belonged to family members. In fact, I could easily pick out my sister's SUV, Carlos's truck, and Matias's car (all Fords, of course). "Everyone is here?" I asked, a note of worry in my voice. "Already?"

"Of course," Sofie said, turning to grin at me. "What did you expect?"

I gave Thomas an apologetic look as we got out of the car. "You're a brave man," Sam said, clapping him on the shoulder before moving to the trunk. "I'll get the bags, you guys go on in."

Sofie led the way up the driveway. Before we reached the steps, the front door was flung open. "Lizzie!"

I ran up the steps to my mother's waiting arms. She smelled like cinnamon and pine needles, like Christmastime and being at home. She held me tight for a long time, as if she was afraid to let go.

"Come on, Mama," Sam said, shouldering past her with the bags. "Let the girl breathe."

"Sorry, sorry," she said, pulling back but keeping her hands firmly on my shoulders. "How are you? You look thin. And pale."

"It's winter there, too, Tia," Sofie said, also pushing past into the house. "Did you think she'd have a tan?"

"Are you sure you're okay?" my mother asked again.

"Perfect, Mama," I said. She finally released me, and I turned for Thomas. He was standing at the foot of the steps. "Mama, this is Thomas." He took the steps two at a time and joined us on the porch. I took his hand, feeling suddenly shy. He squeezed my hand tightly, as if he knew what I was feeling.

"Hello, Thomas," she said warmly, looking him over. "I've heard so much about you. We're so glad you can join us for the holiday."

"Thank you for having me, Mrs. Medina." He released my hand so he could take both of hers, leaning forward to kiss her cheek. She beamed at him, and I knew, like Sofie, he had won my mother over with his charm.

"Come in, come in," she urged, sounding a little fluttery. I stifled a laugh—I couldn't blame her. I got fluttery when he turned on the charm, too.

We stepped into the foyer, and I was immediately assaulted by voices—it seemed every person I was related to was here. "Lizzie!" several called.

"Hello," I called out to everyone. "Merry Christmas!"

There was a general chorus of hellos and Christmas wishes. Before we could take off our coats, my Aunt Maria, Sofie's mom, was hugging us both and welcoming us home. Her husband, Tomas, joined her, as did Sofie's older sister Carla. Then Carla's children were bounding down the stairs, along with my niece and nephew, shouting my name.

We'd barely been in the house for a full minute and I was dizzy already.

"Where's Dad?" I asked my mother. Did I imagine her face fall slightly?

"In the garage with José and Carlos."

I tried to keep my voice light. "Let me guess. They're frying something?"

Everyone around us laughed. "How'd you know?" Sofie said, rolling her eyes. "Thomas, this family wouldn't be celebrating a holiday if there wasn't a heart-attack worthy amount of fried foods."

"Brits like fried food," he assured her. "Fried fish is pretty much our national dish."

"And the girls?" I asked my mother, trying hard to tamp down the irritation that was rising. There was no way my father hadn't heard the outcry over our arrival, even in the garage. And if the girls were somewhere inside, they were most definitely aware that I was here.

"Kitchen," my mom said. "Let's go say hello."

I gripped Thomas's hand in mine and followed her into the kitchen. This room was full, too, with cousins, a great aunt, and, both standing at the sink, my sisters.

"Look who's here," my mother said, her voice deceptively cheerful. I was sure I could detect an edge of warning in her voice.

"Merry Christmas," I said, my eyes on my sisters. Laura smiled and pushed off from the sink, crossing the kitchen to pull me into a hug. As her arms wrapped around me, I saw Maria standing in the same spot, watching us.

"Hello, Maria," I said, once Laura had released me. "It's good to see you."

"Bienvenidos. Feliz Navidad," she said, not sounding at all like she meant the welcome. I was pretty sure her use of Spanish was meant to make a point. Doing my best not to grimace, I turned to Thomas.

"These are my sisters."

"Of course." He shook Laura's hand. "You must be Laura. Merry Christmas."

"Merry Christmas," she said, shaking his hand. Her eyes darted over to me. "We're so glad you could make it."

"And you're Maria," he said, crossing the kitchen to offer my oldest sister his hand. "I've heard a lot about both of you."

"Merry Christmas," she said, and I was glad to see her apparent hostility toward me did not win out over the manners our parents had long drilled into us.

I looked at my mother. "Should I go out and see Dad, or wait for him?" I was sure there was an edge to my voice, but I couldn't help it. I was hurt that he wasn't being more welcoming. I understood that he hadn't been happy with my choice to go abroad. But it was Christmas now, for God's sake.

"I'll get them," she said heading for the door to the garage, and I detected a similar note in her voice. She clearly was not pleased with his behavior either.

I introduced Thomas to the cousins and my great aunt Sonia before I heard the door open again. "Welcome home, little sister."

"Carlos." I smiled, my irritation that he hadn't come in to see me right away vanishing at the sight of him. Carlos, the oldest, would always be where my dad was. It was just a given. They worked at the same plant, usually on the same shift. They spent their lunch breaks together, drank beer in the garage together most nights. Out of all of us, they had the closest relationship. I couldn't blame him for that. But, unlike my oldest sister, Carlos smiled at me warmly and wrapped me up in a big hug, pulling my feet up from the floor the way he did when I was small.

"So," he said, releasing me and looking at Thomas. "This is the boyfriend."

"Carlos, this is Thomas," I said, watching as my older brother sized up my boyfriend. Thomas stood his ground, holding Carlos's gaze without hesitation. "And Samuel already gave him the big brother talk, so you can forget it."

"Nice to meet you, mate," Thomas said, holding out his hand. I released a breath I didn't realize I was holding when Carlos returned the handshake.

I was distracted by the sight of my father standing in the doorway, watching us. I felt a lump form in my throat. He looked the way he had looked the day I left. Disappointed. Or was it sad?

An edge of tension seemed to settle over the kitchen. I realized it was up to me to keep things from getting awkward, for Thomas's sake at least. So I swallowed past the lump in my throat and went to my dad, standing up on tiptoe to wrap my arms around him. "Merry Christmas, Daddy," I said, my voice as bright as I could make it.

After a moment's hesitation, he hugged me back. "Merry Christmas, Lizita," he whispered, his voice gruff. Tears stung my eyes, and I had to blink them away rapidly.

Lizita was a nickname he had given me, a little joke between only us. When I was little, Matias had spent an afternoon teasing me mercilessly because I didn't have a Spanish name like the rest of the family. My dad had caught me crying in the laundry room, and when I told him why, he had wrapped me up in his big arms and told me I could have a Spanish name if I wanted one. He gave me several options to choose from. "Guapo?" he asked, tickling me.

"That means handsome," I pouted.

"You're right. We need something for a little girl. Cerdo?"

"Daddy, I'm not a pig!"

"Hmm," he said, his mustache scratching against my cheek as he held me close. "I call your mother Sofita." Determined to remain upset, I struggled to hold back the smile his nickname for my mom always triggered. Adding an *ita* to the end of the word was a common form of familiarity in Spanish, and I'd always found it to be so nice when my dad used that name with my mom, like he was winking at her with his words. "Perhaps," he said, his fingers moving to tickle me once more, "you'd like to be my little Lizita?"

The combination of his tickling and the funny sounding name had sent me into howls of laughter. I had been Lizita ever since—at least, when no one else could hear him.

When I was sure I wasn't going to cry, I pulled back. "Come and meet Thomas," I said, holding his arm.

CHAPTER SEVENTEEN

The house saw a steady stream of visitors for the rest of the day. Cousins, aunts and uncles, neighbors, friends from church. Even I started to feel overwhelmed after a while. I could only imagine how Thomas felt. At one point, my Aunt Maria pulled him into service rolling dough for her pies. "There is an auction at church," she explained. "To raise funds. My pies always bring in the most of any baked goods."

"I can see why," he said politely, shooting me a panicked look.

"Thomas is a fantastic cook, Tia," I said, winking at him over her head. "You picked a good helper."

He narrowed his eyes at me, but I only laughed. At least helping her, he was only subjected to one of my crazy relatives. Had he remained in the living room with the rest, I was fairly sure he'd be mobbed.

"Lizzie," Carla hissed from the corner. She gestured me over.

"What's up?"

"He's adorable," she whispered. "How on earth did you manage this?"

"Thanks, Carla." I rolled my eyes and went to move away, but she grabbed my elbow to stop me.

"You look like your sister when you roll your eyes like that—don't be a drama queen. I love those movies so much. Do you think you'll get to meet Jackson Coles?"

I affected a nonchalant air as I examined my fingernails. "Oh, I already have. A few times."

She slapped my arm. "Shut. Up. Are you serious?"

"Serious about what?" Laura asked, joining us.

"Your sister met Jackson Coles! More than once!"

"Ooh, really, Lizzie? Why didn't you ever mention it?"

I shrugged. "I don't know. I didn't know you were into those movies."

"Are you kidding?" Laura clutched my arm. "I love them! I totally blushed when Thomas came in, could you tell?"

I looked at her in surprise. It was unlike either of my sisters to be giggly and girlish like this, at least with me. I had memories of them talking about boys when I was little, but I was never invited to participate. "I couldn't tell at all," I assured her.

"Oh, good. I just can't believe you're dating him. He seems really nice. And very into you."

I looked over at Thomas and happened to catch his eyes on me. He winked, and my sister and cousin both gave a little sigh. "See what I mean?"

"He's wonderful," I said, feeling like I might start giggling myself. "I don't know how I got so lucky."

"Because you're beautiful and smart, little sister," Laura said. "Of course he likes you."

"Thanks, Laura," I said, touched and more than a little surprised.

"So, tell me about Jackson," she said, both of them leaning in closer. "Is he as gorgeous in real life as the movies?"

"He's pretty cute," I admitted. "And nice, too. But he's kind of fake. Definitely full of himself. He flirts with everything that moves."

"He could flirt with me," Carla said.

"It'd be nice if your husband heard that," Maria said, coming up behind Carla from the garage and making her jump. "The three of you sound like preteens. Get a grip."

"Oh, you can be all high and mighty," Carla said. "Like you wouldn't take a little flirting from a movie star, José or no José."

Maria looked straight at me. "Mooning after movie stars is ridiculous. It's the kind of thing acceptable in teenagers, not grown women."

Before I could do more than splutter at her incoherently, she had moved on to the living room.

"She didn't mean it the way it sounded," Laura said, looking after our sister uncertainly.

"Like hell she didn't," I muttered.

"I'm with Lizzie on this one," Carla said. "That was a classic Maria Medina burn. Oh well, cuz. Don't let it bother you. She's probably just jealous."

Carla patted my hand before heading off to help my mother refill the drink pitchers.

"You really shouldn't let it bother you, Lizzie," Laura said, watching my face. "You know how Maria gets."

"Yes, I do," I said, still breathing heavily.

"Don't let it ruin your day," Laura urged. "I think it's so nice you brought him home. Mama's been so happy ever since she found out you were coming."

I smiled at my sister, surprised once again at how nice she was being. To tell the truth, Laura often got overshadowed by the much louder, bolder presence of our eldest sister. Maybe it was time for me to start seeing her more clearly, for her own sake.

"Thanks, Laura. Hey, if you want, I bet I could get you Jackson's autograph."

Her face lit up. "Really? Thanks, Lizzie! Oh my God, I have to go tell Carla."

I decided to join Thomas and Aunt Maria at the table. Maybe taking out my annoyance on the dough would help. "Oh, good, Lizzie, you can take over. My hands are bothering me something terrible."

"What's wrong, Tia?" I asked, taking her hand and rubbing her knuckles between my fingers.

"Oh, nothing, dear. You're sweet. The doctor said my arthritis will act up more and more, especially when it's cold out."

"Go sit down in the living room," I told her. "Tell your lazy daughter to come help me."

"Let me get you a drink," Thomas said, jumping up. "What will you have?"

"No, no, dear. I'm fine. Besides, you have flour all over your hands." She patted his chest as she passed and winked at me. "You picked well, Lizzie."

I laughed at the expression on Thomas's face as she left. "I think she has a crush on you."

"I'm pretty sure half your relatives have patted my bum since we got here," he said drily.

"They can't help themselves, you're so cute." I leaned forward to kiss him.

"Gross. You two are not allowed to be that lovey-dovey when I'm single," Sofia said, joining us at the table. "My mom said I'm supposed to help you."

"Yup, get to work."

We settled into an easy pattern; Thomas kneaded and shaped the dough before passing it off to me to roll it flat. Then Sofie laid it in the pie tin and spooned in the mincemeat mixture. We chatted comfortably while we worked.

"So I was talking to Sam," Sofie said. "I said we might need to escape before too much longer. He suggested a few drinks at Dragon Mead."

"Yes, *please*," I said. "That would be great. I've only been here two hours, and I'm getting a headache already."

"You're out of practice," she said. "The noise barely registers for me."

"What's Dragon Mead?" Thomas asked.

"A bar in Warren. You'll like it. They have a really good selection. And you're allowed to bring in your own food."

"I'm up for it. I could go for a beer."

I smiled at him. "You've been a very good sport. Only a few more hours."

"I guess I can manage," he said, sighing dramatically. "If Sofie will let me kiss you again, I might not even complain."

"Screw Sofie," I said, leaning across the table. "You'll kiss me when I say so."

As his laughing mouth closed over mine, I heard my cousin sigh. "This is so totally unfair."

***

Christmas Eve was, if possible, even crazier than the first day. We would all be attending Mass together that evening, followed by a veritable feast at Sofia's parents' house. I was enlisted in the kitchen for most of the day, cooking with my sisters and mom. Thomas had tried to help, but my brothers had insisted he join them in the living room and watch soccer on television instead. "It's okay," I whispered. "Our family is really patriarchal when it comes to this kind of thing. Boys are never in the kitchen. Go watch the footie."

"I don't like it," he said, frowning at me. "Letting you work while I relax."

"You can make it up to me by cooking me a nice meal when we get back. Go on."

He kissed me lightly before following Samuel out to the living room. As he went, I caught sight of Maria staring at me from across the table. I ignored her.

Before too long, I could hear Thomas's voice rising above the rest of the boys. "Bloody awful call! He's offside!"

I smiled and went back to layering tortillas and mole sauce for the enchiladas.

"Will Thomas mind going to church with us, Lizzie?" my mom asked.

"No, of course not. Why would he mind?"

"Well, he's not Catholic, is he dear?"

I looked heavenward, ordering myself not to laugh. I knew she'd been dying to ask that question since I first mentioned we were dating. "No, Mama, he's not. But the Church of England isn't all that different, you know. They even have confession."

"They don't honor the Pope," Maria said, a bite to her voice. "Don't tell me that's the same."

I sighed. "You're right. They don't. But Thomas won't be uncomfortable, Mama." I shot a look at Maria. "Thank you for thinking of him. That was polite of you."

"You're welcome, dear. I just wouldn't want him to feel out of place."

"He goes to Mass with me every week, Mama."

That got everyone's attention. "He does?" Laura asked, eyebrows raised.

I nodded. Partly at my mother's urging, I had found a local church that I liked my second week in London. I found my weekly attendance helped me feel connected to home and my family. Thomas joining me most weeks had been a bonus. "He does. He knows it's important to me, and he wants to share it with me. I think it's sweet."

"It's very sweet," my mother said. "It also sounds serious." Her eyes flitted over to the living room, something resembling concern passing across them. I noticed that Maria and Laura were also looking at me strangely, almost as if they were seeing me for the first time.

I sighed. "Did you guys not realize it was serious? Did you think I was bringing home some guy I barely knew?"

"Of course not, dear," my mother said. She shot a warning glance at her two oldest daughters. "It's lovely that he goes to Mass with you. It makes me feel better to know you're not going alone. I'll have to thank him."

As was often the case, my mother used her implicit kindness and good manners to smooth over a slightly awkward situation. She quickly changed the subject to Laura's ongoing kitchen remodel. But I couldn't shake the feeling that Maria was still watching me with a calculating look in her eyes.

***

It was wonderful to attend Mass back in my own church. I hadn't realized how much I missed the building, with its gorgeous stained-glass windows and yellow stone walls. It gave me a little thrill to have Thomas there with me in the family pew. And when the priest called forward all those wishing to take communion, I didn't think twice about Thomas following me. As we returned to the pew, I caught sight of Maria's outraged face. I tried to put it out of my mind; Maria was very rigid in her spiritual beliefs. A non-Catholic taking communion at Mass was apparently too much for her.

Well, she can just deal with it, I thought to myself. Thomas was every bit as eligible to take the sacrament as anyone else in the room. If she thought I was about to tell him to wait alone in the pew, she had a lot more to learn about me than she realized.

After Mass, we all gathered at Sofia's house. It was all just as I remembered it, the place full of family and love. We sang carols, gorged ourselves on the food we'd spent so long preparing, and passed presents. My parents bought me a beautiful red wool coat. "I thought it looked like the kind of thing a girl might wear in the big city," my mom told me when I went to hug them.

"It's perfect," I said, kissing her cheek and then my father's. "I love it."

Thomas and I had agreed to give each other our presents in private when we were back in London, so I was surprised when my uncle pulled out a gift from him. But it wasn't for me; it was for my mother.

"Thomas," she said, putting a hand to her heart. "You shouldn't have!"

"I wanted to say thank you for welcoming me," he said, in his easy way. I smiled at him, touched.

"I didn't know you'd done that," I said, but his eyes were on my mother. I turned my attention to her and watched as she pulled the wrapping paper off a leather bound book.

I realized what it was before she even read the title. "*Thomas*," I whispered.

"This is beautiful," my mother said, looking up at him. "Did you know *Pride and Prejudice* was my favorite book?"

"Lizzie mentioned it." He shot me a quick grin.

"I named her for Elizabeth Bennet, you know." My mom smiled at me. "This is so special. What a lovely idea for a gift."

"Lizzie and I actually saw that together on our first date. She held it for so long, I thought it would attach to her fingers."

"And then told you it was too much," I reminded him, quietly so she couldn't hear.

"You said I couldn't buy it for you," he said. "You said nothing about buying it for your mother."

I shook my head at him, but he had returned his attention to her. She flipped open the front cover. "Is this really that old?" she asked, covering her mouth.

"It is."

She looked up at him, her eyes shining. "Well, this is a treasure. Come here so I can thank you properly." He went over to where she sat on the couch, and I watched as she wrapped her arms around him, kissing his cheek. She said something in his ear, too quietly for me to hear, and I saw him nod. She kissed him once more before releasing him. She held the book close to her chest for the rest of the night.

"Are you okay?" he asked when he had joined me on the love seat again.

"I'm better than okay. That was a beautiful thing you did."

"I was scared you might be mad."

I rested my head on his shoulder and brought a hand up to his face. Patting his cheek, I shook my head. "Of course I'm not mad. What an amazing present. You made her very happy. Thank you."

"You're welcome, Lizzie."

***

Compared with the craziness of the first few days, Christmas morning was downright relaxing. It was only our immediate family—a big enough group by most standards—for most of the day. In the evening, Sophia's family joined us for leftovers, the kids running around with their new toys while the adults lazily lounged around, eating and drinking.

Our trip went too fast. It seemed like every day there was more family to visit with, more get-togethers to attend. Sofie and I did our best to show Thomas some of our old haunts, but more often than not, we were busy shuttling from one aunt's house to another. When our departure date arrived, I was completely worn out. "I'm going to need a vacation from this vacation," I told Thomas as we pulled our bags downstairs.

"You still have a week until you're back in school," he reminded me. "And I don't have to do any promo work for *Hostile* for another week. We'll have plenty of time to veg out."

I could hardly believe we had managed to make it through the entire trip without my family putting on some major drama. Sure, my dad and Carlos had been all but nonexistent for most of our visit, but at least they hadn't been rude. Laura and Samuel had been downright nice to both of us. And Matias had managed to only tease me a few times.

I should have known it was too good to last. As Thomas went to the living room to say his goodbyes to Sofia's family, Maria grabbed me by the elbow and pulled me into the mudroom.

"Ow," I said, pulling my arm away. "What's your problem?"

"We need to talk." She shut the door to the kitchen and looked at me.

"So talk, Maria."

"You're in love with this boy," she said, her eyes narrowed as she searched my face. It was not a question.

I raised my chin and kept my gaze steady on her. She'd been nothing short of terrible to me the entire time I'd been here. I might have put up with it a year ago, but not anymore. I was done being intimidated by her, older sister or not. "I am."

She shook her head. "Lizzie, give me a break." She sounded slightly disgusted. "What do you expect to come from this?"

"I don't know." It was the truth. I had no idea what would happen to Thomas and me a month from now, let alone in the future. "All I know is that I love him and I have the chance to be with him now. I'm not giving that up."

"You'll get hurt. You know you will. I know you haven't had boyfriends before, and you're probably very taken with the romanticism of all this, but you need to be smart here. You're moving home soon. And he'll still be there. What then?"

"I don't know," I repeated. I was surprised by how calm I felt. Usually the mere thought of what would happen to Thomas and me after I left London was enough to make me worried sick. But not today. "I guess if it's meant to be, it will be."

"You cannot be serious," she said, her voice dismissive. "You sound like a child. How could it possibly work out? He'll go off and be some Hollywood big-shot and you'll be *here*."

"I'm fine with that, Maria," I said, and for the first time I believed it. "I'm fine taking the chance. It's worth it to me. He's worth it to me."

"Lizzie—"

"No, I don't want to hear it. I love him, okay? He makes me happy, Maria. Happier than I've ever been before. And whether that ends in five months or five days, it was still worth it to me to give it a shot."

She shook her head, and it couldn't have been more clear that she thought I was being ridiculous. "Fine, have your fun with him. Just so long as you know it will end, Lizzie. That much is inevitable. The only question is how much time you'll have invested in something that was doomed from the start."

She turned away from me without so much as a goodbye. I felt shocked and wounded. Not so much by her words, but by the way she could be so hurtful, so completely dismissive of me. She thought she knew what was best for me, she always had. And she had zero confidence in my ability to handle things for myself.

I felt tears sting my eyes and blinked rapidly as I saw Thomas and my mother enter the kitchen through the open mudroom door. I plastered on a smile and slipped into the kitchen to join them, determined not to let Maria ruin the last moments I had with my mom.

But as Thomas and I gave our final hugs to my tearful mother and went out to join Sam in the car, I couldn't shake the things she had said to me. Or the fact that she hadn't even said goodbye.

CHAPTER EIGHTEEN

The week after we arrived back in London was one of my favorite times I had with Thomas in all of the months we had known each other. Callie was home in Michigan until just before classes started, so we took the opportunity to hole up in his flat with take-out and movies. We emerged only to take walks in the light snowfall in Hyde Park or take refuge in our favorite cozy pub. For the most part, it was just the two of us, with no distractions and no one to judge us. On New Year's Eve we joined Charlie and the rest at a swanky party at some West End hotel. It was fun to get dressed up and sip champagne with his friends, but my favorite part of the night was returning to his flat and collapsing in front of a roaring fire.

January meant Callie's return and the start of our new term at school. It also meant we were getting close to the premiere of Thomas's new movie, set to debut mid-February.

It was the biggest thing he had done outside of the *Darkness* franchise. Thomas had been in several independent films, but this was the first time he would be the unequivocal star. He'd been excited about the film's release since I first met him, but now I started to detect a healthy dose of nerves mixed in. He wanted this film to succeed.

I was slightly relieved to learn that there wouldn't be a huge premiere for the film. I was already dreading the upcoming *Darkness* premiere, though Thomas assured me I didn't have to go if I didn't want to. *Hostile* was much more low-key. There was a viewing party at a nice restaurant in town, with a modest amount of press there to cover it. Meghan and Carter joined us for the viewing, and I sat with them and watched as Thomas gave a few interviews and posed for pictures with the cast. Then they turned down the lights, and I finally got to see the movie Thomas was so excited about.

He had every reason to be. It was fantastic. One of the best films I could remember seeing. Of course I was biased, but I had a feeling Thomas would be getting rave reviews for the performance. Meghan and Carter agreed with me so vehemently that I knew they really meant it. Our praise did little to ease his nerves; as the official release date, and the release of the critical reviews, drew near, he seemed to get more anxious, if anything.

The morning of the *Hostile* release dawned snowy and cold. I rolled over in bed, reaching out for Thomas, and was surprised to find his side of the bed empty. It was unusual for him to get up without me.

I climbed out of bed and pulled on my bathrobe. "Thomas?" I called. No answer. I used the bathroom and brushed my teeth before heading off in search of him. The smell of breakfast cooking led me to the kitchen. I paused, leaning in the doorway, admiring the view of Thomas cooking, barefoot in sweats and a T-shirt. There was something so appealing about him without shoes or socks, when he was casual and comfortable at home.

I wondered how long he had been up, what had roused him so early. Surely it wasn't a coincidence that he was up early the morning of the film's release, the morning we'd find his movie reviewed in the paper.

"Scale of one to ten; how nervous are you?"

Thomas turned away from the stove. "Morning, gorgeous." He winked at me before redirecting his attention back to the eggs he was scrambling. "And I don't get nervous."

I snorted. "Okay, tough guy."

"I'm serious." He turned off the stove and portioned the eggs out onto two plates. "Toast?"

"Yes, please." I pushed off from the doorjamb and took my seat at his kitchen table. "So you're not nervous about this review at all? Not even a little, tiny bit?"

"Not even a little, tiny bit." Thomas joined me at the table, presenting my plate with a flourish. "For the lady."

"Thanks." I watched him carefully as he dug into his meal, piling his eggs up on his toast. I was not fooled. He met my gaze.

"What?"

"Oh, nothing. Just marveling at how cool and collected you are. I really admire you, you know. Not even worrying about the fact that one of the major paper in Great Britain is reviewing your film today. The first film you've ever had to carry on your own. Your first leading role. I think it's great that you can sit there, so calm and collected, not even considering the fact that all over the country, thousands, maybe even millions of people are opening their paper—"

"Okay, I'm terrified!" Thomas cried, throwing his hands up. "You happy now? I've never been so scared in my entire life."

I smirked at him. "That's what I thought."

Thomas put his head in his hands. "Blimey, Lizzie. I can't even feel my legs. It's like everything has disappeared below the knees."

"You poor thing," I said, getting up and joining him on his side of the table. He pulled me onto his lap, and I curled up there, my head against his chest. "Should I tell you again how brilliant you were?"

He sighed and I could feel his chest tremble slightly. Below my cheek, his heart was beating fast.

"You have to think that. What if he doesn't?"

"Then he doesn't know what he's talking about."

Thomas laughed. "He's only the most respected film critic in Britain."

"Then he should know good acting when he sees it. And you were good." I gave him a little squeeze. "Now that we've dropped the charade, can we please go down to the corner and get a paper?"

He groaned. "I liked the charade so much better."

"Come on," I said. "Eat your eggs so we can go."

"I can't eat these." He pushed the plate away. "I was trying to convince myself I could, but I know I can't."

"Let's just run and get the paper," I said, pulling away so I could look into his eyes. "Get it over with, one way or another. Then we can go on with our day."

"Do you really think it will be okay?" he asked, his voice soft. He looked so scared, so vulnerable looking up at me. I had rarely seen Thomas anything other than collected, affable. I felt a wave of affection for him and kissed his forehead.

"I really, really think it will."

Once we were up, Thomas was in a hurry, insisting we pull our jackets over our sweats instead of rooting around for clean clothes. We'd made several runs to the newsagent in similar states of undress over the last few months, pretty much every time we ran out of chocolate and wine (for me) or beer and cheesy Wotsits (for him). Pulling our boots and hats on, we hurried out into the cold.

"Come on," I said, grabbing his hand and starting to run. I felt excited and nervous at the same time. I was sure the review would be good—you'd have to be crazy to look at

Thomas's work and not be impressed. But what if the reviewer *was* crazy? Or bitter, or jealous, or—

We made it to the newsagent's and skidded inside, both laughing and out of breath from the run. Thomas had a sprinkling of snow on his hat, his cheeks bright from the cold. In his blue wool hat, knitted by his mother years ago, he looked younger than usual. Without thinking, I reached up and grabbed his face, kissing him hard on the mouth.

"What was that for?" he asked, smiling down at me. His eyes were bright and twinkling.

"For luck," I said, but I wasn't sure if that was quite it. I felt something, in that moment. Some kind of shift or premonition. It wasn't a bad feeling, not exactly. But somehow I knew something was about to change.

We found the paper and paid for it, appraising each other over the counter. "Here or home?" I asked.

"Home," he said. "Let's go home."

Then we were running again, back through the snow, which was coming down harder than before. I held the paper to my chest under my folded arms, trying to block the flakes from wetting it.

Inside, we threw off our coats. By now the suspense was absolutely killing me, and I ripped the paper open without preamble. "Do you want to look first?" I asked once I'd reached the entertainment section. "Or should I?"

"You do it." His eyes were wide, scared.

I pulled out the section, wondering what page the review would be on.

As it turned out, I didn't need to look for it. Splashed across the front of the section was a one-word headline.

Triumph!

And below that, smiling out at me, was a picture of Thomas.

CHAPTER NINETEEN

Whirlwind. That's the word that comes to mind when I look back at those weeks following the release of *Hostile*. Things changed so quickly, I had trouble catching my breath sometimes.

No sooner had we finished reading the review than the phone calls started coming in. First was Thomas's mother. She too had been up first thing in the morning waiting for the review. She was crying so hard, we could barely understand her. Next came his agent, yelling into the phone as Thomas stared at me, wide-eyed. While he talked, Callie called my cell phone, screaming about how famous Thomas was about to become. "Britain's next big star," she read from the paper. "A tour de force, breakout performance."

"I've read it, Cal," I said, looking over at Thomas. He was still on with his agent, his expression every bit as bewildered as it had been when he first saw the headline. *He's in shock*, I thought. *Hell, I'm in shock.*

"Did you read the part where the reviewer said he was a shoe-in for a BAFTA? That's like, the British Oscars, Lizzie!"

Then the press started. Thomas started getting calls that very morning, reporters looking for his reaction, requesting interviews, looking for back story. At first, he directed everyone to his agent. Eventually, we took the phone off the hook.

"This is crazy," he told me, wide-eyed. "I was so not expecting anything like this."

"Me either," I admitted. I had assumed the film would be well reviewed, and had even assumed Thomas would be singled out for his performance. But this…this was crazy.

We spent the rest of the day holed up in the apartment, ordering take-out and watching movies. I had thought Thomas would be distracted, his mind on the explosion taking place in his career, but he wasn't. If anything, he seemed overly interested in the film we watched, eager to talk about anything besides the review while we ate, holding me extra close on the couch.

I'm not the only thing he's trying to hold onto, I realized. *He's trying to hold onto his old life. Things are going to change.*

They did change, and quickly. Within days, more stories had been written about Thomas, Britain's new It Boy. People started to recognize him when he was out and about. When he was asked for his autograph, waiting with me for the number eight bus, we both burst into giggles over how surreal it all was. I had a shock the first time I realized paparazzi were following us, two of them snapping pictures of us outside Cocina.

"Guess we'll need to find a new place to eat tomorrow," Thomas said, trying to laugh it off. But I could tell it freaked him out. We stopped taking the bus after that, Thomas insisting on driving every time we went out together. He could justify using the valet now. The next time I went to his apartment there was a newly hired doorman to replace the old buzzer system.

I tried to keep a level head about it all. I had always known he was a fantastic actor and ridiculously handsome.

It had only been a matter of time before everyone else figured that out, too. His agent was booking him on numerous talk shows, and there was talk about a US release in a few weeks, with Thomas and the cast being flown over to the States for a New York premiere and press junket. I could tell Thomas was struggling with the newfound notoriety. His mood seemed to shift from incredulous—"Can you imagine me, on Letterman? What the hell would I have to say?"—to pensive. I did my best to keep the atmosphere light, wanting his time with me, at least, to be as stress-free as possible.

My resolve was shaken the first time I ended up on a gossip site.

It was early March, about two weeks after the *Hostile* release, and I was sitting in my Twentieth Century lit class when I noticed Meredith acting strangely—she kept glancing back at me, a smirk on her face, before whispering to Tonya, sitting next to her.

I felt a blush creep up my cheeks, always uncomfortable with the idea that people were talking about me. While Meredith and I got along okay in the group setting, we had never been particularly close, and from the looks she was giving me, her whispered conversation with Tonya couldn't possibly be a complimentary one.

By break, I decided I'd had enough. "What's your problem?" I asked her, my voice loud, trying not to care that half the class had stopped in the act of gathering their things to stare at me.

She flashed me a grin that did not meet her eyes. "Sweetie, I had no idea you were so famous."

"What are you talking about?"

"Haven't you seen it?" Her face the picture of innocence, she held up her phone. I couldn't see the screen from where I was, but I felt my stomach drop all the same.

"Seen what?"

"You're all over the Internet. I can't believe you didn't know it." She gave me one last smirk before grabbing her purse and flouncing out into the hall, Tonya behind her.

My hands shaking, I reached for my phone and opened the web browser. I stared at the phone for a moment, realizing I had no clue what the addresses were of the gossip sites. *Where's Callie when you need her?* I thought, pulling open a search engine. I typed in my name and gasped as the screen immediately filled with links. Most of the sites looked British, but I was pretty sure I recognized at least one or two from home. I clicked on the link for a site called *Smoke*. As the page loaded, I started to feel faint. It was a picture of me walking into Harrods. It was from the previous Monday; I could tell because I was wearing my red coat. I had popped in to grab a box of Callie's favorite chocolates, a feel-better present since she'd been suffering from a cold. The headline read, "Harper's Cinderella Sweetie."

"Oh no," I whispered, quickly skimming the blurb.

Thomas Harper, star of the surprise smash success Hostile, *is just as princely off camera as on. Sources tell us his girlfriend of several months, Elizabeth Medina, has been enjoying the perks of being connected to a movie star. Plucked from obscurity by Harper, Elizabeth's background has always been much more drab than fab. Studying in London on a scholarship for disadvantaged and minority youth, the American, by all accounts, comes from a much more working-class background than she has been enjoying as the girlfriend of one of Britain's most promising stars. Lucky Elizabeth has been seen around town dining at the Ivy, shopping at Harrods, and getting pampered at Sky Spa. All on Harper's dime, no doubt. Hopefully Elizabeth doesn't grow too accustomed to her flash lifestyle. Sources tell us her scholarship runs out in June.*

I stood, feeling sick to my stomach, and fumbled for my things. "Lizzie?" my classmate Heather asked, sounding concerned. "Are you okay?"

"I have to go," I said, throwing my bag over my shoulder.

"But we're only halfway through."

"Tell him I'm sick. Or I had an emergency. I don't care."

I fled the room, praying I didn't run into Meredith in the hall. All I could think about was getting back to the apartment. My name had shown up in so many links. Were they all like that? What else were people saying about me? The bus stop was crowded. Was it just my imagination, or were people turning to look at me as I approached? Feeling paranoid, I skirted past the crowd and made my way to the nearest underground station instead. The tube would be crowded with tourists and commuters—people in too much of a rush to pay attention to me.

"Elizabeth! Oy, Lizzie!" I spun around and saw a man approaching me. He was dressed in a black leather jacket and blue baseball cap. I paused for a moment, wondering if I knew him from somewhere, when I noticed a camera slung around his neck. "How long have you been seeing Thomas Harper?" he called. "Where'd you meet?"

Screw the Underground, I thought to myself, and turned back to the road, throwing my arm up for a taxi.

"Lizzie, wait," the man called, holding up his camera. "Just one quote. Is Thomas as nice in person as he seems on screen? What's it like dating a celebrity?"

"Come on, come on," I muttered, watching as a black cab blessedly appeared down the street. My heart was pounding and I felt close to tears. People all around were stopping to stare, and I heard the incessant click-click-click as the photographer snapped my picture.

Thank God, I thought, as the taxi stopped in front of me. I pulled open the door and jumped in as quickly as I could. The photographer had reached the curb by now and was bending toward me, taking my picture through the window. "Kentish Town," I told the driver. "Quickly, please."

"You famous or something?" the cabbie asked, pulling out into traffic and leaving the photographer behind. I breathed a sigh of relief, and brought my shaking hands to my head. What the hell was that?

"You okay, love?"

"I'm fine," I said. No sooner were the words out of my mouth did I realize that I was about to start crying. "I'm fine," I whispered, more to myself now, and silently urged the taxi to go faster, desperate to be back in my apartment, where I was safe.

***

It was worse than I had even feared. An hour later, I was pretty sure I had finally seen every link. Not many had been as mean spirited as the *Smoke* article. Most of them simply pointed out that Thomas and I were dating and gave some surprisingly accurate details of our relationship. But the sheer number of pictures of me was what I found shocking. There were at least a dozen different shots. Most were of me with Thomas, holding hands, entering restaurants, getting out of his car. The scary ones were the ones when I had been alone. Shopping, picking up a paper at the newsagent's, going to class. I hadn't even been aware someone was photographing me.

I heard the front door bang open and Callie's voice. "Lizzie? You here?"

"Back here," I called. A moment later, she was in my room. At the sight of me on the computer, she sighed.

"You've seen it, then."

My face crumbled. "Oh, Lizzie," Callie cried, crossing to the room and pulling me into her arms just before my tears started to fall. "It's going to be okay," she said, rubbing my back. "They'll lose interest, you know they will."

"Someone followed me out of class," I managed to croak past my tears. "He was taking my picture while I got a cab."

"It's just a story right now because it's all so new. It will go away."

"What if it doesn't? I'm all over the Internet, Cal." I pulled back to point at the screen. "My family is going to see this."

"Most of it is pretty complimentary," she said. "*Hello* called you an American Beauty."

"You've read all this crap?"

She looked bashful. "I was bored in poetry. Someone mentioned that they saw you online, so I kind of did some searching on my phone."

"You and Meredith both," I muttered. I explained how Meredith had been so bitchy and Callie's eyes narrowed.

"She's just a jealous cow," she said.

"I thought she was my friend. Is everyone going to treat me like that now?"

"No," Callie said firmly. "And if they do, I'll kick their ass."

"Did you see the one where they called me a gold-digger?"

Callie grimaced. "They don't know what they're talking about."

"Yeah, but a million strangers probably won't be as fair-minded as you."

"Screw 'em," Callie said. "Seriously, why do you care what people think?"

"Because it's out there now, Callie. Out there for everyone to see. My family. Future employers. Everyone."

"I'm making you some tea," she said. "You need to get off that thing right now. Come on." She tugged my arm, pulling me to my feet, and gently pushed me down the hall to the kitchen.

Callie deposited me in a chair and pushed a sheet of paper towel into my hand. As I wiped my face and blew my nose, she busied herself with the kettle.

"Have you talked to Thomas yet?"

I shook my head. "I'm supposed to be in class for another few minutes. I ditched at break."

"Good for you," she said. "I mean, not that I'm happy for the reason, but I'm proud of you for being a little rebellious."

A moment later, at exactly one p.m., the time my class was scheduled to end, my phone rang loudly from the living room. Thomas.

"Speak of the devil," Callie muttered as I jumped up to retrieve it.

"Hey, babe," he said. Was I imagining it, or was there an undercurrent of anger in his voice. Not waiting for me to answer, he continued, "Look, I'm going to send a car for you. They should be waiting right outside the building. They'll bring you to my place. I'll explain it all when you get—"

"Thomas," I interrupted. "I'm not in class. I'm home already."

He paused. "You're home? I thought your class went to one. Why are you home?"

I was again overcome with the urge to cry. "I left class early."

For a moment, there was silence on the other end of the phone. "You've seen it, haven't you?"

I nodded, forgetting for a moment that he couldn't see me. "Yeah," I whispered.

"I'm on my way," he said, hanging up before I could argue.

CHAPTER TWENTY

I had never seen Thomas so angry. He couldn't sit still, pacing back and forth across the carpet as I got ready to leave. His agent, Heidi, was waiting for us at his apartment, some new PR person from the firm with her. Thomas was eager to leave, to sit down with them and hammer out some kind of plan for dealing with the press. I wasn't sure what he thought we could accomplish. If I had learned anything about the media during my time in London, it was that the British tabloids were merciless.

"I'm almost ready," I said, peering at myself in the mirror. When Thomas arrived, he had held me close for a moment, demanding to know if I was alright. I assured him that I was fine, but Callie snorted from the kitchen.

"A photographer followed her from class," she told him. "Chased her right into her cab."

I glared at her as his arms tightened around me. He was clearly already worked up enough over all of this. The last thing he needed was to hear more of the gory details.

"Why don't you go wash your face and get cleaned up," he had said, his voice tight. "Then we can go meet Heidi."

I had washed my face and carefully reapplied my makeup. If there were any photographers out there, the last thing I wanted was for them to see me with red-rimmed eyes. The thought of photographers had sent another chill through me and had me rushing to my closet for accessories. A scarf around my neck covered part of my face, if I kept my head down like this. Glasses would help, too. I pulled a few hats off the top shelf and tried them each on, feeling silly.

"What are you doing?" Thomas asked, looking up from his phone. He was sitting on my bed, furiously texting someone. From the look on his face, the person on the other end was getting an eyeful.

"Trying to cover up," I muttered, pulling the Detroit Tigers baseball cap down low over my eyes.

"There's a car downstairs," he told me, smiling ruefully. "We'll be in and out."

"You didn't drive?"

He shook his head. "Not today."

Over at his apartment, Heidi introduced us to a severe-looking woman named Jade. Jade was dressed all in black, her dark hair pulled so tightly back that I was sure her skull must ache. "This is the girlfriend?" she asked, peering at me over her black plastic-rimmed glasses.

"This is Lizzie," Thomas said, visibly bristling. "And she's had a shit day."

"I'm so sorry, Lizzie," Heidi said, taking my hand. "We should have been better prepared for this."

"Yeah, you should have," Thomas snarled. I realized that much of his anger was directed at Heidi. This, apparently, was the kind of thing he thought they should have given us warning of.

"We usually know when a story is going to print," she went on apologetically. "We'll get a call from the paper, asking for comment."

"What happened today?" I asked. Thomas made a scathing noise beside me.

"We've actually been getting calls on you for a while now," Heidi said, her eyes flickering to him before settling back on me. I wondered if any of this was a surprise to him. "Thomas has directed us to not give comments—"

"Because it's none of their bloody business," he snarled.

"Quite right," she agreed. "Unfortunately, they seem to have gotten another source. When they called for comment on this story, the, uh, staff member who answered assumed it was another generic request. We weren't alerted of the call."

From the way she said the words "staff member" and the way Thomas's hand clenched on mine when she did so, I wondered if this person was still employed by the agency.

"Anyhow," she went on, "if we would have had the warning, we could have briefed you ahead of time. I'm truly sorry you had to find out the way you did. And I'm sorry about the photographer at your school. We've already spoken to the dean—"

"You talked to my dean?"

"Yes, we have. We're working with them to set up better security measures for you."

I felt like my head was spinning. Security measures? Meetings with PR staff? Articles about me in the newspaper? None of it felt real.

"Jade is here to talk with you about ways to deal with the intrusion," Heidi said, gesturing at her colleague to take over.

"People you know will start to get calls," she said, her voice strangely dispassionate. I disliked her immediately, and was pretty sure Thomas felt the same. "Your roommate, for sure. Other classmates. It's unlikely they will call your family, the US press isn't as interested yet. But once *Darkness* premieres, if the two of you are still together, the US market will come into play as well."

"What do you mean, if?" Thomas snarled.

"Well, that's something we should discuss," Jade said, oblivious to the dangerous tone of his voice. "The best way to minimize press is to give them little to talk about. It is wise not to get into public rows with each other. No screaming matching at Sainsbury. Public displays of affection are another attention grabber. Lizzie, it's important that you always dress in a way that is conscious of the fact that you may be photographed."

I was so flabbergasted at the idea of Thomas and me in a screaming match anywhere, let alone while at the grocery store, that her last words took a minute to sink in.

"What do you mean?" I asked, confused. "About the clothes?"

"You need to wear knickers," she clarified, her voice still flat. "Everyday. I can't tell you how many photographers will jump at the chance to take a shot of you getting out of a car without your bits covered up."

Thomas jumped up from the couch and turned on Heidi. "I thought you said this would be helpful?" he cried, his voice as near a shout as I had ever heard.

I tugged on his hand, pulling him back to the couch. "It's fine." I rubbed his knuckles, feeling how tense he was. "It's fine," I said again, before turning to Jade. "We don't have to worry about that one. I, uh, always wear knickers."

***

Heidi and Jade talked to us for more than an hour. I was given instructions on how to react to press, how to conduct myself in public, what to do if anyone called or shoved a microphone in my face. By the time they left, I was exhausted.

"What should we do for dinner?" Thomas asked, coming into the kitchen to find me leaning against the counter. "Take-out?"

"I'm not too hungry. I'm actually pretty tired."

"I'll make you a sandwich. You should eat something. Then we can go to bed."

I cleared my throat. "I kind of want to just go home."

His eyes immediately widened, as if in fear.

"Callie texted me that she had movies and ice-cream. It sounds kind of perfect, you know? Just a...a normal night."

"You think you can't have a normal night with me?" he asked, a note of fear definitely in his voice.

"No, Thomas, of course not. It's just been a really weird day. And there are photographers downstairs, and I just...I just want to put on my PJs and chill out."

Suddenly he was next to me, his arms around me tight. "Don't let this change anything, Lizzie, please," he said against my ear. He sounded desperate, almost wild. "Don't...don't leave me, please."

"Why would you think I would leave you?" I cried, struggling to pull away so I could look at his face. When he didn't let go, I wrapped my arms around him, and he squeezed me back all the tighter. "Thomas, why would you think I would leave you?"

"You always said you didn't want this," he whispered, his voice hoarse. "I know it freaks you out, the fame stuff. I know you don't want any part of it. But it's not me, Lizzie, you have to know that. I'm still the same."

"Of course you are," I murmured. "Babe, I know that."

"You almost left me once because you thought our lives were too different. And that was before anyone even knew who I was."

"It was before *I* knew who you were," I said, squeezing him harder. "Before I loved you. Do you think I could leave you now? Just because some idiot took my picture? Come on, babe. You know I wouldn't do that."

He let out a shaky breath and pulled away, his eyes searching mine. "Promise?"

"Of course I promise."

"Okay." He bent and kissed me, his lips almost desperate against mine. He pulled back and stared into my eyes. "I'm so sorry about all of this."

"It's not your fault," I said. "And it's not really that big of a deal."

"Please stay here tonight," he said. "I just...I want you close. I'll know you're safe here."

"I'm safe at my flat."

"I have a doorman, Lizzie," he said. "Your buzzer doesn't even work. Something we'll be fixing, by the way."

He had a point. I shuddered at the idea of a photographer getting upstairs to our front door.

"I can send a car for Callie," he said, knowing I was close to giving in. "She can bring the ice cream and movies here."

"Okay," I said, feeling suddenly tired. "That sounds fine."

CHAPTER TWENTY-ONE

I kept thinking there would be a moment when things calmed down, but it never happened. In some ways, life went back to normal. I went to school and Thomas worked on his next film. We went to trivia on Wednesday nights and ate in our favorite restaurants with his friends and Callie. But now there was the added element of constant media attention. It was a regular occurrence to see photographers stationed outside Thomas's flat. Callie found mention of him online almost every day. She called me one morning, laughing hysterically, and directed me to the very first Thomas Harper fan page.

That was a highlight for me. I told her we needed to alert Thomas. We called Charlie first, of course, knowing he would want to take screen caps with which to torture his friend in their old age. For the next several weeks, we all greeted Thomas by the tagline of the site, shouting, "the Seeeeexiest Man in Bayswater!" whenever we saw him, in public or private. He got pissed after a week or so, but Charlie assured us he secretly liked it.

Mr. Idoni couldn't have been more pleased with the situation. His business was suddenly booming, a result of one of the paper's letting my address slip. I was sure a number of the new, regular female patrons were far more eager to catch sight of Thomas than enjoy Mrs. Idoni's famous gnocchi. But the results for the Idonis were the same. He happily fixed the buzzer and even installed an iron fence on our entrance for more security.

As the release of the new *Darkness* movie approached, Thomas's time became more valuable. He was being sent out on more promotions than he was used to. He said it was because his role got bigger in this film, but I had a feeling they were trying to capitalize on his individual success. Either way, he was suddenly required to give a lot of interviews and attend a lot of parties with important industry people. Sometimes I went with him, but I found the events pretty boring. I never knew who half the people were, and the industry chatter sounded like Greek to me. Callie begged to take my place, and Thomas brought her to a few dinners, to her very great excitement.

As spring started to take shape around us, one event that I would not be able to skip out on approached. The London premiere for *Darkness Falls* was going to be a huge deal. The studio was making plans for a red carpet event in Leicester Square that was sure to draw the A-list of London celebrity. Heidi sat me down a month before the event to discuss my "role."

"Thomas tells me he isn't sure you'll attend," she said, looking concerned and friendly. I liked Heidi, for the most part, but I often wondered how much of her friendliness was an act and how much was genuine.

"He said it was up to me," I told her.

She nodded thoughtfully. "Of course. He wants you to be comfortable. I wonder, though, what Thomas wants. What would make *him* most comfortable."

It was my turn to frown. "What do you mean?"

"It's a big event for him, you know. The success of *Darkness Falls* will only add to the buzz surrounding him. I can't help but think he'd like to share it with you."

"I hadn't really thought of it that way." Thomas had always made it sound like he despised these kinds of events. I hadn't considered that this one might be different, that it might be something to be enjoyed as opposed to just put up with.

"There's also the matter of your relationship and the press."

I stared at her. "Meaning…"

"Oh, just that the press is very familiar with the two of you as a couple now," she said, laughing as if to show me she thought it was all so silly and cute. "They really got behind the whole Cinderella story. I can't help but think there would be some awkward questions for Thomas on your status were he to attend alone."

I felt color come to my cheeks. How did she not understand how offensive I found the Cinderella storyline? It wasn't just cute copy for me—it was my reputation. I wasn't crazy about being known as the poor little girl Thomas Harper rescued from obscurity.

"In other words," I said, my voice colder now, "you think it will be good for Thomas's press if I'm there to reinforce the story. Maybe I should pull out my old glass slippers…"

Her eyes widened. "Of course not. Oh, Lizzie, I'm so sorry if you thought I meant—"

I held up a hand. "Don't worry about it. I'll talk to Thomas."

I did, at my first chance. "Heidi seems to think I should go to the premiere," I told him. "She thinks you'll get awkward questions if I don't."

He looked confused. "Heidi talked to you? About me?"

"Don't worry about it," I said quickly. Fake or not, she was a great agent, and I didn't want to cause any problems between the two of them. "I just want to know what you think. Do you want me to be there?"

"I'd love it if you were there," he said, surprising me.

"Why didn't you say so before?"

He shrugged. "The thing I want most is for you to be comfortable," he said. "But if you were willing to go, yes, it would be nice for me to have you there."

"This is going to be a big deal for you, isn't it?"

He shrugged, but I could tell he was being modest. "It will certainly be different from any other premiere I've been to."

It wasn't really a decision at that point. "Of course I'll go, Thomas. I'd love to."

"Really?" his whole face lit up, and I was once again struck by my ability to make him happy. "That would be so awesome!"

"I can't really pass up the opportunity to see you in a tux, can I?"

He looked so happy that I wished Heidi had talked to me ages ago. "So, what do I have to do?"

"I guess a dress is a big deal," he said, and my face immediately fell. Crap. I had totally not considered a dress. How in the heck was I going to afford it? "Don't worry!" he said quickly, seeing my expression. "You don't have to buy one. For stuff like this, designers donate dresses for the press."

"The press?"

"You know, the whole, 'who are you wearing' thing."

"Oh," I said, my stomach plummeting even farther. I was going to have to answer questions.

"We'll talk to Heidi. I'm sure she'll be able to arrange it."

In the end, I didn't let Heidi get involved. After mentioning the situation to Meghan, she came up with the perfect solution. She had a friend from university, Lorenzo, who was an emerging fashion designer. Having his work featured on the red carpet would be a major opportunity for him. She brought me to his studio, and I immediately liked him. He was originally from Venezuela, and we had fun speaking only in Spanish to irritate Meghan. He put me in several dresses before we decided on a floor-length trumpet dress with a sweetheart neckline and no straps. It was miles away from anything I'd ever worn before, but I fell in love with it immediately. It made me feel sexy and beautiful, two attributes I was sure would come in handy in the company of so many movie stars.

That night, Thomas called me with the best news about the premiere I'd heard so far. "I got two extra passes. Think Callie wants to go?"

"You're kidding," I said. "She's going to *freak*. Who will her date be?"

"Charlie has expressed interest," he said. "I'm starting to wonder if maybe you were right about his crush."

"So can I tell her?" I asked. "Is it official?"

"It's official," he said. "But let me do it. She's going to owe me for the rest of her life, and I want to see the look on her face when she realizes it."

I laughed, feeling better about the premiere than I had since Heidi brought it up. I had a beautiful dress, and was helping a talented designer in the process. And now my best friend and one of my favorite guys would be joining us. Add to that the memory of how happy Thomas had been when I agreed, and I was actually almost looking forward to it.

CHAPTER TWENTY-TWO

The morning of the premiere, I woke up to the sound of our buzzer ringing endlessly. "Callie," I moaned, banging weakly on the wall to her room. "Get the door."

I'd slept badly the night before, nerves about walking the red carpet keeping me awake. I was pretty sure I was going to trip. Or smudge lipstick on my teeth. What if one of the reporters asked me a question? What if I got separated from Thomas? What if it rained and my hair went all frizzy?

When the buzzing didn't stop, I finally gave up and climbed out of bed, pulling my robe around me as I went to the door. I pressed the button on the speaker. "Yes?"

"Delivery for Miss Elizabeth Medina."

Delivery? I never got packages. Suspecting Thomas might have something to do with it, I buzzed the delivery guy up. Sure enough, he presented me with a huge bouquet of lilies in a cut-glass vase.

"Wow," I said, taking the vase from him. "Thank you."

"Can you just sign here," he said, holding out a clipboard. After I signed he flashed me a quick grin. "Somebody messed up, eh, love?"

"No." I smiled back. "He's just *very* nice."

"Ah, isn't that sweet." He winked at me and turned for the stairs. I brought the flowers inside, burying my face in the blossoms and inhaling. I loved lilies.

I set the vase on the counter and realized there was a rather large envelope taped to the exterior. I felt slightly giddy as I opened it. Thomas knew I was nervous and was trying to make me feel better. What a way to wake up.

The envelope felt thicker than I had expected, and it took me a moment to realize there was more than a card inside. I pulled out a thick piece of creamy stationary. The swirly script informed me that the pass allowed both Miss Medina and Miss Owen access to the Spa Blue at eleven that morning for a full day of pampering.

"What did you do?" I murmured, pulling out the card.

Lizzie,

I hope you slept well. I know you're nervous about tonight, so I thought it'd be nice for you and Callie to spend the day together and get your mind off things. The very nice ladies at the spa will also help the two of you get ready for the evening. Please accept this gift from me. I want you to enjoy your day today. I love you. Thomas.

I grinned. Under normal circumstances, I'd be annoyed that he was spending the money on me, but today I couldn't help but be touched by his kindness. He always seemed to have me in the forefront of his mind. It was so sweet. *Besides*, I thought, *Callie would kill me if I didn't accept.*

I smelled the flowers one more time before I headed back to the hallway.

"Hey, Callie," I called out, unable to wipe the smile from my face. "Wake up, sister. You're never going to believe what we get to do today."

***

"I'm pretty sure I'm going to throw up," I moaned, staring at myself in the mirror on the other side of the room.

My hair was up in a towel, my skin pink and shiny from my facial. I didn't look like myself—I looked raw and scared.

"You are not going to throw up," Callie said firmly. "You are going to be fine. Better than fine. Gorgeous."

"I don't feel very gorgeous."

"That's because we aren't finished with you yet." The nail technician patted my knee then eased my feet down into the basin of warm, soapy water. "How's the temperature?"

"It's fine. Thanks, Angie."

"You girls sit and relax for a minute. I'll be back."

Callie sighed happily and settled back into her chair. "Remind me to kiss your boyfriend tonight. This is amazing."

"I'll do the kissing, thank you."

She laughed, then caught sight of the grimace on my face that had nothing to do with her teasing about kissing Thomas. "Oh, Lizzie, lighten up a little. You're supposed to be relaxing, you know? As in, stop worrying about everything."

"I can't help it, Cal," I moaned. "Every time I think about the press, I feel sick to my stomach." I had a mental flash of the hoard of reporters that I knew I'd be surrounded by in a matter of hours and shuddered.

"You're weird, you know that? Most girls would be thrilled to be in the limelight. People calling your name, taking your picture—"

"Talking about my dress, my shoes, my hair. Wondering why a guy like him is with a girl like me."

"Stop it right there," she said firmly, pointing a recently manicured finger at me. "No one will be thinking that. They'll be awed by your stunning good looks and charm."

I snorted. "When have I ever been charming?"

She shot me a grin. "Good point. Are people ever stunned by slightly awkward and shy?"

"You better watch it, lady," I said. "I can get you uninvited from this little soiree real quick."

"What do you want me to say, Lizzie? You shoot me down when I compliment you and shoot me down when I agree with what you're thinking."

I frowned at her; she had a point. "Sorry," I said quickly, not wanting to seem like a brat. "I just hate the idea of people looking at me and talking about me. Whether they think I'm lame or not."

"You need to learn some self-confidence." She leaned back in the chair and closed her eyes. "The whole point of going to a spa is to make you feel good about yourself. Relax. Enjoy the treatments. Think about how nice your nails look."

I looked down at my own manicure. They did look pretty nice, buffed and shaped into perfection with a light coat of ballet-slipper pink. Nothing too flashy. Callie, on the other hand, had gone for fire-engine red. I looked back and forth between our hands for a moment, thinking that they represented more than just a difference in color preference.

"I should change my nails," I said suddenly.

Callie opened one eye and peered at me. "Please don't tell me you think the pink is too much. There is seriously only so much of your crazy I can take in a day."

"No." I shook my head. "I should go red. Like yours."

That got both her eyes open. "Really?"

"Yeah," I said, feeling sure of myself. "You're right, Callie. I need more self-confidence. They're gonna take my picture whether I want them to or not, right? I may as well go all out. Make a splash."

"Hallelujah!" she cried, raising her hands triumphantly in the air and making me laugh. "She finally sees the light!"

"Do you think they'll mind?"

She snorted. "Sweetie, with what your boy paid for us to be here today, I'm pretty sure you could ask them to change the color of your dress and they'd figure out a way."

I felt a clench in my stomach at her words. I'd been trying hard all day not to think about how much all of this was costing. Callie must have caught sight of my face because she quickly changed the subject.

"You could go for a deeper red," she said holding out her own hands. "Because your dress is so dark. When you go red you just want to make sure to avoid an orangey undertone."

"Got it."

Angie approached us, carrying a basket full of pedicure tools. "Angie," Callie said. "We have finally convinced this girl to get a little wild. You wouldn't mind changing the color of her nails, would you?"

"Not at all." She raised her eyebrows. "Wild, eh? I think a little wild could suit you."

I smiled at her, feeling, for the first time that day, slightly excited about the night ahead.

***

Three hours later, I had been buffed, shined, and polished to within an inch of my life. Callie and I had both had hot-stone massages, mani-pedis, facials, and some weird body wrap involving layers of mud and seaweed that we had been assured would give us an unbelievable glow. The spa staff had served us a lunch of finger sandwiches, salads, and fruit with plenty of green tea. I would have preferred a burger, but I had to admit the lighter lunch helped to settle my stomach. After our treatments, we'd been pushed into salon chairs and descended upon by very thin, very tan men in leather capris pants and artfully ripped black tank tops. They washed, dried, teased, and curled our hair until my scalp ached.

"You have no idea the joy this brings me," Callie said, squinting at me from under a mess of curlers. "To see your hair in something besides a braid."

"Does it look okay?" I asked, trying to resist the urge to run my fingers through it. After my nail polish pronouncement, Callie had insisted that I be kept in the dark for the rest of my transformation.

"I don't want you changing your mind because you get scared," she'd said. "You can see the full effect when you're all done up and pretty." After assuring me she wouldn't let me end up looking like a tramp, I'd agreed.

"It looks better than okay," she said. "You'll love it."

I wasn't quite sold. Hunter, the stylist, had straightened and then re-curled my hair, leaving it to flow freely down my back. "What if it goes frizzy?"

"No frizz," Hunter assured me, leaning in to smooth out a lock by my forehead. "Not with the amount of product I put in there. Trust me."

"Okay," I said, taking a deep breath. "I trust you."

"Look at you," Callie said. "Being all open-minded. You're nice like this; you should try it more often."

I stuck out my tongue at her, earning myself a frown from Hunter. "You're about to get your makeup on. No more tongue."

"There goes your social life," Callie said, making me snort with laughter. When Hunter shook his head in disgust, I laughed even harder.

"You're getting me into trouble," I told Callie when he had flounced away to find more hair spray, shaking his head the whole time. "He already thinks I'm not taking this seriously enough. I heard him tell Chase."

"You've disappointed him by not giving a shit about celebrity and fashion," Callie agreed.

"And because I didn't know what root lifter was," I reminded her.

A moment later, a very short woman with spiky purple hair approached. "Lizzie? I'm here to do your makeup, yeah? Name's Peach."

"Hi," I said, eyeing her bone-white face and black kohl-rimmed eyes skeptically. I hoped she didn't think I wanted to look like her.

"What are we thinking for tonight?" she asked, leaning in to examine my pores.

"Uh," I said, not really sure how to converse with someone whose face was a mere half inch away from mine.

"She's looking for old Hollywood glamour," Callie said. "Smokey eyes, dark red lip. She has a red carpet situation and needs to wow them."

"Red carpet, yeah?" Peach asked, leaning back to smile at me. "That sounds fun. Well, don't worry, Lizzie. I'll fix you right up."

She helped me down from the chair and led me across the room to her station. I looked down at the vast array of jars and pots and tubes of color. "Wow," I said, swallowing hard. "I'm not really sure…"

"Trust me," she urged, pushing on my shoulders gently until my butt hit the chair. "I know what I'm doing."

Half an hour later she was done. Per Callie's instructions, she had me face away from the mirror as she worked. All I could see was a blur of her fingers as she rubbed my skin with cream and foundation, then attacked me with a variety of brushes and some weird metal contraption that I was pretty sure curled my eyelashes.

"You look hot," Callie informed me, nodding her head in approval. She'd joined me over at Peach's station to have her own makeup done by a gorgeous dreadlocked man with a hint of a Caribbean accent. She'd been flirting mercilessly with him ever since she sat down; it was hard to believe that she even registered what my makeup looked like.

"Yeah?" I asked, feeling doubtful. It was scary not seeing what the salon staff was doing to me. I wondered if I would come to regret my spontaneous decision to be less controlling. I took comfort in the fact that Callie looked drop-dead gorgeous. Her blonde hair was pulled up in a loose chignon at the neck, her makeup somehow making her eyes look even more blue than usual. I had a feeling she'd be giving every starlet we saw tonight a run for her money. I was hopeful the salon staff wouldn't mess my look up too much when they were capable of making her look like a goddess. On the other hand, she gave them a heck of a lot more to work with.

"You do," she said, meeting my eyes and smiling. "Promise, Lizzie."

I nodded at her, nervousness over the impending evening hitting me all over again. Callie glanced down at her watch. "We actually should get going. We still need to change."

We thanked our stylists. Hunter handed me a small bottle of hairspray to go in my purse, and instructed me to use it liberally throughout the evening. "If I see pictures of you with frizz tomorrow, I'm going to be very disappointed," he said, but gave me a small smile.

"Miss Medina?"

The receptionist was approaching us, smiling her professional, polite smile. "Your car is outside."

"Our car?"

She looked momentarily confused. "To take you home?"

"There must be a mistake," I said. "We didn't use the valet—we took a cab here."

Her face cleared. "This isn't valet, Mr. Harper sent a car to pick you up."

I looked at Callie, eyebrows raised, and a grin broke out over her face. "Awesome! I've been waiting for that perk ever since you started dating the guy."

I shook my head at her, and followed her out of the spa.

"Hell yeah," Callie said, her smile growing wider when we reached the front door. A sleek silver Jaguar was waiting for us at the curb, a uniformed driver holding the door for us. "Thank you, Thomas!"

I laughed, deciding, for once, to just enjoy the experience. Yes, it was too expensive, and, yes, it was completely unnecessary. But it was a gift, and the look of glee on Callie's face was too happy for me to be a buzz kill.

"It's pretty nice," I said, slipping my arm through hers to hurry down the pavement to the car. I had to admit, it was kind of fun—being all done up arm-in-arm with my best friend, slipping into a sleek chauffeured car to zoom us across the city.

The driver let us out in front of our flat. A few patrons entering the restaurant gave us strange looks as we slipped past them into the side door. I couldn't blame them; we were both dressed in sweats with an inch of makeup on our faces and our hair styled to the nines. We probably looked crazy.

Upstairs, I quickly pulled out my cell phone to text Thomas that we were home. Almost immediately, my phone started to ring in my hands. "Hello?"

"Hey," Thomas said. "How'd it go?"

"It was wonderful. How can I thank you?"

When he spoke again I could hear the smile in his voice. "I just want you to have a nice time tonight. Can you do that for me?"

"Of course," I said. "I miss you, by the way."

He laughed. "Woman, you have no idea." There was a muffled voice in the background and Thomas sighed. "I should go. Apparently I have tied my tie all wrong and will be the shame of the entire studio."

It was my turn to laugh. "You better get on that, then."

"We'll be there in twenty minutes?"

"See you then. Love you."

"Love you, too."

"Twenty minutes, Cal," I called out as I ended the call and headed down to my room. I passed at my roommate's door to peek in. "Classy," I told her. "You should go out like that." She was still wearing her zip-up hoodie, but had peeled off the sweat pants. Clad in her underwear, she was jumping on one leg, struggling to pull up a pair of sheer nylons.

She flipped me off as I continued past, hoping I would remember where my own nylons were. In my room, I found that I needn't have worried. Callie had laid them out on the bed, along with a black stretchy tube thing and a lacy thong. She had also covered my mirror with a towel, presumably while I had been on the phone with Thomas.

"What is this?" I called.

"It's called underwear," she shot back, her voice muffled through the wall. "Or knickers, if you want to be British about it."

"Callie—"

She appeared in my doorway, her nylons pulled up to her waist. "You have to wear a thong, Lizzie," she explained, correctly reading the expression on my face. "Your dress is too tight for your granny panties, you'll have VPL."

"I don't wear granny panties! And what's VPL?"

She raised an eyebrow. "Visible panty line. God. What would you do without me?"

"What about this thing?" I asked, holding up the black stretchy tube.

"It's a shaper. It pulls your belly in and smooths you out."

"It looks like a torture device."

"It's not that bad. I'm wearing one, too." When I didn't look convinced, she folded her arms across her chest. "Just pretend you're Lizzie Bennet, okay? Didn't she wear a corset?"

"Fine," I said, turning away from her. "Now leave me alone so I can get dressed."

CHAPTER TWENTY-THREE

By the time our twenty minutes were nearly up, I was once again in danger of turning into a nervous mess. Callie, clad in a black silk sheath that hugged her everywhere that mattered, helped me pull my zipper up and clasp my necklace. "Ready to see?"

I swallowed. "I guess so."

To my surprise. She pulled on my arm. "Where are we going?"

"My room. I have a full-length mirror. You need the whole effect."

She positioned me in the middle of the room, then moved to shut her door, grinning. "Here goes."

As Callie's door swung shut, the full-length mirror on the back came into view, bringing my image with it. For a moment, I was sure I was looking at a stranger.

My hair hung in a thick, silky curtain around my shoulders. Hunter had created huge, soft waves and had somehow managed to keep it from turning frizzy. My makeup was heavy, but appropriate. I didn't know what Peach had done to make my eyes look like that, but they appeared huge and smoky in my face, my eyelashes longer than I'd ever seen them. The cobalt blue dress that I had so loved in Lorenzo's store looked even better now that my hair was down and my makeup was on.

"Thomas is going to flip," Callie said gleefully. "You look ridiculously hot."

"I...wow. I've never felt like this before."

My friend wrapped her arm around me. "You should feel like this more often. Because you're gorgeous, Lizzie Medina. You have absolutely nothing to worry about tonight, okay? You're going to look as good as the rest of them. Better!"

I felt a lump rise in my throat. What had I done to deserve such a sweet, supportive friend? I wrapped my arms around her, careful not to mess her hair. "I'm so glad you're coming tonight."

"Me, too." She laughed against my shoulder. "Do you think that Charlie will be offended if I try to hook up with Jackson in a coat closet?"

I laughed then froze as we heard the buzzer go. "They're here," I said, pulling back so I could stare at her, wide-eyed.

She placed a hand against her heart. "Do you know, I'm actually a little nervous myself! I feel like Cinderella going to the ball."

I laughed and took her by the elbow. "Let's go, Cindy. Maybe we'll find you a prince of your own."

After buzzing Thomas and Charlie up, Callie and I hurried around the living room gathering our purses and slipping into our shoes. "Lord, please help me to not fall flat on my face," I muttered as I stood and tested my stability in the three-inch heels. "Crap, where's that bottle of hairspray?"

I ran back to my bedroom—or, rather, tottered in the heels—to look for it just as there was a knock on the door. I heard Callie open it behind me as I reached my room. "Here you are," I whispered, grabbing the small bottle from my desk and slipping it into my sparkly clutch. I headed back to the living room to the sounds of the others greeting each other.

"You look smashing, Cal," Thomas was saying as I entered the room. He leaned forward to kiss her cheek, his back to me. I stopped short. Even his back looked gorgeous in a tux.

"Wow, Lizzie," Charlie said, looking at me over Thomas's shoulder. "You look so pretty!"

Thomas turned to face me, his eyes widening slightly. "Wow," he said, swallowing hard. "I mean...wow."

I laughed, surprised that I wasn't feeling shy. He was staring at me intently, looking ever so slightly dazed. Something about his expression—or maybe it was the events of the whole day, from the spa to my conversation with Callie—made me feel brave. Beautiful. Sure of myself. I walked to him and took his hands. "You look sexy as hell, Harper. Nice tux."

His face relaxed and he laughed slightly. "Thank you. Speaking of sexy..." he leaned down, brushing aside my hair so he could kiss the base of my neck, sending shivers up and down my arms. He pulled back slightly to whisper in my ear, "You look amazing, Lizzie."

"What about me?" Charlie called from the door. "Isn't anyone going to say how sexy I am?"

I grinned up at Thomas before turning to Charlie. "Hey, Charlie, has anyone told you how adorable you look in that tux?"

He scrunch up his nose at me. "Adorable? Don't you mean hot?"

"Nah," Callie said, looking him up and down with a raised eyebrow. "I think adorable is more accurate. Or cutie-patootie, if you prefer."

Charlie sighed. "I hate you all."

"Do we have time for a drink first?" I asked Thomas.

"We have champagne in the car," Thomas said, looking down at his watch. "And we should probably get going."

"Yay!" Callie suddenly cried, throwing her arms up into the air. We all gaped at her, and she put them down, smiling abashedly at us. "Sorry. I got really excited there for a second."

We all laughed and Thomas ushered us from the apartment. Outside, several of the diners had gathered in the patio area. I caught sight of Mr. Idoni in the crowd and waved at him. He whistled at Callie and me, earning him a slap on the arm from his wife.

We were in a Rolls Royce this time. I was pretty sure Callie's jaw was going to break off, her mouth was hanging open so wide. I felt giddy as I climbed into the car; suddenly, all of this seemed really fun to me. I would probably change my mind as soon as I saw the cameras, but it was hard to be nervous when I was with three of my favorite people in the world. Thomas was grinning from ear to ear, his hand clamped firmly around my waist. Charlie took on the role of bartender, pouring out champagne for each of us as Callie's eyes darted back and forth from the plush interior to the windows.

"You look happy," Thomas said, taking a glass from Charlie and handing it to me.

"This is more fun than I thought it would be," I told him.

Thomas filled us in on what to expect when we reached Leicester Square. "There will be a huge crowd. It's a little overwhelming, to be honest. But there will be a handler to lead you down the carpet. There will probably be some photographers taking your picture—"

Callie gasped. "Really?"

Thomas grinned at her. "A few might. You *are* the date of the new photography sensation Charlie Goodwin."

Charlie gave her a stern look. "Who's sexy now?"

"The handler will get you down the carpet quite quickly, then you'll be inside. Sometimes there are pictures in the lobby, so they might make you go straight into the theater. But if not, you can watch the others arrive from inside."

"What about me?" I asked, trying not to let the nerves invade my good mood quite yet.

"You," Thomas said, looking down at me with a glint in his eyes, "will be staying right next to me."

London traffic was busy and night was starting to fall around us as we inched toward the West End. I felt a palpable sense of excitement coming from each of my companions. Thomas entertained us with stories of some of the more colorful and ridiculous celebrities that might show up that evening. "We might see Richard Hoffman."

"You mean the host of *NightWatch*?" Callie asked with interest. *NightWatch* was a national entertainment program she watched every week.

Thomas nodded. "He usually shows up for these. Ends up totally trashed by night's end and hitting on all the starlets. And you can bet money on Hester Hannigan making an appearance." At my blank expression, he continued, "she was in *Safe House* a while back, this terrible voyeuristic reality show. Total crap. But she caught the fame bug and has spent the last five years trying, with increasing desperation, to cling to a shred of celebrity."

I laughed. "That sounds kind of sad."

"One time she tried to stick her tongue down Tommy's throat to get into the papers," Charlie said. "Feel sorry for her now?"

"No, actually," I said, raising an eyebrow at my boyfriend. He gave a mock-shudder.

"I promise you, no one was more horrified than I."

"We're getting close," Callie said excitedly, leaning into the window to better see out the glass. "I think I see fans!"

Sure enough, the traffic had slowed to a near crawl. Police officers on foot were directing a line of cars toward the square. "This part is perfectly choreographed," Thomas explained, pointing ahead at a cluster of men and women in suits consulting clipboards and looking stressed. "Who arrives when and how much time they get before the next big name comes to overshadow them."

I reached down to clutch his hand, feeling his shake slightly. I knew he had done several of these before, but I had a feeling his reception would be quite different from anything he had ever known. He wasn't just another supporting cast member now; he was a star in his own right. I felt a rush of excitement for him, mixed with pride. He so deserved all these wonderful things to happen to him.

"Here we go," he said, looking over at me. I beamed at him, hoping to convey that he didn't need to worry about me and my aversion to the crowds. I was here for him.

We had stopped next to a long stretch of red carpet. Behind a barricade, a mass of screaming fans waved and jostled each other, stretching along the carpet as far as I could see.

"Holy shit," Callie whispered. "This is pretty intense."

"Just smile," Thomas instructed the three of us. "And listen to the handler. There's nothing to worry about."

Someone opened the door from outside, and a blond head poked into the space. He glanced down at a clipboard before looking back up at Charlie and Callie. "Mr. Goodwin and Miss Owen? My name is James. You can come with me."

Callie shot me a look of excitement and terror. I winked at her. "Have fun."

Charlie climbed out first and helped Callie step down from the car. I watched through the window as James led them away from the car before turning back to Thomas. "You okay?"

"Sure," he said, smiling at me. "How 'bout you?"

I nodded. "I'm just so, so proud of you. And honored to be with you."

His eyes turned liquidy and warm as he gazed at me, making my stomach flip. It was crazy he could affect me so much, even with hundreds of screaming fans and pushy photographers only separated from us by a thin layer of glass. I wasn't nervous anymore. Nothing outside of our own little bubble could touch me. It was just Thomas and me, the way it always was.

A woman stuck her head into the car. "Mr. Harper, Miss Medina. I'm Karen. Ready to go?"

Thomas gave my hand one last squeeze before stepping out of the car. I heard the volume of the fans shoot up exponentially. Before he even acknowledged them and their cries of his name, he turned back and held out his hand to me, helping me from the car.

It felt so surreal, stepping out onto that carpet. The fans were screaming for Thomas, the photographers shouting his name. He wrapped his arm firmly around my waist and waved with his other hand before leaning down and shouting in my ear. "What do you think?"

"It's crazy!" I shouted back. He grinned at me, and I heard dozens of cameras clicking away.

"Now we stand here for a few minutes and let them take our picture."

"Should I step away?"

He kissed my forehead. "Don't even think about it."

"This way, Mr. Harper," Karen said, gesturing down the carpet toward the waiting row of press.

Thomas shook his head and pointed at the barrier and the fans waiting there. "I want to say hi first."

I could tell Karen didn't like it, but she didn't argue either. "Do you want to come?" he asked me. "Or stay with Karen?"

I didn't think the fans would be too thrilled if I tagged along. "Go," I said, smiling up at him. "I'm fine."

He kissed the top of my head before releasing me and jogging over to the barrier, to the great approval of everyone standing there. I stood with a cluster of handlers and organizers, people shouting out orders on their headsets and consulting with each other over clipboards. I smiled as I watched Thomas walk down the barricade, shaking hands and signing the papers and posters they thrust in his face. They were going crazy for him, and even from a distance, I could tell the grin on his face was genuine.

"Lizzie, you look lovely." I turned to see Heidi approaching me. She gave me a brief hug before directing her attention to Thomas. Her eyes gleamed, almost calculating, as she watched him. "That was a nice touch," she said, more to herself than me. "Going to the fans before the press."

"They mean a lot to him," I agreed. She looked back at me and smiled, her face looking more like normal.

"Sorry, I was being a little agent-ish there, wasn't I? He's a dream client, though. He knows so instinctively what to do."

I nodded at her, not sure how to respond to that. Thomas was just being Thomas. He knew those fans had waited for hours to see the cast; that meant something to him.

For the first time, I had the chance to look around and really try to take the scene in. Ahead of me on the carpet, I could make out Killian Cooper, talking to a reporter, a tall, painfully thin blonde on his arm. I didn't see Lola or Jackson yet, but figured they'd probably be last.

"It's time, Karen," Heidi said, looking down at her watch. Karen scurried over to Thomas and whispered in his ear. He nodded, signing an autograph, before reaching for another poster. Again, she whispered in his ear, and I thought I could see him sigh. He shook a few more hands before turning away and following her back to where Heidi and I stood.

"Sorry about that," he told me, once again slipping an arm around my waist. He grinned down at me. "Ready for the madness that is the press gauntlet?"

Karen led us down the red carpet, stopping occasionally so that we could pose for pictures. If it wasn't all so overwhelming, I probably would have been embarrassed to stand there and smile at strangers while they took my picture. Thomas took it all in stride, though, smiling, waving, occasionally putting his free hand in his pocket and staring at the flashes with a squinty-eyed, almost pouty expression that made me think of male models. I laughed and he winked at me. "It's all in the pout, babe."

A few times Karen pulled me away so that Thomas could pose on his own. I didn't mind. I found I enjoyed watching him pose and work the press. He was in his element, a side of him I had never seen before. Thomas the Movie Star. It was fascinating.

As we moved down the line, Karen pulled him forward several times to talk to reporters. Some scribbled down his quotes on the movie and the cast in little notebooks while, to my horror, others had cameramen and conducted recorded interviews. For the most part, I listened to Thomas, a smile plastered to my face, though a few of them asked me a question or two about my dress and what I thought of all this.

"It's definitely surreal," I told a nice lady from BBC 2. "Not like anything I've seen before."

"You're doing amazing," Thomas told me as Karen hurried us further down the line.

"It's kind of fun," I admitted. "It's definitely interesting to watch you work it like a cover girl."

That made him throw his head back and laugh. I heard a flurry of camera activity and wondered, briefly, what these pictures would look like in the morning. Would they show my nerves? Would we look plastic-y and fake? Or would our love, our genuine enjoyment of each other, be evident to anyone who looked at them?

A walkie-talkie on Karen's belt spit out some static before we heard a muffled voice saying, "Coles and Fischer, two minutes out."

"Ah," Thomas said, giving me a mock-frown. "Party's over. No one will care about us anymore when those two get here."

He was wrong. We heard the roar of the fans when Jackson and Lola arrived but no one in our area seemed in any hurry to stop fawning over Thomas. Photographers still called out his name, reporters still clamored to talk to him. A few times, he looked down at me with an almost dazed expression, like he couldn't believe any of this was happening.

"It usually takes me about five minutes to make it down the carpet at these things," he said into my ear.

"I guess I should start calling you Mr. Big Time then, eh?"

I could see Lola and Jackson now. Unlike Thomas, they had chosen to see the press before talking to any fans and therefore made it down the carpet quite a bit faster than we had. I met Lola's eyes over Thomas's shoulder, and watched as hers grew wider. After a rather unpleasant smile in my direction, she flipped her long red hair and turned her attention back to the reporter interviewing Jackson.

When we finally reached the end of the carpet, Karen consulted with someone over her walkie. "Right, you two. They'd like you to come down and do some pictures with the rest of the cast."

I looked at Thomas questioning. "Me, too?"

"Just to start, Miss Medina. Then you can come inside." She gave me a brief smile. "The photographers love you."

This made no sense to me, but I allowed Thomas to lead me back up toward where Lola and Jackson were posing. Lola made a big show of hugging and kissing us both, her hand resting on Thomas's chest far longer than was necessary. Jackson leaned in to kiss my cheek. "You look smashing, Lizzie. The most beautiful woman here."

I smiled at him as he pulled away, winking. It was strange, but I had come to like Jackson much more than I thought I would when we'd first met. He may be pretentious and egotistical, but he seemed genuinely nice. I wondered, if their roles were reversed, how Thomas would have turned out. Would he be different now, if he'd been thrust into the limelight at such a young age? In the few months since *Hostile* had made him a household name, he'd experienced so many new things. It was all so overwhelming. I couldn't imagine him having gone through all this when he was only a teenager, the way Jackson had.

Killian joined us, too, but made no effort to speak to me or introduce his date, who stood staring vacantly at the cameras. "It's a bloody joke," I heard him grumble to Lola as Karen arranged us for the cameras. "They stick me with this twenty-year-old kid, who clearly has no idea what he's doing. Total arse. Has no clue how to handle the press."

Thomas rolled his eyes at me and I giggled. "Just keep smiling," he told me.

After a few moments, they pulled Killian's date and me away so the four stars of the film could pose in various arrangements. Before I left, Thomas kissed me lightly on the mouth. "Save me a seat?"

"You got it." Behind him, I could see Lola glaring at me, but ignored her as I let Karen lead me back to the theater door. In the lobby, I scanned the crowd for Callie and Charlie. "I'm okay," I told Karen, who was still standing close to me. "If you need to, like, get back out there."

She shook her head. "Mr. Harper's people made it clear you were to have a host at all times. In case you need anything."

I sighed. It was a nice gesture, and probably Thomas's idea, but I didn't much like the idea of having a babysitter. I spotted Callie across the room, pushing through the crowd,

Charlie right behind her. "Okay," she said, panting. "That was a trip."

I laughed. "You're telling me."

"Where's Thomas?"

"Pictures with the cast."

That perked Callie right up. "The cast, eh? Is, uh, Jackson here?"

"Yup. And he brought a date."

Her face fell. "Really? Is she prettier than me?"

"Not even close. It's Lola Fischer."

She let out a relieved sigh. "Well, that's okay. They're not actually dating, they just show up places together because they know they'll get written about in the press."

I wasn't sure about that, but didn't press it. "This is amazing," Callie said happily. "There are so many celebrities in here."

"There are?" I glanced around, not recognizing anyone. Callie shook her head at me.

"How you ended up dating the movie star I'll never know. Did you even recognize Thomas that first night?"

I met Charlie's eyes. He was looking at me fondly. I winked at him. "I *did* recognize Thomas," I said. "I didn't exactly remember the name of his character, but I recognized him."

"I play Gideon," a voice said in my ear, familiar arms twisting around my waist. I turned to see Thomas had come up behind us, Lola and Killian with him. "In case you're wondering during the screening."

"I know that now," I told him, blushing slightly.

"Are you actually staying for the screening?" Killian asked, looking at his watch. "Christ. I for one cannot wait to get out of here."

"We're staying," Thomas said. I could tell he was trying not to scowl at Killian. "Some of us actually came to see the movie."

"Oh, that's so sweet," Lola said in her grating voice. "A lot of us duck out the back once the film starts," she explained to me.

"They're all much busier and more important than I," Thomas said, his eyes crinkling up in amusement.

"More important than you?" Jackson said, joining us. "Surely not, Tommy. Not the star of *Hostile*."

Across from me, Callie's eyes had completely bugged out of her head at the sight of Jackson. She looked uncharacteristically pale. "Jackson," I said, gesturing at her. "This is my flatmate, Callie."

I had hoped he wouldn't resist the chance to charm a pretty girl, even if she was a stranger. I wasn't disappointed. He immediately stepped forward and took her hand, bowing low and kissing her knuckles. "Callie," he said, staring right into her eyes. "It's so lovely to meet you."

I had never seen Callie speechless before. I had to admit, I rather enjoyed the sight of her gaping at him, a blush staining her cheeks.

"Did I hear you say you'll be staying for the screening?" he continued. "I usually leave a bit early, but tonight perhaps I'll have to make an exception."

Lola was glaring daggers at Callie, but my friend was far too star struck to notice. "Mr. Coles?" one of the handlers said, stepping forward. "We'd like some pictures in front of the posters. Would the four of you mind joining the rest of the cast?"

"Back to work," I said to Thomas, squeezing his hand. "We'll go sit, okay?"

"Okay." He kissed me. "See you in a few minutes."

As she moved to follow the men, Lola paused in front of Callie. "That's an interesting dress, dear. Who did it?"

Callie's whole face lit up at the attention from one of her favorite actresses. "I bought it at Harrods."

"Off the rack?" Lola said, raising her eyebrows. "Oh, dear, you poor thing. Well, at least now you know for next time." With that, she flounced off toward the rest of the cast. I watched as Callie's face fell, a surge of rage shooting through me.

"Ignore her," I said, grabbing Callie's arm. "She's a horrible cow."

"She is," Charlie agreed, wrapping an arm around Callie's shoulders. She looked slightly shell-shocked. "She's just jealous because Jackson flirted with you. Someone's attention was not focused on her for two whole seconds."

"And because her bony ass could never fill out your dress," I said. "Seriously, Cal, ignore her."

"Wait," she said, holding up a hand. She turned to Charlie. "Did you just say Jackson Coles was flirting with me?"

I laughed. "Couldn't you tell?"

"Oh my God!" she squealed. "He was, wasn't he? Who the hell cares about Lola Fischer?"

"Shh," I said, looking around. "I mean, you're totally right, but we don't need a reporter to hear us say that."

"Let's go sit down," Charlie said, shaking his head. Was I imagining it, or did he look slightly down?

We were directed to our seats in the theater. Most of the other guests were milling around and talking. "Can you even imagine the disgusting amount of name dropping and schmoozing that is happening in this room right now?" Charlie asked, shaking his head.

"Let's sit," I said. "We can people watch."

The room steadily filled with people, an anxious buzz of energy settling over the audience. Once the room was completely full, Mark Holman stood. Everyone immediately fell silent. "Thank you all for coming," he called out, his voice booming. "We're so proud of this film, and I'm sure you'll be able to see why. I have to tell you, this is, by far, the best *Darkness* film yet."

He paused while the audience applauded. Before he started up again, Thomas slid into the seat next to me.

"Sorry," he whispered. "Did I miss anything?"

"Apparently this is the best *Darkness* film yet. By far."

Thomas snorted. "He says that at every premiere."

At the front of the room, the producer was finishing up. "So, please, enjoy! And don't forget to spread the word about the film when you leave here tonight. Let's shatter some records, people!"

Everyone clapped again, and the lights began to come down. I was surprised to feel a bubble of excitement in my chest. Next to me, Callie sat up straighter, her eyes glued to the screen.

As the music started, Thomas squeezed my hand and leaned over to whisper, "Here we go."

CHAPTER TWENTY-FOUR

The after party was a confusing blur to me. It seemed like everyone wanted to talk to Thomas, to compliment him on his performance, to gush about *Hostile*, to hint at the projects they were invested in that he'd be perfect for. For my part, I stayed at his side, smiling politely at the strangers and talking to him in the spare moments he was free of them.

"This can't be any fun for you," he said to me eventually. We'd just escaped the surprisingly aggressive clutches of a tiny white-haired lady who apparently had bathed in Chanel no. 5. She was a major investor in the West End and insisted Thomas would be perfect for a new play her company was putting up. He'd conversed with her politely until learning it was a musical, though she didn't seem at all perturbed by his insistence that he couldn't sing. "Sorry, Lizzie."

"It's okay," I told him. "I'm fine."

He watched my face closely for a minute. "No, it's not okay. You've been so wonderful and supportive tonight. I owe you a better time than this. Let's go find Callie and Charlie and close ourselves up in a hidden corner somewhere."

"Are you sure?" I asked, trying not to let him see on my face how good that idea sounded to me. "Are you, like, allowed?"

"Absolutely. Come on." Before we could walk more than a few feet, Heidi approached us.

"Thomas, there you are. I just saw Jenner Collins and he asked after you. You must come over and meet him."

I felt his arm stiffen against mine. "Actually, Heidi, I was just about to—"

"It will only take a minute," she insisted. "He said something about a project he's starting next winter. I hardly need to tell you what it could do for you, working with someone like that."

Thomas looked ready to argue, but I placed a hand on his arm. "How 'bout you go meet Jenner Collins and I'll go find the others?"

He didn't look happy about it, but he agreed. Relieved to not have to meet another fake, stuck-up celeb, I grabbed a champagne glass from a passing waiter and went off to look for my friends.

"Hello, Lizzie, dear," Lola said, stepping in front of me. "Are you having a good time?"

"I am." With difficulty, I resisted the urge to step on her foot. It was hard to forget the way Callie's face had looked after their encounter.

"Where's Thomas? Don't tell me he left you on your own at something like this. Poor you, you must not know anyone."

"I have several friends here," I said. "In fact, I was just going to look for them, so if you'll excuse—"

"Isn't it amazing about Thomas?" she asked, completely ignoring me. "I did warn you though, didn't I? Back when we first met? I knew things would be looking up for him."

"He's done very well." I wished she would move so I could squeeze by her. I'd had enough of Lola Fischer to last me a lifetime.

"And how are you doing with it all, Lizzie?" she leaned close to me, as if urging me to confide in her. "It must be a nightmare for you."

"It's not," I said. "Thomas and I are doing wonderfully."

She raised her eyebrows skeptically. "You're fine with all the travel? All the obligations? Isn't he heading out to the States with us next week?"

I felt the familiar swoop of my stomach at her words that I always got when I thought about Thomas leaving, but I'd be damned if I let her know she was getting to me.

"I'll miss him, of course. But I'm getting close to exams, so I'll be plenty busy."

"Oh, that's right. You're finishing up school soon aren't you? Well, that will be nice for you to get home, get away from all this craziness." She laughed lightly, but I'd had enough. The image of Callie's embarrassed face fresh in my mind, I took a step closer.

"I don't know what your problem is, Lola, but I'm tired of you always trying to convince me that something bad is happening." Her eyes widened, but I went on. "Are you so desperate for attention that you can't handle other people existing in your immediate vicinity? Thomas and I have nothing to do with you, so stop trying to start shit."

Before she could reply, I turned on my heel and stomped away, my heart beating hard in my chest. I spotted Callie and Charlie on the other side of the bar and made a beeline for them. My face felt hot and my skin was tingly.

"What's wrong with you?" Callie asked immediately when I had reached her side.

"I had...words with Lola Fischer," I told her before raising my champagne glass to my mouth and downing half of it. "I'm just so tired of her."

They were both gaping at me. "What'd you say?" Callie asked.

"I told her she was desperate for attention, that Thomas and I were none of her business, and she should stop trying to start shit."

"Wow," Charlie said, clinking his own glass against mine. "Well done, you."

Callie looked slightly disappointed. "I wish you would have at least called her a bitch," she said. "But I suppose it was fine for your first time."

"My first time what?"

"Bitching out a girl at a party."

I laughed. "Is this something you have a lot of experience with?"

"Oh yeah. Happens all the time."

"So where'd Thomas go?" Charlie asked. "I'm surprised he let you out of his sight."

"Apparently Jenner Collins wanted to meet him."

Callie gasped. "Jenner Collins? Jenner Collins is here?"

"I guess. Why does that name sound so familiar?" I asked.

"Lizzie!" Callie cried. "You are hopeless! Jenner Collins is like the biggest deal in Hollywood! You totally know him—he's from Detroit!"

"Oh yeah!" I realized, belatedly, exactly who she meant. Jenner was a huge action hero, but also ran a theater in the city that was constantly getting rave reviews.

"Oh my God, I would give anything to meet Jenner Collins," Callie said, standing up on her tiptoes to search the crowd.

"He's really not that great, you know," an unfamiliar American voice said. We all turned to see Thomas standing next to a very pretty red-headed girl and a tall, gorgeous man that could only be—

"Jenner Collins," Callie whispered. "Oh my God." Her eyes flickered to the woman beside him. "And you're Annie Duncan. I think I might faint."

The woman, presumably Annie Duncan, laughed. "But then you'd spill your champagne. What good would that do you?"

"Charlie, Lizzie, Callie, this is Jenner and Annie. I got to talking with them and they mentioned they were from Detroit. I thought you girls would like to meet them."

It hit me, again belatedly, that Annie Duncan had starred in Jenner's most recent movie. There had been a lot of local press about her and speculation that she'd be the next Hollywood It Girl. If I was going to go to many more of these events, I was really going to need to start learning my celebrity news.

"Where are you guys from?" Annie asked.

"Sterling Heights," I replied, because Callie seemed too star struck to form sentences.

"Nice. I'm from Ferndale, but I live in the city now."

"We've been here for eight months," I told her. "I think we're both a little homesick."

"I wish I would have known I'd be meeting you," she said. "I'd have smuggled over some Faygo pop and Better Made chips."

I whimpered appreciatively at the thought of real Michigan junk food, and Jenner laughed. "It was very nice meeting you both," he said.

"Maybe we'll see you around sometime," Annie said, reaching out to shake our hands.

"If I have anything to say about it we just might," Jenner said, clapping Thomas on the back and giving him a meaningful look. They turned to go, and it occurred to me Callie had barely said a word.

"Wait!" she suddenly squeaked. They both turned back. "Can I, uh, can I have your autographs?"

I grinned at Thomas as both Annie and Jenner signed the back of Callie's napkin.

As they walked away, I put my arm around my friend's shoulder. "I guess cool and composed Callie was no match for the power of Jenner Collins and Annie Duncan, huh?"

"Nope," she said, beaming. "I don't even care if I looked like a dork. They're huge stars. And they're from *home*."

I knew exactly what she meant.

I had a much better time after that. The four of us did in fact find a quiet little corner where we could eat and drink and watch all the glitterati pass by. Thomas kept up a running commentary about those we could see in the crowd, spilling all the insider gossip Callie could ever wish for. There were some big names in that room, people even I had heard of. I had a feeling Heidi was probably annoyed with Thomas for passing up the opportunity to network.

But I was enjoying his company way too much to care.

CHAPTER TWENTY-FIVE

The next few weeks seemed to happen on fast forward. When Thomas left for LA, I told myself he would be back before I knew it, doing my best not to think about how little time we'd have left by the time he was home. Callie and I both threw ourselves into studying in preparation for our exams, seeing Charlie and our friends whenever we had the time.

In the days after the premiere, it felt like I couldn't go anywhere without seeing pictures of the event. The press had apparently loved Thomas and me and the way we had been so close on the red carpet. It almost felt commonplace now to see pictures of myself smiling up at him when I passed newsagents or went online. Some of the pictures had even made it stateside; I got calls from every one of my siblings, my mother, and most of my cousins. Carla, in particular, was incredibly excited to be related to me. Meredith and Tonya had decided it was in their better interest to be nice to me again; Callie and I both firmly told them to go to hell.

The day before Thomas was set to return, he called with bad news.

"I have to go to Germany."

My heart sank. "Now?"

"No, in a week. They decided they wanted me at the Berlin premiere. Apparently they're making a big push over there, and they need us to do promotion." I could hear the frustration in his voice. I closed my eyes, trying not to cry.

"For how long?"

"A week. Maybe more."

I felt the air leave my lungs in a rush. If he was gone for a whole week, we'd only have one week after that before I left. I couldn't even think that it might be longer.

"You're still coming home tomorrow, right?" I asked, hearing my voice shake and hating myself for it. I didn't need to upset him more than he already was.

"Of course," he said. "Lizzie, I'm so sorry. If there was a way to get out of it—"

"I know," I said quickly, pressing my palms against my eyes to stop the tears that still threatened. "Look, I should finish this work. So we have more time when you get here."

"Okay." His voice was sad. "Call me before you go to sleep?"

"Okay."

We were both quiet for a moment. "I love you," I whispered.

"I love you, too."

***

I was glad I had spent so much time studying while Thomas was gone; now that he was back, I wanted to spend every spare minute with him. Luckily, he seemed to have the same idea. He kept his schedule as clear as possible, seeing to most of his responsibilities while I was in class. He insisted on joining me while I studied, holding my hand while I worked. When I needed both hands to type he held onto my knee instead.

"What are you doing this weekend?" he asked me on Wednesday night while we lay in his bed, wrapped in each other's arms.

"I have a novel to read by Monday. That's about it."

"Let's get out of here."

I squeezed him tighter, liking the sound of it already. "Where would we go?"

"Winchester?"

I pulled back so I could see his face. "Seriously?"

"Yeah. You up for it?"

"Of course!" I'd been wanting to go to the little town where Jane Austen was buried since I first arrived, but had never found the time.

"I figured we could see the cathedral, go visit Miss Austen's house. Would you like that?"

"I would love it. It sounds perfect."

"Great. I'll make the arrangements. I think it will be good for us."

He didn't need to say that this would be our last weekend away together before I left. I had the feeling neither one of us wanted to talk about that, the same way we didn't want to talk about what would happen when I was back in Detroit, besides our vague, unformed plans to "try the long-distance thing."

We left for Winchester after my classes on Thursday. We would spend two nights there before returning on Saturday in time for Thomas's flight. As he loaded my bag in the trunk, I promised myself I wouldn't think about his leaving again for the rest of the weekend.

"It's a good day for a drive, eh?" he said, rolling down the windows.

I looked out at the blue, nearly cloudless sky. So unlike what I was used to in England. "It reminds me of our first date," I told him. "You looked just like this, your hair ruffled in the breeze, the sky blue behind you."

Without taking his eyes off the wheel, he reached over and took my hand. "I think I fell in love with you that day."

I squeezed his fingers between my own, thinking of how familiar they were to me, how vital he had become to me in the months since that day. "I feel like I'm still falling."

As we headed south out of the city, Thomas cranked up the volume on the CD player, the sounds of the Rolling Stones filling the air around us. Thomas sang along for a while until I covered my ears. "You weren't lying when you told that lady you couldn't sing," I teased. He sang louder in response.

It only took an hour and a half to get to Winchester. I was in love with the town at first sight. Winding roads led us through green hills, which gave way to brick buildings. All along the high street a small market had been set up. Thomas had booked us a room in the Old Vine Inn, situated across the square from the cathedral. I wanted to go over and see it at once.

"How 'bout we bring our bags up first, yeah?"

I scrunched up my nose at him. "Well, if you're gonna be all sensible about it."

I was happy we decided to check out our room first; it was gorgeous. "Thomas," I gasped, once he had opened the door. "We get to stay here?"

He laughed. "I hope so, seeing as how they gave us a key."

It was a large room, an entire wall of which was windows. An oak sleigh bed took up another wall, the bedding plush and inviting. Antique dressers and a small writing table took up the rest of the space. I sank down onto the window seat and looked out at the square below, my view partially blocked by the green of the tree branches. "This is perfect."

"I thought you'd like it."

"Have you been here before?"

He shook his head. "Nope. Just did a lot of research online before I booked this place."

I got up and went to wrap my arms around him. "Thank you for this."

He looped his hands loosely behind my waist and lowered his forehead to mine. "I just want to enjoy this time, the two of us, you know?"

I nodded, feeling a lump come to my throat. We were too close to the end now. I could feel it weighing us down. "Let's go explore," he said, kissing my hair. Maybe he could feel it, too.

Outside, we crossed the square into the lawn of the cathedral. The ancient building towered over us. "Wow," I said, staring up at the spires. "That's pretty incredible."

"I like this," Thomas said, gesturing around at the lawn. There were couples walking, kids playing, a few people stretched out on blankets, enjoying the last of the day's sunshine. "I like the vibe."

"Me, too. It's a lot different from London."

"You could say that."

We purchased tickets and entered the cathedral. "This says they have evensong services tonight," Thomas said, looking at a sign near the door. "We could go."

I took his hand. "That would be nice."

It was a beautiful cathedral. Not so grand as Westminster, but I enjoyed the more intimate feel. Thomas consulted a map and led me down the north aisle to the place he knew I most wanted to see.

"Here she is," I said softly, kneeling down to peer at the modest grave of my favorite writer, the woman who wrote the character that was my namesake. The grave marker made no mention of Jane Austen's writing. "The extraordinary endowments of her mind," I read, running my finger along the stone.

"What's this?" Thomas asked. I joined him at the wall.

"Her nephew had this put in," I said, pointing out the plaque that was added many years after her death. "Once her books became known, he published a biography of her to raise the funds."

"The window, too?" he asked, looking up at the stained glass above her plaque.

I shook my head. "That came later, through a subscription."

Thomas waited patiently while I read and then reread the words on her plaque and gravestone, trying to soak it in. I wished that my mother were there with me. There was something about being so near the woman whose books had made my mother a reader that touched me very deeply. When the ache in my chest became too much, I turned to Thomas. "Ready?"

He took my hand, squeezing it, as he led me further into the church. He didn't say anything, but I somehow knew he could tell exactly what I was thinking.

There was much more to see in the cathedral; we ventured down into the crypt, which freaked me out a little, before setting off in search of the Winchester bible.

"This is eight hundred years old," I said, shaking my head. "That's crazy to me. My country hadn't even been founded eight hundred years ago."

"You're a bunch of whippersnappers," Thomas said, affecting a wheezy, old man's voice.

Before we left, we both lit candles. I closed my eyes and prayed for my family so far away from me. I prayed for Thomas, that he would be safe on his trip. I wasn't sure what he prayed for, but he held me close as we exited the cathedral.

"What now?" he asked, looking around at the lawn. "We have a few hours before the service. Want to explore?"

"Would you mind if I write?" I asked.

He grinned at me. "Feeling inspired?"

"Well, it's very romantic here."

We headed back to the square so Thomas could get a blanket from the trunk of his car. We spread it out in the lawn and got comfortable. Thomas read while I worked. I found the words flowing more easily than usual. My heroine was getting ready to make her choice; would she find her way to her one true love?

I knew the answer would be yes. That was the nice thing about romance novels; you could always count on them to have happy endings. You could trust that the characters would make the right choices, and that circumstances, in the end, would work in their favor. It was real life that was complicated. Uncertain. Frightening.

We missed Evensong. Thomas fell asleep reading, and I was so engrossed in my own writing that I completely lost track of time. We decided to head back to the room and get ready for dinner, which we would be eating in the Inn's dining room.

Stuffed and drowsy from the wine, we called it a night. Up in our room, we fell into bed together, neither of us talking much. Like me, Thomas seemed to want to hold on. I fell asleep clinging to him, my face pressed tightly against his neck, so close I could hardly tell where he stopped and I began.

CHAPTER TWENTY-SIX

We spent a lazy morning exploring the town. I found a bookstore; though Thomas sighed occasionally, he waited at my side while I poured over the titles.

"You know," he said, while I weighed two options in my hands. "These are all the same books we have in London."

"I know," I said. "But I like to buy new books in new places. I want it to be just the right one. That way, when I get home, every time I read it, I'll remember that it's the book I bought when I was in Winchester."

As soon as the words were out of my mouth, I regretted them. Thomas and I avoided talking about my return home at all costs. I had a sudden image of myself in my bedroom in Michigan, reading the book I chose and thinking about this day. Feeling sick, I turned away from Thomas.

"Lizzie—" he said, his voice strained.

"I'm just gonna pay for this," I said, trying to keep my words even, bright. I sounded fake in my own ears.

After we left the bookstore, we decided to head over to Chawton, the town Jane Austen had lived in. "They've set up a museum in her honor in her old house," I read from my guidebook. "Score! They have a gift shop!"

Thomas laughed. "I have a feeling you're going to be leaving here with quite a bit less money than when you arrived."

"That's not saying much," I muttered, looking out the car window as we drove along unfamiliar roads.

I was pretty much in heaven at the house. I could have spent the entire day there, but tried to restrain myself for Thomas's sake. He'd been right about me spending my money. I couldn't help but buy new copies of my favorite books, postcards, a Mr. Darcy coffee mug, and a set of *Pride and Prejudice* paper dolls.

"What on earth are you going to do with those?" Thomas asked, laughter teasing his mouth.

"Look at them and cherish them," I said in my most dignified voice. "And maybe even play with them."

He laughed, but didn't tease me anymore.

By the time we had returned to Winchester, it was getting close to Evensong, which I was determined not to miss again. We decided to explore the greens of the Cathedral close. It was beautiful in the grounds; rolling grasses, trees and flowers in bloom, birds singing. I couldn't believe how lucky we'd been with the weather.

Ten minutes before the service, we made our way inside and found seats near the choir. "My mother would love this," I said, looking up at the grand ceiling so far above us. "She goes to Mass at least three times a week."

"Wow," Thomas said. "That's some devotion."

I smiled at him. "She loves the singing."

"Then she would love Evensong," he agreed, taking my hand. "It's mostly music."

The service took my breath away. The soaring voices of the choir filled the great open space and reverberated deep down into my bones. As I had yesterday, I found myself missing my mother. Particularly when we were all asked to sing the "Gloria Patri." The words were as familiar to me as reciting the alphabet, having sung them every week in Mass since I could first speak.

As the reverend got up to read the bible lesson, Thomas leaned toward me. "Are you missing home?"

I shook my head. It wasn't that, not exactly. I did miss my mother, but I didn't feel any compulsion to be home. Rather, it was a deep ache in knowing that the two parts of my life weren't going to be united. I couldn't be here and there at the same time. I couldn't be with my mom and Sofia and my siblings and also be with Thomas. I felt trapped.

The reverend closed his bible and invited us to pray. I squeezed my eyes shut tight and asked God, with all my heart, to help me find a way to hold onto the things that I loved. All of them.

***

I was surprised to find that Thomas's mood stayed upbeat and positive as we neared London the next day. I was dreading his leaving that night, was dreading the passing of the next two weeks. Callie and I had exams this week, and then we'd be finished with school, with nothing to do for the last week except soak in as much of London as we possibly could.

"Where are we going?" I asked, realizing that he was not heading toward Camden, or even Bayswater. We appeared to be approaching the East End instead.

"I want to show you something," he said, looking away from the road long enough to smile at me.

I settled back into my seat, wondering what he might have up his sleeve. Our arrival at our destination did little to shed light on the mystery. "Why are we at Charlie's flat?" I asked, looking up at the familiar brick building.

"You'll see." He took my hand and led me up to his friend's loft. Charlie lived in a very trendy, urban neighborhood. The kind of place that attracted artists and hipsters. I had loved his loft from the first time I visited it. The entire thing was open and bright, with exposed brick walls and ductwork.

To my surprise, Thomas pulled out a key at Charlie's front door. "He's not here?" I asked.

Thomas shook his head. "I asked him to give us some time alone, so I could explain."

"Explain what?"

By then, Thomas had opened the door and was leading me inside. He didn't stop until he'd reached the center of the room. I looked at him expectantly. "You're freaking me out, mister. What's going on?"

"Okay, hear me out," he said, raising his hands in front of him as if to hold me off. He seemed excited and nervous at the same time.

"Okay?" I said, more confused than ever.

"So Charlie just got this amazing new job. He's going to be taking photographs for *View* magazine."

"Wow," I said, impressed. Charlie had told me about the magazine before. They mainly featured high concept art photography, but also included some humanitarian and travel shots. It would be right up his alley.

"The good and bad news is that he'll be based in New York for at least the next year."

It took a minute for the sinking feeling in my stomach to register. "Charlie's moving?" I asked, unsure of why the thought made me so nervous. "Wow, Thomas. I'm sorry. I know you'll miss him."

"I will," he said. "But it does raise a rather interesting possibility."

"What's that?"

He gestured around the room. "His flat will be empty."

I stared at him. I had a feeling I knew what he was suggesting, but somehow I couldn't seem to make my brain work past the leaden feeling in my stomach.

"There's something else, too. Heidi's office is insane since *Hostile*. Apparently my big break was a big deal for more than just me." He gave me a little wink. "She's looking to hire an office assistant, someone to help out with all the extra work."

I was silent for a moment. "Why did you bring me here, Thomas? What is this?" I asked, feeling something like fear creeping into my chest.

"It's a place for you to live," he said, grinning from ear to ear. "Don't you see, Lizzie? You can work at Heidi's office and live here."

I gaped at him. "What? I can't live here."

"Yes, you can! Charlie is out of the country for a year, probably two—"

"I can't afford this place, Thomas." The fear was growing into panic. He couldn't possibly think this would work.

"Lizzie, he'd give you a great deal. The price wouldn't be a factor—"

"Of course it would," I said, knowing my voice was rising, but feeling powerless to stop it. "You know I'm not going to let you subsidize me, Thomas."

He rolled his eyes, and I felt my temper start to rise, battling the fear for my attention. How did he not understand that this wasn't okay? "The job pays pretty well," he was saying, oblivious to the turmoil building in my chest. "And it will give you plenty of time to focus on your writing. And you'll have your own place, so your parents won't have any reason to complain—" At the look on my face he broke off suddenly. "What?"

"They won't have a reason to complain?" I asked, incredulous. "Are you kidding me?"

"Lizzie, just—"

"If I give up the career they sent me to school for and take a job as—what? An assistant? An intern? So that I can stay in a foreign country with my boyfriend. You're right, they'll be thrilled."

"Why are you acting like this?" he asked, his voice tight. "I was just trying to find a solution for us, some way that we could stay together. I thought you wanted that."

"There is no solution, Thomas," I cried, feeling my heart constrict at the words I knew to be true. "I have to go home and you have to stay here!"

"Why? Why do you have to go home? What is there for you? A job you'll hate? That's why I found this place for you, so you can stay, Lizzie! So you can work on something that matters to *you*!"

"I went to school for five years to be a teacher, Thomas."

"Yeah, and then you left as soon as you were finished. As soon as it was time to actually become a teacher, you bailed."

"I did not bail!" I shouted. "I wanted to further my education."

He just stared at me. "We both know that's not true, Lizzie. You came here because you didn't want to start teaching. You came here to escape."

I felt close to tears. He was right, of course, but what did any of it matter now? I was qualified to be a teacher; my parents had spent a good deal of money to make sure I was qualified to be a teacher. My sisters were already sending me job openings. With their connections, I'd probably be in a classroom by fall.

My breath came short at the thought. For one minute, I imagined something different. I imagined what it would be like if I stayed here, if I lived in this flat and worked at Heidi's office. I imagined a life of taking the tube to work, eating my lunch in cafés in town, stopping by the park on the way home. Writing in the evening. Thomas.

Then I imagined telling my parents. Telling my sisters. And the beautiful picture I had just built crumbled in my mind.

"My parents will never forgive me if I give up my teaching career to go to work for your agent," I said, my voice flat. "There's no point in talking about it."

"But—"

"No, Thomas. I mean it. I don't want to talk about this anymore." I turned and walked to the door, leaving him standing in the middle of the room. "Please take me home."

CHAPTER TWENTY-SEVEN

I was determined to enjoy my last weeks in my adopted city no matter what. I hated that Thomas was in Germany. I hated even more that he had left on such a down note. We'd talked every day since he had left, the same as we always did when he was away for work, but I sensed a distance between us that had nothing to do with our locations. I was terrified of how that distance would grow after I left the UK.

"But if you keep worrying about it," Callie said wisely when I confessed this to her, "you'll spoil the last of your time here. You love London, babe. You love it in a way that has nothing to do with Thomas."

She was right. I had come to love everything about this city; the masses of people constantly on the move, the sound of the accents around me, the way so many contrary interests and pursuits could exist at the same time, in the same space. The buildings and the green spaces, the museums and the restaurants. The energy of the place—and the way that energy could fade to a gentle thrum during an afternoon in the park. The fierce love and pride hidden just below the surface of the residents' cool demeanor.

"You don't want to go home feeling anything but great about your time here."

So Callie and I threw ourselves into those last days. We studied for our exams in the parks and cafés we had come to frequent. We visited our favorite restaurants and pubs at night with girls from our class or Thomas's friends. We still went to trivia night—and won, as a matter of fact. And when our exams were over, we did something we had never done before in our months in England; we booked ourselves tickets on the Eurostar from St. Pancras station and found ourselves in Paris two and a half hours later. We spent two days in the City of Lights shopping, eating pastries, and getting lost, neither one of us knowing more than a phrase or two of French.

Back at home in our apartment, our final week ahead of us, Thomas called with more bad news. He was being sent on to France with Jackson and Lola for at least three days. I knew there was nothing he could do about it, his guilt and frustration evident even over the phone. But that knowledge did little to assuage my own dread that things were ending for us in more ways than one.

Callie and I were scheduled to leave London on Saturday morning. Thomas and his friends had planned a going away celebration for us the Thursday before. Thomas assured me he would be home Thursday morning at the very latest, even if it meant being found in breach of his contract with the studio.

"Any word yet?" Callie asked as I checked my phone for the twentieth time that morning. We were out shopping in Covent Garden, trying to come up with a suitable amount of souvenirs to bring home to our family and friends.

"Nope." I sighed and slipped my phone into my purse. "He should be at the airport by now, though. Maybe he's just busy getting through security and everything."

When we took a break to grab a coffee half an hour later, I found out that Thomas's problems were greater than security. The message light on my phone was blinking. "Strange," I said, hitting the voicemail button. "I must not have heard it ring in the shop.

"Lizzie, it's me. We're delayed. I don't know what the bloody hell is going on. Some problem with the weather. I'll call you as soon as I have a new ETA."

My heart sank, but I did my best not to let it show in my face. "Looks like his flight will be late," I told Callie.

She took one look at me and sighed. "New plan. Forget our friends and family, we're going shopping for us."

"What do you mean?"

"I mean, you need to get your mind off Thomas. So we're going to buy us cute new outfits for the fun party being thrown in our honor."

When I had heard Thomas's explanation on the phone, I had felt close to tears. Now I was *sure* I was going to cry. "Do you know," I said, reaching across the table to grab her hand, "that you are the best friend I've ever had in my life?"

I thought she might make a joke, but instead she squeezed my hand back, tight. "Right back at you, babe. Thank you for convincing me to come. I'm so glad I got to do this with you."

We were quiet for a moment, looking at each other, until Callie finally shook her head briskly. "All right, let's snap out of it. We can't just sit here mooning at each other. That cute boy over there will think we're in love and won't hit on me."

"You do know that you're leaving the country in two days, right? Does it really matter if the cute boy hits on you?"

"A lot of things can happen in two days," she said knowingly, standing up. "Ready?"

I wasn't sure, but I thought I saw her wink at him as we walked by.

***

When seven o'clock rolled around, Callie and I were ready to go. We had both picked new outfits—a sundress for me and some miniskirt tank top combo for her—done our hair and makeup, and had a glass of wine to get into the mood. Now there was nothing to do but wait an acceptable amount of time to head down to the restaurant. "We can't be the first ones there, Lizzie. We're far cooler than that."

It was taking everything in my power to not burst into tears and hide under my quilt instead. Thomas was still not back. To make matters worse, I hadn't even heard from him in the past three hours. Our last conversation had consisted of a lot of swearing on his end, and a lot of reassurances that he'd make it in time on mine. Since he hadn't called to tell me the flight was finally taking off, I was now trying to come to grips with the fact that he might, in fact, miss my going away party.

"You okay?" Callie asked, for the hundredth time that afternoon. I felt even worse knowing that she was spending her time worrying about me. This night was for her, too.

"Yeah," I said, trying to keep my voice light. "He'll be here."

But I still hadn't heard from him by the time Callie finally decreed we could go downstairs. Before following her down the stairs, I sent him once last text message: *What's going on? Please tell me where you are, even if it's bad news.*

Someone shouted our names as soon as we entered the restaurant. "Lizzie! Callie! Over here!"

It was Meghan, standing up and waving to us from a table in a near-empty corner. They had strung balloons up on the backs of the chairs and hung a "Bon Voyage" poster on the wall behind the table. As Callie and I made our way toward Meghan, the rest of the guests came into view. I stopped short and put my hand over my mouth in surprise. In addition to Meghan, Carter, Sarra, Mark, and Charlie, Thomas's entire family had come down from Edinburgh.

The sight of them all there to say goodbye to me made tears immediately come to my eyes.

"Oh, don't cry!" Meghan quickly pulled me into a hug. "This is a happy night."

"These are happy tears," I said, laughing and sniffing at the same time.

Everyone stood, taking turns hugging and kissing Callie and me. I introduced her to Thomas's family. When Bryony pulled me in for a hug, she whispered in my ear, "My brother is such a prick. I can't believe he let this happen."

"It's not his fault," I told her, before turning to Charlie. He wrapped me up in a tight hug.

"Any word?" he asked quietly.

I just shook my head, my chest aching with both the joy of seeing so many loved faces and the sadness of knowing none of them was Thomas. I knew he couldn't control the weather or the airline, but I still couldn't quite believe he wasn't going to be here for this.

"Well, look at that. Maybe I was wrong," Bryony said, her eyes on the door.

I spun around and saw Thomas standing in the restaurant's entryway, his eyes scanning the room.

My heart leapt to my throat at the sight of him. He was wearing a suit, with no tie, the top few buttons undone. He looked rumpled and tired and maybe more attractive than he'd ever been. He saw me, and his face broke into a smile.

I didn't think too much about our friends at the table behind me, or the other patrons in the restaurant. All I could think about was getting to him, wrapping my arms around him, feeling him real and alive beneath my hands. He pulled me into him, kissing the top of my head before burying his face in my hair.

"You're here," I said into his chest. "I can't believe you're here."

"I'm so sorry," he said.

I realized, belatedly, that half the people in the restaurant—including Mr. and Mrs. Idoni—were looking at us. "Um, I guess we should go sit down," I said, unable to wipe the goofy grin off my face.

"Probably." But he didn't let me go. Instead, he bent his head and kissed me, hard, on the mouth, bending me backward across his arm like we were characters in a movie. By the time he let me up for air, I was laughing, as were the nearest patrons, and Charlie and Carter were clapping back at our table.

"Come on," I said, my face beet red as I pulled him over to our party. Even as embarrassed as I was, I couldn't stop smiling, and Thomas looked nothing but proud of himself for his little display.

He didn't release my hand when he went to greet his parents and siblings, electing instead to give them one-armed hugs. I didn't blame him. I had little inclination to let a moment pass without touching him for the next two days.

Once we were all settled, a waitress came to take drink orders. "So the flight finally left, huh?" I asked Thomas.

He shook his head. "It was a disaster in that airport, I swear. The entire departure board was delayed or canceled. They wanted to put my whole flight up in a hotel and try to get us out tomorrow."

"How the heck did you get here?"

He smiled. "I took the Eurostar. I don't know why I hadn't thought of it sooner, to tell you the truth."

I gaped at him. "Thomas, you're terrified of tunnels. How on earth did you manage?"

He shrugged. "It wasn't that bad."

I rubbed his knuckles. No wonder he looked so rumpled. Sitting in the airport all day, followed by a two-hour train trip that must have been hell on his nerves, not to mention the travel around Paris to get to the station.

"I can't believe you did that."

"Doesn't matter now." He kissed me again, softly this time. "I told you, Lizzie. I wasn't missing this."

The waitress came back with several bottles of wine, which we passed around the table. When everyone had a glass, Charlie stood.

"I just wanted to say how happy I am that the two of you came to stay." His eyes met Callie's across the table. I wondered, not for the first time, how deep his feelings for her actually went. "We really feel that you've both become a part of our little family here in London. Which means you must stay in touch and come back to visit soon." Now his eyes met mine. "We want to wish you both luck and a safe trip. You'll be missed."

I tried to swallow past the lump in my throat as he raised his glass, the rest of our friends following suit. "To Callie and Lizzie."

"To Callie and Lizzie," everyone echoed. Then we were all clinking our glasses together and hugging again, the table loud with laughter and well wishes. Through it all, Thomas kept my hand firmly in his, refusing, at least for now, to let go.

CHAPTER TWENTY-EIGHT

It was hot in Detroit, much hotter than I remembered for June. The heat seemed to hang oppressively in the air, weighing me down, making me feel sleepy and torpid. The weathermen on TV thought it would finally break when the rain came in, but they were wrong. If anything, the moisture in the air only added to the heaviness. And the constant rolling grey clouds did little to improve my mood.

"You look like shit," Sofia said, standing in the doorway to my parents' kitchen. I blinked up at her, trying to adjust my eyes. I'd spent the last half an hour staring at the computer screen, trying to fill out online job applications.

"Thanks, Sof," I grumbled.

"Are you still jet-lagged?" She came to sit next to me at the table, staring at my face. "You have circles under your eyes."

"I'm not sleeping well." I avoided her gaze, hoping she didn't press much. In truth, my body was still not reacting well to the time change, even after being home for nearly a week. But my lack of sleep was based on quite a bit more than just that.

"So," she said, perhaps wisely guessing that a subject change was desired, "Whatcha doing?"

"Job applications." I rested my head in my palm. "But I'm not making much progress."

She scrunched up her nose. "Looking for a job is the worst. At least there are openings though! That has to be encouraging."

"Uh, huh," I said. The truth was, I was having a lot of difficulty finishing even a single application. I found the questions tedious and couldn't muster up the energy to scan my various transcripts, academic awards, and letters of recommendation. And I had yet to complete even a single long-form question. How was I supposed to know what my teaching philosophy was? Just thinking about everything I would need to do to successfully complete one of these seemed too overwhelming to me.

"It's a waste of time anyhow," I said, not sure if I was talking to myself or Sofie. "I don't even have my grades from the past term yet. I may as well wait."

"But aren't they trying to fill positions now?" she asked. "What if you miss out while you're waiting?"

"They don't hire till August anyhow," I said, not sure if there was any truth to the statement at all. "That's when they know their class needs."

"Oh." Sofie clearly wasn't buying it, but she didn't press. "So, whatcha doing tonight? Want to go out, maybe get a drink?"

I looked down at my watch. It was nearing eleven in London, and Thomas usually called before he went to bed. "Maybe another time, Sof," I said. "I really am pretty tired."

She was quiet for a moment. "You've been home a week, and I've barely seen you," she said, her voice soft. "Your mom says you stay in the house all day, usually up in your bedroom."

"My mom is talking about me?" I asked, my temper immediately rising. "Of course she is." I shook my head. "I don't know why I'd even be surprised."

"Relax." Sofie placed a hand on my arm. "It was in response to a question. I asked her how you were."

"You could have asked me if you were curious, you know. I am right here." I knew Sofie hadn't done anything wrong, but I felt like lashing out. "This family is so ridiculous, nothing changes. Everyone always talking about each other, gossiping. *Jesus Christ*. What is wrong with everyone?"

"Hey," she snapped, her voice controlled but clearly angry. "What's wrong with *you*? First of all, the next time you take the Lord's name in vain like that, I will tell your mother, and I don't care how old you are. You don't talk like that, Lizzie. Not in this house and not around me."

I felt immediately abashed. She was right—I never said that word as a curse. My mother would be horrified if she heard me. Not just disappointed, but hurt. She would consider it disrespectful, to both God and to herself.

"Secondly," Sofie went on, "I *tried* to ask you directly. But you don't return my calls and you certainly never call me. So I asked your mother if you were okay—sue me. Heaven forbid I care."

"I'm sorry," I said, feeling miserable. Sofie was my oldest ally, the one person in our family I could always count on to be on my side. I had no reason to be snippy at her.

"Look," she said, her voice softer. "I know it must be hard for you to come home. I know you miss him. But your whole family is here, and we all love you, Lizzie. You should spend time with us. Get your mind off things."

"I know. You're right."

She watched me for a minute. "But you still don't want to come out tonight, do you?"

"I'm sorry, Sof. I'm just not in the mood. But soon, okay? I promise."

She sighed, but patted my arm as she stood. "Good luck with the application." She walked to the kitchen doorway and paused. "And tell Thomas I say hi."

She probably thought I was crazy, waiting around for a guy to call me, but I didn't care. There was just no way to explain that the best part of my day was the moment I heard his voice. Talking to Thomas was the only time I felt like myself anymore.

I glanced over at the laptop. Maybe I could work on something else, if the applications weren't getting me anywhere. I looked over my shoulder once, to make sure no one had snuck into the house without my knowledge (not that anyone in my family could ever be quiet enough for sneaking), then pulled up my novel file.

I'd been struggling with the final chapter ever since Winchester. I wasn't sure what was making me feel so blocked. I had put the hero and heroine into the perfect circumstance to finally get together and be happy. So why couldn't I just execute it?

Thomas had made me promise I would finish it by the end of the month. On that Thursday night, after the party, we had gone back to my place to sleep. It was kind of sad to be there, with most of my things packed up. He noticed the computer on my desk. "Is this the infamous manuscript?" he asked, peering at it.

I laughed. "It's very infamous, yes. Someday it will be taking the literary world by storm."

He gave me a stern look. "I don't know why you're laughing. You're an excellent writer. If you don't give up, you *could* take the literary world by storm. I know it."

"It's just a silly book, Thomas," I said, moving forward to close the lid of the laptop.

He caught my arm before I had the chance. "Don't say that, Lizzie. Please. I respect your writing. You should, too."

I looked up into his eyes, so honest and familiar. "Okay," I murmured, believing him with all my heart. "I will."

He smiled. "Good. So, how far are you, now? Did Jill figure out that Marcus was the one helping her all along?"

"Oh yeah, that happened ages ago." I sank down onto my bed as he sat in front of my desk, scrolling back in the document.

"Wow, you've been busy. You have like three new chapters since the last time I read this."

"I'm almost done," I admitted. "Pretty much one more chapter. Just the conclusion."

He gave me a dazzling smile. "Seriously? Good for you, Lizzie. That's awesome."

"The problem is, I can't seem to wrap it up. I had so wanted to finish it while I was still here, but that's obviously not going to happen now."

"So? Just so long as you finish it, who cares where you are."

"I know," I agreed. "But my parents' house isn't exactly the cradle of creativity, you know? It's loud and busy and there're always people poking their heads in, wondering what you're up to."

"Don't let that stop you, Lizzie. You'll just have to make the time to do it. You're way too close to give up."

"I know."

He turned back to the screen, absentmindedly unbuttoning the rest of his shirt as he read. "Thomas, seriously?" I asked. "You're actually going to sit there and read that right now?"

He looked up at me, surprised. "I want to know what happens."

"Well, I could tell you what happens," I pointed out. "From over here on the nice comfy bed."

He grinned at me. "Good point."

He pulled off his button-down and trousers, walking in his boxers over to the dresser to pull on a pair of pajama pants he kept there. He paused, staring down at the drawer.

"What's wrong?"

"It's so empty." He sighed. "I keep thinking this is all a bad dream."

For about the millionth time that day, I felt choked up. "Me, too."

Without another word, he pulled on his PJ bottoms and joined me on the bed, pulling me into his chest so tightly I lost my breath. "You don't have plans tomorrow, do you?"

I shook my head against his chest. "Nope."

"Good. We're not leaving this room."

And we didn't. We stayed in my room for the rest of the night and the entire day Friday, only emerging for the bathroom and to bring food back to the bed. The rest of the time, we clung to each other, talking about the ways we would keep in touch, the things we would do to make sure it worked.

"I won't lose you, Lizzie," he had whispered, early on Saturday morning. "I refuse."

I wrapped my arms even tighter around him, wanting to believe him, praying that we could find a way to make it work. I didn't sleep at all that night, and I don't think he did either. Neither one of us wanted to miss a minute.

Now, sitting there in my parents' kitchen, he seemed a world away. How could that have only been a week ago? It seemed like months since I had seen him, since I had kissed him. He insisted on coming to the airport with us, though I tried to convince him it would be easier to say the last goodbye in private.

"It won't be the last," he said, his voice fierce. "Stop talking like that."

It had been hard to say goodbye in public, just like I thought. I couldn't keep from crying, holding him till the last possible second. When Callie finally appeared behind his shoulder to tell me we needed to get through security, when I finally had to actually let go, I felt as if I was tearing a piece of myself from my body.

I sighed, feeling tears well in my eyes again. I'd cried more in the past week than I had in years. I was starting to get sick of myself. It was bad enough that it was hot and humid and grey, did I really need the constant itching eyes and stuffed up head that went along with near constant tears?

I rubbed my eyes and glared at the computer. It was one thing to promise Thomas I would finish, but another thing entirely to accomplish that. How could I write about happy endings when I felt so completely terrible?

My phone rang, distracting me from my self-pity. I felt my heart leap when I saw Thomas's name on the screen. Before I answered, I closed my laptop and started up stairs. I preferred to talk to him in my own room. With the door closed and the lights off, I could almost pretend he was only on the other side of the city from me, instead of on the other side of the ocean.

***

"How are the job applications going?" Callie asked, stealing one of my fries.

I shook my head. "Terribly. I don't know what my problem is. I can't seem to come up with a single answer that doesn't sound trite."

"I think you're just having trouble adjusting," she said. "I know the feeling."

I took a sip of my Coke. "How's your job hunt going? Any closer to making a decision?"

She shook her head. "No. And it sucks. I thought going to London was supposed to help me figure out the next step. But I have no idea."

"We're a couple of sad sacks, aren't we?" I asked. "Look at us, eating in this cheap chain diner. Two weeks ago we were dining in the most trendy restaurants in London."

"Don't remind me," Callie moaned. "I'm so depressed. Did everything feel this lame before we left?"

I sighed. "I'm sure we're just homesick."

"But that's the problem—we are home."

I frowned at her. "I know. But it hasn't been our home for a while. I think we just need to get used to it."

"It just feels so boring here, you know? Colorless, or something."

"Maybe we need to spend some time remembering the things we always loved about home," I suggested. "My cousin Sofie has been bugging me to go out since I got home. We could make a whole night of it. Maybe hit up Royal Oak or go downtown."

"I do like going out in Royal Oak," Callie agreed.

"I think we just got used to everything being right at our fingertips. There is cool stuff around here, it's just more spread out."

"Well, let's find it then," Callie said, taking the last fry from my plate. "Before I go totally stir-crazy."

I slurped the last of my Coke, looking around the restaurant. I'd been home for two weeks and it still felt weird to me. I kept expecting to hear British accents or turn on the TV and find *EastEnders*. I couldn't seem to get my bearings.

"I need to tell you something," Callie said. She looked nervous.

"What's up?"

"You know our last weekend, when I didn't come home and you wondered why?"

"Of course." I leaned across the table. When Callie had texted me that she was sleeping elsewhere that last weekend, I had asked her who she was with. She'd never given me a straight answer. Was I now to finally find out the mystery?

"I wasn't with the guy from the café," she said. "I never even talked to him."

I raised my eyebrows. "Who was it, then? Hot barista guy?"

She shook her head.

"Holy crap, are you blushing?"

She covered her face with her hands. "Stop looking at me!"

"Why are you blushing? Who were you with?"

"Charlie."

I froze, staring at her. She peeked out at me from behind one finger. "Lizzie? Are you mad?"

"Why would I be mad?" I asked.

"You're looking at me like I just grew a second head."

"I'm surprised," I said. "Shocked, more like. When did this happen? Why didn't you tell me?"

"I don't know," she said. "I think I wanted it to be for just us, you know? Without the entire rest of the group having a say in it."

"Okay, but why didn't you tell me later? Wait, why are we talking about this? It doesn't matter. Tell me what happened! Do you like him? Was this something you were thinking about for a while?"

She nodded, smiling in a shy way that made me melt a little. She looked smitten. I'd never seen it on her before. "I liked him the whole time, I think. But I never thought he'd like me back. He's so much cooler than me, you know?"

"Shut up," I said automatically, marveling that Callie thought anyone in the world was cooler than she was, particularly a guy who regularly wore mismatched socks without noticing. "So what changed?"

"We went for a walk after the party. I didn't want to tag along upstairs with you and Thomas." I remembered them slipping away after dinner, saying she needed to make a stop at the newsagent before coming upstairs. When Thomas and I offered to join her, Charlie assured me he'd get her home safely. I'd been so stupid not to realize she'd stayed with him. When she'd texted me later that she'd be out for the night, I'd actually felt a little mad at her, thinking it was kind of mean that she would take a walk with Charlie on her way to hook up with another guy. How clueless could I be?

"So you took a walk together. What next."

She smiled again, looking down. "On the way back from the newsagent, I told him my heels were killing me, and he hailed a cab. Then he told the cabbie there'd only be one stop—his place. He didn't even ask me. I think we both just knew."

"Wow," I said, shaking my head. "This is incredible. I knew he liked you—"

"Wait, what? You knew? Why didn't you tell me?"

"Because I didn't know it would matter to you," I said. "You never acted like you were interested."

"I was trying to protect myself." She shook her head. "Stupid, huh? I thought for sure he'd turn me down. I figured it would be safer to not let on. Think about how much time we could have had if I would have just said something."

"At least you got it together in the end," I said.

"Yeah. At the very end. And now I'm here. And he's there."

I felt a stab of pain at her words. "I know the feeling."

She gave me a wan smile. "This sucks, huh?"

"Wait!" I slapped the table, remembering something. "He's moving to the States! He'll be in New York at the end of the month."

She nodded. "He told me. I might go out and see him. We left it open-ended, so we could both see how we feel when the time comes."

I tried not to feel jealous of her, really I did. But it was hard, knowing that the guy she liked would be on the continent soon.

"Maybe we could both go out there," she said, seeing my expression. "I bet Thomas could come to New York for a few days at least. We could all meet up there. Like old times."

"Yeah," I said, already imagining it. "Maybe we could."

"Ooh, Lizzie, wouldn't it be the best? The four of us in Manhattan together?"

I felt excitement stirring in me. "It would be the best," I said, a grin spreading across my face. "It totally would."

CHAPTER TWENTY-NINE

For the next month, I hung onto the New York trip like a lifeline. I had called Thomas as soon as I got home, even though I knew he was probably already in bed. He hadn't sounded the least bit mad when I woke him up—he was immediately down with the idea.

"A month!" he said before hanging up. "I'll get to be with you in a month! We can make it till then, Lizzie."

I knew that we could. I could do anything for a month. I kept myself busy working on applications and writing multiple versions of the last chapter of my book. I still wasn't happy with it, but at least it was something to do. I wanted to be able to tell Thomas that it was finished when I saw him. I wanted to see his face—I knew he would be proud of me.

My carefully constructed fantasy fell apart two weeks before we were supposed to leave. Thomas got a part in a new movie.

He called me on a Wednesday night. He had just left a meeting with the studio people. I could hear the sounds of the city around him, his voice muffled against the noise. "I got it, Lizzie," he said. "I can't believe it, but I actually got it!"

"What?" I asked, smiling automatically at the excitement in his voice. His emotions had always been so contagious to me.

"That Jenner Collins movie! The one he told me about at the premiere. He wants me for the lead. The lead, Lizzie!"

"Oh my God!" I cried. This was big—huge, actually. Bigger than anything he had experienced so far. "That's amazing. Oh, babe. I'm so happy for you!"

"Thank you! I cannot want to see you so we can celebrate."

"All the more reason to be excited for New York!"

"About that," he said. "Hang on." I heard muffled noises and wondered if he had put his hand over the phone. "Sorry. Just getting the cab. Anyhow, there's a hiccup with New York. I have to be in LA to meet the studio guys that week."

I felt like a lead balloon had dropped onto my chest. It took me a second to realize that he was still talking.

"So I was thinking we could reschedule a little. What would you say to meeting me in California instead?"

I swallowed heavily. I wasn't sure why I was so bothered by the change, but my disappointment was palpable. "I don't know if I can."

"Why?" Thomas asked. "It'd be the same weekend. You were already planning on being gone."

"I was planning on being gone with Callie and a group of people," I said. "I'm not really sure how my parents would react to me going alone to hang out with my boyfriend."

He was quiet for minute. "Are you kidding?" he finally asked.

"Thomas, they're really strict, you know that—"

"You're twenty-three years old," he said. "Almost twenty-four. You're a grown-up, Lizzie. You lived abroad for a year. Are you seriously telling me you have to clear your vacations with them?"

"I live in their house—"

"You're twenty-three!" he repeated. He sounded incredulous. Suddenly, I felt pissed. He was the one who was changing our plans—plans I had looked forward to. He was the one that got to stay in London with all of his friends while I had to come home to sit alone in my bedroom half the time, too miserable to even go out.

"Don't talk to me like that," I snapped. "You don't understand my family, okay? That doesn't give you the right to talk to me like I'm an idiot."

"Lizzie, be reasonable," he said, and I suddenly hated the sound of his posh, calm, English voice.

"It's easy for you to say, when someone else picks up the tab for you to fly to a different country at two weeks' notice." My voice was rising to a shout. Somewhere in the back of my mind, I knew this was stupid—why was I lashing out at Thomas, of all people? But I couldn't seem to stop. "I paid for my plane ticket already, Thomas. And it wasn't just a drop in the bucket for me."

"I would buy your ticket to LA, Lizzie, it's really not something to get worked up about."

"There you go again!" I shouted. "Acting like I'm some charity case, like you're way too righteous to care about something as mundane as money—"

"I'd rather not have this conversation in a cab, Lizzie." His voice stopped me short. He sounded tired, and sad. Just a minute ago he'd been so happy. I'd ruined that.

"Thomas—" I began, my voice shaking. What was I doing?

"I need to call my mother," he said flatly. "She'll be wanting to know about the meeting. We'll talk about New York later, okay? Maybe I can arrange something."

"Thomas, I'm sorry—"

"It's fine," he interrupted. "We'll figure it out. Goodbye."

Before I could answer, he had clicked off. I held the phone in my hand, horrified at myself. I had just ruined one of the biggest moments of his career. I had let my own issues get in the way of his news. Who cared if he couldn't go to New York? Did I expect him to turn Jenner down? Refuse the role? Over a weekend? He was even offering me a way to see him regardless. And I had thrown it back in his face.

It wasn't until I climbed into bed a few moments later that I realized he hadn't even told me he loved me before he hung up. And I didn't blame him at all.

***

The New York weekend came and went. Callie went and came home hinting that an East Coast move might be on the horizon for her. It was hard, knowing what Thomas and I should have been enjoying. Harder still to know that he was so much closer, in my very country, and I wasn't seeing him. The next time we talked, he had urged me, again, to come out and see him. I had been sorely tempted, but just couldn't drum up the courage to tell my parents that I was going all the way to LA to stay with my boyfriend. Alone. In a hotel room. Thomas could judge all he wanted, but I was pretty sure my dad would have refused to let me back in the house. You could call it ridiculous or old-fashioned, but it was what they believed. And I was clearly too much of a coward to go against them.

"Let's look on the bright side," Thomas said before hanging up. "At least I'll be in the States come winter. The movie shoots in LA. That's closer than London."

We made tentative plans for him to come to Detroit in September, the first time he had more than a day or two off. I told myself we could hang on until then, that we'd be fine.

But I had my doubts. I was scared by the way I'd reacted to his news. What kind of relationship did we have if I couldn't even be happy for him in a situation like that?

Maybe we would have been able to hang on. September wasn't too far off, not in the grand scheme of things. I'd already been without him for two months—what was one more? We might have been fine—if it weren't for the picture.

I saw it on a Friday morning in late August. I was staring out the window in my room, completely ignoring the blinking cursor on the computer in front of me when the phone rang. I'd been sitting there for more than an hour, unable to muster the motivation to type a single word.

I picked up the phone, eager for a legitimate distraction. "Hello?"

"Hey, it's me," Callie said. "Where are you?"

"Home," I said. "Working on my résumé." It was a lie, of course. I hadn't even opened my résumé. I had wanted to try to write a little, thinking it might make me feel better, but I hadn't even managed to attempt that.

On the other end of the phone, Callie took a deep breath, and I was suddenly worried. "What's the matter?"

"I need to tell you something, and you're really not going to like it. But I don't want you to hear it from someone else..."

"Callie," I said, a warning note in my voice. "What?"

"There are a bunch of stories online about Thomas," she said, her voice coming out in a rush.

"Aren't there always stories about Thomas these days?"

"Yeah, but these are about Thomas and...someone else."

I felt the blood rush from my face. Oh God.

"Who is it?" I whispered.

"Lola," Callie said, sounding miserable.

Maybe it's just work stuff, I told myself, my heart pounding as I opened my web browser. *They were probably just doing something for the movie...*

I pulled up *Hello!* and couldn't help but gasp. There, on the front page, was a picture of them. And it was clear from the way he was helping her into a cab that it had nothing to do with work. I felt sick.

"Oh no, you're looking at it, aren't you?" she said. "You shouldn't look at it. It won't do you any good. You know they're always making this crap up, Lizzie. It doesn't mean anything."

"I have to go," I whispered, certain I was going to throw up at any minute.

"Lizzie, wait—"

I didn't give her a chance to finish before I hung up. I didn't throw up either. Instead, like a masochist, I scrolled through each picture of the two of them out together. At Cocina. The realization that he had taken her there, to a place we'd been together, caused another sharp pain. When I'd seen everything there was to see on TMZ, I googled his name. More sites came up, more pictures, more captions. *Thomas Harper and his on-screen, off-screen love interest.* "Oh God."

I couldn't remember anything ever hurting like this. Not even leaving London. Nothing ever felt like this. I couldn't breathe, I couldn't think. All I could do was stare at picture after picture of the two of them together.

I wasn't sure how much time passed before I heard the shrill ringing of my cell phone. Assuming it was Callie again, I ignored it, not anywhere near ready to talk to her. When it rang for the fifth time, I finally picked up. "Cal, I can't—"

"It's me."

Thomas. Shit.

"Lizzie? Are you there? Lizzie, come on. Talk to me."

My mouth was dry, a huge lump in my throat. I wasn't sure I could get sound out, but I finally managed to say, "Hello."

"Callie called me."

Great. Thanks a lot, Cal.

"She said you saw pictures online...from last night."

"I did," I said, tasting something sour at the back of my throat. "I'm looking at them now, actually. You look good. So does she."

"It wasn't a big deal, Lizzie. We ended up in the same restaurant, so we ate together. That's all."

I felt like I'd been slapped. He was actually admitting that he had dinner with her? That was as good as a date.

"How nice for you," I whispered.

"What's wrong? Look, I know you don't like her, but I couldn't have just refused—"

"Was this the first time you just so happened to have a dinner date with someone else?"

He was quiet for a moment. When he spoke again his voice was measured. "Hang on. What exactly do you think happened last night?"

"I'm reading all about it right now, Thomas," I said, trying to keep my voice steady. "How the two of you seemed inseparable. How you couldn't keep your hands off each other throughout the whole meal. It's obvious from this picture that you weren't getting into separate cabs. Where'd you go after?"

He was silent for so long, I began to think the connection had gone out. But he was still there—and he was pissed. "Are you fucking kidding me?" he asked, his voice positively dangerous. It was a little scary—Thomas never got angry, not at me. "You actually believe some total shite written on a gossip site? You actually think I would do something like that to you?"

"I know what I see Thomas."

"Then you need your eyes checked. I ran into her with a group, Lizzie. There were several of us from the film. Of course we ate together! I didn't even sit next to her, let alone touch her. A photographer happened to get a shot of me helping her into her cab—which she took alone, by the way."

He broke off, breathing deeply. I had never heard him so upset. I felt dazed, off balance. I had gone from thinking everything was ruined to suddenly realizing that nothing had changed.

"I didn't know," I said, swallowing.

"Yes, you did!" he yelled, and I winced. "Of course you did! Or you should have. Because you know me! If you think I could do something like that—fuck, Lizzie, then you don't know me at all. What in the hell are we doing here?"

"I'm sorry," I whispered, tears coming to my eyes. He was right, of course he was. The second a question came up, I had jumped to conclusions. When he had never once given me a reason to doubt him.

"You don't get it, do you?" he asked, my apology having no effect on his anger. "I didn't want any of this. It was your call, Lizzie, to go home. To refuse to see me in LA. The only thing I wanted was you."

"So it's my fault?" I asked, the tears falling now. "Because I came home? What, are you punishing me?"

"I'm not punishing you!" he cried. "God, what do you think of me? Nothing happened, Lizzie!"

"Thomas—"

"This is too hard," he said. "To be away from each other. It's not good for us."

"What are you saying?" I asked, ice cold fear dripping into my chest. "Are you...do you want to break up?"

"What is wrong with you today? I didn't say break up! I want you to come back, Lizzie. There is a job and a flat for you right here, less than ten miles away."

"Nothing's changed, Thomas," I said, feeling so sad my knees suddenly felt weak. "We still live two very different lives."

Thomas was quiet for a moment. "You know what," he finally said, his voice bitter. "We do. I'm living the life I want. I'm willing to take a risk to have the career that I want. The relationship that I want." He paused and I knew, instinctively, that his next words would hurt. "And you, Lizzie, clearly are not."

"Thomas—"

"You know what the saddest part is? It's not that you won't take a chance for me. It's a big deal, I get that. I would never ask you to give up the things you wanted just to be with me. The saddest part is that you won't take the chance for yourself. You'd rather stay there, miserable, in a job you hate, than take a fucking chance."

"That's not true," I cried, but even as I said it, I knew it was a lie.

"Oh, really? How's the book coming, Lizzie? You finish up that chapter yet?"

"Thomas!" I cried, his words hitting me as hard as if I'd been slapped.

"Good luck with the job search," he said, his voice so bitter and angry and sad that he didn't even sound like himself anymore. "I hope you're very happy with where you end up."

"Thomas," I said again, my voice breaking in pain on his name. But he wasn't there. For the first time ever, he had hung up on me. And, for the first time, I couldn't help but wonder if he had given up on me entirely.

CHAPTER THIRTY

Callie found me in my room twenty minutes later, sprawled on the bed. I had cried until my eyes ran dry, until I felt lightheaded and sick to my stomach. Now I was lying, mute and numb, staring at the ceiling.

"You look like shit," she announced, standing in my doorway.

"Thanks," I muttered, rolling over and throwing an arm across my face so I didn't have to look at her.

"Nope," she said, striding to my bed and grabbing my arm, pulling it from my face. "We're done with the moping in bed part. You and I need to talk."

"What's there to talk about?" I croaked. "I basically told him I don't trust him, and he rightly told me to go to hell. I'm a terrible girlfriend, and now I'm getting exactly what I deserve."

"Bull shit." Her tone was enough to make me look up at her in surprise. Her face was twisted in frustration and…anger?

"You're mad at me, too," I muttered. "Awesome."

"You know what, Lizzie? I've had enough of you feeling sorry for yourself! It's bull shit," she repeated. "And it's really pissing me off. So you're going to get out of bed, go wash your face, and come with me to get some food. You look like hell, and you haven't had a proper meal in who knows how long."

"Callie—"

"Do I look like I'm going to take an argument from you?" she snapped. "Get. Up."

I was a little bit afraid of my friend, to be honest. She looked so fierce, so unlike her normal pretty, happy self. I scrambled out of the bed, and she graced me with a smile. "Good. Now go wash your face and meet me downstairs."

Twenty minutes later, Callie and I had settled into a booth at a kitschy little Italian place we had frequented after exams. "It kind of reminds me of home," she said wistfully, looking around, and I knew she meant London. I felt a little stab of pain in my already overworked heart and said nothing.

"So, you talked to him."

I looked up at her. "Yeah. Thanks, by the way. For calling him. I really appreciate it."

"Well, you wouldn't answer my calls. What was I supposed to do? It's ridiculous that you would think he would do anything. Especially with Lola." She made a face. "Gross."

"I heard all this from him, Cal. I'm already aware that not trusting him makes me a bad person."

She shook her head. "So what did he have to say?"

I sighed. "He said they just ran into each other. And that it was ridiculous for me to think he'd do anything."

"He's right."

"Thanks," I muttered. "I got that part. He then proceeded to tell me that I was a coward for not staying there and going after what I want. Because apparently it's just as easy as that."

"You know what, Lizzie? I think you're full of crap."

My mouth dropped open as I gaped at my friend. "Excuse me?"

"You're in love with him. Really, honestly in love."

I was silent for a moment. "Well," she snapped. "Aren't you?"

"Yes," I said, "but that doesn't change the situation."

She snorted. "God, Lizzie. Do you know how lucky you are?"

"Lucky?" I asked, feeling my temper start to rise. "You call it lucky to be separated by a frickin' ocean from the guy you love?"

"You can tell yourself that all you want, but it ain't the ocean that's keeping you from him."

"We live in different countries, Callie—"

"So? There are airplanes, you know. This is the twenty-first century."

"So, what? We should just keep doing the long-distance thing? You can see how well that's worked out so far."

"That's my point, Lizzie. You aren't separated from him because of the distance. You're not with him for one reason: you're scared."

It was quiet for a moment while I stared at her, my mouth open. "*What?*"

"You're terrified. Terrified to stand up to your family for once and tell them what you really want."

"That's not...that's not true."

Callie laughed bitterly. "Okay. Sure. You're not scared of your family. Uh huh."

My face was burning. "You don't know what they're like."

"But I know what *you're* like. And that's the part I don't understand."

"What do you—"

"You act like you're some meek pushover. Like you're too weak to stand up for what you want. But that's not you, Lizzie. It's *not*."

"It's hard for me sometimes," I said, looking down. "I'm not as confident as you, okay?"

"Bull shit."

I stared at her, shocked. She'd been the one telling me I was too self-conscious for years. "Is that your phrase of the day or something?"

She ignored me. "Lizzie, think about what you've done this year. You went to London for an entire year. Against the wishes of your family. No one else did that for you—you did it. And the apartment thing. You're the one who took charge and found us a great place. You're the one who negotiated with Mr. Idoni to get us a decent rate."

She has a point, a little voice in my head whispered.

"And Thomas—you dealt with all that crap from the tabloids, from Meredith and Tonya, from complete strangers. You didn't let it stop you from getting what you wanted. You even stood up to Lola frickin' Fischer, for God's sake."

I had done that. Everything she was saying was true. And there were other things, too, things she didn't know. Like how I had kissed Thomas first, way back on our first date. How I had written nearly an entire book. How I still hadn't applied for any of the jobs my sisters had found.

"You're so much stronger than you give yourself credit for," Callie said, her voice soft. Though I had cried myself horse already, there was a new lump in my throat. "So be strong, Lizzie. Tell your parents what you actually want."

"They only want what's best for me," I whispered, the lump growing larger. "I don't want to disappoint them."

"I know they love you." She placed her hand on my arm. "And I'm not saying that I know you better than they do, or that I know better what's good for you. But I do know that in all the years I've known you—five years, Lizzie!—I have never seen you happier than you were with Thomas. They weren't there to see it, Lizzie, but I was."

She looked me straight in the eyes. "And you know I'm right."

***

I spent the next two days in a fog. With the school year fast approaching, my sisters had started to get concerned about my lack of interviews, a concern that they, of course, shared with my parents. I had to endure a whole family critique on my résumé in an attempt to figure out what was going on. I, of course, knew exactly why I hadn't gotten any interviews, but there was no way I could tell any of them that.

"I just don't think you're taking this seriously enough, Lizzie," Maria had said before leaving for the night. "Districts are already making their decisions. You're moping around here all day and missing out."

I just stared at her blankly. I couldn't muster up the energy to even pretend that I cared. She sighed loudly. "Next week we are going from school to school to hand deliver your résumé. Maybe it will help show that you have some initiative." When I started to complain, she held up her hands. "No arguing. There is absolutely no reason for you to not start the school year with a job. Tomorrow we'll go shopping and find you a nice suit."

"Ooh, shopping," Laura said, joining us in the foyer. "I'll come, too. It will be fun, Lizzie. The three of us haven't been out together in ages."

"Maybe because some of us have responsibilities while the other mopes around all day reading."

I felt a flash of anger at my oldest sister, but it, too, was quickly numbed by the energy-sucking fog.

"Fine," I muttered. "We'll go shopping tomorrow."

My sisters showed up around lunchtime the next day, Maria bringing her kids for Mom to watch. In the time since I had been home, I hadn't noticed much improvement in their behavior, in spite of Maria's insistence that she and José were being much stricter now. Of course, my mother smothered them with kisses the moment she saw them, completely ignoring the fact that JJ had already knocked over the hall coatrack.

"I think this is so nice," my mom said, dishing out salad and rice to each of us. "The three of you shopping together. It seems like it's been so long since you girls have hung out."

I noticed her eyes flicker to my face for an extra beat and felt a surge of guilt. I'd pretty much been a whiney brat since I'd been home, staying up in my room whenever possible and avoiding the family at all costs. It must be hurting my mother.

"It will be nice," I said brightly. "I'm really looking forward to it." I figured the way she beamed at me was worth the lie.

"JJ!" my mom called. "Sofia! Time to eat!" Though my mother was probably the best cook in the entire city, she had appeased the kids with frozen chicken nuggets and French fries, two food items that appeared to make up the bulk of their diet.

Sofia skidded into the kitchen and immediately burst into tears. "Those don't look like ours!"

"What's wrong, nieta?" my mom asked, scooping her up and kissing her reddening cheeks. "Did your abuelita get the wrong ones?"

"Yes!" Sofia sobbed. "I like the dinosaur-shaped ones."

"Sofie, stop crying," Maria demanded. "Mama, put her down. She needs to learn to not be spoiled."

It was funny, as soon as Maria opened her mouth Sofia's tears stopped, almost as if by magic. *Smart kid*, I thought to myself. *She knows who she can get her way with and who she can't.*

"JJ!" Maria shouted. "Your grandmother called you!"

JJ came barreling into the kitchen and jumped into my lap. "Oof," I muttered. "Watch out, buddy."

"Mail came," he said. "You got a big letter, Aunt Lizzie."

"I did?"

"Yup. I hid it though. You're going to have to go find it."

I sighed. "JJ, bring the mail in, please."

"Nope." He wrapped his arms around my neck and started using my stomach as a ladder. "You have to look."

"José Junior!" Maria said, her voice harsh. "You listen to your aunt and go and get the mail."

He looked at her, a mutinous expression on his face, and for one moment, I thought he might disobey her. But she narrowed her eyes further, making him gulp and jump down. "All of it!" she called after him as he scurried into the living room.

"That was freaky, Maria," I told her. "I had flashbacks of you babysitting me and scaring me half to death."

Maria rolled her eyes, but I thought I saw a smile tugging on her lips. "You were the worst to babysit. You were constantly asking me questions. You wanted to know everything."

"Lizzie was a sweet girl," my mother admonished, tapping the top of my head. "She never got into any trouble. Not like the rest of you."

I beamed at my sisters, who both coughed out the word "bull."

"Here you go, Auntie Liz," JJ said, entering the room much more subdued than before. "And here's the rest Abuelita."

He slid the stack of mail onto the counter before handing me a large, manila envelope. I flipped it over and saw a London postmark. Thomas's handwriting.

My heart started a gallop in my chest. We hadn't talked since our disastrous conversation three days ago. Surely he must have sent this before I'd screwed everything up so badly. I stood, not caring about lunch or the fact that everyone was staring at me.

"I'll be right back," I muttered, making a break for the stairs.

Safely in my room, I sat at my desk and stared down at the envelope. It felt heavy in my hands. What had he sent me? With trembling fingers, I tore the flap from the top of the envelope and turned it over, and a thick, canvas-bound volume fell into my lap. I turned it over to see the front and gasped out loud.

An Untitled Love Story, by Elizabeth Medina.

Slowly, I flipped open the cover. Sure enough, they were the words I had written. All of them. Thomas had had my manuscript printed and bound. He'd made it into a book for me, a book I could hold in my two hands as proof that I'd created it. I quickly thumbed through the pages until I reached the back. He had left the last chapter blank, waiting for me to finish.

Tears blurring my eyes, I reached into the envelope, hoping for a note. I wasn't disappointed. A folded piece of cardstock fell into my hands.

Lizzie,

I thought you might need a reminder of how far you've come. I'm so proud of you, for the talent and hard work it took to write this book. Please don't give up. Finish it. I'm dying to know how it all turns out.

I love you, my sweet girl.

Thomas.

I was having trouble breathing, the tears coming fast now. It was one of the nicest things anyone had ever done for me. There were a lot of people in my life who wanted what was best for me. My parents, my siblings, even Callie. But out of all of them, Thomas wanted what would make me happy. Thomas wanted me to have what *I* wanted.

"Lizzie!" Maria called from downstairs. "We need to go!"

I quickly wiped my eyes, trying to take deep breaths. "Okay," I called back.

"Hurry, please. I only have a few hours until José comes home."

I set the manuscript on my desk and found some tissues. I had to get a hold of myself. My sisters would know immediately that something was wrong, and they would be merciless with their questions until they found out what it was. I blew my nose and slipped down the hall to the upstairs bathroom where I could splash water on my face.

When I emerged a few minutes later, I looked put back together, calm.

But inside, my heart was hammering and my mind was spinning. Something felt different at the core of me. I'd been sleeping all summer, feeling sorry for myself and moping. Going along with life like I had no say in where it was headed. Now I felt awake for the first time. With the new consciousness came an anxiousness, almost like a fear. Like there was something I was supposed to do that I was forgetting.

Seeing my book like that had altered something in me. And I wasn't sure I would ever be able to change it back.

CHAPTER THIRTY-ONE

My sisters dragged me to three store before they were satisfied we'd found the best outfit at the best price. In the end, we settled on a black slim skirt and fitted jacket. In my mind, it didn't look all that much different from any of the other options, but I had learned long ago to never argue with my sisters when it came to clothes.

By the time we reached the house, I was desperate to be alone. I had to get up to my room where I could think. I had to make sense of the whirlwind of thoughts in my mind.

But of course nothing could be that easy in my family. Both of the girls came in with me, and JJ and Sofie insisted on telling us every detail of their time at Abuelita's house.

"It's getting late, Maria," my mom said, glancing at the wall clock. "You'll never have time to get dinner done before José gets home. Why don't you eat here? We can make extra."

Since sharing a meal at my parents' house happened at least twice a week, Maria had no objections. Instead, she pulled on an apron and got to work on dinner, taking out her phone and sending a text to her husband while whisking something on the stove.

I felt like screaming. Why couldn't there ever be any peace or privacy in this house?

"Lizzie, chop the veggies for salad, will you?" my mother asked. "I need to get the laundry out."

I was pretty sure the last thing my shaking fingers needed was a knife, but I did as my mother asked. Laura called her husband Frank, inviting him along as well, and then joined us at the counter. For a brief moment, it felt like old times. Standing with my sisters in the kitchen, cooking and talking, getting ready for a family meal. My mom had already called Carlos and the twins as well. Soon the house would be full, the way it usually was.

There's nothing wrong with this, I realized. If I hadn't met Thomas, I probably could have been very happy here, with my family. I never would have been lonely. I never would have been on my own. I would have had traditions to pass onto my own kids. It would have been a very nice, meaningful life full of laughter and love and family.

But I *had* met Thomas. And that had changed everything.

I knew now what I needed—to hear his voice. To apologize for my behavior. To thank him.

I took the first chance I could to escape. "Do you think Mama was going to use this pork or the chicken?" Maria asked, peering into the fridge. "I suppose it doesn't matter, there's enough of both."

"I'll ask her!" I threw my knife down and ran from the kitchen before my sisters could question me. I took the stairs two at a time, calculating the time in London. It would only be ten, surely he'd be able to talk. Unless he was out—I pushed that thought away, determined to never doubt him again.

I stopped short upon entering my room; my mother was standing with her back to me, in front of my desk, my unopened manuscript in her hands.

"What are you doing?" I squeaked. She turned to face me, startled.

"Lizzie, you scared me," she said, putting a hand to her heart.

"What are you doing?" I repeated, feeling panicked. Had she read it? What would she say? Would she tell the family? I couldn't bear the thought of my brothers and sisters teasing me, not about this. Not about something I had worked so hard on, put so much of myself into.

"I was bringing your laundry up." She pointed at the basket on the bed. "And I saw this sitting out." She looked down at the bound stack of papers in her hands. "What is this, sweetie?"

I felt color flood my face. "It's just…it's just something that I wrote."

"You wrote this?" her voice was quiet. Measured. "Is it a novel?"

I nodded.

She looked at it for a moment, silent.

"Mama—"

"Why didn't you tell me you were writing a novel?"

It was my turn to be startled. I was not expecting that. "Well, I didn't know…I thought you guys might think it was dumb."

Something changed in her face. "Elizabeth Medina, are you serious?" She sounded angry. Why was she angry?

"What do you mean?"

"Why would you think I'd think this was dumb?" she demanded, holding out the manuscript. "Are you *serious*?"

I was baffled by her reaction. "Mom, I'm sorry. I just thought…everyone always gives me a hard time. Because I spend so much time reading and thinking about books and—"

"You wrote a novel," she interrupted. "Lizzie, that's amazing. And you thought I'd tease you about it?"

I suddenly realized what was going on. She was hurt.

"Not you, Mom," I said, feeling terrible. "I didn't think you would. But Carlos, and Maria—"

"Over my dead body," she said firmly. "I won't allow it." She looked back down at the manuscript. "What is this book about? When did you write this?" She shook her head. "What a wonderful thing. I wish you had told me, mija."

Suddenly I was crying. I buried my face in my hands, all the sadness of the past few months breaking over me in a wave. My mother hadn't called me mija—my daughter—since before I left for London. I had never realized how much I missed it until that moment.

I felt her arms come around me, gentle and familiar. "Eliza, Eliza," she whispered, rubbing my back. "My sweet girl. You've been so sad for so long. What is it, mija? You can tell me."

"I don't know what to do, Mama," I wailed, wrapping my arms around her and burying my head in the crook of her shoulder.

"Come and tell me, mija," she said, pulling me to the bed. "We'll figure out what you should do."

With her arm wrapped firmly around my shoulder and my face buried in her neck, I told her everything. About how Thomas had asked me to stay, about the job he had found for me, and how it would enable me to write. I told her how I had refused him, how much I regretted my behavior since I'd been home. How I dreaded teaching. I told her how happy I had been, studying books all day and writing all night. That Thomas's friends had become my friends, too, better friends than I'd had anywhere. How I had felt more like my true self than I ever did before. I told her how I wanted nothing more than to go back to London, but was so sure it would be wrong to give everything up just for a man. And after I told her all these things, I simply sat and cried, letting her run her fingers through my hair until I was calmed.

Finally she spoke for the first time since sitting down on the bed. "Lizzie, do you know how you got your name?"

I hiccupped. "Of course. You named me after your favorite character in your favorite book."

"But why do you think she was my favorite character? What do you think I saw in her that was so important to me I wanted to give her name to my last child?"

I was quiet. I had never really thought about it.

"Elizabeth Bennet was a strong woman," she said, when it was clear I had no answer for her. "She was intelligent and mature and could laugh at the silliness of the world around her. She was a good and loyal daughter, yes. But she stood up for herself. She did not settle. She went after what she wanted, even when her parents disagreed." I lifted my head to stare at her. What was she saying?

"Elizabeth knew that love was more important than security, more important than money, and yes, even more important than the desires of her mother." She smiled at me then. "I wanted you to be strong like that, mija. That is why I chose her name for you."

"Mama..." I whispered, overcome by her confession.

"Also, your father wanted to name you after his aunt Silvia, and I could never stand that woman."

I laughed and she joined me, rubbing her hands gently across my back. "A mother wants her children to stay close by, Lizzie. But more than that, much more, she wants her children to be happy."

"I don't know how I can be happy," I said, feeling the same sense of hopelessness that had plagued me for weeks. "Not without him."

"Then isn't that your answer?"

I stared at her. "Are you saying...you think I should go back?"

"I think you should do what would make you happy, Lizzie, and forget about what everyone else wants."

"You and Dad taught me to be independent," I said, twisting my fingers in my lap. "What would it mean if I give up my education and leave my home just for a guy?"

"If it was a choice between a career you loved and a man, I might give different advice," she said.

"But Dad spent all that money on my school so I could get a good job and take care of myself." I closed my eyes again, imagining what my father would say if he knew I was even considering this.

"It doesn't matter how much money Dad spent on your school if you'll end up unhappy as a teacher. Of course, I wish you would have told us you didn't want to teach before you started college."

"It's...it's not always easy to tell you guys things," I said softly. "Our family is a little...opinionated."

She laughed. "That is true. And we haven't always encouraged you to go your own way." She paused. "Do you love Thomas, Lizzie? Do you really love him?"

"I do." I squeezed my eyes shut tight, knowing it was the truest part of me, my love for Thomas.

"Then I think there is nothing more important in this life than love. Not a career, particularly not one that won't even make you happy. Not what other people will think of you. Not even the opinion of your family."

It felt like a great weight had lifted from my shoulders. Before I could tell her that, before I could even thank her, she sat up a little straighter. "Now, mija, tell me about this book you wrote."

I looked at her, and was surprised to see tears in her eyes. "I'm very proud of you," she whispered, "and I want to hear all about it." She touched my cheek gently. "Tell me about what you wrote, Lizzie, while I still have you here and close to me."

In that moment, I wanted her to wrap me up in her arms again. To hold me close and never let me out of her sight. But she had raised me to be stronger than that so, instead, I took a deep breath, swallowed past the lump in my throat, and told my mother all about my book.

CHAPTER THIRTY-TWO

The sun was shining in London.

It was bizarre, crawling along the crowded streets in a black cab, the city teeming just outside my window. It almost felt like I had never been away, like the last three months had been a bad dream. Hyde Park Corner came into view and my stomach dipped. Almost there now.

My phone beeped, and I pulled it from my purse. I had a text from Callie. *Are you there yet? Did he freak?*

I typed out a quick reply, letting her know I was still in transit. Her question made me, if possible, more nervous than I had been. *Did he freak?*

Oh crap, what if he *did* freak? What if he wasn't happy to see me? We hadn't talked in a full five days. Maybe it had been a bad idea, thinking I should surprise him. There was a very real chance he'd still be mad at me.

Then I'll make it up to him, I told myself firmly. There was no going back now. I was in this for the long haul, no matter what happened in the next fifteen minutes.

Fifteen minutes. I swallowed hard and looked out at the park next to me. Londoners and tourists alike were out in force, walking dogs, riding bikes, lounging in the grass. Enjoying the last few hours of a perfect late summer day.

With any luck the perfection would last. Only a few minutes now.

***

Two hours later, I was sitting on top of my suitcase, wishing I would have brought a jacket. With the sun setting, it was getting chilly. And I was pretty sure the clouds above me were getting greyer. It would probably rain soon.

Of *course* Thomas was out. It was my own fault, planning this ridiculous surprise. I should have just called him as soon as I decided and let him know I was coming. Instead I had envisioned some romantic reunion. For all I knew, he was out of town. I felt like crying; what would I do if he didn't come home soon? I only had about fifty dollars left to my name, having spent every bit of my savings account, plus a nice contribution from my brother Sam, on my last-minute plane ticket. There was no way I could get a hotel room in London for less than fifty quid.

You'll just have to call Meghan, I told myself. No biggie. But I hated the idea of any of Thomas's friends knowing I was in town before he did.

Another beep from my purse, another text. This one from Sofie. *Just call him*, she urged. *Find out where he is.* But I had come too far now to ruin the surprise by calling. Besides, I was starting to feel vaguely sick that he'd still be pissed after our last conversation. I wanted to explain myself in person.

If he's not back in an hour, I will, I wrote back.

Her next text came after only a minute. *I hope he hurries. I don't know how much longer I can hold your mother off.*

I felt a little pang, thinking of Sofie at home in my parents' kitchen. I wondered who else was there, who else was waiting to hear how this little experiment went. My mother, for sure. And Sam. Maybe Matias and Laura. Definitely not Maria. And definitely not my dad.

Telling them all what I planned to do was one of the hardest things I'd ever done in my life. After my conversation with my mother, she had gone downstairs to help finish dinner, leaving me in my room to try and get myself together. And try to get my courage up enough to go downstairs.

By the time I felt ready to face them, everyone had arrived for dinner. The addition of so many faces did little to make me feel better. Samuel was the first to notice something was wrong.

"You gonna join us or you gonna stand there in the hallway?" he asked, grinning at me as he brought a few beers to the table. He paused, catching sight of my face. "Lizzie? You okay?"

I cleared my throat. A few heads turned in my direction, but everyone else carried on talking; it took a lot more than a cleared throat to get everyone's attention in this house.

"You guys?" I tried. "Hey, everyone?"

"I think Lizzie has something to say," Sam said, his eyes still on mine, curious. I shot him a small smile before turning to the rest of the family. Everyone was looking at me now, even the kids, waiting for me to talk. Great.

"I've decided to move back to London."

I had never heard our house so quiet. Laura's mouth had actually dropped open. Across the room, I met my mother's eyes. They were sad, but steady on mine.

Maria got her voice back first. "What are you talking about?"

"I've decided I want to live in London. I have a job and an apartment lined up. I'm going as soon as possible."

"I don't understand," Carlos said, squinting at me. "I thought you were teaching in the fall?"

I shook my head. "I never got a job. And that's okay with me. Because I don't want to be a teacher."

Now every head swiveled in my father's direction. His face was red, and I gulped. I had a feeling I was about to see a new level of his anger.

"You are not moving to London," he said, his voice even. "Stop with this ridiculousness, Lizzie, and sit down. Before you upset your mother."

"My mother already knows," I said. "I told her this afternoon. I'm doing this, Dad."

My father turned to her, livid. She met his gaze. "You're okay with this? With her giving up her career?"

"I want her to be happy," she said softly. "I don't think teaching will make her happy."

"It won't, Dad. I'm sorry. I should have told you sooner."

He slammed his hand down on the table, making Laura jump beside him. "You went to school to be a teacher, Lizzie! It's a good career. You will not throw this opportunity away. I won't allow it!"

It took every ounce of strength in my being to hold my ground. "I'm sorry. I really am. But I'm going."

For a moment, I thought he might actually throw something. Instead, he stood up. I was pretty sure I could see his hands shaking. "I'm not talking about this anymore. But you can forget about this entire thing, Elizabeth. You're not going."

He grabbed his beer and stomped out of the kitchen. A moment later, we heard the door to the garage slam.

I felt like crying, but I ordered myself to stay strong. Surely the hardest part was over.

"You have got to be kidding me, Lizzie," Maria snapped. "Look at what you're doing to your parents."

"I'll deal with my parents, Maria," I said. "It's not really your concern."

"Not my concern?" Her eyes narrowed. "You think it's not my concern when you continue to drag this family on a rollercoaster of your selfishness?"

"Why is it selfish to go for what I want?" I cried, feeling the tears build behind my eyes. "It's my life, Maria! No one else's. I'm not asking any of you for anything!"

"You're asking your parents to throw away the money they spent on your schooling so you can run off with some boy in another country. Because that's what this is really about, isn't it?"

"I want to be with Thomas," I said. "But even more than that, I want to try to find a life that makes me happy. A job that makes me happy. Why is that a problem for you?"

"You're a child," she cried, throwing up her arms. "Look at what you're doing to your mother."

"That's enough, Maria," my mom said, her voice sharp. "Your sister doesn't need our permission. She's an adult. And she's allowed to make her own choices."

"You're okay with this?" Maria asked, incredulous. "I can't believe that."

"I want you to be happy, Maria," I said, the tears falling now. "I'm so happy you have the kids and José and a job you enjoy. Because I want you to be happy." I turned to Laura and my brothers. "I want that for you, too. For all of you. Because I love you very much. Can't you want that for me?"

"We do, Lizzie," Carlos said, his voice calm, almost condescending. It was like I was ten again and my big brother was explaining something to me in the tone he reserved for clueless little sisters. I had a feeling he didn't believe for a second that I would go through with it. "Of course we do. But we don't want you to do something you'll regret, either. Not teaching? Moving out of the country? That's not you."

I wiped my face, done crying now. They might not understand, they might not support me, but it didn't matter anymore. "I know you think that, Carlos. But it's time you all trust me to make my own choices." I took a deep breath, knowing that the battle was over. I had faced them, stood up to them, and still didn't feel the slightest bit inclined to change my mind. I was sure about my decision. I was ready. "I've made my choice. I'm moving to London."

A slamming car door made me jump, pulling me from my thoughts. I peered down the street, wishing Thomas would hurry. It was starting to drizzle now. I pulled my sweater closer and ducked my head to keep my face from the rain. Maybe it was time to call it quits. I could phone Meghan right now and she'd probably—

"Lizzie?"

I jumped in surprise. Thomas was standing a few feet from the porch.

"Thomas! Uh, hi," I stammered, jumping up. "I mean...well, hi."

He stared at me, clearly shocked. "What are you doing here?"

I took a deep breath. Time to tell him everything. But the words wouldn't come. I'd planned out my whole speech a dozen times on the plane, all the apologies I wanted to make, my explanations. Facing him, I couldn't think of a single thing I'd wanted to say. All I could do was stare at him. It had been months. He was so beautiful.

"Lizzie?"

"I didn't apply for any jobs," I blurted. It was the first thing I could think of.

He looked confused. "What do you mean? Lizzie, what's going on? Are you okay?"

"I didn't apply for any teaching jobs," I said, wanting to make him understand how important that was. "All summer. I kept filling out applications but I didn't send in a single one."

"Okay," he said, still sounding unsure. "Is that...is there a reason why?"

"Don't you get it?" I asked. "You were right, Thomas. About me. I don't want to be a teacher."

His face cleared a little bit. "You're not going to teach?"

I shook my head. "No. I'm not."

We were both quiet for a moment, staring at each other. Finally he cleared his throat. "So, if you're not going to teach, what are you going to do?"

I wished he would smile, that he would walk closer. Anything to show me that he was happy to see me, that my next words would be welcome. But he didn't. And that was okay. I could take the lead—I'd gotten pretty good at it.

"I want to stay here, with you. I want to find a job, work with Heidi if the spot is still open. Write at night." I took a step down toward him. "I want to be where you are, Thomas. Wherever you are. Always."

It felt like an age that he stared at me. His expression, usually so easy to read, was inscrutable. Just when I felt sure he was going to turn me down, he moved, so quickly it took my brain a moment to catch up. Then he was kissing me, his arms around me, pulling me down from the step. It had been too long since I'd felt his lips against mine, but they were as familiar as if I never left. I had come home, here in Thomas's arms, in a way I hadn't back in Michigan. This was where I belonged.

He pulled back, staring down into my eyes. Still, he didn't smile. "Can we just recap?" he asked, sounding breathless. "Just so I don't misunderstand. You're moving here?"

I nodded.

"You're going to live in London. Full time?"

I nodded again, waiting.

A smile broke out on his face, so broad it took my breath away. "I take it you're okay with that?" I whispered.

"I guess," he said, laughing.

"Are we done with the recap?" I asked, moving my face closer to his.

"What's the hurry?"

"I'm going to kiss you again, and I didn't want to be rude and interrupt."

"By all means, Lizzie," he said, smiling. "You go right ahead."

I stared into his eyes, thinking of all the kisses we'd shared. That moment in Edinburgh when I decided to stop being afraid. Our first kiss, in the London Eye, when I had felt so much like I was falling. Hundreds of kisses later, that feeling had never left.

I brought my lips to his again and leapt, one more time.

~

Interested in reading more from this author? Check out her two best-selling series below.

Love Story Series

In Search of a Love Story is the first in the three-book series, in which you meet Emily Donovan, a self-described romance novice, as she searches for her very own love story.

An Unexpected Love Story, is the second in the Love Story series, where we follow along with Brooke Murray as she attempts to save her parents' inn, find true love, and run a business-all while wearing the perfect pair of heels!

In the final book in the Love Story Series, *An (Almost) Perfect Love Story*, we learn more about Ashley Phillips. She has always believed in love, but does she have what it takes to fight for love when her perfect love story turns out to be not so perfect after all?

Three Girls Series

Come along for the crazy ride as Ginny McKensie and her best friends deal with an unexpected pregnancy in *Three Girls and a Baby*.

Follow Jen Campbell as she struggles to plan the perfect wedding—and find her very own happily ever after in *Three Girls and a Wedding*.

Join Annie Duncan as she continues her search for the perfect leading role—and the perfect man to go along with it in the third and final book of the series, *Three Girls and a Leading Man*.

Reunite with Ginny, Jen, and Annie and catch up with Kiki Barker-Thompson as she attempts to create the perfect fairy tale life in *The Truth About Ever After* (a Three Girls book).

ABOUT THE AUTHOR

Rachel Schurig is the best-selling author of the Three Girls series, available now in paperback and ebook. Rachel lives in the metro Detroit area with her dog, Lucy. She loves to watch reality TV, and she reads as many books as she can get her hands on. In her spare time, Rachel decorates cakes.

To find out more about her books, visit Rachel at
rachelschurig.com
Join the mailing list for updates and exclusive content!
Visit her author page on Facebook
(https://www.facebook.com/RachelSchurigAuthor)
Follow her on Twitter (https://twitter.com/rems330)

Printed in Great Britain
by Amazon.co.uk, Ltd.,
Marston Gate.